THE
GOLDEN
TRINITY

Praise for
Robyn Nyx's work

Never Enough

"Nyx's debut is an entertaining thriller with two well-realized heroines. But readers who can handle the gory content will find it well balanced by plenty of romance and copious amounts of sex, as well as a solid cast of supporting characters and some insightful handling of contemporary social issues." *Publishers Weekly*

"If you are a sucker for fast paced, gritty crime thrillers that will make you neglect your household chores and read way past your bedtime, well fellow book lover, this is certainly the story for you." *The Lesbian Review*

The Extractor Trilogy

"Nyx balances the task of developing emotionally complex characters and creating a plot that is well paced and full of action on a grand scale. The story is captivating, and the best part is that it's the first in a fantastic trilogy." *The Lesbian Review*

"I genuinely couldn't have predicted what did happen though, and urge everyone to read this trilogy if not for the imaginative story, then for the intensity of how people's actions affect not only their own lives but the lives and feelings of others. So good! Robyn has perfectly captured all that moral uncertainty between doing the right thing legally and then doing the right thing morally." *LesBiReviewed*

"The redemptive power of love is a huge take-away from this book. There were more than a few times where I found myself on the verge of tears while reading some of Landry's conversations with her best friend Delaney." *Victoria Thomas*

Music City Dreamers

"Fans of the show Nashville will love Music City Dreamers by Robyn Nyx, for its angsty drama involving megastars and aspiring singers, songwriters and record executives. This is also not the stereotypical Nashville of bros and whiskey you often see on CMT." *NPR*

"I really enjoyed this story and I am so glad Ms Nyx made this foray into lesbian romance. She has captured the passion and intense emotions of the two women, as well as weaving a fascinating story." *Kitty Kat's Book Blog*

The Golden Trinity

"Ms. Nyx tells an awesome story with real characters, and that to my mind is the goal of a good book." Lesbian Reading Room

"What an excellent book and I demolished it in one go! I had such a great time reading Uncharted and would be happy to pick it up again tomorrow. The pace was perfect and felt like I was on the adventure with Chase and Rayne. For the last 30% of this book, my heart was in my chest with all the excitement." *Les Rêveur*

LesFic Eclectic Volume One

Robyn Nyx has put together a fantastic collection, and brought to us some amazing new talent as well as stories from some of our already loved and established authors in the genre. Engaging readers with new writers is always fantastic, and the new writers included in the Lesfic Eclectic are all absolutely brilliant." *LesBiReviewed*

LesFic Eclectic Volume Two

"I have read the seasoned writers before such as Anna Larner, Robyn Nyx, Brey Willows, Jenn Matthews and Anne Shade as always blew me away with their storytelling. A little something for everyone is the tagline across the cover, and I couldn't agree more. I highly recommend grabbing a copy of Lesfic Eclectic, a bottle of vino and taking one story at a time." *Les Rêveur*

By the author

The Chase Stinsen Adventures
The Golden Trinity (Book One)
The Copper Scroll (Book Two)

Music City Dreamers

The Extractor Trilogy
Escape in Time (Book One)
Change in Time (Book Two)
Death in Time (Book Three)

Never Enough

Edited by Robyn Nyx
LesFic Eclectic Volume One
LesFic Eclectic Volume Two

THE GOLDEN TRINITY

Robyn Nyx
2021

Cataloging information
ISBN: 9781838066871
CREDITS
Editor: Jan Stone
Cover Design: Robyn Nyx
Production Design: Global Wordsmiths

Butterworth Books is a different breed of publishing house. It's a home for Indies, for independent authors who take great pride in their work and produce top quality books for readers who deserve the best. Professional editing, professional cover design, professional proof reading, professional book production—you get the idea. As Individual as the Indie authors we're proud to work with, we're Butterworths and we're *different*.

Authors currently publishing with us:

E.V. Bancroft
Valden Bush
Helena Harte
Karen Klyne
AJ Mason
James Merrick
Robyn Nyx
Simon Smalley

For more information visit www.butterworthbooks.co.uk

to Molly
Chase the Rayne :)
Robyn xx

Acknowledgements

I always wanted to call this book The Golden Trinity, and in this fresh re-issue, I got my wish. I need to thank Ginette Murray, a real-life archeologist, for her invaluable consultation, fact-checking, and research. And as always, to Brey Willows, my wonderful wife and authory partner, who puts up with every repetitive conversation we ever have about the world of writing and sits by my side for every sentence I create.

Dedication

To Brey, the woman I'm privileged to share my life, dreams,
and words with. You made this all possible,
and I can never thank you enough.

CHAPTER ONE

Paris, 2018

URBAN SPELUNKER. CHASE could add it to her résumé but supposed that the suits at Stanford wouldn't be impressed. Nor would they add any danger money to her fee. She adjusted the face mask that was doing a pretty awful job at keeping the earthy, metallic tang of death at bay. Not for the first time that night, she lost her footing slightly and instinctively grabbed at the wall. It seemed terribly disrespectful to stick her fingers in someone's eye sockets. Dead or not, that was just rude. But needs must. She didn't fancy taking a gulp of the dank water she was wading through. Who knew how much of it was actually liquefied human? She prodded the toe of her rubber shoe along the wall and found a ledge. "Sorry...to all of you," Chase muttered as she used the eye and nasal orifices of multiple skulls to edge toward dry land.

She pulled herself up onto the damp ground and squelched her way beyond a collection of skulls and bones that stretched between the ground and the ceiling, arranged like giant vases. The ends of limbs, thousands of them, looked like downturned hearts broken from the overwhelming weight of death pressing down on them. "This is a great advertisement for cremation," she whispered before wondering why she was bothering to be quiet. It wasn't like she could disturb anyone down here...So why was there another source of light other than her flashlight? Chase slowly advanced toward it on a four-inch-wide stone walkway between two black pools of foul-smelling liquid.

Then just like any good horror movie, "CHUNKY CHASE STINSEN!"

She swiveled to face the direction of the hollering, twisted her ankle, and lost her footing. Chase sprawled backward and felt weightless for the tiniest fraction of a moment before the filthy water broke her fall and she was submerged in its darkness. She came up for air, her arm outstretched to find purchase on something, anything. A strong hand wrapped around her wrist and pulled her from her putrid predicament in one tug. She landed on her feet and wiped the sludge from her eyes just in time to see Rayne Marcellus lift the skull of Joan of Arc from its stone altar.

Chase pulled her face mask down. "What the hell are you doing here?" She'd just spent three hours wading through freezing cold pools of God-knows-what. To lose another treasure to Marcellus? How many times could this keep happening?

"That's no way to greet a fellow professional, now is it?"

Defeat ripped through Chase like a hurricane. She raised her eyebrow. "I'm not greeting a fellow professional though, am I? I'm saying a cordial hello to a well-heeled grave digger."

Rayne brought her free hand up to her chest and feigned offense. "Chase, your words wound me. But I forgive you. I expect the raw burn of repeated failure is the only thing making you speak to me with such disrespect."

Chase went to move toward Rayne, but the giant brick shithouse of a woman who'd pulled her out of the water stepped forward and blocked her path.

"Think about your next move, Stinsen," Brick Woman said as she crossed her arms across her considerable chest and smirked.

Chase clenched her jaw, irritated that Rayne's new team member knew her name. It sounded more like a dare than a warning. She'd been training hard for the last month. Capoeira. Tae kwon do. The gym. A quick scenario of her versus Brick Woman played out in her head, but it wasn't a happy or bloodless ending for Chase. She held up her hands. "Fine." She craned her neck around the mountain of a woman and jutted her chin toward Rayne. "If you're good with taking something that belongs to people of this country." It was likely a waste of breath, but Chase held on to a sliver of hope that one day Rayne might surprise her and locate her missing conscience in the sea of money she'd made raiding tombs for billionaires. "She's their saint, not yours."

"I don't need her or anyone else to be my saint." Rayne smiled as she held up the skull and inspected her prize. "Isn't it amazing how we all look more or less the same when our flesh is long gone and we're reduced to bones?"

Rayne's esoteric observation seemed out of place, but it was something Chase had gotten used to over the past few years. She occasionally

THE GOLDEN TRINITY

wondered what it might be like to have a real conversation with Rayne, away from dead and ancient artifacts, far from this cutthroat competition they'd cultivated…like old times. Sharing a good bottle of wine from Rayne's renowned collection before…Chase shook the intrusive thought away, not caring to admit that her wondering was more than occasional.

"Earth to Stinsen." Brick Woman waved her hand in front of Chase's face.

"And yet still some of us are more valuable than others," Chase said. No doubt Joan of Arc's skull was already bought and paid for by some private collector with more money than taste. Someone who'd keep her on a shelf for their rich friends to gawk at, ignorant of the history and struggle of an amazing woman.

Rayne shrugged. "As in life, in death."

Another philosophical pearl. Rayne opened her leather satchel and placed the skull carefully inside. At least she was treating it with the respect it deserved. For now. "Doesn't it ever bother you that you're selling history to the highest bidder instead of facilitating its restitution to the whole world?" Chase asked.

"Then what would you do for a living?"

Rayne smiled again, a mischievous sparkle in her eyes. Chase wished Rayne was a man. Or at least not such an alluring woman. It didn't seem fair that God would have bestowed so much talent on one person. Intelligence, beauty, strength, Rayne Marcellus had everything Chase could want in a woman. But Rayne's lack of a moral compass meant Chase's actual attraction to her, beyond a wild fantasy, was way south of never gonna happen.

Brick Woman turned and gathered the floor lights they'd set up. An equally sizeable companion appeared from around the corner with a duffel bag—they looked like two oversized, matching book ends—and Chase watched, frustratingly helpless, as yet another priceless archeological find disappeared from her grasp.

Rayne winked before walking away with her two henchwomen a few steps behind, covering her back. Brick Woman tossed a dismissive sneer as she turned the corner, leaving Chase holding her flashlight…and little else. The suits at Stanford weren't going to be understanding about yet another loss to Rayne Marcellus.

CHAPTER TWO

Syria, 2019

CHASE CLOSED HER eyes as another round of artillery bombardment somehow managed to echo across the vast emptiness of Syrian desert. Where once this land had boasted some of the finest examples of Hellenistic buildings and art, now landmines and dynamite traversed the rubble and ruins of a history ISIS forces were determined to destroy. She backed up a little closer to the smooth stone of the temple column and tried to breathe as quietly as a whisper on a wild wind. She concentrated on controlling the thudding of her panicked heart against her ribcage, and the thoughts spiraling around her mind cursing her for taking this job. Though a few years had passed since ISIS had beheaded the director of antiquities and displayed his mutilated body on a column much like the one she was now pressed against, the image was fresh. It would never leave her and had haunted her for the few nights prior to this trip.

"I don't want you to go."

Chase smiled, holding tight to the pride she'd felt when Noemie's protective nature had kicked in. But it was rich coming from a young combat medic who'd already completed two fifteen-month tours of Iraq and Africa.

"I'll be fine. I always am. Anyway, isn't it me that's supposed to be the one that worries?"

The angry spitting of fully automatic machine gun fire jolted Chase from her memories and pulled her back into the cold darkness of the desert night. She pressed the heel of her palm to the side of her head. If she wasn't fully in this moment, right now, if she wasn't aware of every little thing that was going on around her, she could find herself the next ISIS proclaimed idolater on a column all her own.

She moved slowly around the pillar. In the distance, though not far enough, distinct golden flashes of gunfire dappled the night sky like stars raging at the gods. She wondered what Queen Zenobia would make of those weapons on her territory and bet she'd have liked them plenty back in 270 CE. Maybe then she wouldn't be in the tomb that Chase was hunting down now. She retreated back around the ancient stone and retrieved her pack from the ground. She hoisted it over her shoulders and pulled the straps tight. With all the portable lights, camera, and laser scanning equipment in there in addition to her usual gear, it weighed a damn sight more than she was used to. Happy coincidence that she'd been training hard for over a year. It'd given Chase the results she wanted so jacking her pack around didn't present a problem. And Rayne Marcellus wouldn't be making comment about her physique the next time they had a run-in.

She lifted the thermal imaging scope to her eye and scanned across the hundred-and-eighty-degree area that lay in front of her. She didn't register any warm bodies on two legs close enough to be of concern. It was go time.

***

Chase dropped her pack to the floor, released her climbing rope, and quickly tied a double constrictor knot around the vertical bar of the iron gate. She walked to the crude, blasted hole in the ground and tossed the rope length down it. She focused her Maglite and could see a few curls of unraveled rope at its base. The satellite imaging had been able to show the underground structure beneath the castle, but the Stanford techs hadn't been sure of its depth from the castle floor and had estimated it at two hundred feet. Seeing the relatively little amount of rope gathered on the cave floor, Chase was glad she'd insisted on a three-hundred-foot rope. She fixed the Maglite to her harness, turned back to the gate, and refastened its chain to keep it from swinging open while she rappelled into the cavern.

Chase stepped onto the edge of the crater and tautened her line before slowly lowering herself until her legs were level with where the ground had given way when the Ms7 earthquake had hit Syria three days ago. Thousands had died, and the underground structure Chase now held herself over had been revealed. She was the archeologist they'd called to go in. They knew she was the only one crazy enough to disregard the risk of being caught by ISIS. Or at least that's what her carefully cultivated reputation made them think. As she began to sweat with the heat and exertion of the undertaking, being discovered by extremists was at the absolute forefront of her mind. But there was no way she'd be anywhere else right now.

She released the descender and welcomed the cooler air as she traveled downward. The rappel gave her time to think about the legend she was hoping to prove as fact. Chase had long been fascinated with Zenobia, the Warrior Queen of Egypt. Her rule in the traditionally masculine world of the Arabian desert had motivated Chase to become an archeologist, after it had first given her the strength to accept who and what she was. And in between paying gigs and lectures, she dedicated her time to discovering the truth behind Zenobia's disappearance once she was defeated by the Roman Emperor Aurelian. Chase didn't want to believe the story of her being married off to a Roman senator or of her committing suicide. She wanted to unearth a hero's death and the loyalty of her staff that saw her body hidden from those who would parade her through the streets as a warning to other women, or men, who might have the gumption to defy the Roman Empire.

And that's exactly what the new batch of unearthed Vindolanda tablets described.

Chase hit the ground loudly and dusty chalk plumed beneath her trusty old engineer boots. Noemie was always prompting her to buy new ones, but they'd been on more adventures than Lara Croft. Chase wasn't superstitious as such, but neither was she prepared to see what happened if she bought herself a shiny new pair. She released herself from the rope, unclipped her flashlight, and watched her breath cloud before it dissipated upward. Every hair on every inch of her skin stood at attention, gathering heat and preparing her for fight-or-flight. She'd gotten this far. Nothing was going to make her flee what she'd been seeking for over two decades. Chase ran her tongue over her dry lips and swallowed, but there was no moisture. She pulled a water packet from the leg pocket of her cargos, ripped it open, and squeezed the cool fluid into her mouth. She stuffed the packaging back, knowing she couldn't leave a trace of her visit here.

Chase swung her pack around, accessed the back pouch through a side zip, and pulled out her iPad. She accessed the pictures of the carefully drawn maps on the skin-thin shards of alder wood found in the most recent discovery at Vindolanda. Previous pieces found had dated between the first and second century, but this trove covered the last few decades of the third century. They detailed Zenobia's rise, fall, and most importantly, her final resting place. The Vindolanda Trust had contacted Chase because she was the world's leading expert on Palmyra's Rebel Queen. It had taken five months to piece together three different accounts of the last few days of Zenobia's life according to soldiers who'd served under her but had switched alliance to the Roman Empire after her defeat. The tablets claimed Zenobia had been slain in battle, defending her people and her empire to the last. But before the Romans could claim her body, Zenobia's soldiers had smuggled her away from the fray. According to the soldiers, she was mummified with her handmaiden and hidden in a hypogeum deep in bedrock. This, where Chase now stood, could be that very hypogeum. Hidden for centuries and built over by the Mamluks a thousand years later in order to further protect the Empress of the East from ever being discovered.

The anticipation of what Chase might now find pressed against her chest and made it difficult to breathe deeply. The crypt was supposed to be less than a quarter of a mile long with only one access point. That access point had remained a secret as Zenobia's people meant it to, and deciphering the tablets, maps, and messages hadn't led to it. If it weren't for the earthquake that had collapsed the ceiling where Chase had entered, it might have taken her years to locate. She shook off the thought that thousands of people had died so that she could profit. Chase pointed her flashlight along the open chamber and wished Zenobia's people had made the relatively short trip across the water to Cyprus and buried her there. At least then they would have been able to excavate the area properly and give the Warrior Queen the worldwide audience she deserved. Their laziness meant Chase would only be able to take photos and laser scans of the Queen's sarcophagus to build a 3-D model. If she did find what she was looking for down here, she'd be loathe to leave it. It would only be a matter of time before ISIS heard about it, sent in excavators of their own, and in typically misogynistic fashion, desecrated and destroyed it. She comforted herself with the thought that at least she would have salvaged something real to give substance to the legend.

The chamber steadily became narrower, and the little moonlight from the hole she'd come in through had long faded. Dust danced around the shaft of light she was holding, and the absence of any kind of critters was vaguely reassuring. She was no Indiana Jones—slithery snakes had never scared her—but not having to share the increasingly small space with other oxygen-munching animals was still preferable. The webbing she walked through was another thing. Spiders didn't consume that much oxygen, surely, but damn, the stuff stuck to everything. The corridor became too small to walk upright and Chase was forced to crawl. She looked again at the maps of the area on the tablet. There was no indication that the corridor was anything other than ten to fifteen feet wide. There'd been only one way to go. *I couldn't have gotten lost.* She pushed the iPad back into her pack and pressed on.

The light from her flashlight bounced back at her, and she reached out to touch the cold flat stone that blocked her path completely. She shone the light around all of its edges. There was no sign of rubble around it, and Chase concluded that its construction was purposeful. It couldn't have been the result of the earthquake because at its base was a sharp-edged gap, indicating that the stone would descend into a possible space beneath it…if only she could locate a way to open it. She focused her flashlight on the ceiling, methodically scanning the left side, right side, then floor of the corridor leading to the stone. On each surface, bar the ground, was a three-inch-square hole. Chase figured each hole might contain a lever linked to the door to enable its release. Either that or they'd trigger a booby trap and her search for Zenobia's tomb ended with her skewered three ways in this tiny corridor like some unfortunate extra in an adventure movie. Nope, that wasn't happening. Chase wanted to be the hero of this particular adventure.

She tentatively probed the opening of the overhead square, finding nothing until she was in up to her elbow. She felt something hard, wrapped her hand around it, and attempted to wiggle it in every direction. There was more give when she pushed it away from her. She hitched her feet onto the side wall, still slightly anxious that the lever might release the floor instead of the door, and pushed. It gave way surprisingly easily, and Chase saw the stone wall tremble a little. She released the breath she'd been holding and moved across to the other side to repeat the process. Once again, the stone trembled as the lever moved something ancient within the walls. She explored the final hole in the ceiling. The lever wasn't as deeply embedded, but it didn't want to move as readily as the others had. She took off her backpack, pulled out her crowbar, and repositioned her pack over her shoulders. Only once had she been stupid enough to leave her pack on the ground doing something like this. She'd fallen thirty feet into a muddy pit, and when she emerged some time later, her bag been picked over by the locals. They'd left her with the only thing they couldn't make use of, her cell phone. It was an expensive mistake she'd vowed never to make again.

Chase fixed the crowbar into the hole, braced her feet against either wall, and put her entire weight behind it. She pushed, released, pushed, and released until it suddenly dropped away, and Chase fell forward with the force. Her right shoulder smashed into the stone wall as it began to drop, and she managed to roll away from it as it plummeted downward at speed. Chase peered into the darkness beyond the blockade, and the beam from her flashlight illuminated a dark shape in the chamber. The tomb? She swallowed hard and got to her knees to move closer. Chase estimated the distance between her and the tomb was less than twenty feet, but as she inched closer, the space seemed to treble. She'd been searching, hoping, working for this moment for the best part of two decades and now it was within touching distance. The final resting place of the Warrior Queen.

As she drew nearer, the intricate carvings on the stone became clear. Zenobia stood proud at the top of the frieze, with her four children at her feet. Her army and people populated the remainder of the picture. Chase translated the writing across the edge of the tomb lid and whispered, "The noblest of all the women of the East."

She ran her fingers over the carvings on the relief, feeling the bumps and crevices of its artistry. She'd hoped the casket would be ornate, that her people would've had the time to have created something worthy of her. Like most leaders, Zenobia had probably had the sarcophagus made to her specification years before her death, but under the circumstances of the battle, Chase feared they might not have been able to stow her away in the thing she'd created for her journey to the afterlife. Chase closed her eyes and imagined Zenobia's people in this chamber, robbed of the ability to hold a procession, in hiding from Emperor Aurelian's forces. Chase was sure they would have managed a eulogy to mark the queen's passing but doubted they'd risked a feast. They would've been too busy trying to stay alive and undiscovered and needed to draw the invading Romans away from the tomb.

Chase shook off the melancholy of the muted celebration of the Warrior Queen's life. This ending was definitely better than the Roman myth of being paraded through the streets weighed down by gold. The awareness of her current position and potentially imminent discovery by hostile forces brought Chase out of the past. She shrugged her backpack from her shoulders, pulled out the set of portable lights, and scouted the chamber for the best place to position them. It took Chase less than fifteen minutes to set up the lights, camera, and suspended laser scanner, something she'd practiced maybe a hundred times as she'd prepped for this. She didn't want to be here a moment longer than she had to be, lest she be discovered. She ignored the stone steps in the corner of the chamber. Though it would have been the entrance and exit for Zenobia's people when they buried her here, Chase had no way of knowing what blockade was at the top of it. And since she'd had no luck finding it, there was little point exploring it now. She'd found what she'd came for, and she'd leave the same quiet and unassuming way she'd arrived.

She looked through the viewfinder and altered the camera settings to suit the lighting conditions. She allowed herself a smile. She'd done it. She'd found Zenobia's tomb and she was going to share it with the world.

***

"We've attracted too much attention. We should abort."

Rayne shook her head. Usually, she'd always listen to Ginn's advice—she did have almost three decades of military training and experience—but tonight, she knew she couldn't. It wasn't that her client was paying her four million dollars for this jaunt. And it wasn't because this had been months in the staging and had cost over a million dollars to see through. It wasn't even that her reputation might suffer a little if she came away empty-handed—that was solid enough to take a few hits. While all of that mattered, Rayne couldn't take Ginn's advice for one simple reason.

Chase Stinsen.

Rayne knew Chase was already here. Had probably already found the tomb. The Warrior Queen *was* Chase's specialist subject. Rayne would've been disappointed if she and her team had found Zenobia's tomb before Chase, and perhaps even a little upset on Chase's behalf. Finding Zenobia's tomb was the equivalent of the Holy Grail for Chase. If Rayne had found it first, it might've broken her, and Rayne didn't want that. She enjoyed their competition, and no one else in the business was close to either of them.

It'd be almost boring without Chase around.

Rayne certainly didn't want to be the reason Chase slipped off the raiding radar, and she definitely didn't want to be responsible for her death. While Rayne had overseen everything, she'd been happy to let Ginn and Tonyck plan this insertion carefully. This was Syria, not a tiny part of Africa with a small, friendly tribe nearby. Getting caught was a death sentence, and it wouldn't be a quick, merciful one, she was sure. This place had been G&T's playground for a good few years. They knew how it worked, they knew which locals they could tap for information about the ISIS forces…and they were trained killers. Something Rayne tended to push to the back of her mind for the most part. She always got the job done, but she wasn't quite a by-any-means-necessary kind of person.

"Seriously, Rayne." Tonyck placed her hand on Rayne's shoulder. "We can't guarantee your safety if go any farther."

Rayne nodded. They hadn't managed to navigate their way through Palmyra as quietly as they planned, and it wouldn't be long before they could expect a well-armed posse of insurgents piling up with nefarious intentions. "I know what I'm asking. I'll triple your claim bonus when we get out of this alive." She motioned toward the spot G&T had rigged to blow. "But I want that sarcophagus, and I'm not leaving Stinsen here to pay for our clumsiness."

Neither of the twins had any love for Chase. To them, she was just a bump on the log, the competition they had to beat. But she was also an innocent, and Rayne knew their training wouldn't allow them to leave her behind.

Ginn nodded and clapped her sister on the shoulder. "Let's get this done."

Rayne watched them do their thing from a safe distance and checked her watch. She could be doing something, or someone, much less dangerous at three a.m. Maybe Chase would be so grateful for this rescue, she'd finally be inclined to share Rayne's bed for the night. More likely she'd deduce, correctly, that it was Rayne's presence that had necessitated the rescue in the first place, and get all up on her high horse about it. Chase's morals got in the way of so many good things.

The small blast shot pieces of the rock across Rayne's path, and she looked across to see G&T giving her the thumbs-up. Rayne quickly moved to the hole the C4 had created and shone her flashlight through it.

THE GOLDEN TRINITY

Stone steps descended into a darkness blacker than the devil's heart. She scrambled through and dropped directly onto the steps. Tonyck shoved her pack and MPX through to Rayne before tugging herself through with some difficulty.

"Maybe you need to lay off the protein," Ginn whispered as Tonyck hit the ground.

"Maybe *you* need to make the holes bigger." Tonyck dusted her jacket off and threw her pack back over her shoulder.

Rayne rolled her eyes at the identical twins. It was like watching someone poke fun at themselves in the mirror. "Just get your ass in here."

Ginn pushed through their packs and equipment, before Tonyck pulled her equally muscular sister through the intentionally small passage. Once they had the tomb, they'd blast a much more conspicuous aperture from which to escape. Mac would land the helicopter, they'd secure the cargo, and leave the village with everything, and everyone, intact.

At least that was the plan.

Ginn began to hammer a cleat into the wall and prepare the winch to tug the tomb up the steps. Tonyck clipped the carabiner at the end of the galvanized steel roll of cable onto her utility belt.

"Once this is set up, I'll be down to join you," said Ginn.

Even in the dim light of the cavern, Rayne didn't miss the glance the twins exchanged. They were usually so cool and unaffected by things that would have most people soiling their Calvins, but tonight their worry was seeping from every pore. The look they shared seemed full of unspoken emotion and the possibility they might not see each other again. An uneasy anguish plucked at Rayne's stomach, and she tried to retrieve her customary composure, again ignoring the nagging doubt she had about taking this commission.

Rayne took the lead, checking the steps for potential fragility. She'd counted two hundred and eighty when light from below began to illuminate their path. Tonyck tapped her on the shoulder. Rayne knew it was to halt her path so she could check the situation, but Rayne shrugged her off. The only person who'd be down here before her was Chase.

"It's fine." Rayne unclipped the safety clasp from her handgun holster and withdrew her Delta Elite Rail, more for Tonyck's benefit than any concern for her own safety. She didn't look to check Tonyck's reaction—a predictable raised eyebrow and clenched jaw—and continued her descent.

Rayne rounded the corner after the final step to see the impressive portable setup Chase had assembled. A scaffolding construction supported a suspended laser scanner that was busy traversing up and down the rails, capturing a 3-D image of Zenobia's tomb. Chase was positioned behind a camera, which Rayne assumed would be a Canon since she swore by Nikon and they were diametrically opposed on just about everything they'd ever discussed. Rayne would have startled her with what had become her traditional greeting, but Chase looked substantially less chunky than when she'd seen her last in the Paris catacombs. Her tight Under Armour sweatshirt revealed distinctively shaped shoulders and bulging biceps even though they weren't under any tension. Her now broad shoulders tapered into her waist, and she was wearing cargo pants that sheathed an impressively tight looking butt.

When Tonyck prodded her in the back, Rayne wondered just how long she'd been staring at Chase's rear view. Rayne batted Tonyck's hand away and holstered her weapon. "Dwayne Johnson sent me to get his wardrobe back."

Chase spun around, her foot caught a leg of her camera tripod, and it began to tumble toward the floor. She caught it before it crashed onto the hard surface and cursed.

"Jesus, Marcellus. You scared the crap out of me."

Rayne stifled a laugh at Chase's reaction, but Tonyck wasn't nearly as politic and guffawed loudly.

"Nervous much, Stinsen?" Tonyck asked before coming around Rayne and dropping her pack to the ground to unload her rope rig.

Chase settled the tripod and turned to face Rayne. "Why are you here? And what the hell is she doing?"

Rayne smiled. How to put it? "I have a client—"

"A rich, stupid, and ignorant client, always. But there's nothing you can take away here without attracting a lot of attention. And not the kind of attention you crave."

"Are you going to take these down? You probably wouldn't like the way I'd do it." Tonyck stood at the head of the tomb, gripping one of the scaffolding columns.

Chase moved around the casket to face Tonyck. Rayne noted she didn't look quite as hesitant squared up to her as she had in France. She had a new, and attractive, confident aura to match her super fit physique. It suited her enormously. But if she were a gambling woman, she'd still put her money on Tonyck. Rayne would happily tend to Chase's wounded body though.

"Get your ham hands off my equipment," Chase said.

She caught hold of the pole but didn't attempt to remove Tonyck. Sensible decision. "Leave it, Tonyck. You don't want to break anything she can't afford to replace."

Tonyck grinned, released her hands, and stepped back. "Then she needs to break it down in the next three minutes or I will."

Tonyck went back to setting up her rope rig, and Chase glared at Rayne, clearly waiting for an explanation. She had a way of looking rather adorable when she was mad, which she usually was when they met.

"Quit staring at me and tell me what the hell is going on," Chase said, not moving from her position. "I got here first. I'm halfway through the scanning, and I've just started the photographs. I'm not taking down my equipment for anyone. *Especially* not you."

Rayne couldn't blame Chase for her defensiveness. She hadn't had a win in their last four unofficial competitions. It'd been pretty even up to then, but Rayne saw the need for some extra help and had the means to employ it. Subsequently, she found Ginn and Tonyck. With the extra help, the rivalry had skewed in Rayne's favor, and Chase's previously playful demeanor took a decided turn to the persistently disgruntled.

"Not even if ISIS is about to descend on us?"

Chase tilted her head and put her hands on her hips. "What did you and your goons do?"

Tonyck looked up. "You should be really careful about how you refer to the people who are gonna save your ass, Stinsen."

Chase straightened and made herself a little taller. If it weren't for the fact that they were all in danger of losing their lives, Rayne would have been enjoying the butch cockfight.

"As far as I was aware, I didn't need my ass saving," Chase said toward Tonyck before turning back to Rayne. "I managed to get down here without alerting anyone, and I was going to get out exactly the same way. Just me, my equipment, and my data. So I'll ask again. What did you and your goons do?"

Tonyck began to rise from her knees, but Rayne waved her down. Chase had every right to be angry and suspicious. Rayne pulled her ponytail tighter and sighed. "We believe we may have blown our cover in the village."

"*We believe we may have blown our cover?*" Chase placed her hands on the tomb and leaned toward Rayne. "This isn't a pirate wreck in the Florida Keys, Marcellus. We're in the middle of a war-torn country, and there are people out there who'd happily blow our heads off…after they've dragged our bodies through the streets on live TV. Are we in danger or not?"

Rayne shook her head; would Chase ever let Florida go? She heard Ginn coming down the steps behind her and saw a flash of relief on Tonyck's face. "We are. But we have a plan."

Chase threw up her hands. "Great. That's awesome. You and the army twins have a plan. I feel so much safer now. Just how long have we got before a troop of heavily armed fanatics come tearing down those steps and blast us all to pieces?"

"No one's blasting us to pieces on my watch, Stinsen," Ginn said as she joined her sister building the rope rig. "Move your shit and let us do our job."

Chase was silent for a moment. Rayne could almost see the cogs turning. Maybe she'd considered having a go at Tonyck, but now that there were two of them, she had no chance. Still, it seemed like Chase's ego was having a hard time backing down.

"Let me help." Rayne moved toward the laser scanner and switched it off. Chase looked at her as if she were about to stop her but didn't.

"FUCK!" Chase turned away, smashed her fists on the wall, and hung her head.

G&T raised their eyebrows, shook their heads dismissively, and returned to their work. This wasn't something they could possibly understand. All they comprehended was the need to work as fast as they could to get everyone out alive. Rayne hesitated, a novel and undesirable response she was unfamiliar with. Should she comfort Chase or gently rib her, as had become Rayne's way of communicating with her? This was Chase's Holy Grail, her passion. It wasn't just a commission or a client. It went far beyond that, and though Rayne had no such attachments to any historical period, or anything for that matter, she empathized with Chase. Rayne had read Chase's papers on the Warrior Queen and the subtext was clear: Zenobia meant far more to Chase than just another archeological find. She seemed to have made some deep, meaningful connection with the long-dead ruler, and to Chase, it must have felt like Rayne had strolled in and ruined everything she'd worked toward.

Rayne measured her approach to Chase. She reached for her shoulder but pulled back before she made contact. Given the situation, Chase could be forgiven if she turned around and whacked Rayne in the face. "We don't have much time, Chase. If you don't want to leave your equipment behind, we need to pack it up."

Chase swung around to face Rayne, and her contempt was as clear as Crater Lake.

"You think I care about the equipment?" She took a step closer to Rayne. "I can buy new equipment. I can't buy the chance to scan this tomb again." She poked Rayne in the chest. "You've seen to that. ISIS will descend on this place and destroy every last piece of history buried here."

Rayne ignored the aggressive physical contact and motioned to the twins, who now had their rig almost ready. "We're not leaving the sarcophagus here, Chase. It's coming with us."

Chase furrowed her brow. "What are you talking about? There's no way you can get her out of here."

Rayne chose to overlook the reference to Zenobia's actual physical presence, given there'd be nothing left of her but bones, and that was if they hadn't cremated her. "Trust me, I'm making it happen."

Chase scoffed. "Like I could ever trust you again."

She pushed past Rayne and began to quickly disassemble her apparatus, tossing the aluminum frame into a canvas pack. Tonyck stood and came around to the head of the tomb. She lifted it clean off the floor while Ginn pushed the inflatable net bag over the edge and into the middle. Tonyck released the tomb, switched to the opposite end, and Ginn pulled the bag to encase the tomb entirely.

"What are they doing?" Chase had cleared her laser scanner and moved on to her camera and tripod.

"Protecting the tomb for the trip."

"Of course they are." Chase strapped her tripod to the side of her pack and looked completely unconvinced.

Aware she was getting nowhere with Chase and even more aware that she didn't want to waste any time, Rayne shrugged and picked up the end of the netting. She closed the loop, unclipped the safety notch, and pulled the release wire. All the tiny pockets of foam within the net began to expand until the tomb was no longer visible. Rayne took a sideways glance at Chase and smiled when she saw that Chase looked suitably impressed with the ridiculously expensive, glorified inflatable bag. Rayne stepped back while G&T wrapped the rope rig around the casket and tightened it off. Tonyck unclipped the carabiner from her utility belt and refastened it to the one at the head of the tomb.

Ginn looked back to Rayne. "Good to go, lady boss. I'll send the signal to Mac when I'm topside," she said and jogged back up the steps.

Moments later, the chamber shuddered with the blast of explosives at the surface. Chase jumped but tried to cover it up by running her hand through her hair and affecting a look of nonchalance. Tonyck shook her head but said nothing. The cable on the tomb tautened, and it began a slow ascent up the steps with Tonyck guiding it.

"Ready?" Rayne asked. Chase nodded, unusually silent. "Do you want some help with your pack?"

Chase muttered something under her breath and looked mortally offended. "I've got it."

Rayne suppressed a smile. It was almost too easy to tease a butch, but as femme as she was, Rayne could handle her share of any workload. She turned to follow Tonyck. "Then let's get out of here." The casket's progress was pretty slow, necessitating something short of a turtle crawl behind it. Rayne milked it a little, exaggerating her walk in case Chase was checking out her ass. She suspected Chase was probably far more concerned with a potential gunfight once they were out of the chamber, which was also what Rayne should be troubled by. But she had faith in the twins. They'd never failed her yet, and despite their initial reluctance to continue with the mission, their energy had settled, and they seemed assured everything would turn out okay.

"When did you start packing?"

Rayne resisted a sexual riposte and tapped the butt of her pistol. "Like you said, this isn't the Florida Keys."

"Are you any good?"

Chase sounded either impressed or disbelieving. Rayne couldn't decide which, but Chase should know by now that Rayne could do anything a butch like Chase could do, *and* do it in high heels without breaking any nails. "G&T wouldn't let me have one if I wasn't."

"Let you? Aren't you the one calling the shots?"

Rayne smiled at the dig but didn't rise. "I'll be the one firing the shots if I have to. That's all you need to know." Rayne wished she could have seen Chase's face. It *sounded* like she might even be smiling. Rayne's own smile disappeared when she heard Ginn's hollering. The whirring of helicopter blades deadened Ginn's words, but her urgency was unmistakable. The spatter of gunfire punctured the short silences between the blades slashing through the night sky, and Tonyck turned back to face her.

"Stay low. Conserve your ammo. Shoot single shots where you see the sunbursts," Tonyck said before clambering over the tomb to join her sister. She turned back briefly and pointed toward Chase. "And keep her out of the way."

Rayne swallowed hard and pulled her Colt from its holster. Shooting at sunbursts instead of paper targets sounded only slightly less ominous than shooting at people. The tomb shifted suddenly and disappeared from view. Rayne could see bursts of gunfire maybe a quarter of a mile away. She had no idea what weapons they were using or what range they might have. She was only hoping that they didn't have anti-aircraft missiles. G&T said they'd always carried arsenic capsules in a false filling in their teeth in case they were captured and the future looked grim. Rayne wondered if they'd kept them. They had no backup team in case this operation went south. What would she do if they were captured? She didn't want to think about that right now. Getting out of here had to be her only focus.

She pulled down her night goggles and ventured out, careful to keep low as Tonyck had instructed. She glanced back at Chase to see she had a phone in her hand. Was she sending a final text just in case they didn't make it out of here? Who to? Rayne didn't think Chase was seeing anyone.

Another burst of gunfire startled her from her absurdly misplaced musings. "Follow behind me."

Rayne saw Chase clench her jaw. She clearly didn't like the idea of being rescued by someone she saw as a damsel no doubt, but she had little choice. This was a dangerous place to give playtime to Chase's ego so she ignored it and moved forward. The twisted air from the invasion of the helicopter blades made the dust plume upward in vicious mini tornadoes and gave them some natural cover. Rayne could see Tonyck working hard to fix the tomb to the custom-built cargo carrier beneath the chopper while Ginn laid down cover fire forty feet away to draw enemy fire from her sister. Rayne moved beyond Tonyck and the chopper and dropped into a ditch, pressing herself against the compacted dirt.

Chase thudded down beside her. "What are the chances of us getting out of here alive?"

Her voice sounded calm considering their surroundings, and Rayne was glad Chase seemed to be relatively cool in a crisis of this magnitude. Both of them were archeologists, and neither of them were battle trained. But they both knew the risks of this particular undertaking. At least Rayne had brought a team qualified to deal with this fallout. What was Chase thinking, coming in here alone? Rayne quelled the pique she felt rising. Chase shouldn't be her concern, and yet she here she was, about to return enemy fire on her behalf.

Rayne ignored the question she didn't want to answer and slowly raised her head above ground level to wait for an attack. It wasn't long before a whole surge of sunbursts lit up an area of palm trees, and the rounds kicked up sand just in front of her. Submachine guns, and in range. Her own fire would barely cover half the distance between them and whoever was attacking them, but it would give them more than one target to aim at. That way, they couldn't be sure of how many of them there were. She steadied her arms on the ground, just like Tonyck had taught her. Closed her right eye. Ignored her hammering heart. Braced her arms and shoulders. Took a deep breath. Slowly squeezed the trigger.

Without ear defenders, the reverberation of the gunshot surprised Rayne. She tuned it out and refocused. Another shot. Still powerful enough to shove her shoulders back a few inches, but she was more prepared for the noise this time. Ginn shot flares of fire from her MPX just to the left of her, and their attackers returned the favor. Rayne was soon through her first magazine. She drew back into the hollow, released the empty clip, and slammed another into the magazine seat. She was back over the ledge and firing a slow and steady stream of shots in double quick time. Rayne registered the proximity of the shots heading her way. Some thudded to the ground close enough to feel vibration in the dirt, others tore open the air above her head, echoing their deadly intent as they passed.

"G! Rayne! We're a go. Get over here."

Rayne couldn't recall ever being more elated to hear Tonyck's voice. She retreated from the edge of danger, caught hold of Chase's arm, and tugged her toward the helicopter. She heard the heavy footfall of Ginn close in before she felt her strong arm wrap around her back and propel them all forward. They ducked beneath the hurtling chopper rotor and Ginn made sure Rayne was the first one in. Rayne turned to see Ginn all but throw Chase into the cabin.

"Get us the fuck out of here, Mac." Tonyck stepped onto the landing skids and continued to fire as Mac steered the Huey in the opposite direction to the attack.

Rayne backed up and settled onto the canvas covered bench. Chase hitched herself up to sit beside Rayne. Tonyck was already seated on one of the outward facing benches, her gun trained on the disappearing landscape of the Palmyrene mountain belt, and Ginn perched similarly on the opposite bench.

Rayne holstered her weapon and stretched out her hand slowly. She hadn't realized how hard she'd been gripping her gun, and her fingers felt like arthritic twisted steel. She used her other hand to rub it out and pushed away the latent panic at the back of her throat. They were safe, and she had the casket. She glanced across to Chase, who'd dropped her head between her knees and had her hands on the back of her neck. Her pack lay discarded between her feet. Rayne once again admired the distinct lines that separated her delts and biceps. Her attention traveled along Chase's back to appraise her ripped lats, and Rayne allowed herself a moment to imagine digging her nails into that back while Chase fucked her.

She'd transformed her body in the year Rayne hadn't seen her, and the transformation was impressive. Rayne had always had a soft spot for Chase, but her new hard body ramped her attractiveness up a level and made the conquest even more appealing. Rayne tugged out the wrap holding her hair up and enjoyed the weight of it falling over her shoulders like a comforting blanket. She leaned in to Chase's ear and whispered, "Let's go to my place."

CHAPTER THREE

Cyprus, 2019

CHASE TURNED UP the heat on the shower and pressed her head to the smooth tile. The Palmyran desert sand pooled around her feet before snaking off toward the drain and disappearing. She closed her eyes tight. *She* could've disappeared tonight. In the heat of the fight, she hadn't wanted to contemplate what would have happened if the ISIS forces had overcome Rayne and her team. But now, in the safety of the penthouse suite at the Royal Casale, Chase couldn't switch off the part of her brain that insisted on going to that dark place. The image of al-Asaad's mutilated body etched itself on her eyelids, and she opened them quickly. It could've easily been her hanging from one of those columns right now. One thing that had come out of this was that she'd be carefully considering the potential danger in all future assignments. Up to today, it had been easy to be gung-ho, but being faced with her own mortality had been quite the wake-up call. No amount of physical training could have prepared her for what had transpired that evening.

A big part of her wanted to be angry with Rayne. Chase was more or less convinced that it was Rayne who had attracted the unwanted attention, but she had no way of really knowing that patrol wouldn't have come her way regardless. For all she knew, it could have been a routine scouting party that attacked them and had nothing to do with Rayne's presence. In which case, Chase should be on her knees thanking Rayne and her team for saving her skin *and* Zenobia's tomb. In the afterglow of survival, she'd almost forgotten that not only had they gotten away from Syria with their lives, Rayne had rescued Zenobia's legacy from certain desecration by a historically disrespectful occupying force.

Chase stopped herself from getting carried away with thoughts of Rayne being suddenly altruistic. She'd been there for a client, as always… but Rayne hadn't been obliged to take Chase with her. More than simply take her with them, Rayne had protected Chase. She'd risked her life by firing back. She hadn't taken cover and waited for the gorilla girls to clear the path. Rayne had taken an equal responsibility in getting them out of there, and now they were safely ensconced in a luxury hotel over three hundred miles away.

She couldn't deny that she'd been more than a little impressed with how Rayne handled the situation. She could even have been a little turned on by it all if she hadn't been fearful for her life. There was something about a woman like Rayne taking control that scratched for her attention. But it also dug at her prowess and taunted her for not taking care of Rayne.

She heard a gentle knock on the bathroom door. "Yeah?"

"Are you hungry?"

Rayne's question was ambiguous. For food or something else? The way her hot breath had caressed Chase's ear in the helicopter with the offer of going to her place inferred Rayne could be offering something other than a meal. But Chase wouldn't be going there. As grateful as she was for the extrication from certain death, Rayne Marcellus was still a glorified tomb raider, and that didn't sit well. It didn't matter how off-the-charts sexy she was. And no doubt, Zenobia wouldn't be made available for the whole world to celebrate.

Chase's stomach grumbled for her attention, outstripping the need for anything else. "I'm starving. I'll eat anything other than pork, thanks."

"No problem."

Rayne's response was immediate, and Chase wondered if she'd read something into nothing. Rayne could have any woman she liked. She wouldn't bother with…Chase looked down at her body. She was no longer the chunky woman Rayne teased mercilessly. She had rips and bumps, muscles instead of a shapeless form. Chase wasn't anywhere near the size of Rayne's two shadow mountains—she didn't want to be—but she had more confidence in her body than she'd ever had before.

She put the distracting thoughts aside and lathered up, wanting to wash away the whole experience. She'd figure out how to get home later, but right now all she wanted to do was eat and sleep for a few hours. Hopefully, this suite had two bedrooms.

***

Chase wrapped the silk bathrobe around her, folded up the arms, and shoved them over the elbows. She looked in the mirror and shook her head. There was no way to butch up this robe at all. Another knock on the bathroom door made her jump.

"Your clothes, madam. Fully laundered."

Chase opened the door to a young woman in a service uniform holding a neatly pressed pile of her clothes. "Thank God…thank you." There was no sign of Rayne, and Chase couldn't offer a tip so she just smiled in what she hoped would convey her apology and closed the door slowly. She stripped out of the offensive garment and redressed. When she emerged from the bathroom again, the dining table was covered in a whole range of dishes and Rayne was seated at the head of the table with her two bodyguards on the opposite side, facing her. Neither of them looked up from their food to acknowledge her so she figured that a deadly battle didn't make them civil acquaintances. Rayne smiled and motioned for Chase to join them. She poured herself a coffee and sat beside Rayne. It all felt strangely normal considering they were being shot at a few hours ago.

"My client says they're a direct descendant of Cleopatra, just like Zenobia," Rayne said after a swallow of orange juice. "Her genetic material has had a lot of years to get around, so I'm not questioning the validity of their claim."

Straight to business then, which reminded Chase that her scan was only two-thirds complete. Was Rayne having an attack of conscience and felt the need to justify her actions? "Okay. And you're telling me this, why?"

"My client has agreed to let you complete your laser scan and take as many photos as you wish, on the understanding that you never reveal the fate of the tomb, particularly to your employers. As far as anyone is concerned, the casket was left beneath the city, most likely to be destroyed by ISIS." She waved toward her muscle mountains. ~~muscle Marys~~. "And we were never there."

Agreed to? Meaning Rayne must have asked on Chase's behalf. That was unexpected. Had a close shave with death finally given Rayne the principles Chase hoped she'd one day discover?

"G&T have put your equipment in the ballroom, along with Zenobia's tomb." Rayne pushed a keycard along the table toward Chase. "It's perfectly secure. You have until noon before we move it."

Chase reached for the keycard and Rayne put her hand over Chase's.

"As a favor to me, my client has offered that you can visit the tomb to conduct further tests for your own purposes only…if you can prove you can keep your mouth shut."

Chase's hand tingled beneath Rayne's soft touch and she shivered. Rayne looked amused by her reaction but didn't say anything. Tonyck stopped eating long enough to glare at her. Was she being protective or was there some deeper attraction to her boss? Chase suspected it might well be both. Unless she was straight, which Chase unapologetically doubted, how could Tonyck *not* be attracted to Rayne? And if Tonyck was, Chase expected her twin sister would be too.

Rayne withdrew her hand, and Chase checked her watch. It was just before nine a.m. If she wolfed down a quick breakfast, she'd have two and a half hours to conduct her scan and take as many photographs as she needed. The natural lighting would make them far superior and less grainy than the ones she'd managed in the tomb *and* they wouldn't have the scaffolding in the way if she shot them first before setting up the laser scanner. "I don't know what to say, Rayne."

"Thank you would be a damned good start," Ginn said before she shoveled another forkful of food in her mouth.

Rayne shook her head. "With our history, I expect that's not a phrase Chase will find easy to say to me."

History. Trust. Chase remembered how much she'd enjoyed working with Rayne on that joint expedition in the Florida Keys almost a decade ago. It could've been the beginning of an unstoppable pairing. Their skills complemented each other perfectly, but Rayne had screwed her, and Chase had worked solo ever since. Was this about second chances? Did saving her life mean the slate should be wiped clean, or was it simply a hiatus in hostilities? An armistice of sorts? And once Chase left this idyllic island, she should expect normal service to resume?

"I'm sorry. I *am* grateful." Chase shifted in her chair to face Rayne, trying to ignore the tank twins' presence. She wouldn't have chosen to do this in front of them, but she pressed on regardless. "Thanks for getting me out of Syria alive." *If the patrol was coincidental and not entirely your fault.* "And thank you for the opportunity to complete my scan. You know how much this period of history means to me, and I'd love to spend more time studying Zenobia's tomb…but you're asking me to lie to get what I want."

THE GOLDEN TRINITY

Chase leaned back in her chair and ran her hand across the back of her head. She tried to read Rayne's expression, but it was like the shutters had come down over her soul the moment Chase had said "but." This was such an impossible situation. "I believe in everyone having access to our world history. Not just the ones who can afford to hire the best grave robbers in the business." Rayne's jaw clenched at the description, but as far as Chase was concerned, it was a title well-earned. "You're offering me something that I've wanted since I was an undergrad. But to take it, I'd have to abandon the morals I've built my life and reputation around." Voicing the thought diminished her appetite considerably, and Chase pushed away the plate of food that had been prepared for her. "I'm not like you. I just can't do that."

Rayne shrugged, and any emotion or reaction she had to Chase's words weren't visible.

"Your loss. I didn't think it would be so easy for you to surrender your life's passion." Rayne swirled the juice in her glass as she spoke. "Would your morals prefer it if we'd left her casket for ISIS to desecrate?"

Rayne drummed her manicured, painted nails on the table. Her face might not have given anything away, but her words and body language gave away at least some of what she was feeling. Her indignation was misplaced. Rayne had no right to get up on a horse of any height. She was a thief in every other walk of life.

"I'd *prefer* it if you let me take the tomb to Stanford and then on to a suitable museum for everyone to appreciate. I'd *prefer* it if you didn't take it to one ridiculously rich woman who thinks she's a long distant relative of two great queens when in fact, they're probably a nobody trying desperately to be a somebody."

The twins stopped eating. They dropped their cutlery to the table noisily and glared at Chase. She'd been rude considering Rayne's hospitality, but running her mouth off had always been a problem that got her into trouble. She might be able to hold one off long enough to sprint away, but she didn't like her chances with both of them bearing down on her. Surely Rayne wouldn't let them put a beating on her just because Chase had told her how she felt.

"I think you've outworn your welcome, Stinsen."

The words came from the one that might or might not have been Ginn. Chase hadn't been interested enough to study them to tell them apart.

Rayne held up her hand, presumably to stop her from speaking on Rayne's behalf. She tapped her expensive watch, a Tag Heuer Chase recognized from a billboard ad. Chase glanced down at her own Casio. Their worlds were so far apart, they might as well live on different planets. She'd been stupid to think that Rayne could possibly have changed.

"You'd better make the most of the time you've got left with your precious Zenobia then. Your equipment is there." Rayne pointed to the door. "Tonyck will take you down."

Chase looked at Rayne's heavies and didn't like the sneer that played on their faces with Rayne's final phrase. It felt like they were itching to knock her around and the only thing stopping them was a lack of tacit permission from their boss. Chase pushed her chair from the table and stood. She wanted to say something else to Rayne but wasn't sure what, and she didn't want to offend her further in case Rayne *was* tempted to sic her dogs on her. Rayne had focused her gaze through the floor to ceiling windows. She was otherwise enchanted with the glorious view of the Mediterranean Sea. More likely she was just done with Chase.

Tonyck was already at the door, but Chase shook her head as she walked toward it. "I don't need an escort. I can find my own way, thanks."

She didn't move and looked beyond Chase for further instruction from Rayne. Chase turned to see Rayne shrug and wave her away dismissively. It shouldn't have surprised her. It certainly shouldn't have hurt her. And yet, an inexplicable cattle prod-like stun to Chase's chest got her attention. She exited the room and closed the door quietly behind her before she said or did anything she might regret.

Chapter Four

New York

RAYNE RELAXED INTO the director's chair in the corner of her seventieth-floor office. From here, she could the horses at Central Park and the long line of shivering tourists desperate to hitch up and be wrapped in a heavy fur blanket, just like they'd seen in the movies. From this distance, they looked like Monopoly pieces and the park was the game board. On the corner, a tiny dot in a booth was selling five-dollar cups of hot chocolate for the ride. No doubt he would be doubling the price today. Tourists were known to pay any price for something toasty when temperatures hit minus double figures in the city. The memory of meeting Jack in a dirty street in India's Orissa district made an appearance in the movie theater of her brain. He'd helped her out of a sticky bartering situation that, without his linguistic skills, would probably have seen her exchanging her freedom for the artifact. In return, she'd flown him over to her city. She'd helped him become a US citizen and start his own catering business. Getting his papers had been difficult. The current president's xenophobia was at an historically dangerous level, but Rayne's considerable connections were able to slice through the bureaucracy and make Jack's American dream a reality.

"Ginn and Tonyck are here, Ms. Marcellus. Shall I send them through?"

Her receptionist's voice cut into Rayne's peaceful memories. Rayne smiled. Hearing someone else introduce her team still made her laugh. She pressed the intercom on the table beside her chair. "Thanks, Jenny. Please do."

G&T came through the doors looking extremely pleased with themselves. "Hey, lady boss."

"You both look very fresh considering you've just done a round trip to LA in twenty-four hours. Get yourselves a drink and tell me everything."

Tonyck grabbed two bottles of mineral water before they both flopped down onto the sofa opposite Rayne. She shifted her position to look at them and grinned. "You got more than money on your trip, didn't you?" Rayne asked, suspecting she already knew exactly what kind of extras they got from one of her favorite clients, Kera Espinosa.

Ginn cracked her bottle open and nodded. "She was *very* grateful for the African ruby. She said she was disappointed you didn't deliver it because she would've liked to have thanked you personally."

"But you softened her disappointment considerably, yes?" Rayne winked. Kera had a notoriety for loving women that blew Rayne's reputation for ephemeral dalliances out of the water, but she wasn't certain Kera would go for the twins. She was known for her love of femmes.

Tonyck laughed. "She said she'd been thinking about a 'sister sandwich' since you hired us. Wanted to know what it might feel like crushed between two walls of muscle."

Rayne raised her eyebrows. She'd wondered exactly the same thing, but a sense of professionalism had stopped her from finding out. She'd probably drop Kera a line for a more vivid description from her perspective. Kera's skills as a raconteur all but matched her almost god-like ability between the sheets. Rayne was slightly sorry for missing out, but she'd promised the twins a special bonus on top of tripling their cash for the Syria debacle, and they seemed particularly grateful.

Rayne couldn't stop her train of thought from barreling along the tracks to Chase Stinsen. Not that she'd expected to, but Rayne hadn't heard from Chase since they loaded Zenobia's tomb onto her client's private jet and left her on Cyprus to find her own way home. Rayne knew she should've offered her passage from the island, but she'd still been smarting from Chase's complete destruction of her character and profession. And the knockback was something she wasn't used to and wasn't inclined to *get* used to either. They'd had a brush with death. Rayne thought it was completely natural to celebrate their escape with a few hours of life-affirming, break-the-bed, head-exploding sex. But Ms. Morals was having none of it. If she wouldn't share her bed, she wasn't getting the chance to share her plane.

And the twins had made their feelings on Chase very clear. They would have rather fucked her up for her disrespect to Rayne than share any more oxygen with her on a luxury jet. They weren't just her employees. They'd become her friends, and she valued their opinion. She somehow felt they would've been disappointed with her if she'd offered Chase a seat on their flight after the way she'd spoken to Rayne. So she didn't. Nor did she make any effort to say good-bye or speak to her at all after Chase had left their breakfast table. She sent G&T down at noon to transport the tomb to the waiting jet. She'd given them strict instructions not to engage further with Chase and not to touch any of her equipment unless it obstructed movement of the tomb. They'd looked disappointed. Rayne knew they would do anything for her, and if she'd asked them to take Chase outside and teach her a brutal lesson in respect, they would have. And, she suspected, they would've enjoyed doing it a little too much.

Rayne looked at her desk. This month's issue of *Archeology* teased its readers with the promise of a "Zenobia: The Warrior Queen special feature" in its next release. She had no way of knowing if Chase would reveal everything that transpired that night, despite Rayne asking her not to. Rayne had alerted her lawyer, and she was on the case, demanding to see the article before it went to print if Rayne or her team were mentioned at all. Act now and save yourself an expensive lawsuit, her lawyer had warned the publication. Rayne had considered calling Chase to ask her outright, but her lawyer vetoed the idea. "No fraternizing with the enemy," she'd said with the dramatic flair she was known for in the courtroom. When had Chase become the enemy and not just healthy competition? Whatever, now it was just a waiting game.

"Rayne?"

She returned her focus to Ginn and had an unfamiliar rush of gratitude for the twins having crossed her path. Her parents wouldn't have been impressed with the strange gust of emotion. *Every relationship is just another business transaction.* It was an odd code to begin teaching a child at eleven years old, but she learned her lesson well and for the most part, it had stuck.

"You guys should take a vacation." Rayne leaned forward and tapped them both on their knees. "You've earned a break."

Tonyck looked puzzled. "We only just got back from Africa."

"That was work. You need to relax." Rayne got up and faced the city she loved so much. It was a city with an insular population that made her parents' code very easy to live by.

"We spent a week in a five-star spa hotel, getting massages and mud baths. I couldn't be more relaxed." Tonyck joined Rayne at the window and put her arm over Rayne's shoulders. "Do *you* need a break?"

The softness in Tonyck's voice belied her rock-like appearance. Beneath their gruff and impressively built exterior, the twins had a quiet emotional intelligence they kept hidden from everyone but Rayne. "Maybe." Rayne patted Tonyck's hand and moved from beneath the considerable weight of her arm. They were close, but that kind of intimate physical touch—more intimate than a kiss in many ways—still made Rayne a little twitchy. She sat behind the safe barrier of her solid oak desk and picked up the email Jenny had printed off for her earlier this morning. A man named Stan Turner wouldn't stop calling, insisting that he had the opportunity of a lifetime for her. Jenny heard that a lot, and thus far, it'd never been true. And neither she nor Rayne had ever heard of a Stan Turner, so the likelihood of his claim being true was less than minimal. He said he'd send her proof and that Rayne would definitely take the meeting as soon as she saw it.

She studied his proof again. Ancient Mayan symbols decorated what looked like part of a map. The colorful trio of images in the top was what had captured, and now held, Rayne's attention. Legends, myths, and lore surrounded the existence of the Golden Trinity, but that's all there had ever been. A treasure hoard to dwarf all treasure hoards. A career-defining find. Something to make Rayne more than just a "glorified grave digger," as Chase was fond of calling her.

She moved a piece of hair from over her eye that was bothering her. Just like Chase Stinsen. Chase's near-constant presence in her mind was becoming distracting and irritating. Why she kept thinking about Chase was beyond her and beyond frustration. Sure, Rayne would've enjoyed a couple of hours in the sack with her, but it didn't happen. Why couldn't she just let it go? Had she gotten so used to women throwing themselves at her that "no" was a word alien to her comprehension? Deep down, in a placed she buried all the things that she couldn't control or understand, a place her parents had encouraged her to cultivate and hide from everyone, often including herself. In that place, she knew this was all about Florida. Young and hungry, Rayne had thought and hesitated too little when the decision to capitalize on their work at Chase's expense had presented itself. Her head had been too easily turned by the lure of a fast fortune, and Rayne had known that Chase's moral compass wouldn't allow the sale of their find, even just a third of it, to a private collector. Lauren Young was fifteen years older than Rayne and had everything Rayne wanted: fortune, fame, and the ability to charm anyone and everyone out of anything and everything. Lauren promised she could mold Rayne so that she could have it all too. All she had to do was double-cross her partner.

Rayne looked over at Ginn and Tonyck. Tonyck had retaken her seat and they waited, respectfully, for Rayne to pick up the conversation. They'd only been working for her for a little over eighteen months, but they already knew when to keep quiet and not press further. She switched her mind back to Stan Turner and his promise of a lifetime opportunity. If what he'd sent her was genuine. If it was a tiny piece of a large map that could lead her to the Golden Trinity, she'd be foolish not to at least meet him to see what he actually had. On its own, it was nothing. It was a tease, with no intention of delivering anything more substantial. But if he'd somehow managed to discover a complete map and he'd called only her, it wasn't something she'd be passing on.

"I'm going to California for a couple of days." Rayne folded the printed email and slipped it into her handbag.

Tonyck's gaze was searching. "Are we coming with?"

Rayne shook her head. "It might be nothing. I'll call you if it turns into something." She called Jenny on the intercom. "Jenny, get me a flight to Los Angeles this afternoon, please. Call Turner and arrange a meeting for tomorrow." The return flight? Rayne could look in on Chase at Stanford while she was in the area, lawyer's advice be damned. "I'll call you from LA to organize a return flight if I need one." If Turner's map turned out to be genuine, she'd be heading south of the border immediately.

"No problem. I'll send the details to your cell," Jenny said. "Where would you like to stay?"

Rayne ran through the list of her favorite city hotels; it was a short list since most of them were pretentious, overpriced, and lackluster. "Book me in at the Vervida." She recalled her last stay there had included a thank you gift from Kera in the form of a cute butch with a terrible weakness for femmes in extraordinarily high heels. Kera had also provided a pair of killer six-inch Jimmy Choos in leather softer than a baby panda's butt. Rayne couldn't have done much walking in them, but the heel fit in the cute butch's mouth perfectly, as did much of the rest of her. Maybe when she called Kera later, she'd see if her friend was available tomorrow night.

There was no better way to relax after a meeting than with a short-haired woman on her knees.

"Who's Turner?"

Ginn's question echoed distantly and returned Rayne to the room. "I don't know yet. Speak to Jenny. She'll give you the information she has on him so far. See what you can find because we couldn't find anything of interest." Rayne pushed out of her chair and picked up her handbag, eager to get home and pack the perfect outfits for the trip. "Email me whatever you unearth. Call me if it's something I need to prepare myself for before the meeting. Jenny will give you the details when it's organized."

"Be careful," Tonyck said, her concern evident in the faint lines around her eyes.

"It's just a meeting, T."

Tonyck let out a short huff of breath the way she did when she doubted something.

"It's never just a meeting, lady boss."

Rayne touched Tonyck's shoulder as she passed her. "I'm sure there's no need for you to worry. I had my tracker checked after Africa. It's working perfectly. You'll always know where I am." She winked, thinking about meeting with Chase. "Unless I don't want you to know."

Tonyck sighed. "We can't protect you if we don't know where you are, Rayne."

Her serious tone made Rayne smile. It was rather nice having people so concerned for her welfare, even if she was paying them to do so. She stopped as she opened the door and smiled at the twins. "You know I appreciate your anxiety over my safety, but I'll be fine. I'll send word on the Batphone if I need your help."

Tonyck lifted her water bottle as if to throw it at Rayne. "You're mocking us. Get out of here."

Rayne flashed a smile, closed the door behind her, and turned into a waiting Jenny.

"Your flight is booked from JFK for two thirty p.m. You land at LAX at a quarter to six. Your usual driver, Adele, will be waiting for you at the gate and will take you directly to Vervida. I've sent the tickets to your cell." She tapped off a series of items on her tablet and looked up. "I've booked your regular table at the hotel restaurant for the first two evenings with a hold on it for the following two evenings, should you choose to extend your stay. Chef Michaela will prepare your food personally."

Rayne smiled, recalling the last time she'd tasted Chef Michaela's food, and later, Chef Michaela herself. With the delightful combination of her *and* the cute butch, that weekend had been a particularly good one.

"Mr. Turner would like you to join him for lunch tomorrow at two in his penthouse suite at the Rodeo Grande."

Rayne raised her eyebrow. A private meeting was standard. That Turner was residing at the Grande indicated he had more means than she and Jenny had given him credit for. Or he was ramping up a horrific credit card bill that he'd be paying off for the next decade. *Or* he was just a damned fine con artist, and he'd be leaving without paying the bill at all. Rayne wanted to know which scenario she was walking into. "Call the Grande. Check who's in the penthouse." She glanced back at her closed office door. G&T wouldn't be impressed she was having a closed meeting without them present when they hadn't done a thorough background check. "Let me know as soon as you find out." If he was a conman ~~the latter~~, she'd still take the meeting, of course, but she might borrow a bodyguard from Kera for company.

"Is there anyone else you'd like me to contact for a meeting while you're in the area?"

Rayne shook her head. "I'll look in on Kera Espinosa if I have time, but I'll call her myself." She neglected to mention that she might call in on Chase while she was there; she didn't want her, the twins, or her lawyer knowing about that possibility. And if Kera's cute little butch friend or Chef Michaela were free, maybe Rayne wouldn't be tempted to follow through anyway. There seemed little point pursuing a rekindling of their friendship. And yet, the guilt wouldn't allow Rayne to put it behind her either. Rayne had made her choice a decade ago, and she'd made her fortune since, just as Lauren had predicted. Chase hadn't let Florida go, and if saving her life didn't convince her to leave the past behind, Rayne suspected that nothing would.

CHAPTER FIVE

"I'M SORRY, CHASE. But we can't afford to have a shark like Teri Harper coming after us. I need you to cut any reference to Rayne Marcellus or anyone connected with her."

Chase rubbed the palm of her hand hard across her forehead. How was it that Rayne was nearly three thousand miles away and still managing to mess with her life? "I don't understand why, Barry. Every word of the article is true."

"Unfortunately, Chase, that's irrelevant. It's your word against hers, and you have no proof that Ms. Marcellus was anywhere near Palmyra or Zenobia's tomb. Our lawyers aren't budging on this, and the publisher isn't prepared to take the risk. This isn't the *Washington Post*. If you refuse to rewrite the feature, none of it will be printed. It's that simple."

"Fine. I'll take it out." Chase hated having to compromise her integrity, but she wanted it published. She wanted to share the photos of Zenobia's tomb and the 3-D model they'd created at Stanford with more than the student body. "When do you need it by?"

"End of next week, latest." There was a pause on the other end of the line. "And thank you, Chase. You've made the right decision."

Carry ended the call before Chase could respond.

"I doubt that." The right decision for them to avoid legal action, maybe. Chase scrolled through her phone contacts to Rayne's office number in New York. She should call and tell her exactly what she thought about her latest stunt. She couldn't believe Rayne would threaten to sue the magazine. Chase recalled that she'd said as much in Cyprus, but she thought Rayne was bluffing.

She placed her cell on her desk and turned to the window to enjoy a little summer sunshine. A lone student who hadn't gone home for the summer trekked across the grass and copped a squat beneath a willow tree. She pulled a book from her backpack and settled against the willow's trunk, apparently instantly absorbed. Part of her would've liked to have been back in their shoes, her whole life in front of her again. She wouldn't make the mistake of trusting Rayne again, that was for sure. She rocked back in her chair and grabbed her stress ball. Who was she kidding? She'd fall for Rayne's charm in any parallel universe in any circumstance, no matter how many chances she got to have a do-over. When they met, Rayne was everything Chase felt that she wasn't: beautiful, intelligent, fascinating. Her self-esteem had improved plenty since Florida, and she now knew her own worth…though she'd never call herself fascinating… or beautiful for that matter. But she *was* intelligent. And she had a certain appeal to enough women to keep her from being a completely clichéd professor, married to her work and with no time for anything else.

If she thought about it long enough, and she'd thought about it plenty in the ensuing decade, Rayne had broken something inside her when she'd betrayed Chase and she'd never cared to fix it. She was happy enough, and her work *did* keep her too busy to have anyone long term in her life, as a lover or a friend; both required more time and attention than she had to give. The only person she always found the time for was Noemie, and since Noemie had joined the army a few years ago, she demanded less attention than she had as a rootless orphan teenager.

Chase glanced at the picture of Noemie on her desk, taken on the day she passed her basic training. Chase's pride had been beyond containment on that day. It wasn't as though Chase raised Noemie—she'd done that herself against all odds—but she'd been there for the past nine years when no one else really had. She'd been a kind of adopted mum, though she would've preferred to have been identified as an adopted sister. But that wasn't what Noemie needed. She needed a parental figure where none had ever been before. The students who asked if Noemie was her little sister always got preferential treatment over those who asked if she was Chase's daughter. There was only a thirteen-year age gap, for God's sake.

Chase's phone vibrated on her desk with an unknown number. She hated those when Noemie was on active duty. Every unknown number that rang during those times raised an army of ants in her stomach that made her nauseous.

"Chase Stinsen."

"Hi, Chase Stinsen."

Think of the devil and she calls. Why did she always address her with her full name? Even Rayne's telephone voice was smooth enough to…to what? Chase pushed the unfinished sentiment away. "Have you called to gloat? Because if you have—"

"Whoa, slow down. Gloat about what?" Rayne asked.

Her surprise sounded genuine enough but that didn't change the facts. "I just got off the phone with the editor at *Archeology Today*. You won, like always."

Rayne sighed. "I did ask you not to include me and my team. My client would've sued me if anything had gotten out about their involvement. I know you don't rate what I do, but I take my client's privacy very seriously."

Chase noted Rayne's non-gender specific use of a pronoun, just as in Cyprus. Either her client was gender-fluid or more likely, she was being clever enough not to reveal even the slightest detail about them. Whatever Chase thought of Rayne, her professional discretion had always been beyond compromise. It was a shame Chase wasn't able to say the same about her professional morality. "That's probably because they're criminals and would end up in jail if you revealed who they were." Chase knew she was being inflammatory, but she was damn sore about her article, and Rayne was to blame for all of it.

"Wow, that's very judgmental and completely untrue. Well…not completely."

There was a playfulness in Rayne's voice that almost made Chase smile. At least it wasn't a video call; Chase didn't want Rayne knowing she could still make her laugh. "I'm mad at you." She hadn't intended to be so matter-of-fact about it, and it sounded childish. Rayne had a knack of getting her to say exactly what was on her mind without ever asking directly.

"Saying it aloud is the first step to getting over it," Rayne said, sounding like she was making no effort at all to control her amusement.

"I don't want to get over it, Rayne. This is my career, my profession. Editing you, the tank twins, and your Cleopatra descendant client out of the story is going to make it impossible to write." Chase paused. She wouldn't have a full scan if it hadn't been for Rayne's presence and actions. She softened slightly. Rayne could've gotten considerable kudos for her inclusion in Chase's article, had she been able to tell the full story. Maybe Rayne hadn't acted completely selfishly.

"I'm sure that whatever you write will be perfect, Chase. You don't need me in it. *You* found Zenobia first, and it's possible that if it hadn't been for the ISIS patrol, which may or may not have occurred as a result of our presence, you would've gotten everything you needed and escaped undetected. Tell *that* story."

That was the closest Chase had ever come to receiving a compliment and a confession from Rayne, and she had enough sins to keep her saying Hail Marys for at least a year. "What *have* you called for? I'm busy." She checked the time. "I have a class in five minutes." It was an obvious lie, and she didn't care to analyze why she'd felt the need to fabricate a fantasy lecture. Rayne was on the other side of the country and still she affected Chase in ways she didn't appreciate.

"Aren't all your students on summer break?"

Chase glanced across at the student still beneath the tree. "Some stayed back for extra tuition. What did you call me for?"

"Teacher's pets. Do you they bring you shiny red apples? I'd bring you a shiny red apple."

"And it'd probably be poisoned. What did you call me for, Rayne?"

"Ouch. But anyway, I called to invite you to dinner. I'm in Frisco for a meeting about the Golden Trinity. I wanted to talk to you about your article to see if we could come to a compromise, but that's a moot point now… Still, dinner at the Vervida should be hard to turn down, no?"

The Golden Trinity? She marveled at the way Rayne dropped *that* into the conversation as casually as if she were talking about something as everyday as the fog over the Golden Gate Bridge. And the Vervida? Perhaps the most exclusive and sought-after reservation in the city. It cost more to dine there than Chase made in a month. *And* the cherry on the cake, Rayne had wanted to talk about a compromise?

"It's not a moot point. I'd like to hear your thoughts on making the article hang together without a huge chunk of the truth included." Chase sounded more combative that she'd wanted to. Dinner at a fancy restaurant with an even fancier—perhaps the fanciest—woman was a rare treat. And maybe it would yield a positive spin on her article which, until Rayne had called, was feeling very daunting.

"How is it that you manage to make an acceptance sound like a rejection?"

Chase could hear the amusement in Rayne's voice again. It wasn't easy to offend her, though Chase knew exactly how to smash that button if she wanted…and sometimes even when she didn't, like in Cyprus. "I'm sorry," Chase said, adopting a formal accent. "I would simply love to dine with you. What time were you thinking?" The sound of Rayne's free laughter reminded Chase how much she used to love making Rayne giggle just to hear it.

"How does eight work for you, Madam Chase?" Rayne asked.

"Perfect."

"Shall I send my driver to pick you up?"

Now it was Chase's turn to laugh. Rayne had a driver. Chase had a beat-up Chevy truck. "And have you know where I live? I don't think so. I'll meet you there."

"You think I don't already know where you live, Chase Stinsen?"

Rayne hung up before Chase replied. She didn't know whether Rayne was messing with her or not. It was exactly how she felt Rayne liked her to be—constantly on her toes and unsure of herself. *So why am I meeting her for dinner?*

***

Chase held her tie up while she released her seat belt. She let it go and smoothed it down. There was no way she wanted a pull in this tie. Even in the outlet sale a year ago, it had been an extravagant purchase. It had hung on her tie rack since, waiting for the perfect occasion to warrant a hundred percent mulberry silk appearance. As the Vervida valet tugged on the door of her truck to open it, Chase was confident this was *definitely* the occasion for her fancy tie.

She stepped out onto the steaming sidewalk, the unseasonal heat evaporating a quick shower, and left her door open for the valet to climb in after he'd given her a ticket. He looked neither impressed nor hopeful of a decent tip as he struggled to navigate the stick shift, grinding the gears and making everyone look their way. Chase didn't know whether to be more embarrassed for herself, rocking up to a top-class hotel in a low ride pickup truck, or for him, who was glowing redder by the second.

Chase left him to it and smiled at the doorperson as they opened the door. She couldn't read their expression, a skill no doubt essential in their line of work, and she tried not to let her sense of not fitting in creep in. She'd been invited, she looked smart enough, and she was meeting one of their guests. Chase belonged here…at least for the next couple of hours.

She walked in and took in the opulent décor. The hotel was styled like the interior of the Vatican. Huge frescos adorned the ceilings and walls, with such artistry and skill that they looked almost 3-D, as if they might reach out and touch the patrons. Recesses in the walls held life-size statues of Catholic saints, while the floor was littered with the remnants of Roman deities, discarded and unloved. It was an accurate representation of the real Vatican and reminded Chase of an early trip as a student that had saddened her. She'd hated seeing the blasé manner in which Pagan history had been treated, carelessly labeled with meaningless numbers and scattered in corridors with little or no explanation. Some of the larger pieces and statues were appropriately displayed, but for the most part, it all felt like an afterthought. Tens of thousands of pieces of amazing archeological artifacts treated with such disrespect. The trip sealed her desire to commit her career to restoring the history of communities and cultures to its rightful place. Something fundamental that she and Rayne disagreed on entirely.

"Ms. Stinsen?"

A woman dressed in Vervida uniform touched Chase's arm.

Chase smiled. "Yes?"

"If you'd follow me, I'll take you to Ms. Marcellus's table." The woman turned but kept a gentle grip on Chase. "She's been waiting."

Chase noted the touch of chastisement in her voice as though Chase was late. She followed and checked her watch, three minutes past eight. She'd aimed to be on time, but the traffic on the 101 South had caught her out. Ms. Bossy Pants set a cracking pace through the reception and into the glass-walled elevator. "How did you know who I was?" Chase asked, more a desire for small talk than an actual interest. She found being in such close proximity to people in an elevator without making conversation, plain weird. Rayne was the exact opposite; she hated random strangers asking how her day was going or what her plans were. Chase smiled, remembering the times she would deliberately engage in conversation just to irritate Rayne.

Ms. Bossy Pants raised her eyebrow and appraised Chase's appearance with a lightning quick scan. Chase could see she wanted to say something very specific but was figuring out how to temper her words. Chase didn't think Ms. Bossy Pants cared for her feelings as much as she didn't want to upset Rayne by insulting her dinner guest.

"Ms. Marcellus described you perfectly," she said and looked at the elevator doors as if they couldn't open quickly enough.

Lucky for her the high-speed elevator got them to the thirtieth floor in record time.

Ms. Bossy Pants exited with a curt, "Follow me, please."

Chase surveyed the restaurant as she deliberately trailed slightly behind. The walls and ceiling were glass, delivering a spectacular unimpeded view of the Bay Bridge. The blue lights on the bridge reflected beautifully on the still water, which was why Chase liked it far more than its older and ugly companion, the Golden Gate Bridge. Every table was occupied, and yet the noise of conversation was just about bearable; any louder and Chase might've considered slipping in her protective earbuds. She wondered if Rayne knew the levels would be okay for Chase or whether it was just coincidence. Rayne had probably long forgotten Chase's difficulties in concentrating if there was much audio stimulation from other sources.

Ms. Bossy Pants needn't have bothered leading the way. Chase saw Rayne way before she would have seen anyone else. No one stood out in any room quite like Rayne Marcellus. Christ, if the sun exploded tomorrow, Rayne could be its stand-in. She radiated an energy and presence that ensured she was the focus of the room for almost everyone, and even if they weren't looking at Rayne, you could bet your inheritance they were thinking about her. Her Italian father had gifted his ebony hair and dark eyes. Rayne had said that ended up being all she wanted from him when it became clear to her that his approval and fatherly pride depended entirely on whether or not Rayne was successful at everything she did. From an amateur psychologist's point of view, it explained a lot about the way she behaved. It could even be an excuse, but at some point Chase believed every daughter or son had a responsibility to themselves to emerge from the shadow of their upbringing and learn how to be their own person. It was an easy philosophy to carry when Chase's family life had been pretty much baggage-free.

As it became clear that Chase was heading for Rayne's table, she felt the gaze of almost every woman-loving person in there, on her. Chase was comfortable with how she looked, and she knew that she might as well have a label on her forehead or a comic bubble over her head proclaiming her sexuality. Short hair, androgynous, now with muscles. She was an easy spot, but damn it, she didn't care. She'd been proud of who she was for a long time, and no bigoted assholes ever made her feel ashamed of how she presented. She knew what the straight guys would be thinking: There's no way she's meeting her for a date. Maybe they're adopted sisters or best friends. Beautiful people always had to have a regular looking best friend.

"Chase," Rayne said and raised her glass. "You're looking very handsome tonight."

Chase touched her tie, a little self-conscious at Rayne's none too quiet greeting, though she appreciated the blatant way she announced her appreciation. "Thanks." Accepting a compliment didn't come too easily. Rayne smiled the way she did when she knew she'd made Chase squirm and motioned to the seat opposite her.

"Please, sit."

Chase didn't miss the way Rayne swept her gaze over Chase when she thought she wasn't looking. Or maybe she knew damn well Chase would see her and didn't care. Rayne had never held back her desire to bed Chase, but Chase had no wish to be part of Rayne's collection of conquests. She wasn't against one-night stands—they were about all she was prepared to commit to—but she couldn't bring herself to sleep with Rayne. Her complete self-interest and greed made her particularly unattractive, and Chase had learned to keep her physical attraction under control quite easily since her Florida betrayal.

Chase ordered a soda and settled into the plush leather seat. She began to wonder if it had been a good idea to meet her number one competitor, but she wanted to know about the Golden Trinity and Rayne's ideas on the rewrite of her article without her and the tank twins in it. All she had to do was stop glancing at Rayne's cleavage in the tight, low cut dress she was wearing and concentrate on her words.

"Have you eaten here before?" Rayne asked.

She took a sip of wine that probably cost more for a glass than food for an entire African tribe for a week. Chase couldn't decide if Rayne was goading her or if it was a real question. She decided to let it slide or it was going to be a painful night for both of them. "I'm sure you won't be surprised to hear me say that I haven't." She reined in the temptation to compare her modest income to Rayne's ill-gotten gains, important especially given that Rayne was picking up the tab tonight.

"Then you're in for a culinary treat. Chef Michaela's specialty is a sea bass dish to trample over hungry babies for. It's still your favorite?"

If Rayne was picking up on Chase's ambivalence, she wasn't showing it. It was as if she'd rewound the clock, acting like they were still friends and colleagues, remembering her favorite food. Where was the vaguely disguised animosity of the past few years? Had their brush with ISIS given Rayne some perspective on what was important in life? Was she trying to make up for what she'd done to Chase? But then there was the hungry baby metaphor that was still very much the regular Rayne. Chase had always secretly liked Rayne's politically incorrect and black humor, though she'd chastise her for it and feign offense publicly. Rayne had a sense of freedom Chase was still searching for in the caves and tombs she explored but so far had come up short.

"I'm tired of fighting, Chase. I don't expect you to forgive me for Florida, but I want to be done with the constant battling with you."

Rayne must've seen the phantom cogs over Chase's head. She frowned and shook her head. "Is that why you hired your gorilla girls? To keep the playing field level?"

Rayne flashed a femme fatale look. The kind that always got their victim into trouble. The look that would have Chase doing Rayne's bidding, no matter the cost. Chase shook it off and waited for a response.

"You know I hate to lose…"

"So what you're actually asking me to do is back off so you can win every contest without a competition? That's how you want to stop the fighting? With me stepping out of the ring?" Chase thumbed the dripping condensation from her glass of soda. She wished to be that cool right now.

Rayne sighed, pushed her own glass to the side, and leaned across the table. "That's not what I meant—well, when I first hired G&T, it *was* to get ahead of you. But they became more than that, and they seem to enjoy protecting me. But after Zenobia…you could've died." Rayne retrieved her wine. "We should be working together."

Chase laughed. "Tried that, got screwed, and *didn't* get a T-shirt to show for it. In fact, I almost *lost* the shirt off my back."

Rayne looked a little wounded, vulnerable even. Chase clenched her jaw. She wasn't falling for this, whatever *this* was.

"Won't you ever let that go?" Rayne asked.

Her eyes seemed bereft of any emotion, but there was a slight tremor in Rayne's voice that gave her away. How had she managed to make Chase feel sympathy for *her*? Chase was the injured party here, but Rayne was right…she really couldn't seem to let it go. "Let's talk about something else. You mentioned you were taking a meeting about the Golden Trinity? Is that for real?"

The waitress returned, and Chase let Rayne order. It saved Chase the embarrassment of looking for the cheapest item on the menu. Rayne ordered some dishes in a perfect French accent. Well, it sounded like perfect French to Chase, but she couldn't profess to having an ear for European languages, other than Spanish, and that was only because of its similarities to the South American dialects Chase was familiar with.

The waitress left them alone again, and Chase waited for an answer or something pithy about not sharing such information with the competition.

"I don't know if it's a hoax yet. We're looking into the guy's background." He sent me a piece of a map, and if it turns out to be genuine, it could be the first real evidence the Golden Trinity actually exists."

"Who's the guy? What line of work is he in?" Chase asked the questions but didn't expect a straight answer or an answer at all.

"Stan Turner. He's in the logging business, mainly in the Brazilian rain forest. Jenny thinks he might have had an illegal operation at some point, but she can't find anything to prove that categorically. He seems to be doing everything by the book. And he's got a contract that has something to do with sixty million acres of rain forest being released by the Brazilian government." Rayne shrugged. "I suppose with that amount being free range, he can make a fortune."

Chase ran a hand across the back of her head. Not only was Rayne being open and honest, but her last comment sounded like she might even be growing a fledgling conscience. "Is he into palm oil? All that orangutan killing is heinous."

Rayne's expression went blank. "What have orangutans got to do with palm oil?"

"The loggers are taking their habitat and slaughtering them if they get in the way." Chase tapped the screen of Rayne's phone. "Don't you use this to keep up with current affairs? Or is it just for your FindHrr account?"

Rayne surprised Chase by laughing at her little dig.

"What, you think I can't use it for both? Isn't the whole point of these phones so you don't need any other gadget in your life?"

Chase smiled as the waitress brought their first course. It was a fish dish of some description—she could tell that much from the aroma rising in the steam—but beyond that, she was stumped. It looked good though there wasn't an awful lot of it. This was obviously one of those restaurants where the presentation outweighed the importance of quantity. She could've snorted the small portion.

"Don't worry, there are another five courses coming," Rayne said as she speared her own piece of the same dish. "I remember how much you like your food, but it looks like you've been eating plenty of proteins and not much fatty stuff recently." Rayne waved her now-empty fork in the general direction of Chase's biceps. "Why the sudden change?"

Why the sudden change of subject was Chase's unvoiced question, but she decided not to push it. Rayne had already told her far more than she'd expected her to. "A few reasons, I guess." Chase wasn't about to tell Rayne she was the main one. "Noemie came back from a tour super-pumped, and I could barely keep up with her when we played racquetball." Chase shook her head at the memory. "I taught her how to play the damned game, and she kicked my ass."

Rayne tilted her head and gave her one of those false sympathy looks. "Aww, can't have her beating her hero, can we? Do you remember the first time you beat your dad at anything? For most people, it's a mixed emotion moment, but I loved it. I couldn't wait for it to happen…and I couldn't wait to do it again."

Chase knew Rayne's childhood had been difficult, but she hadn't shared much detail about it even when they were friends. "What did you beat him at?"

"Chess."

Rayne didn't miss a beat. The excitement she'd clearly had when she'd done it was almost visibly tingling beneath her skin. Chase nodded. "Such a great game."

"It was that day. He thought it was a fluke," Rayne said. "But I destroyed him in six moves the second time." Rayne pierced her last piece of fish with vim. "He never gave me a third opportunity."

"Guess we know where you get your loathing for losing then?" Chase said.

Rayne's eyes seemed to darken a little, and her expression hardened.

"I don't like to lose because I wasn't *allowed* to lose as a kid, at anything, or to anyone."

Chase wanted to reach over and put her hand over Rayne's to comfort her in some way. What the heck was happening? "That's a lot of pressure for a kid."

Rayne put down her fork and pushed her plate away decisively. "So what are your other reasons?"

Chase acknowledged Rayne's need to return the focus to Chase. "I wanted to look in the mirror and really like what I saw. I've always loved strong women, defined muscles, six-pack abs. I figured if I was going to make the change, I'd better get on with it before I got too old to make it happen."

Rayne flashed a wicked grin. "Do you have a six-pack?"

"Yeah, a few in the fridge at home," Chase said.

"Ha ha…do you?"

Chase swallowed the rising panic in response to Rayne's flirting and clenched at the thoughts of Rayne exploring Chase's new lines and bumps. "That is for me to know," she said instead of standing, pulling up her shirt, and flashing her bumpy abs like she had the urge to.

Rayne smiled and licked her lips. "And for me to find out?"

CHAPTER SIX

A KNOCK ON the door woke Rayne from an alcohol induced slumber. She opened her eyes and focused on the ceiling in an attempt to divine where she was. As the delicate hand-painted blue willow trees adorning it sharpened, she remembered she was at the Vervida in San Francisco. She had a potential client to meet. The Golden Trinity could be real.

She reached for the water bottle on the bedside table and swallowed half of it before there was a light tap on the bedroom door.

"Room service, Miss Rayne. Hello?"

Rayne would usually have switched the do not disturb on, but she couldn't remember how she got down to her room, or in it, or…she looked under the comforter to see she was still fully clothed in her now extremely wrinkled DKNY dress. Jenny would pitch a fit when she saw the state of it.

"I'm in bed. Would you come back later, please?" Rayne asked, her voice a little croaky and dry, no doubt from being unconscious on her back all night long with her mouth wide open. Attractive. She hoped Chase was long gone before she started sleep-drooling. If it was Chase who'd tucked her in bed…it could've been a hotel staff member for all Rayne remembered.

"Of course. But I have a Gatorade and a Snickers for you. Your friend left strict instructions that they should be delivered to you at eleven a.m. She said that you had a very important meeting at one, and even if you threw your heels at my head, I was to make sure you had these things." The lady paused and tapped the door again. "So may I please come in and earn the generous tip from your friend?"

Rayne smiled widely. So Chase still cared. And she'd remembered Rayne always consumed a gallon of Gatorade and a Snickers after a heavy night on red wine. They seemed to be the only things that ever kept a monster truck from rolling around in her head the morning after. Rayne didn't know how they worked better than any painkillers on the market, but thanked the lord they did. "Sorry, yes. Please come in."

"Thank you, Miss Rayne."

The lady came in smiling genuinely, looking as if she really enjoyed her job. Rayne always appreciated people who exhibited a sense of fun no matter their profession. She scanned the name tag on her uniform. She liked to acknowledge people by their names where possible, no matter how short their interaction. "Thank you, Sarah," Rayne said as Sarah put the supplies on her bedside table.

"No problem, Miss Rayne. Would you like me to run the shower?"

Rayne shook her head. The service at the Vervida went beyond an evening turndown and chocolates on the pillows, but Rayne still liked to do things for herself. She retrieved her purse, took out a fifty-dollar bill, and offered it to Sarah. "No shower, but thank you, and thanks for these."

Sarah smiled and held up her hand. "That's not necessary, Miss Rayne. Your friend already took care of that."

Rayne sat up and extended her arm. "Please, I insist. I'll be terribly upset if you don't."

Sarah tilted her head before accepting the bill. "Thank you, Miss Rayne. That's very kind of you." She turned to leave but paused at the door. "There's nothing else I can do for you?"

"Actually, I'd really appreciate it if you could brew up a fresh pot of Blue Mountain before you left."

Sarah seemed to light up at the prospect of being some use.

"Absolutely, Miss Rayne," she said and pulled the door closed behind her quietly.

Rayne uncapped the Gatorade and used two hands to hold the giant bottle. She drank a third of it before she put it down and unwrapped the Snickers bar. The first bite felt like a little piece of heaven exploding in her mouth, and it obliterated the rancid taste of bitter, repeating wine and bed mouth. If God did make womankind, they were her pièce de résistance, but a Snickers would have to be her second-best invention.

She'd just finished it and washed it down with the remaining drink when her phone beeped to indicate a text message.

Hope the usual remedy works. Have a good meeting. Let me know if TGT is for real?

Rayne smiled at Chase's text. After an initial frostiness, they'd slipped back relatively easily into their old banter. The conversation and wine flowed, though Chase switched to soda water and didn't partake of the vintage she'd handpicked at all. Rayne couldn't recall much beyond the fourth course, other than Chase had getting a little irritated about the Zenobia article. God, Rayne prayed she hadn't promised any appeasement in her drunken state. Her lawyer would go caged lion crazy if she had.

Rayne reluctantly peeled herself out of bed and went to the bathroom. She turned on the side shower, not wanting to get her hair wet from the overhead waterfall fixture, slipped out of her dress, and stepped in. Sometimes the soothing rhythm of steady water over her body stimulated her memory, and she wanted last night's events to return, especially how she'd ended up in her hotel room. Sadly alone, but Chase was a chivalrous sort and would never have done anything sexual with Rayne in her consent-absentia state. Rayne was almost rueful about that, but if and when she ever bedded Chase, she wanted to remember every moment of it. Not that having Chase would be special in any way, other than how long she'd made Rayne wait, obviously. Rayne just liked to commit every outstanding sexual encounter to memory so she could play them over on her occasional solo evenings. And she had no doubt that Chase would be exceptional in bed. She had very little to base her confident assumption upon other than the few tales of a couple of mutual friends slash lovers over the years. Maybe it was about the way Chase carried herself, a confidence and self-assuredness held back by a little insecurity and buoyed by the need to be the best. Chase's ambition was raised from the embers of a fire far different from Rayne's. Her need to be the first, best, and only was far more pathological than Chase's. Hers was born from the counter-balancing motivations of willful neglect and over-the-top, constant pushing from her parents. But that upbringing had given her the tools to overcome anything and become the person she was, a successful and respected antiquities hunter. Well, respected in enough places to soften Chase's *lack* of respect for her. Rayne poured the beautifully-scented shower gel onto a loofah, and the bergamot began to soothe her aching head.

Pieces of last night's dinner conversation began to replay in Rayne's head. Why had she been so open about the Golden Trinity meeting? Why had she shared the memory of beating her father at chess? The feeling of melancholy at the distance between her and Chase had been growing since she'd left Chase to find her own way home from Cyprus. Maybe she needed to go back to her shrink for a few more sessions. It seemed that the experience in Syria had affected her far more deeply than she wanted, and she should address it before she went soft.

And asking Chase to work with her, what was she thinking? Chase had chosen her path and the high ground. It hadn't gotten her much further than a half decent tenure at Stanford and a reputation for being a bit of a saint. So what? Would Rayne trade her position, at the top of her game, with multimillionaire clients, and adventures all over the world in first-class style? For what? A middle of the road existence and a beat-up truck?

Rayne scrubbed the sudded-up loofah across her chest when the answer she wanted to say didn't pop up front and center. Would she want to give this up? Jetting across the country for a business lunch and staying in top class hotels when the room service included making her morning coffee from one of the rarest beans in the world? She wouldn't swap that for a regular job. She'd be crazy to even consider it, especially just for the approval of a woman. Just because that woman was Chase Stinsen, someone Rayne had always admired far beyond mere sexual attraction. Far better for Chase to join *her*. Together they'd be unstoppable, but Rayne had blown that chance in Florida when she followed Lauren into this life.

Rayne rinsed off, wanting to wash away this nonsensical reflection along with the soap. Last night had been nice. It had proved they could get along while they both orbited their own worlds. Maybe that should be enough. It was certainly an improvement on relations prior to Syria. And they'd have to come up against each other again in the pursuit of another ancient artifact. Being too friendly would make beating Chase to it awkward. Friends but not too friendly then?

She stepped out of the shower and wrapped a heavy cotton towel around her. The Golden Trinity. That's what she should be focusing on right now. If Stan Turner was for real and his map legitimate, Rayne could be about to embark on the biggest adventure of her career. And she liked working solo. Right?

***

"Tonyck wants you to know that she's extremely unhappy about them being benched for this meeting," Jenny said.

Rayne lowered her phone and checked the report Jenny had sent over a few minutes ago. Turner *did* have an illegal logging operation, but he was also trying to go straight. Finding the treasure of the Golden Trinity would probably mean he'd never have to fell another tree. His finances appeared to be in order, and Jenny commented that his accountant must be a particularly talented one. But he was definitely at the Rodeo Grande with the means to pay for his penthouse suite.

She raised the phone back to her ear. "How does Tonyck think I managed *before* I employed her and her sister?"

"She says you've been lucky, and luck runs out," Jenny repeated after Rayne had already heard Tonyck respond in the background.

"Super. That's not ominous at all. I'll be fine. We're meeting in one of the most exclusive hotels in San Francisco, not down a back alley in the Castro." Rayne's driver pulled into the lobby front of the Grande and stopped the car. "Look, I'm here. I'll check in in a couple of hours with an update." Rayne tipped her driver after she'd opened the door for her. "Thanks, Adele."

Adele smiled, nodded, and went back around to the driver's seat. "I'll be waiting in the parking lot beneath the hotel, Ms. Marcellus. Give me a call when you're ready."

"Will do." Rayne straightened her skirt and swept her hand through her hair. "If I don't call, be sure to send the cavalry," Rayne said to Jenny and hung up before she heard Tonyck's inevitable cursing. She couldn't resist teasing her. Her over-protectiveness was sweet but suffocating and a little bit stifling. It might be worth having a serious conversation with them on her return to redraw the boundaries of their roles and responsibilities.

A quick inquiry at the desk led to a hefty security type escorting her up the elevator and to Turner's penthouse. When they got to the sixtieth floor, Turner was already at the opened door to his suite. Rayne recognized him from a picture in an earlier email Jenny had sent.

He held his arms out wide to great her. "Welcome, Ms. Marcellus. I'm really glad you agreed to meet me."

In the twenty feet from the elevator to Turner's door, Rayne took in all she could to supplement Jenny's profiling. Expensive suit, a subtle gray pinstripe, perfectly tailored and fitted. High quality English brogues in oxblood red. Matching shirt and gray tie. His outfit declared he was a serious businessman, but he fidgeted in it just enough to indicate a certain discomfort. The tie reminded her of Chase's tie last night. It had probably cost more than the rest of her outfit, but Rayne loved that Chase had succumbed to the temptation to have at least one top quality garment in her wardrobe. And she'd looked hot enough to make Rayne want to have Chase fuck her fully clothed. She bet she'd look amazing in a custom made three-piece suit.

Rayne refocused on Turner and extended her hand. "When I saw your evidence, Mr. Turner, it was impossible for me to decline."

Turner smiled widely and revealed a mouthful of shiny new teeth. Business must be good. Rayne registered they weren't his own and wondered what had happened to his natural set. Accident? Drugs? Beating?

"Please, come in." Turner stepped back inside and waited for Rayne to enter before he closed the door with her escort remaining in the corridor.

Two other men were present; a bespectacled guy sat on the couch in a cheap suit and white gloves. Some sort of antiquities guy maybe. He looked up and gave her a quick smile. The second guy stood by the window and was dressed much the same as Turner but looked even more uncomfortable. Something about the way he stood, awkward and ready to bolt, indicated he'd probably be far more at home in jeans, boots, and a shirt. Rayne suspected he was one of Turner's workers or perhaps a good friend who worked with him. She ruled out lover since Jenny's report included details of Turner's penchant for *female* sex workers.

They both looked harmless enough, which reinforced Rayne's decision to come alone as a solid one. Turning up with G&T would've screamed mistrust and been a bad beginning to their business relationship.

Rayne scoped the large oversized armored-looking briefcase on the table in front of specs guy. It wouldn't have been out of place at an arms deal. Turner was certainly taking this seriously and clearly believed what he had was genuine. She sat beside specs guy and drummed her fingertips on the case. "Is this the map?"

Turner nodded. "Yes. Yes, it is." He parked himself directly opposite Rayne and placed his hand on the case. "Would you like to see it?"

Rayne held back the sarcasm that leapt to mind. "Most definitely."

Turner twisted the case around so that it was facing him, and Rayne could only see the edges. He took his time unfastening the clips, apparently wanting to build Rayne's anticipation.

"Are you ready to have your mind blown?" Turner asked with more than a hint of the dramatic.

Rayne laughed gently. "I hope so." And she hoped she hadn't wasted her time coming here. Turner was excitable, which meant he might be gullible too. Could be that some entrepreneurial kid from an indigenous tribe had done a finger painting, dragged it around a few cedar trees, and sold it to Turner for enough money to keep his tribe fed for a year. As Turner lifted the lid slowly, Rayne could see a glass box within the case. A crowd of butterflies began to stir in her stomach at the slight prospect that she was about to see something people like her had sought for centuries. Turner finally pushed open the case and turned it around for Rayne to inspect.

Fig tree bark. Logosyllabic Proto-Mayan language. Markings and glyphs in white, red, yellow, black, and green, representing the world as Mayans saw it. She touched the glass, traced the drawings with her fingertips, and allowed the possibility to become a reality. A previously undiscovered piece of twelve-hundred-year-old history, so close she could almost taste it…through its hermetically sealed box.

She looked up at Turner, and if it was possible, his smile had grown so wide that the corners of his mouth almost reached his ears. He clearly registered Rayne's unspoken acknowledgement that what he had was truly genuine.

"Where did it come from?" she asked, her fingers still resting on the glass lest she remove them and the parchment disappear. She dropped her gaze back to it, desperately trying to take it all in and memorize it all.

Turner pointed to the other guy. "Rich came across it when he was inspecting a felling site. The tree had been cut just above some calloused wood, and he could see a corner of something that just didn't belong there."

"Calloused wood?" Rayne asked, having never heard of the term.

"Think of it like a tree's version of scarring. If the bark is breached in any way, the tree compartmentalizes the wounded area to prevent bacteria getting in and further damaging the tree. It's self-healing which allows the rest of the tree to recover." Turner paused, as if to ensure Rayne had understood what he'd explained before he moved on. She nodded, so he continued. "The wound was deep into the exposed trunk—impossible to tell the number of years because tropical trees have no discernible growth rings—but Rich could tell it had been there a long, long time."

Turner glanced over to Rich and smiled, but Rich said nothing. Rayne stopped herself from asking whether he was mute or just rude.

"If you're wondering why he hasn't said anything, it's because he can't. His tongue was cut out by a drug gang."

Rayne silently reprimanded herself for being a judgmental ass and at the same time, wondered if Turner was a mind reader. "Jesus, a drug gang. In Brazil?" Rayne knew little of the drug trade in South America, other than a vague idea that it was mainly a Colombian thing.

"Yes. There's a war going on between Brazilian and Colombian gangs. Rich stumbled across a trading point on the Japura River when he was... hiking. He was lucky to only lose his tongue. The rest of his party lost their lives."

Something about the way Turner hesitated and said "hiking" indicated Rich was involved in something a little less palatable than walking in the rain forest. Nothing Jenny had pulled up pointed to Turner being involved in drugs. That was something Rayne stayed well away from. She had no desire to lose any extremities, especially not her tongue. What kind of a lesbian would she be without that? She kept her amusement to herself, but the question remained and it needed addressing.

"Hiking?" Rayne asked. "I have no wish to offend you, Mr. Turner, but I have to be sure. Do you have any involvement in what you've just described?"

"Drugs are where you draw the line, Ms. Marcellus?"

The accusation in his tone struck hard. Rayne had cultivated a reputation for dealing in the dark and moving in the shadows; she couldn't argue with that. And yet, the inference that she could do anything for a trade bothered her. She looked again at the ancient scribbles beneath the glass barrier. She wanted this job, but still... This must be how Chase felt when Rayne offered her the chance to study Zenobia behind closed doors. Christ, was this what she'd become? Hesitant and soft? Maybe she should be wearing a WWCD bracelet: What Would Chase Do? "We all have to draw a line somewhere, Mr. Turner. Even someone like me." The atmosphere had changed in an instant, and Rayne regretted her stubborn decision not to bring G& T.

Turner laughed abruptly and ended the weird, tense silence. "Absolutely, Ms. Marcellus. But no, I have no connection to any drug dealing activities. Rich and his party were scouting for fresh logging areas. I admit to being an illegal logger in the past. I'm sure your background check illuminated that particular section of my history. But I'm no drug dealer."

Rayne didn't care for his smug smile, but she was satisfied with his response. She could usually divine a liar pretty easily, and his answer seemed genuine.

"Should I continue, or have I lost you?"

WWCD? "Please, continue."

"Rich cut out the top section of the trunk to reveal a box sealed with wood sap." Turner tapped the glass gently. "Luckily, he didn't open it immediately. He had a feeling it might be something important, and he's seen enough treasure hunt programs to know the importance of limiting contact with the atmosphere." Turner sighed and leaned back in his chair. "When we started the company over two decades ago, we spoke of discovering some wildly fantastical treasure, but we never though that it would actually happen."

Rayne appreciated his enthusiasm, but her assessment of him had changed direction somewhat. Where she'd originally thought him rather mellow and harmless, a harder edge had pushed through the pretense and caused Rayne to reconsider who he really was and what he might be capable of.

"What made you think this was linked to the Golden Trinity?" Rayne asked, though she'd read the tale that a tall tree held the secret to the greatest treasure of them all. She just didn't expect an illegal logger to share her interest in fairytales and folklore.

He clenched his jaw. "I'm not an educated man, but I like history and grew up on adventure stories and Indiana Jones. When we ended up working in South America, I read about the treasure hoards and the Spanish conquests. The fall of the Mayan culture intrigued me greatly, and the thought of all their considerable riches—the Golden Trinity—hidden somewhere in the Brazilian rain forest, what's not to love?"

"Indeed." Rayne smiled, but her mind was on fast-forward through the possible scenarios. To what lengths were Turner and his mute colleague prepared to go? They needed her expertise, clearly, but had they thought about the dangers of such an expedition? Booby traps and spiked, deep holes weren't just the folly of fiction. Where did Turner think theat inspiration came from? She was certain he'd want to come along for the discovery, but she was also sure he wasn't the type of guy who liked roughing it in the jungle with rattlesnakes sliding over his bedroll. Or whatever creepy crawlies were native to Brazil. "How do you see this working, Mr. Turner? What exactly do you want from me?"

He smiled widely, and Rayne was once again drawn to the bright newness of his teeth. Maybe he'd been with his buddy, Rich, when they were looking for a new site and the drug gang had knocked all of his teeth out.

"I want you to decode the map and lead us to the treasure."

He made it sound easy. Rayne looked again at the bark. Mayan mythology had been her PhD thesis. That's why he'd called her. That, and her reputation for always delivering, except the occasions where Chase beat her to it. But Chase was the expert on logograms, not Rayne. "Us, who? I have my own team."

"I know that, Ms. Marcellus, but who knows what or who we might come across on this adventure. I've hired my own team of ex-military personnel to accompany us."

Ex-military personnel. Read dishonorably discharged mercenaries, guns for hire with no compunction against doing whatever needed to be done. "And if we come across indigenous tribes?"

His smile took on a more menacing edge. "Then they'll need to get out of our way or take the consequences. You're a raider of tombs; you have a reputation for getting your clients their commission regardless of what might stand in your way. Surely you wouldn't let a few hermits stop you from finding the Golden Trinity? If something gets in my way, I chop it down. Logs, animals, people, what's the difference? They're just an obstacle to overcome or eliminate. I was under the impression you shared this philosophy. Am I incorrect? Do I need to contact my second choice hunter, Oscar Owen?"

Rayne swallowed the ball of disgust that rose in her throat. Owen would think nothing of slaughtering innocent people to get the Trinity. Rayne had only had the misfortune of crossing paths with him once before, and before he knocked her unconscious, he told her that the only reason he wasn't going to kill her was because she was too sexy to die just yet. "Get in my way again, and I might have to rethink my position," he'd said before delivering a powerful backhand that knocked her off her feet and into a ten-foot ditch. Rayne had tried to convince herself she'd hired G&T to get ahead of Chase. Buried in her head was the truth that she'd done it to protect herself from Owen. She hated to admit being afraid of anyone or anything, but that vicious bully of a man warranted special attention. She wanted to think that in the same situation now, with Tonyck's training, she'd be able to take him. She was faster. She didn't have to be stronger.

But no doubt he'd hide in plain sight alongside a gaggle of mercs with guns trained at her head like last time. Owen didn't entertain the notion of a fair fight. To him, it was win at any cost. But if she could get him alone, she was sure it'd be a different story.

"And I was thinking we could see if Chase Stinsen might be interested in joining us. I've been told that her grasp of ancient cartography is second to none. She'd be very useful in understanding the map, don't you think?" Turner's voice cut across the lengthy silence.

Rayne nearly sprung across the table to take out Turner's eyes with her thumbs. This world wasn't Chase's purview, and Turner's words sounded more like a threat. Chase would say no to any approach by him, but Rayne wasn't sure that would be the end of it. Would he take her by force? Christ, what was she supposed to do? If she took the job, maybe she and her team could prevent any bloodshed and minimize the impact of their expedition on any Brazilian tribes. There was no way she could allow Owen to go in her place. That would be more irresponsible than anything she'd ever done in the past. If she took the job and was successful, she'd be writing her name into the history books. Not only that, Turner was offering triple her usual fee with a ten percent bonus from the sale of anything they found over the total value of ten million dollars.

"There'll be no need for that, Mr. Turner. I have all the skills you need." Rayne held out her hand over the briefcase, smiling as she took another glimpse of the map and Turner shook her hand. "You've hired yourself the best tomb raider money can buy." She didn't care much for the moniker, but if it was good enough for Hollywood, it was good enough for her. Who'd play her if her story was made into an adventure movie? She'd play herself. Acting in front of a camera couldn't be that hard, she'd been acting in front of people every day of her life.

CHAPTER SEVEN

CHASE HIT THE beat on the uppercuts on a strange autopilot.

"Twenty-nine, thirty, thirty-one, thirty-two. Switch," shouted the super-fit body combat instructor, barely out of breath.

On days when Chase felt like this, it was the instructor's face she envisioned pounding on. Not that she had many days like this, distracted by thoughts of Rayne. It had been over seven hours since Rayne's meeting about the Golden Trinity. It wasn't like Rayne had promised to check in or let Chase know how it had gone. She hoped Rayne didn't think the hangover cure was a bribe and had taken it in the spirit with which she'd sent it.

Which was what spirit, exactly? After Chase had tucked Rayne into bed, she'd wanted to purge both their heads of the entire night. Aside from the relatively major issue of the Zenobia article, they'd slipped back into flirty friend mode in no time at all. How had Rayne done that? She'd tempered Chase's anger at her, not just for Florida, but for the loss of Joan of Arc's skull too. Rayne had been unusually honest, and that had nudged Chase away from her regular method of dealing with Rayne and her charming bullshit. Especially disarming had been Rayne's willingness to share intimate details of her relationship with her father with minimal prodding.

A firm shove to her shoulder knocked her out of her musings and back into the studio.

"What's with you? Are you just doing your own thing?"

Chase looked sideways at Noemie and shrugged. "It's been a weird couple of days."

"Tell me about it after class." Noemie gave her another shove. "Concentrate."

Chase laughed at the swap in roles and picked up the moves again. Used to be that Chase was the one demanding that Noemie focused on her training. Now that she was in the army, it seemed the tables had turned.

She managed to keep herself focused on the remaining tracks. After the cooldown, she retrieved her towel and water and headed for the showers with Noemie shadowboxing Chase's kidneys.

"So what's with you? Some egghead at the university?" Noemie asked through the glass that separated the shower cubicles.

"You won't be impressed when I tell you," Chase said as she lathered her peppercorn body wash across her stomach. The definition of her abs made her smile, and she was glad no one could see her being so vain.

"Then it can only be Rayne Marcellus or Lucy Dawson. Which is it?"

Chase didn't answer for a moment. Lucy Dawson was a name she hadn't heard in a long time. Unpleasant memories of their few years together flashed in her mind. Noemie hadn't liked Lucy from the start and told her so, which made for a rocky relationship. Lucy had quickly grown incredibly jealous of Chase's bond with Noemie and tried to make it as difficult as possible when she spent time with Noemie. And her jealousy wasn't limited to the kid. She'd hated Chase being with anyone but her, including friends and colleagues. By the end of it, Chase had become a veritable hermit, so she finally pulled the plug.

"Wow. Lucy Dawson. She didn't go quietly into that good night, did she?" Chase said.

"That's an understatement. She was batshit crazy. Didn't she try to keep *everything* you owned and everything you'd bought together?"

Chase laughed as she let the water run over her head, and she rubbed the sweat from her hair. "She was a good lesson for you. Run away as fast as you can the moment they start getting possessive."

Noemie tapped the glass. "You didn't learn the lesson too quickly. How was I supposed to pick it up?"

She had a point Chase couldn't argue with. "Did I ever tell you she tried to tear up all the cards you gave me?"

Noemie hit the glass again, this time a little more forcefully. "No way? Tell me she didn't do it."

The slight change in Noemie's voice would have gone unnoticed by anyone else, but Chase felt it as sure as if she'd seen Noemie's big brown eyes tear up. Chase pressed her palm flat again the glass. "Don't be crazy. She was never getting her hands on those," Chase said, sweeping away Noemie's subtle emotional moment. Noemie wasn't one for overt shows of sentimentality and preferred them to be ignored on the few occasions her tough shell slipped to reveal her marshmallow underbelly. Noemie had pretty much hated school, especially English, so when she wrote anything, it was important and it was from the heart. Chase treasured every one of her cards. She knew Noemie well enough not to talk until she'd processed her episode of vulnerability so she waited for Noemie to open up the conversation in her own time.

"So that means it's the Marcellus woman," Noemie said after a few moments of silence while they finished showering.

Chase wrapped her towel around herself and opened the shower door to see Noemie already waiting outside, her arms crossed, and the kind of serious look on her face that always made Chase laugh.

"I thought you hated her after what she did to you?" Noemie asked.

Chase put her arm over Noemie's shoulders and guided her back to the lockers. "Hate is a very strong word, Noemie. I don't think I *hate* anyone. Takes up too much energy, you know?"

Noemie rolled her eyes. "I know, *Mother*. But still, isn't she, like, your number one enemy?"

Chase shook her head as she retrieved her kit bag and tossed it on the bench. "We're often in competition, *yes*. Is she my enemy? *No*."

Noemie wagged her finger. "I know what's going on here. This is colleagues to friends to almost lovers to enemies to friends and maybe to lovers, isn't it?" She did a little dance as if she'd just figured out an age-old riddle. "This is like the stuff in those books you were always trying to get me to read, isn't it?"

"You'd like them if—"

"If I'd just give them a try," Noemie parroted in her best Chase impression. "I know, I know." She sat on the bench and pulled on her jeans. "Am I right?"

Chase tucked her tank top into her sweat pants and zipped up her bag before answering. "No, that's not it...exactly." She shoved her feet into her sneakers and stood. "C'mon, soldier. I thought you have to be able to get dressed in the time it takes a sparrow to fart?"

Noemie sighed as she quickly pulled her stuff together. "I do. So when I'm not on duty, I like to take my sweet time." She swept her long jet-black hair over her shoulder theatrically. "Looking *this* good takes time."

Chase shook her head at Noemie's vanity, before silently reminding herself that she'd just been admiring her own body parts in the shower.

What the heck? She'd worked damned hard to get those abs. Pride could be a virtue as well as a sin. "Let's go."

They made their way back to Chase's truck and got in. As usual, Noemie made a big show of the passenger door sticking.

"When are you going to buy a new truck?" Noemie asked, strapping her belt on.

"Never." She turned the key, and the truck took a little extra time before it kicked into life as if to warn Chase against trading her in. "I've told you, as soon as you roll that puppy off—"

"The lot, you lose a hundred thousand dollars. Yeah, yeah, I know."

"Knowing didn't keep you from putting a down payment on a brand new Mustang with your first army paycheck though, did it?" Chase asked, not even trying to rein in the motherly chastisement.

Noemie grinned and flashed the look of supreme cuteness that she'd mastered in her early teens. It was a look that usually meant Chase forgave her anything, including the time Noemie had totaled her previous truck during the one and only driving lesson Chase ever gave her.

"Enough about me. Back to you and the Marcellus woman. What gives?" Noemie asked, clearly unwilling to let it slide.

"You could just call her Rayne."

Noemie shook her head. "That implies a friendliness I don't feel. What gives?"

Chase pulled out of the lot and headed home. "We went for dinner last night—"

"Dinner?" Noemie slapped the dashboard. "Hadn't she just left you stranded on some remote Greek island?"

Chase had to laugh at Noemie's reaction. She'd always been a black-or-white kind of girl. There were no shades of gray. Cross her and she'd slice you out of her life with the precision and finality of a cutthroat razor.

"Cyprus isn't remote. It's one of the larger islands. There were commercial flights leaving every day."

"I don't need a geography lesson, thanks, Mom. *I've* been traveling the world for the past few years too, you know? Tell me how you got from deserted to a hot dinner date?"

Chase swung her truck into the strip mall and parked at Crunch to get them a healthy, post-workout takeout. She could've argued that it wasn't a hot dinner date, but Chase couldn't deny that thinking of it that way hadn't crossed her mind. In another time, or maybe in a parallel universe, maybe it could've been exactly that.

"I'll tell you everything over a big box of falafel and poached eggs."

They made small talk with the owner, who it turned out happened to have been born in Cyprus. Noemie could talk the hind legs off a donkey, and by the time their order had been freshly prepared, they had his whole life story and why he'd opened his little business. Chase had been going there for six months and only knew his name was Andreas. She smiled at how far Noemie had come from the almost mute kid she'd met over a decade ago. Simultaneously, she wondered if she'd gone the other way and stopped communicating with people outside her academic circle. Why hadn't she thought to ask about his life? Because she was always so preoccupied and insanely busy, she didn't have time for small talk. She was always rushing from one place to another and usually ordered and paid online and picked up at the side kiosk. But the way Andreas had lit up when Noemie engaged him made her think she'd cut herself off from the wider world. No doubt Andreas was delighted someone as exotic and beautiful as Noemie had bothered to talk to him, but either way, it was something for Chase to think about.

"Tell me about your latest conquest," Chase said after they got back in her truck. So started an epic, blow-by-blow, text-by-text description of Noemie's most recent love interest. As Chase pulled into her drive, Noemie ended the tale with a final-sounding, "I've had enough." Chase was sure Noemie only meant she'd tired of the antics of this one, and she was ready for the next adventure.

"I'll see Eve when she's back from Fiji, anyway. I liked Eve."

Chase liked the appropriately named Eve too; Noemie's first taste of lesbian lust was also an army girl. And she'd kick-started Noemie's long-held ambition to do something meaningful with her life. Neither she nor Chase knew what that might turn out to be, but serving her country definitely fit that description. Eve was a few years older than Noemie, but Chase approved of her in a way none of the subsequent ones managed.

Noemie unlocked the front door, grabbed plates and drinks from the kitchen, and launched herself onto the couch. Chase put their takeout boxes directly onto the plates, and they dug in. Chase hadn't realized how hungry she was until she saw she'd polished off half the box without taking a break. When she looked up, Noemie sat cross-legged, staring at her between bites of food.

"First of all, it wasn't a date." Chase pointed her fork at Noemie to preempt her inevitable interruption. Noemie sighed and motioned a zipping of her lips. "Second, we have a lot of history together, and that makes it easy to slip into old patterns of behavior. Third, it was a business meeting of sorts. I'm about to publish an article about Zenobia—"

"The Warrior Queen in Syria?" You remembered? I'm impressed."

Noemie snorted. "You went into a war zone with nothing to shoot but a camera. Of course I'm going to remember." She gently poked her fork into Chase's thigh. "Losing you...that'd be the end of me."

Chase swallowed the bowling ball of emotion that surged up her throat from her heart. They looked at each other for a long moment before Chase broke the gaze and pulled Noemie into a hug. Memories of many days and nights in Noemie's teenage years flooded Chase's mind and threatened to escape in the form of tears. All those times when Chase had run out of words to comfort and reassure, Noemie's favorite thing had always been record-length hugs. She always held onto Chase so tightly, as if her very existence and sanity, as if her tenuous link to a better life, depended on it. These days, her hugs tended to be only a little longer than the average one, but this one harked back to those times. Chase had come to understand that it was Noemie's preferred method of communicating. She blinked away the soft burn of her own emotion, aware that every period of army leave resulted in their past resurfacing.

Noemie eventually pulled away, and Chase resumed the conversation as if nothing had happened. "Her lawyer threatened to sue the magazine if I didn't remove all mention of Rayne and her tank twins. So the magazine is being chickenshit. They won't publish it at all unless I edit them out. I was hoping I could change Rayne's mind..."

"But?" Noemie asked and shoveled a half ball of falafel into her mouth.

Chase shook her head. "It was a fool's errand. Rayne has to protect the client who commissioned her to retrieve the tomb. She has to protect her own reputation."

"Huh. What about *your* reputation?"

Chase ran her hand across her forehead. Rayne didn't concern herself with that small detail, so why was Chase making excuses for Rayne? The fact was that if the magazine wasn't cowering behind their legal department, Chase would have no reservations in publishing the article as it stood. To hell with Rayne's reputation, though she didn't see how it could be damaged given how heroic Chase had written her. At least up to the part where they packed Zenobia up in a crate and shipped her off to a shady claimant of ancestry rather than a museum where her story could be told and would live on. Chase wished she had a lead on Rayne's client. She would've loved to play a part in reclaiming the tomb for the Syrian people.

"Rayne's a bit short-sighted when it comes to the needs of other people." As the words left her mouth, she wondered why and how Rayne had managed to slide so easily back beneath Chase's skin. She'd been angry with her, so why had she tipped the staff and made sure Rayne had a wake-up call and a hangover cure? Making sure Rayne made it to bed safely had been only right. The state Rayne had drunk herself into sealed Chase's responsibility to get her back to her hotel room without the possibility of being accosted by some unscrupulous sort, and there'd been plenty of interest in Rayne over the course of the evening. But Chase's aftercare? Where the hell had that come from, and why? Rayne paid for an expensive dinner. So what? She could afford it, and it didn't mean Chase owed her something in return.

"I'm struggling to see your issue. Are you just pissed at her for all those reasons you've listed? Or are you pissed at yourself for not telling her what a first-class ass she is?" Noemie waved her fork around. "Oh, oh, I've got it. You're not used to losing, and this feels like you have."

Noemie looked at Chase, waiting for confirmation that one of her guesses was on the money. None of them were, and yet all of them were. She couldn't understand why she was so worked up about Rayne. She'd been trying to convince herself that her distraction was about Zenobia and the article, but there was an annoying niggle in her conscience telling her that was only part of it. "All of that, none of that, and more." She chased a piece of poached egg around the box though her appetite had left her.

Noemie looked exasperated. "This," she motioned in a circle around Chase with her fork, "this is why I'm working my way through the alphabet of girls' names with no strings attached."

"I think you might have the right idea," Chase said, but she was unable to stop thinking about her old friend. Rayne hadn't replied to her text about the Golden Trinity, and she hadn't called to tell her how the meeting had gone. Chase didn't know why she'd asked her to call, nor why she'd expected her to. They weren't friends *or* colleagues. No doubt she wouldn't see Rayne again until their paths collided in pursuit of another precious piece of history that some bigwig figured they had a right to buy because they had more money than morals.

And yet, here she was, checking her phone like a teenager for something, anything from Rayne.

CHAPTER EIGHT

RAYNE SETTLED INTO the plush seat of the town car and stared into the blackened privacy glass that separated her from Adele. Her reflection bounced back at her blankly until it rolled down to reveal her smiling driver.

"Where to, Ms. Marcellus?"

Rayne held up her finger to indicate she needed some thinking time and appreciated when Adele simply nodded, turned around, and returned the partition.

She pulled her phone from her purse, unlocked it, and navigated to contacts. Jenny. Tonyck. Chase. She needed to speak to each of them for different reasons but couldn't decide which one to start with. She flicked through to Chase and hovered her thumb over her number before scrolling through to Jenny and committing to the call rather than overthinking why she'd want to speak with Chase first.

"Yay for everyone. You haven't been murdered or mutilated," Jenny said without waiting for a greeting.

"Mutilated? You spent some time mulling over possible scenarios, did you?" Rayne asked, glad to be instantly grounded by Jenny's no-nonsense attitude.

"I've had no choice. Glum and glummer have regaled me with all the potential outcomes of you taking meetings with mysterious men without them." Jenny somehow sounded both confounded and entertained.

"You could've kicked them out of the office, Jenny. As tough as they are, they wouldn't dare to defy you." Rayne was only half-joking. Though Jenny was officially a little person, her personality and authority were anything but, and both Ginn and Tonyck knew better than to get in her way if she was on the war path.

"They were amusing me, but I was one tale away from banishing them, yes. Are we taking the job? Is his map for real?"

Rayne looked at her nails. She'd need to shorten them for this adventure.

"In a way. And yes, very real. Whether it will actually lead to the Golden Trinity is something we'll find out soon enough."

"Explain. How can you take a job 'in a way,' Ms. M?"

"Take G&T into my office, video call me in an hour, and I'll explain everything. I'll email you a shopping list shortly." Rayne hung up and tapped on the privacy glass. "Take me back to the hotel, please, Adele."

"No problem," Adele said once the glass retracted once more.

Rayne relaxed into the seat and closed her eyes. Her brain worked better when she shut out the world visually. Which made her think of Chase again, who suffered with too much audio stimulation. She remembered Chase explaining that her brain didn't want to focus on one thing because it wanted to listen to everything. But sometimes it became oppressive, and too much noise resulted in her simply shutting down and listening to nothing. It wasn't the same for Rayne, but the blackness of her eyelids made everything slow down a pace or two. What was Chase going to say about all of this? She'd been lucky enough never to cross swords with Owen, but that didn't keep her from holding very strong opinions on both him and his methods. She'd want to help, surely. Rayne wanted Chase to be a part of what was rapidly shaping into a crazy plan. But she'd be asking Chase to put herself in danger if things went wrong. And there were so many variables and unknowns that made even Rayne a little twitchy though she liked to think of herself as fearless. Tonyck would most likely be inclined to veto everything, but she could rely on Ginn to be gung-ho with her.

Rayne opened her eyes and took a deep breath. What was she thinking? She could've just declined the commission and let Turner try to hire Owen. He was no expert in Mayan language. He probably wouldn't even know where to start and the expedition would have faltered before it had really begun. No indigenous tribes massacred. No Golden Trinity treasure. No damage to Rayne's reputation. *Damn it, Chase. This is all your fault.* WWCD? Rayne was about to find out.

***

"Your shopping list doesn't seem to match the commission you went to Frisco for," Jenny said, her expression giving no indication of humor. "Did you take an impromptu second meeting for something a little less legal?"

THE GOLDEN TRINITY

Rayne shook her head. "It's all connected. It just got more complicated than I anticipated. Tonyck, how fast can you pull everything together?"

Tonyck leaned closer to the camera. "We've got almost all of what you need in the stockroom, but we'll have to visit the doctor to get the tranquilizers."

Tonyck narrowed her eyes and affected her super serious look. Rayne had only ever seen four expressions: serious, very serious, super serious, and "Oh, fuck" serious. The latter she'd glad only seen just once in Syria.

"What are we doing, lady boss?" Tonyck asked. "Seems like we're packing for two jobs."

Rayne held up her hand. "Let me preface this with a question. If innocent people had to die for us to complete a job for a client, would that be okay with you?"

All of them looked mortified, and she heard "Fuck, no," and "What kind of a question is that?" She didn't need to parse out the simultaneous responses; Rayne got the answer she hoped for.

"Good. I'm glad we're in agreement." She gave a quick rundown of her conversation with Turner, starting with the details about the drug gangs and finishing with Turner's nonchalance at killing indigenous peoples if they were to get in his way.

Tonyck smashed her fist on the conference table. "We should've been there. We could've taught him a lesson in humility." She raised her hand, and Ginn fist-bumped her.

"Hell, yeah," Ginn said. "We'll get on a plane right now and come do it."

Rayne rubbed her hand over her face and sighed. Sometimes they could both be a little too quick to violence. "I have a plan, hence the strange shopping list. I've told Turner I'll take the job and—"

"What the—"

"Shut up and listen," Rayne said, her irritation flaring at Tonyck's interruption. Jenny sat serenely, patiently waiting for the plan. G&T could learn a few things from her. "I've told him it'll take us two days to prepare and instructed him to charter a plane to take us to Rio on Saturday. I've asked him to remain at the Grande so I can go see him with any last-minute queries and to drop our expedition equipment off as it arrives. I want Jenny to get you and our gear here as soon as possible. Once we're together, we'll take a trip to the Grande and relieve Turner of the map.

When we've secured the map, we head to Rio on our charter—another job for you." Rayne pointed to Jenny. "We follow the map and find the Golden Trinity for ourselves." Rayne rolled her neck, and the ensuing cracking noises reminded her she should book a massage for later...after she'd spoken to Chase and got her onboard. She turned her attention back to her iPad to see all three of them with raised eyebrows and quizzical looks. "What's the problem?"

"You want us to steal a map and find the treasure?" Tonyck asked.

"Yes. Exactly that," said Rayne, feeling particularly pleased with herself. She was preventing genocide and should still end up with a life-changing and career-defining archeological find.

"It sounds more like a movie plot than a plan based in reality," said Tonyck. She pulled on her ear as if that mighty empty it of what she'd just been told. "And you're serious?"

Rayne shrugged and held out her hands, palm up. "Of course I'm serious. Why wouldn't I be?" She didn't understand Tonyck's reticence. "It's not like what we do is always a hundred percent aboveboard. What's the problem?" she repeated.

Tonyck looked at Ginn, who nodded and grinned in the way that meant she was ready for anything. Rayne knew she could rely on Ginn to be on board.

"There's no problem if that's what you want us to do. But if something goes down and we end up in prison, you're paying for our legal fees. We don't want to end up with a public defender, no matter what crime we get caught for."

Tonyck managed to say that all in such a way that made it clear she and her sister would still follow Rayne into hell in a paper helicopter. A gentle warmth radiated through her with the thought that these tough army girls had her back. It was understandable they just wanted to be properly insured against any blowback. Rayne smiled, appreciating their loyalty and willingness to go along with her plan. Her crazy plan. If two ex-military specialists thought it was a wild idea, what the hell was Chase going to think? Once this call was over, she'd find out. She *didn't* want to contemplate what G&T would think of Chase joining their little adventure…

CHAPTER NINE

CHASE CHECKED THE time when her melodic doorbell announced a visitor with a tinny version of the national anthem. After their healthy dinner, she and Noemie had settled down in front of the TV for ice cream and a movie. They'd earned it, and the dessert was the half-fat Ben and Jerry's chocolate cookie flavor, so it only half counted as a cheat treat. Noemie initially resisted, but the smell of it soon had her collecting her own spoon to dig in. Chase discarded the empty tub and started to get up, trying not to wake Noemie from her post-workout nap.

"Where are you going?" Noemie asked as she rubbed her eyes and shifted from the cuddle.

"Someone's at the door." Chase was sure she looked as confused as she felt. Midnight visitors weren't a usual occurrence and hadn't been since college. She stopped at the mirror in the corridor to finger-comb her waxed hair into something reasonable and to check her teeth for errant pieces of falafel. Even uninvited, late night callers deserved a certain level of personal presentation. She opened the door without thinking to slip on the safety chain. When the thought did occur to her, she figured she was safe enough with super soldier daughter only a few feet away. She flicked her porch light on to reveal Rayne standing in her doorway holding a bottle of Winter Jack. Noemie couldn't save her from whatever this was.

"You have no idea how hard it is to get this drink in the summer," Rayne said, holding aloft the fancy bottle as if that were somehow enough to explain her presence.

"What are you doing here?" Chase asked, not bothering to withhold her rising irritation. She'd wanted a simple text, maybe a phone call. She hadn't wanted an impromptu visit, especially since Chase had never given Rayne her address. "And how do you know where I live?"

"Who is it?" Noemie shouted.

She obviously wasn't worried enough to raise herself from her pit. Rayne raised her eyebrow and looked impressed, and there was something else in her expression, but it left her eyes before she spoke again.

"Bad time? Are you…" She looked Chase up and down, taking in the oh-so-sexy tank and sweats combo. "You can't be entertaining?"

Rayne had clearly concluded that Chase's outfit wasn't suitable for whatever she meant by entertaining. "I'm not." Chase didn't owe Rayne any further explanation, especially not at this hour. "It's Rayne," she said, loud enough for Noemie to hear.

"Huh. What does *she* want?"

Rayne looked puzzled that whoever the woman was in Chase's house, she knew who Rayne was, and her tone wasn't exactly welcoming.

"Now we've both asked, and you still haven't answered." Chase leaned her hand against the doorjamb but kept her other hand on the door so that it was only half open.

Rayne waved the bottle again. "I'll tell you if you let me in."

The brief uncertainty was gone, and Rayne acted as though she dropped by every other day. Chase *did* want to know about Rayne's meeting though. "Fine." She pushed the door open and stepped aside for Rayne to sweep past her and strut toward the living room without looking back.

Chase blew out her cheeks and quietly closed the door. At least she didn't have any early morning lectures or work since the students were on summer break. Rayne had come all this way to see her, so Chase expected she'd be seeing the sunrise.

"Noemie? I heard you'd joined the army as a combat medic."

Chase flopped back down beside her.

"Oh, yeah? How'd you hear that?" Noemie asked.

They didn't travel in the same circles. How on earth would Rayne know that information? Chase nudged Noemie in the ribs. "She did. She's on leave for a month." Chase chewed the inside of her cheek before she added, "She's heading back out to Iraq in two days." She hadn't wanted to acknowledge or address the fact that Noemie was leaving already. Their time together was so precious, and it always disappeared with intolerable speed. She heard Noemie swallow hard before she gave Chase a return nudge in her ribs.

"I'm whacked," Noemie said, rising from the sofa. "See you in the morning for our run." She tapped Chase on the leg and was at the door before she turned. "Try to keep the noise down. I'm a light sleeper." She winked at Chase and trotted up the stairs, slipping and yelling, "Ow," at the third or fourth stair as she always did.

"Night, night," Chase shouted up after her. "Love you." Rayne's presence had almost stopped her from adding the last bit, but Noemie needed to hear it more than Chase needed to keep any emotion hidden from Rayne.

"Love you too," Noemie said and closed her door loudly.

"Wow." Rayne whistled. "She's all grown up now."

"She is." Chase hoped her tone would indicate she didn't want to talk about Noemie further. It was late, and she was tired. The body combat had wrecked her and all she wanted to do was crawl into bed, pull the comforter up to her neck, and sleep until her crazy daughter jumped on her in the morning for their park run. "Why are you here?"

"Okay." Rayne held up her hands. "Have it your way. No small talk…" Her grin widened. "The Golden Trinity might exist after all. I think Turner's map is real."

Chase inched forward. "No way. You're sure?"

"As sure as I can be without doing carbon testing on the bark, but I'm sure it's the real deal. The colors, the markings, how it looks…it fits the lore of the treasure and the tree."

Chase stood, her energy suddenly revitalized and too much for a static position. She paced the room. What to say? Turner hadn't come to her, though her knowledge of logograms was superior to Rayne's, that and her cartography skills. Of course he hadn't, because he wanted the treasure for himself and Rayne would have no compunction about where it ended up, as long as she got the glory for finding it and made another cool, bank-busting commission. Suites at the Vervida didn't come cheap, and Rayne had developed a taste for the high life early in her career.

So why had Rayne turned up on her doorstep? She couldn't think that Chase would help her. She tried to calm the fleet of fireflies in her stomach. "That's great. When do you leave?"

Rayne bit her lip and twisted the rope ring she'd worn since Chase knew her. Both were surefire signs something was coming that Chase wouldn't like.

"As soon as we've stolen the map from Turner," Rayne said.

Rayne threw the matter-of-fact statement in casually, but it struck the serene waters of Chase's head like a bouncing bomb. She turned quickly and stared at Rayne. She had to be joking, right? "Sorry, what? It sounded like you just said you were going to steal the map from your client."

Rayne raised her eyebrow and nodded. "You heard right. You didn't want small talk." She picked up the bottle she'd brought with her and offered it to Chase again. "Now do you want that drink?"

Chase dropped back onto the couch and rubbed her eyes. "I was ready for bed…"

"I'm up for that. This'd make for great post-sex pillow talk," Rayne said and winked.

Chase coughed and ignored the invitation. "Glasses are in the kitchen." She pointed in the general direction. To her surprise, Rayne got up and headed out, giving Chase some time to gather her thoughts. Rayne's bombshell of her planned theft still didn't explain her presence. Unless Rayne wanted Chase to be the voice of reason she always used to be for her, and she wanted Chase to talk her out of it.

Rayne returned with two glasses full of ice, filled them with the liquor, and offered one to Chase. "You still prefer it iced, don't you?"

Chase accepted the glass and nodded, taken aback that Rayne had remembered another trivial detail.

"Do you remember when I bought you your first bottle? You drank all of it over ice before I read the label—"

"And it was supposed to be heated. Yeah, I remember. I can't believe you do."

Rayne shrugged. "I remember everything about those years."

Chase took a long drink to avoid looking into Rayne's eyes, which were calling for her to jump in. What was her end game? Other than the obvious, and Chase wasn't falling for that. "Back to stealing the map…" Chase said and leaned into the sofa, affecting a relaxed pose she certainly didn't feel.

"Okay. We need to liberate the map from the Grande. Ginn and Tonyck are on their way with everything we need for that part of the operation. Once we have the map, we'll board a chartered jet to Rio, hire a local guide, and find the Golden Trinity." Rayne smiled and sat back in her chair as if that should explain everything.

"Why do you keep saying 'we'?" Chase knew Rayne had her team, and her gorilla girls were imminent. But the "we" sounded more inclusive than that.

"I'm glad you ask." Rayne raised her glass. "I want you to come with me. Hence, we." She sipped her drink but made a face like she didn't fully appreciate the taste. "Like old times."

Chase blinked hard. Where to start? Old times had been successful until Florida, and Florida *was* a success for Rayne. She laughed. It seemed like the only reasonable response to the nonsense Rayne had just fed her.

"Look. I understand your reaction, and most likely, your trepidation, but—"

"No shit? How terribly wonderful of you," Chase said, mimicking Rayne's particularly proper way of speaking. "There's so many things wrong with *everything* you've just said that I'm struggling to decide how to prioritize my responses." Rayne opened her mouth to talk, but Chase thrust a finger up to silence her. "Firstly, no to being any kind of accomplice to your crazy criminal activity. Secondly, no to working with you even though it *is* the Golden Trinity. And thirdly, just no. No to everything." Chase put her glass on the table a little too heavily, reminding her that Noemie might already be asleep. She lowered her voice to a whisper. "I don't understand why you're here, Rayne. I don't understand at all."

"Can I speak now?"

Chase caught the edge of impatience in Rayne's voice, and it scratched at her own patience with this whole situation. "No. You don't get to do that. You turn up at my house, a house I haven't even given you the address to, at midnight with some wild tale and expect me to work with you? *I'm* the only one in this room who has the right to be annoyed. Okay?"

Rayne began to raise an eyebrow to give Chase that look that always made her feel a little bit admonished and a little bit turned on. Tonight though, she was in no mood to be either of those things, and she was glad when Rayne didn't follow through on the full expression.

"I'm sorry, and you're absolutely right," Rayne said, put down her glass, and clasped her hands in front of her. "I needed to act fast, and I just expected you to be ready to jump with me without much thought. I was wrong."

Chase wiggled her finger in her ear. She couldn't be hearing right. Rayne had said the two things that Chase couldn't recall her ever admitting to: being sorry *and* wrong. This, the Zenobia thing, and the meal last night were really making it look as though an alien mind swap had occurred. She looked like Rayne. She sounded like Rayne. But she couldn't *be* Rayne.

"Turner is a loon. He wants the treasure no matter the cost. And I don't mean money." Rayne ran her hand through her hair and sighed. "He'll go through any tribes he comes across, and he said he'd hire Oscar Owen if I didn't take the job."

Rayne fell silent, and the gravity of her words settled on Chase's mind like a lead weight. Owen's reputation was a particularly vile one. The thought of Rayne being mixed up with him flipped her stomach and not in a good butterflies kind of way. His penchant for violence and his flagrant disregard for women were well known in the business, but he always managed to stay out of Johnny Lawman's hands. If Turner was willing to contract Owen's services, he was bad news in every way.

"I need your help, Chase. I need your expertise with the map. You'll understand it better than I can, what colors they used and why, the meaning of the positions of symbols. I can do this, but I can do it faster and better with you. I don't know if Turner has made digital copies of the map, so stealing it doesn't necessarily stop him. This could turn out to be a race, and me stealing the map will give us a head start in getting to the Golden Trinity and making sure everyone on the way is kept safe and away from harm. Once we have the map, Turner's bound to recruit Owen." Rayne reached out and touched Chase's knee gently. "I know what I'm asking of you. I understand you're reluctant and that you still might say no… But I have to ask."

Rayne had been opening and closing her hand over and over as she spoke, a little tell that meant she had something else to say. But what more could there be? Chase wanted the whole picture for her to even consider Rayne's plea. "There's something else…What is it?"

Rayne looked away for a brief moment and shook her head. "Isn't that enough?"

"No, don't do that. You don't get to pick and choose what I should or shouldn't know. This isn't just another expedition. You're asking me to put my life at risk to join you."

Rayne looked away again and ran her fingers over her forehead. "How can you still tell when I'm holding something back?"

Rayne's body language was talking up a storm. Chase smiled. "If I told you that, you'd stop doing it. Spill."

"He mentioned your name and expertise." Rayne clenched her jaw and her fist. "I think if I pushed him into this corner, he'd come and get you, whether you wanted to go or not."

THE GOLDEN TRINITY

Chase closed her eyes and shut out everything but her own thoughts. The Golden Trinity might or might not be real. Either way, it had put the lives of innocent people at risk. And Rayne had laid that at her feet. She must have known how Chase would react when given the story, or at least hoped for that reaction, but did Rayne have any choice either? Doing the right thing was unfamiliar territory for Rayne. It was Chase's playground. Teaming up again was a bad idea on so many levels, but Chase couldn't see a way to avoid it *and* live with herself. The possibility of Owen slicing through people with a machete as though they were troublesome vines sickened her.

And Rayne. If anything happened to her…she squeezed her eyes shut tighter against the invasion of images of Rayne coming head to head with Owen. Finally, there was the Golden Trinity. If—a big if—it was real and they found it, Chase could ensure it went to the Brazilian government and their people. And she'd stop Rayne from profiting from it on the black market.

She opened her eyes and met Rayne's gaze. There was a vulnerability there that Chase hadn't seen before. She had no chance of kicking her out and letting her get on with it. Chase had a lot of questions, but right now she could see that Rayne just needed an answer. God, she knew she was going to regret this. "I'll help you, but I'm having nothing to with whatever your plan is to steal the map. I'm sure your gorilla girls can handle that without me."

Rayne smiled. "You won't regret it, Chase. I promise."

Chase nodded, amused by Rayne's optimism and sure that she would almost certainly regret it. "But we have to discuss what happens to the Golden Trinity *if* we find it."

"Sure." Rayne raised her glass. "To saving lives and finding the largest haul of treasure in recorded history."

Chase clinked her glass to Rayne's and knocked it back. She was going to need more than a little liquid courage if they came face-to-face with Oscar Owen.

CHAPTER TEN

"THIS IS *MY* plan, Tonyck," Rayne said, frustration scratching at her mind like steel nails down a chalkboard. "I won't stay out of the action." She punched the penthouse level button with a little more force than intended and caught the alarm. A high-pitched bell rang twice before someone's disembodied voice filled the metal box.

"Is there a problem?"

"Apologies. There's no problem. I caught the alarm when I pressed for another floor. Everything's fine."

Tonyck glared at Rayne, the unspoken tension clear in her eyes.

"There's no need for emergency services?" the woman asked.

"No, no. All is well, thank you." Rayne pushed her hair behind her ear and avoided further eye contact with Tonyck.

"Okay. Could you depress the alarm to deactivate the emergency response, please?"

"Of course," Rayne said and did as asked, conscious that the last thing they needed were any cops in the building when they were about to perpetrate a crime. "Apologies again."

"Fine," the woman said, and an electronic clunk sounded the end of the conversation.

The possibility that the voice might still be listening hushed the lecture she'd been in the middle of delivering to Tonyck.

Tonyck took her reticence as an opportunity to defend herself. "All I'm saying is, be careful. This is new territory for you." She ignored Rayne's widening eyes warning her to stop speaking. "The map is your focus."

Rayne clenched her jaw, the only way she could stop herself from responding. *She* was the one who decided whose focus should be where. She concentrated on the flickering lights of the hotel floors as they came and went in an effort to distract herself from her anger. They had a plan and she'd stick to it, of course. She respected both Tonyck's and Ginn's experience in hostile situations, and she didn't begin to believe that she knew better. But she wouldn't be rushed away if something went wrong or they had to deviate from the plan. Tonyck's suggestion that Rayne simply get out of there and out of harm's way if there was trouble wouldn't fly. Rayne had no intention of doing anything of the sort. She might pay G&T danger money, but she didn't pay them to take the fall for her. All of this has been her idea, and she'd see it through. No matter what.

Rayne quickly navigated her way through the sequence of events they'd planned. Once the elevator door opened on Turner's level, there would be no going back.

"Second thoughts?" Ginn asked as if she'd reached into Rayne's mind and pulled them out for inspection.

Rayne shook her head, willing the elevator to move faster. As exciting as she'd thought doing something this flagrantly illegal might be, she now wanted to get it over with so they could start the real adventure of finding the Golden Trinity. Tonyck tapped Rayne's upper arm. When Rayne looked at her, Tonyck had narrowed her eyes. "You know you actually see less, not more, when you do that?" Rayne motioned to Tonyck's face. "It doesn't give you the power to see into my mind." The elevator pinged to sound its arrival at the penthouse. "Everything's going to be fine."

The doors opened to reveal the same guy on door duty as before. She nodded to Tonyck, their sign to indicate there'd been no change. Tonyck had been concerned that the ex-military team Turner had mentioned might already be present. She didn't visibly relax, and Rayne felt her own shoulders tense in anticipation of any changes they might find inside Turner's suite. His door opened and Turner came into view.

"Trouble with the elevator?" the door guy asked.

He nodded to G&T with what Rayne had come to learn was the military nod, their version of gaydar.

"Just me being clumsy and catching the alarm," Rayne said as she stepped out of the elevator and approached. Each step felt unsteady, and she straightened, summoning the sashay swagger she usually affected so easily. Now wasn't the time to allow nerves to creep in.

"That wouldn't be something I would have thought you to be, Ms. Marcellus," Turner said.

He smiled and Rayne saw that unsavory look in his eyes she'd come to expect in men like him, a sickly mixture of desire and entitlement. She pushed down her answering desire to punch him in his smug face. He'd obviously become very used to women servicing his every whim, even though he had to pay for the privilege. She returned his smile and stopped at the doorway waiting for him to move aside.

"Come in," he said, barely moving.

Rayne slipped past him, careful not to touch any part of him. She wondered if he thought of her as bought and paid for in ways other than for her treasure hunting expertise. He'd be sorely disappointed. She turned to see him attempt to close the door on G&T, but Tonyck slapped her hand against the heavy wood.

Turner looked at Rayne. "Do they need to come in?"

Rayne nodded and pointed toward them both, reining in the small hiccup of panic that bubbled in her stomach. She couldn't execute their plan by herself. "They have the equipment I said I was dropping off with you."

Tonyck pulled on a strap to her backpack with her free hand, and she mixed her accompanying expression of obvious impatience with a snarl.

"Of course," Turner said and stepped aside with an exaggerated shake of his head. "I'd forgotten about the equipment."

Rayne turned around and was relieved to see the briefcase containing the map was parked under the table in the living area. Turner's mute buddy, Rich, sat on the couch opposite and nodded to her. He raised his glass and pointed to it, she assumed to offer her one. Could it be this easy?

"That's okay. I'll help myself." Rayne walked over to him as casually as she could manage. "Can I top you up?" He nodded and Rayne's heart rate quickened. "Gin?" Rich shook his head. "Vodka?" He nodded again. Rayne took the glass, walked beyond him, and set it on the side table where a colorful array of bottled spirits were arranged. She retrieved the small baggie of crushed Rohypnol from the inside of her bra and emptied it into the inch of vodka in Rich's glass. She reached for the Absolut as she swirled his glass to mix the drug.

"Sorry, Ms. Marcellus," Turner said as he swept up to Rayne's side. "Rich can be such an ass when it comes to looking after a woman. Allow me."

He positioned himself so close to her that her level of discomfort forced her to step away. She slipped the empty baggie into the pocket of her trousers and kept her focus on Turner. The pulse in her throat felt like it might jump out of her mouth. "It's not a problem."

"Nonsense. You're our guest. You shouldn't be serving yourself. And you definitely shouldn't be refilling that lazy drunk's glass."

Rayne glanced across at Rich who'd responded to Turner's comment with an extended middle finger. In another situation, she might've sympathized with Rich. She couldn't imagine not being able to communicate verbally.

"What's your poison?" Turner asked.

He smiled and Rayne controlled any visual response. His grin seemed to be getting more sexually loaded every time he directed it her way. She pointed to a distinctive bottle that attracted her attention because it looked like a pear-shaped woman. "I'd love to try the Appleton Fifty."

Turner raised his eyebrows and looked impressed. "Great choice. That's the most expensive spirit on the table. There were only eight hundred bottles of this made, you know? It's smooth enough that you should enjoy it neat," he said, pouring three fingers' worth into a lead crystal tumbler then offered it to her with a flourish. "Enjoy five hundred dollars of liquid elegance."

Rayne balked and held up her hand. "Goodness, I couldn't possibly." Expensive liquors didn't excite Rayne, and his pretentiousness chafed at her growing desire to smash the glass over his head, grab the briefcase, and run. Every additional moment in Turner's company made her more determined to thwart his continuing exploitation of South America. First timber and now hidden treasure.

"Once you find the Golden Trinity, liquor like this will flow like tap water." Turner took Rayne's hand and pressed the glass into her palm. "I insist."

His hands felt like frog skin on hers, and she withdrew with the glass as quickly as possible without spilling the ridiculously priced drink. It took all her restraint not to snatch up a napkin from the table and wipe away the feeling of slimy mucus from her hands. She took a short sniff of the rum, intrigued to discover how the smell of a five-thousand-dollar bottle of rum differed from a twenty-dollar special. Her nostrils filled with a hint of cinnamon, but above that, she couldn't detect any of the other top, middle, or bottom notes or whatever the hell it was she was supposed to be able to smell. She glanced over the top of her glass to see Turner waiting expectantly for her verdict. Rayne sipped it and nodded. "It's magnificent."

Turner filled Rich's glass with vodka, while keeping his gaze on Rayne.

The white powder had dissolved, so half their plan was in motion. Rayne flashed a look Tonyck's way and blinked once to confirm she'd dropped the drug.

"If you want it," Turner said in Rich's direction, "you need to fetch it." He wafted the glass in the air and a few drops fell onto the carpet in movie-like slow motion.

Tonyck wandered over. "I'm happy to serve an old member of my unit," she said as she took the glass from Turner with no resistance, went back toward the sofa, and handed it to Rich.

Rayne twisted her rope ring while she tried to convince herself that Rich being ex-Special Forces wouldn't alter Tonyck's loyalty. She cautioned herself within seconds; Tonyck was making sure Rich received the drug. Being in the Special Forces didn't make him any less of a murderous asshole.

"How did you two come to work for Ms. Marcellus?" Turner asked after he'd made his own drink and clinked his glass to Rayne's.

Tonyck had dropped the equipment bag beside the door and retaken her position beside her sister. "We answered a Craigslist ad," she said without missing a beat.

Rich grinned widely, snorted, and a strange laughing sound emerged from his mouth. He raised his glass toward the twins and downed the contents in one gulp. Tonyck winked and the corner of her mouth turned up slightly. Turner cleared his throat, noticeably uncomfortable at being excluded from their inexplicable in-joke. Rayne had no idea either so she shrugged and shook her head.

"I expect it's some military humor we couldn't begin to understand," Rayne said. They needed him to relax and sit down. She had another baggie of Rohypnol in the right cup of her bra with his name on it. "Would you show me the map again? I'd like to begin some exploratory translation of the symbols."

"Of course." Turner moved to the case and waited for Rich to remove his empty glass before he laid it on the table.

He pressed his fingerprint to the lock panel and slowly lifted the lid as if he were once again revealing it for the first time. Rayne reacted as she had when he'd initially revealed it to her. Clichéd, she knew, but the sight of it truly did take her breath away. She traced the edges through the glass trying to imagine what it might feel like.

"Still finding it hard to believe?" Turner asked, his fingers tracking the glass toward Rayne's.

She withdrew her hands and put them over her mouth, trying to make it less than obvious that the thought of touching him in any way repulsed her. "It is quite unbelievable, Mr. Turner—"

"Stan. You should call me Stan."

She gave a quick smile. "Then you should call me Rayne…I went back to my hotel after our initial meeting in something of a daze. Even though I'd seen it so closely, my brain still refused to believe it was real." Turner was lapping up her reverence, becoming more wide-eyed with each word, so she ramped it up a notch. "I woke several times that night, certain I'd been dreaming, sure that you couldn't possible exist, and that it had all been a wild fantasy." Tonyck rolled her eyes and shook her head slightly. Rayne ran her middle finger over her eyebrows slowly and looked at Tonyck long enough for her to receive the message. Turner leaned over the briefcase, his excitement obvious, but Rayne doubted it was for the map.

"I'm so glad you share my enthusiasm, Rayne."

Rayne pointed to the map, every inch of the bark used in one way or another. An artifact like this made non-destructive carbon dating worth the extra expense over traditional carbon-14 dating. Even removing a tiny piece of the map might have affected their ability to read it accurately. "I do love the new carbon dating process," Rayne said.

Turner took a sip of his drink, reminding Rayne she had yet to get the drug anywhere near him.

"I don't understand why more museums aren't trying the process. Where else do they let someone get away with an acid *and* an arson attack?"

Turner chuckled at his own clever humor, and Rayne felt a measure of truth in his words. How many arsons had he set to cover his tracks in the Amazon? After speaking with Chase, Rayne had spent a little time reading about illegal logging the previous night, and as she had, guilt had crept up. Why hadn't she checked into that *business* before agreeing to meet him and entertain the notion of him becoming a client? Had her ethical standards slipped so low, unnoticed, that Jenny thought she wouldn't balk at how he'd made his fortune? She'd thumbed a lengthy email to Jenny questioning the moral turpitude of the company but then deleted it. Rayne was responsible for the final decision on client suitability. She couldn't blame Jenny or anyone else. She'd abdicated rather than delegated, and Turner had been a much-needed wake-up call. Wouldn't Chase be proud? "At least it proved your theory correct. Imagine spending that kind of money only to find that an artistic aboriginal kid had made it and stuffed it in a tree to fool the *karai*." Turner looked like he didn't understand. "White people." Rayne glanced at Rich. His eyes were beginning to look too heavy to keep open. The window to drop the drug into Turner's drink was closing quick, and there didn't look to be a legitimate opening coming anytime soon. She looked across to Ginn, and she nodded, beginning to move into position behind Turner. Plan B then.

Turner tutted. "You insult me if you think a witless child could ever put one over on me." He knocked back his drink and rose from the couch, his ego obviously wounded.

"Please don't misunderstand me, Stan. I certainly don't lump you in the *karai* category. You've been around them long enough that they couldn't begin to outwit you. I have no doubt."

Turner didn't respond. He filled his glass and returned to his seat on the couch opposite Rayne.

"Flattery will get you everywhere." His brow furrowed as he focused on Rich, who was now snoring like Darth Vader. "That boy can't take his liquor. That's why I don't let him drink the liquid gold." He tapped his glass. "Perhaps you'd like to tell your bodyguards to leave so we can talk about our plans in a more…relaxed atmosphere."

His meaning was clear. Relaxed equaled naked. Rayne smiled as she saw the twins move silently to the rear of Turner. "Perhaps you'd like to go fuck yourself."

She savored the millisecond of his confusion at her rebuke before Ginn clamped her giant hand over his mouth. She yanked him backward, and Tonyck quickly administered Plan B to a vein in Turner's neck. He was immobile and unconscious in seconds with minimal noise or movement. Ginn slowly released him and slid him back onto the couch. Tonyck put her finger to her lips and approached the door. She checked the small screen for the corridor camera and gave a thumbs-up sign. Ginn joined her and stood to the side of the door. She pulled out her own pre-prepared needle and nodded to Rayne.

Rayne took a last sip of the rum. It'd be a shame to waste it since Turner's pretentious claim that it was liquid elegance was irritatingly on point. It was the best she'd ever tasted. She resolved to liberate the rest of the bottle along with the map. She gave Rich a little shake to ensure he was fully unconscious before she joined the twins at the door.

"Just get him all the way in," Tonyck whispered.

Rayne suppressed a sudden giggle that arose from nowhere. This wasn't a situation that warranted laughter. She dismissed it as nerves. What they were in the middle of was new, and yes, exciting, but it definitely wasn't something to giggle at. She pressed her lips together in case another bout surprised her and nodded. She opened the door. "Could you come in and check Mr. Turner? He's had something of a turn." Rayne stepped aside to encourage him to enter.

"What happened?" he asked, stepping into the trap. "Was he—"

He didn't get to finish the sentence. As Rayne closed the door behind him, Tonyck stunned him with a blow to his neck. She kicked the back of his knees, and he thudded to the floor. She wrapped an arm around his thick neck and put her other hand over his mouth while Ginn plunged her needle into a small section of neck Tonyck left open. She held him as his thrashing slowly stilled. Rayne watched, impressed by their slick takedown. It took both of them to drag him over to the sofa.

"I'll get the map," Rayne said. She opened one of the backpacks the twins brought and pulled out another pack, smaller but the perfect size for the glass box containing the ancient bark. She moved around the twins who were busy securing their three drugged victims in para rope, and slowly lifted the airtight box from the briefcase. She couldn't stop a wide smile. Relieving the bad guys of an ancient artifact, fighting the good fight, protecting the innocent tribespeople…now she *really* felt like a tomb raider.

Chapter Eleven

Chase didn't have the vocabulary to put what she felt into words. Not adequately. Wonderstruck. Astonished. Overwhelmed. None of them perfectly described her reaction to what she was looking at. And there were so many layers to its existence in any ordinary circumstances—a piece of history possibly two and a quarter thousand years old, a map to lead them to an astonishing haul of treasure people had sought for centuries, only the fifth remaining record of Mayan language on bark.

But Chase wasn't in any ordinary circumstance. This was a Rayne situation, and that complicated *everything*.

Chase resolved to parse out what was going on into smaller, more manageable chunks. Trying to juggle the situation as a whole was just too much. The approach didn't sit well. She was used to dealing with complex scenarios with little trouble, and the last thing she wanted to appear was incompetent. She could do this. She'd *been* doing this her whole career. She just had to temporarily ignore the danger and threat of violence, or worse, that sat menacingly at the back of her mind waving for attention.

The map. That was the reason Rayne wanted her there. It was, almost unbelievably, sitting before her now in a sealed case. It'd be cumbersome to lug around on their expedition, but Chase expected that the interchangeable tank twins would take turns. And as much as she disliked everything about them, after seeing them in action in Syria, Chase was begrudgingly comforted by their presence.

The feeling apparently wasn't mutual.

"She's dead weight, and she's going to slow us down," Tank Twin One grumbled.

Chase looked up from the map at her. "Could you both wear name badges? You're like a pair of pedigree poodles, and I can't tell the difference."

Tank Twin One raised her eyebrows and snarled. "You wanna see this poodle throw a punch, shortstop?"

Rayne placed a hand on Tank Twin One's shoulder. "This is Tonyck, and her slightly younger sister," she pointed to the other one who looked amused rather than furious, "is Ginn. Tonyck has deeper frown lines on her forehead, her Special Forces tattoo is on her right shoulder, and generally she's more serious." Rayne removed her hand and gestured to the other one. "Ginn's tattoo is on her left shoulder, her skin's softer because she moisturizes daily, which Tonyck blasts her for and calls her Ginger Beer, some sort of English slang for queer. And she sports an almost perpetual grin."

Chase didn't want to know about Ginn's skin. And how did Rayne know that? And why was Chase bothered that Rayne *did* know that? "Why are they named after a cocktail? Mean parents or your nickname for them?" Chase couldn't stop herself from wanting to push Tonyck's buttons. Every time they'd met, Tonyck's reception had been less than welcoming, especially now that she realized it was Ginn who'd pulled her from the Parisian sewer. Chase didn't understand why since she'd never done or said anything untoward to her. She'd decided to give it right back instead of wasting more time trying to analyze it. It looked like Rayne had to suppress a laugh.

"It's a nickname they got in the military," Rayne said. "Ginn's full throttle approach occasionally needs watering down, and her big sister does just that."

"Older sister," Ginn said. "Not bigger sister."

She flexed her bicep and Chase had it down for nineteen inches. She was over six feet tall so it didn't look disproportionate to the rest of her, which was symmetrically sizeable. At only five foot five, Chase had decided she couldn't train to be much bigger or her head would look like a shrunken head on a voodoo doll.

"Older *and* bigger," Tonyck said.

Without getting out the measuring tape, Chase couldn't comment either way. Tonyck may have edged it. Her long-sleeved shirt looked like it was struggling to contain her biceps, chest, and back, but she also had a bit of a belly that indicated a guilty leaning to chocolate or alcohol. Ginn's stomach looked flat enough to iron her shirt on. That's how she'd tell them apart from now on, but name badges still wouldn't hurt. She uncapped a bottle of water and drank. Long-haul flights always made her super thirsty.

"Chase has an unparalleled grasp of Mayan calligraphic art and is an expert in ancient cartography," Rayne said, relaxing back into her seat. "She's vital to interpreting the map correctly. Animals become colors with a misplaced glottal stop. I don't want to think I'm heading toward a yellow brick road only to discover I'm walking into a pit of snakes."

Chase laughed and water spluttered from her mouth. Rayne offered a napkin, smiling mischievously, but Chase shook her head and wiped it away with her scarf. The knowledge in Rayne's joke evidenced she was no airhead when it came to decoding glyphs either. Once again, Chase was struck by the injustice to most regular people that Rayne had been blessed with beauty, brains, and a kick-ass sense of humor. It simply wasn't fair to anyone else.

"Is that the same scarf you were wearing in Syria and Paris?" Ginn asked.

Odd that she'd observed and remembered Chase's accessories, but she nodded.

"It's her lucky scarf," Rayne said.

Rayne got up and approached Chase. She reached down and ran her fingers along an edge of the scarf, and her nails grazed Chase's bare collarbone and chest. Chase clenched against the response between her legs and swallowed. It sounded like it echoed around the cabin.

"I think it makes her look like a wildly adventurous National Geographic photojournalist."

Rayne's words caressed her ego as delicately as her fingers had caressed Chase's skin. Damn, she knew exactly how to rev a girl's engine. In truth, Chase only wore it because that was exactly what Rayne had said when she'd first tried the new look. Rayne released the material and continued beyond Chase. Chase glanced over her shoulder to watch as Rayne somehow managed to walk elegantly at fifty thousand feet. If Chase tried that in heels, she'd be facedown in some fat guy's lap. Rayne closed the cockpit door behind her.

"Best keep your focus on what you're here for and keep your eyes off the lady boss."

Chase knew it was Tonyck talking before she turned to meet her confrontational glare.

"I could say the same to you," Chase said. Tonyck flushed pink and her head twitched to the side.

"My focus *is* the lady boss. We're here to keep her safe from everything…and *everyone.*"

"Who's going to keep her safe from you?" Chase asked. Her heart thumped against her chest, and she was sure even the captain would hear it. Chase hated confrontation but wasn't afraid of it. Even if its source had about forty pounds of muscle and six inches of height over her.

Tonyck moved to rise from her seat, but Ginn put her arm across her chest and grinned. "I like you. You've got some *cajones* for a little guy."

"Thanks?" Chase said, unsure as to why Ginn had called her a guy. But she'd take that over constantly butting heads with a walking wall. Tonyck still glared so Chase looked away, happy to let her continue to bore holes of fire into Chase's skull. As long as Tonyck had Rayne's back, she could act like a belligerent butch as much as she liked.

***

The approach to the Manaus landing strip roused mixed feelings. Chase couldn't wait to suck in lungfuls of non-conditioned air, though the temperature would probably be high enough that each breath would coat her throat with heat. On the other hand, the capital of Amazonas was a study in opposites, a dichotomy of privilege and poverty. Cruise ships moored to a side of the city where brightly colored high-rises and status symbol buildings such as their opera house abounded. But the vista changed where Manaus met the rain forest, where stilted houses crushed together on softly rising hills, their fasciae a palette of weather-beaten, pale, pastel panels. It angered Chase that the look had been appropriated for the shabby chic look in fashionable restaurants and bars across the US, ignorant of the poverty from which it came. This wasn't an unusual sight in South America, hell, the world over. Chase had seen it on many expeditions, but its impact pressed heavy on her heart wherever she went. If they found the Golden Trinity, the people in these slums could benefit and finally have the life they'd come here for. *If* their government used the vast income to provide better, safer housing. It was a big *if.* Chase rested her forehead on the small window. She stared beyond the harsh orange glow of the city lights into the comforting darkness of the rain forest.

The epic task before them suddenly weighed on her chest. Turner had told Rayne where he'd found the map. She and Rayne had studied it before they left SFO to get a rough idea of where it referred to. From that, the destination airport was Tabatinga, via Manaua. Chase was as certain as she could be that the top right corner of the map correlated to where the Itaquai met the Ituí River. The possibility that she could have made a mistake sat at the forefront of her mind. Could she afford to ignore it? They'd checked, doubled-checked, and checked again. The positioning made sense in relation to where the map had been hidden, south of Atalaía where Turner planned to decimate newly available areas of rain forest for profit.

Chase had done some digging while she waited for word from Rayne that she'd secured the map, and what she'd discovered had blown away the lingering doubts about joining Rayne's crazy quest. She recalled the images of a small previously uncontacted tribe that had left her in tears. Their butchered bodies, mutilated by machetes, left distorted and displayed as a warning not to get in the way of the *karai*. White men were claiming this land as their own and had no compunction about slaying whoever stood in their way, much the same as they had done in North America. A single bow lay clutched in the hand of the only adult male of the six dead. An arrow as long as the bow itself lay impotent beside him. It had been no match for the savage attack that had befallen them.

The location where the gruesome tableau was found was too close to where Turner had felled the tree that yielded the map to be coincidental. And this was simply a taster of how far they'd go to make their fortune. Chase still had so many concerns if they actually found the Golden Trinity. Would Rayne betray her again? Had Rayne realized she needed Chase once she'd seen the map? Was that the ruse behind her sudden bout of morality?

She parked all her worries to concentrate on deciphering the map. She had a chance to stand between genocide and greed. Even in school, she'd never been one to look the other way when the resident bully victimized the weaker kids. Getting a beating when she stepped in to help a woman in a bar fight hadn't diminished her drive to defend people unable to protect themselves either. This was no different. More dangerous, sure. Potentially fatal, accepted. But she couldn't and wouldn't stay at home when she knew she could help.

The wheels bounced on, off, and then back onto the ground, jerking Chase from her thoughts. She felt a gentle touch on her forearm and opened her eyes to see Rayne above her. How did she look so put together and fresh after sixteen hours of moisture-sucking pressurized air?

Robyn Nyx

"Grab your gear, Chase. Our next plane is waiting for us."

Chase ran her hand over her face firmly, trying to smoosh some energy in there. If she could wake her face up, maybe her body would follow. "No transfer time?" She unbuckled her seat belt and stretched.

Rayne swept her gaze over Chase's upper body and shook her head. "We've got the charter to Tabatinga waiting for us to load up. No time to waste, muscles." Rayne winked.

Chase left her arms in the air a moment longer, enjoying Rayne's attention mostly because Tonyck was eyeballing the exchange. Chase could see her jaw clenching and unclenching in ill-disguised contempt. "What about immigration?" Chase relaxed her arms and stood. She slung her backpack over her shoulder, grabbed her river bag in her other hand, and waited for a response.

Rayne laughed and caressed the side of Chase's neck briefly. "They do things different down here…especially when you load their palms with a bunch of Benjamins."

Chase shivered at Rayne's touch, and she bit at the inside of her lower lip. Who was she kidding? She couldn't play this game. Novice versus champion wasn't a fair match. She nodded, said no more, and Rayne walked away. Well, she glided really, but Chase didn't want to dwell on that.

Chase gave Tonyck a cheeky wink and jogged to catch up with Rayne. "I know I said that I didn't want any part of whatever you did to get the map, but I can't seem to kill my curiosity…" Chase wiped her forearm across her head, the oppressive humidity hitting her entire system as soon as she left the conditioned comfort of the plane.

Rayne glanced sideways at Chase and smiled. "What do you want to know?"

"How do you walk so damn fast in heels?" Chase asked, not sure why she prioritized that irrelevant question.

"Practice." She cast another look Chase's way, mischief playing on her lips. "You'd be stunned at what I can do in heels."

Chase didn't doubt it, but she didn't want to know either, right? Right. "Turner *is* alive, isn't he?"

Rayne halted instantly, and Chase nearly fell over herself to stop on the same dime.

"That's not a serious question, is it?"

94

There was a lack of playfulness in her voice, a seriousness Chase hadn't heard before.

"Tonyck and Ginn, they're pretty hardcore. Situations turn bad. Accidents happen..." The inference hung in the air, almost visible such was its presence. Rayne blinked and tugged her ponytail over her shoulder before she continued her assault on the tarmac toward the other plane.

"If anything had gone wrong. I would've told you, Chase. I would never knowingly put you in a situation of that magnitude."

Rayne's heels clicked on each metal step as she climbed up into the much smaller plane. Chase focused on the silk-wrapped wedge of Rayne's shoes instead of her swim model's ass.

Rayne reached the top and turned to face Chase, who paused a few steps down. Maddeningly, it increased their height difference farther and reminded Chase that no matter how hard she trained her body, she'd never be taller than Rayne. Her own lack of height had always gnawed at her inner sense of butchness. She should be six foot, or at least five ten. She wanted to look down on her girl, wrap an arm *over* her shoulders protectively. Maybe she'd invest in some Cuban heels...if they made it home.

"Satisfied?" Rayne asked before strutting inside the plane without waiting for Chase to answer.

Chase took the last couple of steps with one stride, caught her toe, and nearly fell into the plane. Maybe she could look into being stretched.

She dumped her bags into an oversized seat and dropped into one opposite Rayne, already settled and staring out the window as intently as if Cirque du Soleil were performing on the wing.

"What kind of head start do you think we have on Turner?" Chase asked, waving her hand in front of Rayne's face.

Rayne batted her hand away and turned her attention back to Chase. Her intensity was almost as stifling as the humidity.

"We left them tied up and pumped with a hefty dose of Rohypnol and hung a 'Do Not Disturb' sign on the door. Tonyck said they'd be awake after eight to ten hours. He's in the penthouse so it's not like anyone could hear them shouting. I suppose they'll be reliant on the diligence of the hotel staff. We could have a ten-hour run on them, or it could be as many as twenty-four hours. Then they'll be tracking us, with or without the map. Turner will want what he thinks is his. Our footprints aren't as invisible as we need them to be."

Rayne pulled the tie from her hair. Chase quickly looked away to avoid the inevitable shampoo ad-like cascade of Rayne's hair falling over her shoulders. Chase's life would be so much less complicated if Rayne had simply been a model instead of her chosen profession. Chase could've watched her from afar, admired her in the sleek, glossy pages of fashion magazines (that she would never admit to owning and would hide away like a teenage boy hides porn). But instead, their paths appeared inextricably linked, and they were fated to crash into each other's lives repeatedly. Chase had sometimes daydreamed their destinies were intertwined and that they would keep smashing together until they realized they were supposed to face this existence side by side. Those kinds of thoughts usually came after Chase had watched a ridiculously clichéd Hollywood rom-com movie or read a soft and fluffy lesfic book (again, something she'd never admit to owning and her collection was stashed away in a trunk beneath her bed).

Those kinds of thoughts she shoved away because they were as unwanted as they were painful. Chase knew she'd just be a sidekick to the Rayne show, and she wanted to be the hero of her own life. *She* wanted to rescue the damsel in distress. Fuck knocking the clichés. They existed because sometimes they were true, and Chase embraced that one. But more than that, Rayne stood in the way of any kind of real partnership, friendship, or something deeper. Rayne's ambition and selfishness left no room for anyone else in her mind or her heart.

CHAPTER TWELVE

CHASE FINALLY FOUND an empty wooden stool, picked it up, and joined the rest of the group. Rayne had commandeered the only table in the rudimentary bar, and the few seats around it were filled by Rayne, the tank twins, and a local Tonyck had met on their way from the airport into Tabatinga. Maybe it was a bar. There was no one serving, but there were glasses on shelves, and Ginn had brought in a bottle of rum. Chase didn't know if the meeting was prearranged or whether Tonyck had just started a conversation with the first English-speaking Brazilian she'd found. They weren't exactly forthcoming with their plans. Rayne's quick explanation of, "It's just a short stop for provisions, transport, and a guide," had done little to settle Chase's growing concern about Turner, and worse, Oscar Owen. Alongside that, however, the bubbling in the pit of her stomach that came with any adventure, the excitement, had increased tenfold. Syria had been intense, but when Chase took the time to reflect on it, she realized it had been the best experience of her life. She was processing the notion that she wanted more, more adventures, more danger. The possible thrills of hunting down ancient artifacts got her out of bed every morning, but this added risk plugged a hole Chase had been ignoring.

Sitting here now, with a recently purchased machete hanging from the belt on her cargo pants, sweat darkening her camel-colored shirt, and her lucky scarf dipped and soaked in rainwater to keep her cool, she felt invigorated in a way she'd only dreamed about. *This* was the life she'd envisioned when she became an archeologist. This was her chance to become the hero she was desperate to be.

Chase took off her Oakleys and hooked them onto her scarf. Rayne looked across and winked. She was incorrigible. With everything going on, she could still happily flirt as if there were all the time in the world for it.

"I have the boat you need, and I have perfect guide for you," the local said. "Do you have the dollars we agreed?"

The man's skin looked like tanned, lived-in leather. He'd probably never heard of sunscreen, much less used it. His white button-down linen shirt was three sizes too big for him or he'd recently lost some serious weight. But there was something about him that gave the visual impression he was unbreakable, like his spirit ran through him in braids of stainless steel.

"Money isn't a problem, Pablo." Rayne slid a stack of fifty-dollar bills across the table. "As agreed."

"For the guide." Pablo grinned at the sight of a wad of greenbacks and moved to take them when the door to the tavern slammed against the wall.

Everyone turned or looked toward the unexpected and loud intrusion. Chase, closest to the door, saw one guy and three women dressed head to foot in matching urban camouflage. While the guy was relatively average size, his posse were weighty, hefty women who wouldn't have looked out of place on a prison rec yard. Chase clenched her teeth to stop from laughing. Their uniforms were of little use in the dense, lush green Amazon forest. Her urge to laugh drifted away quickly as she took the rest of them in. Each sported a machete on their belt, and the guy wore a shoulder holster with the butt of a handgun peeking out of it. In her peripheral vision, the tank twins edged their chairs away from the table, and Tonyck pushed the briefcase containing the map farther under the table to conceal it from view.

The guy with the gun walked forward with an exaggerated roll of his right hip as his left leg limped behind him almost imperceptibly. Chase suspected he'd affected the roll to hide the physical defect of a slightly shorter leg. He swept his hand through his greasy looking hair and shook his head, slowly and theatrically.

"*Americanos*? In my town? Pablo, my eyes must be deceiving me, because it *looks* like you're in the middle of a business deal with the pretty lady." He rubbed his eyes and nodded. "Yes, that is what this looks like. But that can't be, because you know you have to run everything you do by me…don't you, Pablo? You know that."

His European accent seemed out of place. Siberia seemed like a long way to come to run a small town like Tabatinga. His little gang fanned out from behind him, and one of the women put her hands on Pablo's shoulders to keep him from going anywhere.

"Nicolai. It's just a conversation," Pablo said and pushed the dollars back toward Rayne. "The lady was eager. The lady misunderstood."

Nicolai continued past Chase and stopped beside Rayne. He offered his hand. "It's a pleasure to meet you, Miss…"

"Miss Congeniality," Rayne said, ignoring his hand and keeping her expression serious.

Ginn snorted and Chase covered her own amusement by wiping her hand over her mouth and chin. It was as casual as she could manage. Nicolai frowned, clearly not a Sandra Bullock fan. He dropped his hand to his side.

"Did you misunderstand my friend? Did you offer him payment for something he cannot deliver without my express permission?" Nicolai picked up Rayne's glass and emptied it onto the floor.

Chase glanced at the tank twins. Tonyck could take the one with her paws on Pablo. Ginn could disable Nicolai. The other two were on either side of Chase, both slightly in front of her. The woman on her right turned and eyeballed Chase. She flared her nostrils, and her nose ring glinted in the single beam of sunlight that penetrated the boarded windows.

Rayne brushed away a wisp of hair that had escaped the white bandana she'd wrapped around her forehead. Even in fatigues and this oppressive heat, she managed to look like a hot Calvin Klein model on a jungle-themed catwalk.

"I don't believe so. I think we understood each other just fine. The only one who seems to be confused here is you," Rayne said and gave Nicolai a sweet smile.

He smirked and moved Rayne's ponytail from over the bare shoulder and ran his finger along the strap of her tank top. "How so, pretty lady?"

Rayne placed her hand over his fingers and smiled again. "Because you seem to think you're in control here."

In one swift motion, Rayne twisted Nicolai's hand and pulled him downward with force. Chase watched, awestruck, as his head bounced off the table. Within a millisecond of Rayne's action, Tonyck was up and at the woman holding Pablo, and Ginn barreled toward the woman on Chase's left.

Energized, Chase twisted up, yanked her chair from the floor, and drove it across the chest of the woman with the nose ring. She fell backward onto her ass, but Chase didn't give her the time to recover. She kicked her across the jaw, sending her onto her back. Chase stepped forward but saw the woman's kick at her leg too late to avoid it. Air rushed past her, and she hit the dirt floor hard, the breath knocked out of her.

"Fucking *blanco*," nose ring woman said as she landed a punch.

Chase tensed and absorbed the blow, before she slammed her forearm across the woman's face. The accompanying crack gave Chase an unusual sense of satisfaction. The force of the strike sent her tumbling to Chase's side, and Chase was quick to follow up. She straddled her and pinned one arm beneath her knee. Chase held the other one down with her right hand and drove her left fist across the woman's jaw. Once, twice, a third time before she ceased her struggling beneath Chase's weight.

Chase slowly extricated herself and stood to see the others had been similarly neutralized. Rayne and the tank twins looked at her. The corner of Ginn's mouth turned up in a small grin. Rayne raised her eyebrow and gave Chase a smile accompanied with *that* look like she wanted to push Chase on the table and devour her. Tonyck's expression was harder to read, but Chase thought it'd decreased a few notches of contempt.

"So the new muscles aren't just for show then?" Rayne nodded toward the semi-conscious goon at Chase's feet.

Rayne's memory was obviously selective. Chase had taken up MMA training at around the same time they'd become colleagues the first time. Her failed attempt at being a Good Samaritan in that bar fight made Chase realize she had to get better at defending herself if she was going to continue trying to help people. And sometimes, attack was the best form of defense.

"I guess not," Chase said, putting a little swagger in her voice. It wouldn't hurt for the tank twins to see she could take care of herself and wouldn't be the "dead weight" Tonyck had anticipated. And despite her best intentions to the contrary, Rayne's approval was annoyingly important.

"Pablo." Rayne leaned across the table and pushed the undisturbed pile of dollars back toward him. "Perhaps we should conclude our business on the way to the riverbank?"

Pablo scooped up Rayne's money, nodded, and rose from his position at the table where he'd apparently remained unaffected by the ruckus around him.

"Absolutely. We'll pick up Effi on the way. She is expecting of us. Then I go back for your belongings." He pocketed the dollars, buttoned the flap, and patted it as if to make sure it hadn't disappeared. As he passed

Nicolai, he gave him a sound kick in the gut and smiled when Nicolai groaned. "Just because he is ex-military, the silly man thinks this is his town. I've endured much worse than him."

Out on the street, Pablo pulled his shirt open to reveal an ugly, poorly-healed wound that started at his collarbone and disappeared into the waistband of his jeans. At a few inches wide, Chase figured it could be a machete wound, but it looked like his skin had almost been peeled back from his ribcage.

"Gold prospectors," he said directly to Chase.

She'd studied it a little too long. "I'm sorry. I didn't mean to stare. Why did they do that to you?"

"Because I wouldn't be a good little slave for them."

He jumped into a battered old Jeep. The engine unwillingly sputtered into life and a cloud of diesel plumed into the air, scarring the bluebird sky. Rayne slid into the passenger seat. Chase got in and scooched across to the far door. Ginn followed, but for unknown reasons, Tonyck came around to the far door. She glared at Chase until she shrugged and scooted over to the middle. Tonyck climbed in and took up far more room than she actually needed, making Chase feel like fresh cement between two bricks. Tonyck positioned the steel briefcase in the well, and it banged against Chase's shin. She closed her eyes and counted to five, choosing to think about Pablo's past experience rather than her current position.

"Did you escape from them?" Chase leaned forward so only the edge of her ass was perched on the back seat.

"I did…because of Rayne. But my family was not so lucky."

She caught his glance in the rearview mirror and saw tears pool in his eyes before he quickly looked away. Tonyck shoved her knuckles sharply into Chase's kidney.

"Had to ask, didn't you? Asshat," Tonyck whispered.

Chase didn't respond. Tonyck was right; she shouldn't have pried. But she wanted to know how Rayne had helped him escape. She focused her attention on her surroundings, trying to get her bearings in relation to the airport, but Pablo twisted the car this way and that, left and right along increasingly narrow and muddy backstreets. The shacks and buildings began to meld into each other, impossible to tell apart. A particularly large pothole jolted their ride so hard, Chase bounced from her seat. On landing, her ribs ached where nose ring woman had landed a punch. Chase slowly dropped her hand from the front seat and pressed against the spot. It didn't hurt enough to be broken. It hurt just enough to let her know she was on a kick-ass adventure.

***

Tonyck and Pablo traveled to the airport and back twice for the group's supplies. Chase wondered if Tonyck would bring her gear at all, but she'd done her a small disservice. She found her backpack and river bag squished beneath a box of tools on the second trip. They packed everything into a boat that had seen better days. The paint had long abandoned its efforts to maintain its good looks, and the windshield was so deeply and comprehensively scratched from abrasive cleaning products and maybe even the odd bullet that seeing through it was near impossible. The outboard looked like it had been stolen from a museum for the oldest engines in the world. If this part of the Amazon wasn't brown, it would be once that rust-bucket started oscillating its oxidized propellers. Chase suspected the rust might be the only thing holding the boat together.

"Is this thing the best you can afford?" Chase didn't bother to conceal her incredulity. They needed something to last a couple of weeks at least.

Tonyck rolled her eyes. "What's the matter, *princess*? Not luxurious enough for you?"

Chase clenched her fists deep in the pockets of her cargo pants. "I was thinking of you, actually. I don't see any mirrors for you to fix your makeup."

Rayne stepped between her and Chase. "We don't want to draw any unwanted attention to ourselves."

"*Banditos!*" Pablo called from his position amidst the electrics.

"The bandits around here are ruthless, and they'll take whatever they can get their hands on." Rayne pulled a dirty tarp over their bags and packs. "You don't want to be stripped naked and tied up, do you, Chase?" She smiled and wiggled her eyebrows. "Or do you?"

Ginn laughed and clapped Chase on her back hard enough to make her stumble forward. She barely caught herself from falling headlong into the boat. Heat to rival the ambient temperature crawled up her neck and onto her face.

"Aww, you've made her blush. The quiet little archeologist likes it rough." Ginn kept laughing. "If all the paracord goes missing, we'll know where to look first."

Chase stepped into the boat and stuffed her bags beneath the tarp without response. She dropped onto one of the few canvas-covered flat cushions on the side of the boat and pulled out the laminated paper copy of the map, along with a topographic map of the area. Pablo rocked back on his knees and tapped on the second map with a nail-less finger and traced a huge circle around the region they were about to venture into. Chase wondered if his nail had been removed during torture by the gold prospectors.

"All of this used to be protected," he said before he turned back to whatever pressing maintenance he was doing beneath the steering wheel.

Effi, their guide, plopped down beside Chase and looked at the map over her shoulder.

"Over thirty thousand square miles of land inhabited by the uncontacted tribes. While the FUNAI is in flux, it's open season on everyone. Drug traffickers, loggers, gold prospectors. All types of ruffians are like kids given the keys to the candy shop. The *flecheiros* and the *flecheiros* have their work cut out trying to stop the invasion of *brancos*."

"*Caceteiros?* I've heard of flecheiros, arrow people, but not *caceteiros*." Chase shuffled away from Effi a little. The oppressive heat wrapped around like a woolen blanket, and the nearness of another body increased her discomfort.

"Head bashers," Effi said matter-of-factly. "People have no other language to describe them other than how they kill people."

"Delightful." Rayne tossed Chase and Effi a banana each. "Keeps the cramps away."

"Thanks, Rayne." Chase peeled the fruit and devoured it in three bites. It was the first fresh thing she'd eaten in nearly twenty-four hours. She contemplated Effi's observation and began to speculate how many other ways of murdering intruders the Amazon aborigines had. Was it possible that they were all offshoots of the same tribe, only distinguished by their methods of massacring marauders? She hoped that Effi had a sound grasp of languages other than English and Brazilian Portuguese. Chase studied Portuguese and had a workable understanding of Tupi-Guarani. Over forty languages sat under the Tupi-Guarani umbrella, so her knowledge gave Chase a better than average chance of making herself understood. Chase's and Effi's combined communication skills might be all that would stand between them and getting their heads caved-in.

"How do you know so much about the area, Effi?" Chase put Effi in her late thirties, and she spoke as if she'd attended college in the US such was her level of English.

"I was a *sertanista* in FUNAI for over a decade. I worked alongside Alejo Rocha and his son for two years. I learned more in that time than in all my previous years."

She looked wistful, and there was a sadness behind her eyes that Chase figured came from Rocha's brutal end. Effi couldn't have been there when it happened because everyone in the base at the time had been butchered.

"I was in a party of five who'd gone back to Tabatinga for vital supplies." Effi looked beyond Chase, beyond the forest, recollecting the memory. "We came back to a horror movie. Limbs separated from their bodies. Headless colleagues. Torsos hacked into pieces. But the worst had been saved for Alejo and his son. They were nailed to the wall, gutted with their insides outside." Effi shuddered and scratched at the back of her shaved head. "*That* image is seared onto my eyeballs. I see it every night when I try to sleep."

The boat's engine kicked in and disturbed the gentle silence that seemed to have fallen around them from the moment Effi began to recount the horrific attack. Chase wondered if Effi was in the right headspace for this expedition. Her mentor had been slaughtered just two months ago, and they'd be passing by the scene as they progressed along the Itaquaí. This trip would be difficult enough without losing their guide before they'd really begun. "Are you going to be okay?" Chase had to put it out there. The lives of everyone in the boat might depend on it.

"You want to know if I'm traumatized and whether I'll go crazy when we revisit the place where it all happened?" Effi nudged Chase's thigh with her knee but didn't wait for an answer. "You have nothing to worry about, my friend. Out here, I have seen it all. My colleagues have also been murdered by the very people we tried to protect, not just the *brancos* and others who seek to exploit our resources. What I have seen only makes me more determined to continue Alejo's work. There is much fear now and much lawlessness." Effi smiled and the fading sunlight shadowed her face, giving her an angelic outline. "We are already recovering, and outposts are once again being manned. FUNAI will rise from the ashes of its headquarters, and we will fight again. This land will once again be protected." She nudged Chase once more. "In the meantime, it's your job to keep our most vulnerable people safe."

Chase nodded as the solemnity of Effi's words settled on her conscience. No pressure then. Pablo gunned the boat upriver and the engine grunted against the current. Chase slid down in her seat, pulled her ball cap down low over her forehead, and closed her aching eyes that were so heavy they hurt from the lack of sleep over the past day and a half. Effi's words echoed as she slipped into welcome slumber...*It's your job to keep our people safe*. Chase had every intention of living up to Effi's expectations. And to Rayne's.

CHAPTER THIRTEEN

CHASE LOOKED CALM and peaceful sleeping. Rayne marveled at her ability to switch off whenever she needed to, irrespective of surroundings, noise, or situation. With the constant drone of the outboard and Pablo's incessant babbling, Rayne had no chance of resting her mind or body. It didn't matter how many meditation classes she took, Rayne needed complete silence and darkness to sleep. Ginn had taken the opportunity to rest too, and Tonyck took first watch at the boat's bow. She scanned the shores and white beaches in timed sections, her eyes never stopping unless something drew her attention. She rested her AK47 on her legs, but her right hand and trigger finger stayed in ready position. Her unwavering alertness, even after nearly forty hours without sleep, comforted Rayne. She felt safer than ever with the sisters by her side.

Her gaze wandered back to Chase. She made Rayne feel safe in a different way, safe in her soul. She wouldn't ever share that with Chase. No doubt she would think Rayne was playing her for a fool. But whenever Chase was around, it was as if she'd caught hold of Rayne's leg and was keeping her from floating away, from losing herself, losing sight of who she really was.

Chase impressed Rayne with how she'd handled herself at the bar. She'd summarily dispatched one of Nicolai's henchwomen and made it look relatively easy. Chase must have taken a punch or two, but she hadn't mentioned it and showed no signs of any pain. Rayne would have jumped at the chance of a closer inspection to ensure Chase was still healthy, had it arisen.

Effi caught her appraising Chase and grinned as if they'd shared a private joke. Rayne didn't look away. She wanted Effi to grasp that Chase was off limits to her. She'd already shown far too much interest in Chase for Rayne's liking, and Chase had looked far too interested in Effi's history. Rayne shouldn't be trying to figure out if Chase was interested in Effi, or vice versa. She had no legitimate claim to Chase's affections. In the cold light of their history, she was probably the last person in the boat Chase would be interested in. Who Chase might or might not want in her bed shouldn't even be on Rayne's mind. They were seeking the legendary Golden Trinity; every switchback in the river had perilous potential; the tribespeople they were trying to protect might try to kill them; and by now, Turner and Owen were undoubtedly picking up their trail. Any one of those things should be occupying her immediate thoughts, but instead, Rayne's concerns circuited her relationship with Chase.

She had no idea why and how Chase had burrowed into her head and wouldn't go away. Was Rayne so used to getting her own way that Chase's refusal to be a transitory lover had tripped something in her head that simply *had* to make it happen? Part of her wanted to believe that shallow and frivolous explanation which suited Rayne's lifestyle. It wasn't like Rayne's every waking thought and moment revolved around Chase. It was mostly a case of out of sight, out of mind, but when Rayne stepped out of living in the moment, when she gave herself time to process and contemplatively reflect on her life…those were the occasions when thoughts of Chase were prominent.

And maybe she'd been a ridiculous cliché when she'd betrayed Chase in favor of a different life with Lauren Young. Maybe she'd self-sabotaged any semblance of a future with Chase because she had felt herself falling into a one-way love affair. On those isolated periods when she analyzed their interactions, she knew that Chase simply didn't *see* her, not in the way Rayne wanted her to. Rayne's overly sexual way of being embarrassed Chase. Some days, Rayne would deduce that Chase was being obtuse, not seeing what was right in front of her and not reacting as she otherwise would. If only she realized. Other days, Rayne would accept that she just wasn't Chase's type, and perhaps their early interactions had sealed Rayne permanently and immovably into friendship territory. And after Rayne's betrayal, enemy status.

"Why don't you get some shut-eye, Rayne?"

Tonyck's question was almost lost over the clamorous cacophony of the outboard in its unceasing conflict against the current. Rayne ran her hand over her face and yawned involuntarily at the mention of sleep. The sun had ducked behind the forest and only a fading rose band, reluctant to rest, hovered above the forest line. The boat's mounted spotlight was the only other illumination, and the dense forest looked dark as the devil and just as foreboding. She joined Tonyck at her self-instigated sentry station. "I need silence to sleep. Ginn and Pablo are talking like they've got to put the whole world to rights before the next sunrise." Rayne had packed her Bose Sleepbuds, but they were no match for human and engine noise, and topping out all were the animal calls she was too tired to distinguish or name.

"I can shut her up, easy…if you actually wanted to sleep."

Tonyck narrowed her eyes the way she did when she knew there was more at play.

"We covered our tracks as well as we could, didn't we?" Rayne had been thinking about Turner and Owen since Chase had asked about them. It had set her wondering how big a team he'd assemble. She'd settled on fifteen. It wasn't an educated guess. She just didn't want to think there could be more.

"You know the answer to that. When someone who looks like you travels anywhere, people see you. They're not looking for you, but they can't help it. And you're hard to forget. So when someone else starts asking questions, they're easy to answer." Tonyck shrugged and traced her finger along the barrel of her rifle. "We bribed the people we could bribe. We bought loyalty where it was for sale. But we've passed through two major cities and a boomtown. We're all pale faces in South America, even with your impeccable tan, and we've been in a fistfight in what I'd only loosely describe as a bar. So far, this hasn't been a trip where we can—"

"You're not making me feel much better. Your pep talk kinda sucks." Rayne pushed her shoulder against Tonyck's, and they laughed. "Does it get better?"

"My pep talk or our future?"

"Either. Both." Rayne sighed and rested her elbows on her knees. "We're doing the right thing, aren't we?" The question had been circling her consciousness since they'd left Turner tied up in his penthouse suite and hightailed it from the hotel with the two thousand-year-old-plus map.

"You're not worried that you're doing the wrong thing," Tonyck whispered, seemingly aware that they were sharing a conversation Rayne wouldn't have with anyone else on the boat for various reasons. "You're worried that what you're doing might get everyone here killed."

Rayne tutted and shook her head, but it convinced neither Tonyck nor herself. "I thought soldiers were supposed to be dumb-ass robots who just follow orders and don't think for themselves?"

"The clue's in the name: *Special* Forces." Tonyck put her hand beneath Rayne's chin and lifted it. "Everybody here believes in what you're trying to do here, Rayne. You know?"

Rayne offered a tight-lipped smile but didn't affirm Tonyck's statement. Tonyck lifted Rayne's chin farther so that Rayne had to look at her. "More than that," Tonyck said, "everyone here believes in *you*."

Rayne closed her eyes against the soft burn of threatening tears. Tonyck's words meant more to Rayne than she would ever know. She'd wanted her parents to believe in her for so long, and they never did. In her twenties, she'd wanted *anyone* to believe in her, but that never happened either. In this decade of her life, she thought she'd managed to outgrow the naïve notion. Yet, here it was again. Rayne wasn't sure she deserved their faith. She was trying to do several things with this expedition, and some of them were mutually exclusive. Her initial and primary goal was to prove the Golden Trinity existed by locating and discovering it. Oh, how she wished it had remained that simple. Why couldn't Turner have been a nice, genuine philanthropist instead of a psychotic would-be murderer? Without that twist, she wouldn't have been forced to recruit Chase. But that consequence held its own advantages. *And* a serious disadvantage. Chase wanted any find to be properly catalogued and gifted to the Brazilian government. A government that had recently reduced its funding to FUNAI and offered ten million square feet of Amazon to loggers and gold prospectors. What was the alternative? The uncontacted tribes didn't need millions of dollars worth of gold…unless they could use it to buy their homeland once and for all.

And there was the little matter of the glory. This would be the find of the millennium, not just the century. A treasure unequalled in value. A historical find that would seal Rayne's reputation and legacy. If the legends were true, Rayne would be able to name her price for every future job.

Where *did* Chase fit in? Her expertise was going to be vital to interpret the map. She hadn't wanted to admit that its vast array of symbols and colors had her second-guessing her interpretations. Even before Turner announced himself to be a ruthless genocidal maniac, Rayne had been racking her brains to figure out whose expertise she could call on, because she was damn sure Chase wouldn't have helped. Rayne had lured her here with the lore of the Golden Trinity and the added altruistic goal of saving the lives of hundreds of uncontacted tribespeople. But Rayne hadn't been completely honest. The thought of all that treasure going to a museum was unimaginable, and she had no intention of letting that happen.

Tonyck nudged her gently and she opened her eyes. The rebellious band of light had succumbed to the darkness, and now the sky was alight with stars. She tugged her lightweight jacket closed and zipped it up.

"You okay?"

Rayne nodded. "Sure. I'm just not used to this hero role."

Tonyck chuckled. "More like antihero. I'm not sure your motivations are pure enough to qualify for hero status." She motioned to Chase, still sleeping and still looking incredibly cute. "I think that little shit is the hero of this story."

"Maybe you're right." Rayne *did* like the idea of Chase being the hero, and she knew that's what Chase wanted to be, was even born to be. All those action movies she watched, the new, stronger physique she'd been building, her ever-present sense of morality, of what was right and wrong. Chase didn't quite know it yet, didn't quite believe in herself enough, but she was hero material to her core. "But where does that leave you and Ginn?" Rayne was enjoying thinking of their adventure as a story, something to tell her kids at night, not that she'd ever any. It made it seem less real, less frightening. She could go back to facing the stark and dangerous reality of what they were doing when the sun bid them good morning.

"I guess we're sidekicks—your sidekicks," Tonyck added quickly. "I'm not taking orders from mini Gertrude Bell over there."

Rayne laughed quietly. Chase would love being compared to the famous writer and archeologist, though her opposition to women's suffrage was an ugly blot that didn't apply to Chase. "Like Hawkeye to Black Widow?"

"More like...whoever it was who stands at Loki's side when he was fucking with Thor." Tonyck chuckled. "You'd make a great goddess of mischief."

"Would that mean Chase is Thor?" Rayne grinned and pulled her hood over her head to give more protection from the hungry insects she could see dancing in the boat's spotlight. "I think she'd look weird with long, flowing hair. But she'd smash his Ragnarok style." Rayne's mind drifted to placing Chase in Thor's outfit, all metal breastplate and muscular biceps. Happy place.

"Wake her up, and we'll give you a live action version of the 'Contest of Champions.' I'll be the Hulk." Tonyck flashed a wicked grin and drove her fist into her other palm.

"You're so bad." Rayne shook her head. "What have you got against her? You've been giving her shit since the day you met." Did Tonyck harbor a modicum of professional jealousy? Chase had a successful career, and she was celebrated for her work keeping relics in their home nations. Tonyck had been studying for a degree in history before she joined the military. Perhaps Chase served as a reminder of a life Tonyck missed out on, reminded her of regrets she couldn't release.

"What have I got against her?" Tonyck whispered and leaned slightly closer to Rayne. "How about how easily she can hurt you? You told me all about how close you two were, and now look at how she treats you. I can't handle that." She eased back slightly, picked up her flashlight, and shone it into the never-ending darkness of the forest.

Rayne had no response, at least none she would voice. Tonyck had made her point and fallen silent by retreating back into her defensive duties. Rayne had offered no immediate riposte refuting Tonyck's logic because she didn't want to be accused of protesting too much. But the longer she didn't say anything at all, the more Tonyck would continue to believe it to be true.

"That's not the case. I'm not easily hurt." Rayne shifted and rocked on alternate ass cheeks. The cushions on the boat barely qualified to carry the name, and her butt had slowly been going numb for the past fifteen minutes. Tonyck gave her a sideways glance, but the dim light made it impossible for Rayne to get a read on her expression.

"No?"

"No," Rayne said, with more belief and force the second time.

"Because *nobody* can hurt you?"

Tonyck's mocking tone dripped like salt on an open wound. Hadn't Rayne worked hard to make that true? "Exactly. Anyway, Chase is too gentle a soul. She doesn't want to hurt anybody." She tried not to be too defensive of Chase but feared she failed.

"Tell that to the woman she beat unconscious this afternoon."

"That was different. She had no choice. Chase would never choose to hurt me." The conversation was becoming muddied, and Rayne wanted it to end.

"Sometimes when two people are so intrinsically different, they don't have to make a choice to hurt each other. It just happens."

Rayne shook her head. "What do you know about it? What do you know about Chase?"

"Hey." Tonyck placed her free hand on Rayne's shoulder. "I'm sorry. Sometimes my pop psychology takes me down roads I shouldn't go. Ignore me."

"Just give her a break." Rayne bristled even as Tonyck acknowledged her demand. If she were a cat, her fur would look like she'd just stuck her paw in a socket. She appreciated Tonyck backing down, but she wasn't stupid and she wasn't taking back anything she'd said. She'd planted the seeds and she'd watch them grow while Rayne struggled with the inner turmoil, while she tried to figure out why she was so quick to jump to a defensive stance on anything Chase-related.

Rayne stretched out her legs and leaned back. Her body took up six cushions, but she may as well have been lying on a bed of piranha teeth for all the comfort it gave. "I'm going to try and get some sleep." She pulled the drawstring on her hood tighter. "Pablo said it'd be another couple of hours before he moored the boat for us to make camp. Are you swapping out with Ginn?"

"No. I'm good."

Tonyck's response was neutral and gave no hint of emotion as to how she felt about Rayne's outburst. That's what it was. An outburst, and it was so unlike her. In the available time frame, Rayne had thought she'd considered everything for this expedition. Logistics. Supplies. Guides. But she'd never truly stopped to think about how she might feel working with Chase again. She'd given it such little thought because they were going to be in the jungle, searching for treasure, trying to stay alive, and attempting to protect the Amazon's Indians. Surely something as trivial as their close-quarters relationship shouldn't have to figure into her calculations at all...

She pressed her head farther into the cushion as if that might somehow stop her from thinking so hard. The vibration of the engine through both water and wood penetrated the meager fabric of the makeshift pillows. Sleep would be an evasive mistress tonight. She focused on picturing the map instead. She thought about shifting that final stone in the wall that would lead to the Golden Trinity. Legend boasted that El Dorado, the City of Gold, was a pauper's palace compared to the Golden Trinity. They were thoughts she could get on board with. Gold was forever. Being around Chase was not.

CHAPTER FOURTEEN

CHASE DREW THE heel of her palms across her eyes and blinked hard to focus in the blackness. The boat slowed to a standstill and bobbed gently in the water.

"Let's go." Effi jumped up, grabbed two big expedition bags like they were packed with feathers, and hopped into the shallow row boat they'd towed with them.

Chase slung her pack over her shoulders and strapped her river bag across her body. She let Rayne get into the skiff first and was about to follow when a heavy hand slapped across her chest.

"Age before stupid," Tonyck said and joined Rayne.

Ginn laughed. "You'll get used to her."

Chase tightened the straps on her backpack and stretched her back muscles, allowing Tonyck to pass rather than let herself be woman-handled by the elder tank twin. "Or she's like grits. You either love or hate her." She motioned to Pablo. "After you."

Pablo patted her on the shoulder as he passed. "Thank you, my friend."

His courteousness tempered Tonyck's boorishness, and she let herself relax. "How long are the watch periods?" Chase asked Ginn, knowing they couldn't leave the motorboat unattended without coming back to find it stripped bare or gone completely.

"That's not for you to worry about. Me and Smiley over there will be taking watch."

Chase tried not to take Ginn's response as dismissively as it sounded. "I'm happy to do my share, Ginn."

"I'm sure you are. But have you ever had to shoot at a live target with one of these puppies?"

Tonyck lifted the AK47 previously nestled alongside her leg and waved it in the air a little too carelessly for Chase's liking. Chase rested her hand on the hilt of the shiny new machete she'd bought at a Tabatinga market stall. It wouldn't be much defense against a barrage of bullets from any *banditos* prowling the river at night, but she'd grown up in Texas; she was holding a gun before she could write with a pen. "I've shot plenty of guns."

"But have you ever had to shoot in anger?" Ginn waved Chase off the boat. "You're needed for things others than keeping us safe." She pointed to the backpack Tonyck had at her feet in the rowboat. "You read that. I shoot this. Deal?"

Chase smiled, wondering how the twins could be so vastly different in personality when they'd obviously forged the same path in life. "Deal."

She stepped into the skiff and didn't bother to set her gear down. The sandy riverbank was only about fifty yards away. Effi made quick work of getting them to shore. Pablo jumped into the river when it got too shallow for Effi to paddle.

"Move quick or your toes will make a light snack for the piranhas." Pablo smirked but held the boat steady while everyone splashed into the cool water and quietly jogged to the sands. Clearly, Chase wasn't the only one who was uncertain as to whether or not Pablo had been teasing about the nocturnal habits of the carnivorous fish.

Chase and Pablo pulled the boat out of the water and into the tree line. He swiftly secured it to a tree trunk with a thin steel cable and lock.

"It's not much, but it should slow down any would-be thieves," he said by way of explanation.

Tonyck shone her flashlight into the impossibly dark wall of trees. "We'll fashion a clearing a few feet into the forest. That way we can keep a clear line of sight to the main boat."

"Not your first foray into the jungle?" Effi asked.

She looked impressed, and although Chase didn't want it to, it irked her that Effi was happy to pander to Tonyck's epic ego.

Tonyck shook her head. "I've been around."

Chase caught the wink Tonyck sent Effi's way and wished she hadn't. She wasn't in the jungle to observe the courting habits of a wild gorilla.

"I look forward to hearing all about it," Effi said.

"Okay. Bivvy building time then?" Chase's level of discomfort increased incrementally with every exchange. She unclipped her own flashlight from her front backpack strap and focused it into the foreboding forest. It looked only a smidge more inviting than a pool party with Pablo's piranhas , but it had to be better than watching Tonyck flirt with

Effi. Chase withdrew her machete from its sheath and made her way into the trees. She moved branches and vines with the blunt edge of the blade rather than chopping needlessly. There was little use trying to save the Indians if they destroyed their home needlessly to do it.

Chase smelled Pablo before she saw him beside her in the gentle green glow of the snap light he'd hung around his neck. She'd be certain to stay upwind of his camp bed tonight.

"I told you my story," Pablo said as he pushed through the vegetation doing its best to stop his progress. "What is yours?"

After Pablo's watery eyes in the car, Chase hadn't asked any more questions. She didn't know Pablo's story. He'd only revealed only a tiny piece of it, and that was like looking at one old Polaroid in a shoebox chock full of them. "There's not much to tell, Pablo." A ground vine caught Chase's shoes and she stumbled forward, catching her balance to stop from falling headlong into the bush. "Shit."

"Everybody has a story, Ms. Stinsen. Tell me how you and Ms. Rayne met. I am interested to know how people connect and stay connected."

Pablo's phrasing struck home. She and Rayne had connected, and it seemed no matter what either of them did, their connectedness simply wouldn't sever.

"Ooh," Effi said, close enough for her breath to brush Chase's neck. "I would like to hear this story also."

Chase's flashlight revealed a small clearing, just about perfect for their small camp with enough thin trees to erect their cover. "Ask me again when we're all set up."

Pablo and Effi grunted and huffed past her. Their shadows elongated in the false light and began to look like the tall trees they were closed in by on all sides.

"Chicken," Rayne whispered in Chase's ear.

Chase hadn't clocked her approach, despite how wet and squelchy the ground was underfoot.

"Jesus. Creep up on a woman, why don't you?"

"They won't forget, Chase. You'll have to give them something."

Rayne rested her hand momentarily at the base of Chase's back, making her shirt stick to her skin. "You're the one who likes to talk." Chase stepped away from Rayne's searing touch. "*You* spin a tale for the eager audience. They probably want to hear it from you anyway." Chase was aware how petulant she sounded but was too tired to care. A few hours of shut-eye on the boat had done little to satisfy the chunky little sleep demon that tugged at her eyelids and sat on her shoulders, making each step three times heavier than it should be.

"This expedition is going to feel a lot harder if you're always snapping every time we speak."

Rayne's voice softened, and that serious tone slipped back in again. Rayne was right, of course. Chase had agreed to work with her and her team. No one had forced her hand. She should quit being such a little...

"Let's set up camp together and take some time to talk." Rayne put her hand on Chase's shoulder and squeezed. "We're working too close to be assholes with each other all the time."

Rayne moved past Chase without waiting for a response, though it was implicit in her silence. Tonyck came up on her left in the path Pablo had forged but still managed to barge Chase's shoulder.

"Leopards don't change their spots."

"What the hell are you talking about?" Chase asked as Tonyck's considerable bulk began to block the light from the rest of the party in the center of the clearing.

"Once an asshole, always an asshole," Tonyck called back.

"You'd know because you've tried so many times and given up, huh?"

Tonyck halted, and Chase almost walked into her back. She turned around and Chase looked up at her, swallowing down the flight response and refusing to be intimidated.

"The lady boss wants you here because she thinks she needs you." Tonyck lowered her voice and prodded Chase in the chest. "Let her down, and you'll have me to answer to." She shoved Chase and continued into the open space.

Chase steadied herself, suppressed the desire to throw a rock at Tonyck's head, and rubbed her chest where it felt like Tonyck had dented her sternum. She rolled her shoulders and shuddered a little at the ensuing crunching of bones, before she joined Pablo at a tree he was in the process of butchering. She dumped her bags on the ground and waited to catch it.

He inclined his head toward Tonyck. "She is *durão*. You say, a tough guy. They push and push. They don't stop pushing until you fall down or you push back." He swung his axe clean through a branch four inches in diameter. "Which will you do?"

Chase caught the branch as it fell and tossed it onto the ground. Effi picked it up and carried it over to the edge of the clearing. "I'm not interested in fighting her. She's just an employee. Rayne won't allow her to do anything off-plan."

Pablo sighted his axe on another branch. "Nobody is ever *just* anything. And Rayne will not always be around to protect you… In this place, it is easy to get lost."

Chase took the next branch and repeated the procedure. Pablo's words were loaded with omens, and she didn't appreciate the inference that she needed Rayne to protect her. *She* should be the one protecting Rayne, not the other way around. Fuck it. She wanted to sleep. Not analyze or interpret. Not think or forecast. Just sleep. That wasn't happening until she'd made her jungle tent. Pablo felled another branch in silence, and Chase took it to a spot she claimed as hers.

She retrieved some paracord from her backpack, pulled her buck knife from her belt, and rested the end of a branch against the tree she'd chosen. She tied the branch loosely to the tree at around six feet, lifted it, and walked to the second tree, edging along the branch. Chase cut another length of paracord and tightly tied the branch to the tree. She retraced her steps and pulled on the slipknot to tighten the binding around the tree. It looked pretty straight. It probably wasn't strong enough for her to practice high beam walking across it, but it only had to hold a light piece of tarp so it'd be fine.

Chase returned to the edge of the clearing and hacked a good dozen or so palm leaves for a base layer beneath the tarp to set her gear on. She arranged them far less carefully than she usually would and comforted herself with the knowledge it was only for one night. She pulled out her tarp from the back zip compartment of her backpack, unfolded it, and tossed it over the branch acting as the roof strut. A few more lengths of paracord, some pegs knocked into the ground, and her tent was complete. She unpacked her hammock and tied it beneath the tarp before pulling out what Ginn had called a "wafer half bag." When she'd tossed it to Chase to pack, she'd been amazed. It weighed less than a decent-sized bar of chocolate at around six ounces.

Chase knelt down and pushed her backpack and river bag inside. Someone approached and stood beside her. She recognized Rayne's fading perfume and didn't need to look up to identify her jungle houseguest.

"Room for two?" Rayne dropped her own gear and sleeping bag onto Chase's palm leaf floor.

Chase jumped up and knocked her head against the roof branch. "Oww." She reached to press her hand on her throbbing skull, but Rayne beat her to it. Rayne shone her flashlight on the back of Chase's head as her fingers gently pushed Chase's hair this way and that, searching for blood. Chase didn't move. The feeling of Rayne's fingers in her hair was soothing, the kind of touch she'd love to fall asleep to. She jerked herself back into reality. "Any damage?" Chase remained in place, still reeling from Rayne's casual bag drop. She didn't know whether she might collapse either. And that wouldn't be cool.

"Nothing visual." Rayne used her other hand to cup Chase's chin. "How do you feel?"

Flustered. On fire. "A little lightheaded." Chase leaned against the closest tree, away from Rayne's caress and closed her eyes. She was too weary and Rayne was too close. She felt Rayne's hands rest on her waist.

"Kick off your boots. Let's get you horizontal before you collapse."

It wasn't the smoothest line Rayne had used trying to get Chase into bed, but Chase could barely speak, let alone quip. She allowed Rayne to guide her down to the palm leaves. She unlaced her boots and pulled them off. Chase watched as Rayne fashioned a loop over the central branch and clipped Chase's boots onto it with a carabiner from her belt. She lifted the tarp and slid them underneath it so they didn't act as rain catchers. Chase pulled off her damp socks and stuffed them in the mesh front of her backpack. She shuffled under the tarp to take off her pants but stopped when Rayne snuck in beside her.

"You were serious?" Chase had packed the gear Ginn had given her at the airport. She'd assumed everyone had the same. "Don't you have your own tarp?"

"No."

Even in the dim illumination provided by the scattered glow sticks and flashlights, Chase could still see Rayne's eyes sparkle mischievously. "At least look away." Chase motioned to her belt. "Give me some privacy."

Rayne smiled widely. "You're shy even with your hot new body?"

"It's not new. It's just…better." Chase looked away and grinned, her ego suitably buoyed by Rayne's continued attention to her improved physique. Impressing women had been one of the motivating factors in working so hard.

Rayne nudged her shoulder. "I can hear you smiling."

"You still have to look away," Chase said and turned back to Rayne.

"Let me show you how it's done in the jungle." Rayne leaned back onto her shoulders, thrust her hips in the air, and swiftly maneuvered herself out of her pants. Rayne's slender thighs packed enough muscle to show they were strong, but were still shapely in that incredibly feminine way that made Chase melt, suck in her breath, and want to reach out and trace every inch of skin from her hips to her toes—all at once.

"You're staring."

Chase swallowed and gathered her courage. "You told me to watch."

"I didn't say you should adopt that predatory look in your eyes."

Rayne was clearly amused. Chase figured she must be used to this and every other sort of attention from almost everyone. She admired Rayne's ability to use it to her advantage, but she didn't want to be manipulated by her natural desire. Rayne was stunning. Chase truly couldn't stop her physical response, but she *did* have control of her own head. "You're a beautiful woman, Rayne. I'm queer and you'd be exactly my type…in another life. Without our history."

Rayne looked away toward the rest of the camp, and Chase took the brief opportunity to yank off her trousers. She rolled them up and stuffed them into her river bag before pulling out her mosquito net and fixing it to the loops of her hammock.

"Will our history always be a wedge between us?" Rayne busied herself fixing her hammock and net adjacent to Chase's. "It's not all bad…"

Rayne's half-question, half-statement hung in the air between them. Chase got into her hammock and slipped her legs and ass into the wafer bag. She zipped the mosquito net closed.

"What you did, Rayne, was a massive betrayal. If someone ever did the same thing to you, are you saying you'd forgive them and move on? So easily?" Chase tentatively shifted farther along the bed to get comfortable. "You're right. Not all of our history is bad. A big chunk of it…" *were the best times of my life.* "A lot of it was really good fun." Chase's pulse quickened, and she took a few deep breaths to regain control. Being in such close proximity to Rayne had always had this effect on her. She'd need to figure out a way to handle it on this expedition. For now, she simply said no more and turned off her flashlight hoping to signal an end to the difficult conversation.

She felt Rayne swing up against her as she crawled into her own hammock and secured the insect protector around her. Her flashlight dimmed.

"Chase…"

"Yeah…" It was too soon to feign sleep.

"I've never said sorry for Florida. I've never apologized for how much I hurt you, professionally and personally…"

Chase felt light pressure from Rayne's hammock shifting against her before her fingers rested on Chase's arm through the nets. Chase was glad for the enveloping blackness around them. She didn't want Rayne to see the tears in her eyes.

"I'm sorry, Chase. I truly am."

Rayne's touch was gone and the warm breeze hit Chase's skin where it had been, reminding her how brief Rayne's sincerity could be. Chase willed herself not to move, not to respond, not to speak. She'd waited eight years for those words. She'd longed for a heartfelt apology, and she was desperate to believe Rayne meant it. It would take more than one apology to rebuild the trust Rayne had smashed with a wrecking ball.

But it was a suitable start…

CHAPTER FIFTEEN

CHASE WOKE TO the smell of open fire cooking, and her stomach growled its approval. She knew they'd have to hunt and kills animals she'd barely heard of, let alone tasted. She felt the solid presence of Rayne beside her and didn't try to resist the urge to see her sleeping. Chase loved waking before the women who'd shared her bed to watch them sleep. Only for a little while, not for a creepy, intense, and lengthy period. Although some might argue that anything lasting longer than a quick glance was creepy. But Chase had always found something so peaceful and comforting about sleep. The silence was meditation before the world assaulted her brain.

Falling asleep beside someone was usually an ultimate declaration of trust. It was trusting them not to kill, rob, or otherwise abuse her. Usually. Except when she was all but forced into a situation which necessitated sleep among people she barely knew, never mind trusted. That word again. Rayne, again. Part of Chase wanted to trust her. The part that had agreed to accompany her on this insane expedition that would probably turn out to be the greatest adventure of her life. And perhaps it was that holding back Chase's willingness to let Rayne in again. If this ended up being the ultimate adventure, would everything else be bland and beige without Rayne beside her?

"Do you have a fetish for watching women sleep?" Rayne opened her eyes and caught Chase enjoying her.

"I like the silence," Chase said. Excuses seemed unnecessary. She'd spoken to Rayne about it when they were friends. She knew all about Chase's atypical way of being. "The world is generally too busy talking. Life is so loud. I like the moments before people feel obligated to fill them with noise."

Rayne smiled, and the softness behind her eyes spoke of understanding. She'd never judged Chase even when Chase had judged herself in all her weirdness.

"Lots of people aren't comfortable with silence." Rayne turned sideways in her hammock to face Chase. "It gives them too much time to think about everything they regret in their lives."

Chase raised her eyebrows. "I'd never thought about it that way. What about you? Where do you fall on the spectrum between absolute silence and constant noise?"

Rayne ran her hand over her hair, still in a ponytail. Chase imagined long hair wasn't conducive to lolling around in a string hammock. She liked how low maintenance her short hair was...but she did love the feel of long hair trailing a path along her naked body.

"That's the spectrum, is it? They're the two extremes as defined by the Chase Stinsen school of logic?" Rayne asked, and a smile played at the corner of her lips.

"Yeah." Chase could tell Rayne was teasing her and didn't mind. "They're the parameters. Answer the question."

Rayne frowned and stuck out her bottom lip. "You've gotten bossy. Is it the steroids?"

"I've always been this way. It's not 'bossy,' it's straight talk." Chase gestured toward Tonyck, busy burning breakfast. "Have your tank twins spoiled you with their sycophantic nonsense and you've forgotten how to have a simple conversation?"

"'Tank twins'? Nice. I think they'd like that." Rayne poked at Chase through her mosquito net. "Well...Ginn would probably like it. Tonyck might just beat you up for it."

"What *is* her problem with me?"

Rayne waved her hand in the air. "I don't know. She's a military woman with a certain way of doing things. You're an academic with a different way of doing things. Sometimes people just clash. Is she still giving you a hard time?"

Rayne looked away, but before she did, Chase saw something in her expression that didn't match her words. Rayne knew precisely why Tonyck didn't like Chase; she simply wasn't saying.

The rumbling in her stomach and need for sustenance trumped her desire to understand Tonyck's motivation for hating her *and* Rayne's reason for lying about it. She unzipped her net, swung her legs out, and jumped onto the ground after a quick check for anything slithering or crawling across the leaves. The butt or the breasts? Chase had to bend over to get her pants from her bag; which view would be best to offer Rayne?

"The ass," Rayne said.

Had mind reading become another of Rayne's extensive skills? "What?"

"Your hesitation. You're wondering how to retrieve your pants without giving me a hot flush. I'm saying I don't mind overheating so I'd prefer that you stick your butt in the air...if I'm allowed to have a preference."

"You're not." Chase turned sideways and gave her neither. In her hurry to pull on her pants under Rayne's sexually loaded stare, Chase got her toe caught on the inside lining and toppled to the ground. "Don't you laugh."

Rayne ignore the warning and giggled.

"You've got such a cute laugh," Effi said, approaching their area with two sticks crammed with skewered cubes of cooked meat.

Chase rubbed her hand across her mouth. She would've liked to have said something similar, but she hadn't. She missed out on the breathtaking smile Rayne gave Effi for the compliment. Why was she jealous? Chase didn't want those smiles for herself...did she?

Chase finished dressing and accepted the appetizing offering gratefully. She went to take both, but Effi pulled the second one back and waited for Rayne to escape her bed. She gave Chase a quick grin as if they were playing a game. Chase didn't want any part of it and ignored her. Rayne didn't bother to put her pants back on, and Effi didn't bother to hide her appreciation. Chase was sure Rayne noticed but didn't dignify it with any recognition, making it Chase's turn to grin.

"This is really good," Rayne said after taking a bite. "What is it?"

Chase held up her hand to stop Effi from speaking. "Are you sure you want to know?"

Rayne smiled and put her hand on Chase's shoulder. "Always the protector." She touched Chase's cheek gently before turning to face Effi. "Tell me. I'm not as fragile as this one seems to think I am."

"Monkey," Effi said, seeming to take a certain amount of pleasure in the revelation.

Chase inclined her head and Rayne shrugged, outwardly unaffected by the thought of munching on monkey meat. "Needs must," Chase said, but she was thinking about whether she really saw Rayne as fragile, or whether she simply *wanted* to see her as fragile to pander to Chase's caretaker sensibilities.

"Let me know if you would like more. It's another full day's journey on the boat before we reach the old FUNAI HQ. It will be a while before we eat something fresh again."

Effi smiled at both of them before she walked away, leaving Chase to wonder about Effi's flirtatious nature. Ginn and Chase were the only women in the group she hadn't shown an interest in. It wouldn't have fazed Chase if it had just been Rayne on the receiving end of Effi's attentions. That was always to be expected. But to be overlooked in favor of the mean tank twin, that was tough to take. Not that Chase would be interested in Effi, but who didn't find it flattering to be desired?

"Where are you at?" Rayne waved her had in front of Chase's face.

"Sorry. I was just wondering what type of women Effi was interested in." Chase leaned back against the tree, pulled off a chunk of meat, and popped it into her mouth. She tried not to think of a cute little monkey swinging through the trees before its life was ended for their breakfast. They were going to be eating all sorts of meat and fish she'd usually avoid, although she'd never seen monkey meat on the menu of any of her local restaurants.

Rayne stepped closer to Chase and stood between her open legs. "Are you jealous?"

Rayne reached out and traced her fingers along Chase's collarbone. Chase's skin tingled at her touch, but she subdued any overt physical reaction. Had Rayne placed her other hand down Chase's shorts, she wouldn't have been able to hide *that* response.

"Of Tonyck? Nope, she's not my type." Chase looked across at Tonyck, needing an ardor dampener. Rayne had a hypnotic Medusa effect, but Chase was melting instead of turning to stone.

Rayne put her hand on Chase's cheek and gently brought her around to face her. "Not of Tonyck or Ginn...of me. Am I your type?"

Chase pulled the inside of her lip between her teeth and bit down. If she could feel a little pain, maybe it'd distract her from her raging reaction to Rayne. She couldn't move Rayne's hand. If she tried, she worried that their fingers might entwine by some magical spell, never to be separated again. If she succumbed just once, she was sure her body would override her mind and demand Rayne again and again. "Please...don't."

Rayne's eyes flickered, something registered though Chase couldn't know what. She smiled, the one Chase had seen many times when they were friends; the smile she'd never seen her give to anyone else. Rayne took her hand away but stayed close.

"Effi is one of those people who flirts with anyone and everyone to make themselves feel good, because in here," Rayne pressed the palm of her hand on Chase's heart, "she doesn't mean it. Stick around, she'll get to you."

Chase was glad of the chest muscle she'd built and trusted it would be protection enough for Rayne not to feel her heart thudding against her ribs. "You know her that well?" Chase had the feeling Rayne might also be referring to herself.

"No. I just know her type." Rayne stepped to the side and leaned against Chase's tree.

Chase was simultaneously relieved and wounded by Rayne's movement. "We're in the middle of the Amazon with someone you don't know? Kind of feels a little reckless."

"I know and trust Pablo. I've known him since I helped him escape the gold prospectors. He knows Effi. That's good enough for me." Rayne pushed off the tree and began to walk away. "Monkey tastes pretty good. I'm going back for more before it's all gone," she said into the still, humid air.

Chase didn't respond. Words wouldn't come because Rayne's casual mention of her involvement in saving Pablo's life had just blown her mind. Before she'd fallen asleep last night, Chase had mentally created a blackboard in her mind. One side, pros. One side, cons. Rayne's name scribbled in chalk at the top. She'd populated the cons column first, and it hadn't been hard. She'd chalked in the pros, and they were more numerous than Chase had expected before she'd begun the list. But the cons still outnumbered the pros, and that's how Chase needed it to remain to maintain the status quo she'd accepted. Rayne was a selfish, shallow woman who wouldn't know the right thing if it walked up and announced itself. After they'd parted ways, framing Rayne that way made it easier for Chase to keep her at a distance. And nothing Rayne had done, to Chase's knowledge, in the past four years had indicated any anomaly with that picture…

Until she showed up on her doorstep with tales of the Golden Trinity and saving Amazonian Indians.

Until Chase learned that Rayne had somehow rescued Pablo from certain death with no obvious benefit to herself.

What else had Rayne been up to, unbeknownst to Chase, that would add more items to the pros list? And if that column became longer than the cons, if Rayne's mind and soul, if her heart matched her outward beauty… how was Chase supposed to maintain professional boundaries with the most physically desirable woman she'd ever met? More pressing than how she'd do that, was *why* she'd do that.

CHAPTER SIXTEEN

RAYNE SAT BESIDE Pablo at the boat's helm and took a deep breath of the Amazon air. She spent so much time in smoggy, filthy cities, that the taste of clean air often eluded her memory. Moments like this reminded her of one of the few good memories of a childhood vacation in Zion. The muddied, brown, and murky water of the Itaquaì River was a fitting simile to the rest of her childhood recollections. But this reminded her of a good day; a clear, bright, bluebird sky, no man-made machinery to be heard, and an accompanying three beat call of condors. The feeling of reaching the trail end of Angel's Landing at twelve years of age and looking out across the park had never left Rayne. She'd sat at the very edge and dangled her toes at 6000 feet on 270,000,000 years of rock layers. She'd felt invincible and untouchable…and alone. Years had passed, friends and lovers had come and gone, shared their paths for transient periods before parting ways. Those same three emotions remained. Rayne had conditioned herself to the evanescent nature of relationships, platonic or otherwise. No one to rely on her equaled no unrealistic expectations and no one to disappoint.

The only person she didn't feel so alone in the presence of was Chase. But inevitably, Rayne had disappointed her too. She thought back to breakfast and practically pinning Chase to a tree. *Please…don't.* The same words, sentences, phrases could be heard so many different ways by different people. To many, Chase's words would have sounded like a plea for Rayne to simply leave her alone. Rayne hadn't interpreted it that way. *She'd* seen the look in Chase's eyes that accompanied those words. She'd seen the conflict between what Chase had said and what she had meant. That wasn't born from any arrogance on Rayne's part, taking no for yes wasn't one of her faults. It came from knowing Chase because Chase had let her in and allowed her familiarity. And Rayne's understanding had been supplemented further when she felt Chase's reaction to her unplanned disclosure regarding Pablo. Confusion abounded, and Chase had said nothing. Rayne had walked away, as she often chose to do, but this time it was to give Chase the space and opportunity to process what had transpired. She'd come to learn that Chase didn't tend toward spontaneous judgment, decisions, or actions unless pushed. Rayne didn't want to push. If Chase was ever going to come to her, she wanted it to be after quiet deliberation. She glanced back at Chase who was leaning back on the boat, propped up by her arms, triceps bulging from the edges of her rolled-up shirt. Who was Rayne trying to fool? She'd gladly take her in the heat of the moment too.

"We should be at the FUNAI HQ before nightfall, Ms. Rayne. I've been told that some of the outer huts survived the fire," said Pablo. "I am expecting we'll be able to sleep indoors tonight," Pablo said, "which is good because there might be big rain."

"Excellent." They were lucky this expedition had fallen toward the end of the rainy season. Rayne didn't mind trekking in the rain, but the problem lay in never being able to get anything properly dry in the humid heat and making a fire was damn near impossible. Rayne didn't fancy getting trench foot even for the biggest treasure haul in history. "You're sure no one else has already taken up residence there?"

Pablo shook his head and steered the boat to the mid-channel of the river where the likelihood of being attacked was vastly reduced. "I do not think so. Anything of value was stripped not long after the tragic attack, mostly by *banditos* or lone wanderers looking to make a quick sale in the town. There is nothing of interest there for the tribes, and they would have stayed away from such an obvious building anyhow." Pablo sat back in his seat and pulled his cap farther over his forehead to shield his eyes from the strong morning sun. "You have to remember the history here, Ms. Rayne. When the white man first came to their land, the Indians opened their hearts and arms to those people, brought them gifts. Exploitation, slavery, and slaughter have been vicious lessons, but they have been well learned. They avoid contact wherever possible, but if it happens, now they greet outsiders with the sharpened end of their bamboo arrows or the smooth surface of a rock club."

Rayne applied bug spray to bits of her uncovered flesh. She offered the bottle to Pablo, but after he'd eyed it to ascertain its nature, he broke into a wide grin. He slapped his bare forearm several times with his hand.

"I am crocodile skin, Ms. Rayne, weathered and impenetrable. The mosquitoes would break their spiky noses if they tried to stick them in my flesh."

Rayne looked at Pablo's skin, most of it uncovered since all he wore was an oiled-up tank top, shorts, and sandals to keep his feet aired. "I guess you do resemble a distressed leather couch." She focused on the visible part of his chest scar and shuddered, recalling seeing Pablo's chest sliced open with a machete. As if sensing her memory, he reached over and placed his hand over hers, his bumpy calluses evidence of the labor-heavy life he led.

"Thank you, Ms. Rayne."

In his eyes, she saw the sorrow and joy he must live with every day. The cruel double-edged sword a survivor of any traumatic or catastrophic event carried with them was both burden and rebirth. "You need to stop thanking me. You say it every time we meet," Rayne said, affecting a chastising tone more to cover her own faltering voice than to actually reprimand him. The fact that she'd found Pablo before he bled out but hadn't gotten there soon enough for his wife and daughter, haunted her still. "Besides that, you helped lead me to the Golden Raft of Fonte. There was never a debt to be paid, but if there had been, you did it a hundred times over by doing that."

Pablo squeezed her hand before returning to the steering. "And yet, you still sent me a substantial finder's fee." He laughed, picked a ready-rolled cigarette from the engine controls, and lit it. "You are not fooling me with your tough lady boss act," he whispered. "And I think that your Chase will realize that on this adventure with you."

Rayne snatched Pablo's cigarette and took a drag. "She's not my Chase." She coughed the incredibly strong, foul-tasting smoke out and handed it back.

"You are not a smoker, Ms. Rayne." Pablo looked puzzled.

"And you're not a scruffy looking Cupid." Rayne clapped him on the back. "But I *am* tough."

Pablo smiled and clamped the cigarette between his lips. "There is tough *here*." He flexed his bicep and kissed it. "And there is tough *here*." He tapped on his heart with two fingers. "You are constantly seeking treasure you can hold, Ms. Rayne. Treasure you can find and sell to the highest bidder. You think it is made of gold or platinum. You think it is from ancient times. The treasure hunt you do not realize you are on is for a treasure far more precious, far more fragile. You are hunting for a heart to hold, a heart that will hold you."

Pablo chuckled and turned his attention back to his course. Apparently, he'd decided that he'd dispensed enough jungle philosophy for Rayne to be getting on with. She concentrated on the river, winding this way and that, and resisted the nagging temptation to turn and look at Chase again. There was treasure to be found, and Turner had to be on their trail by now. The fragility of life echoed in the forest that enveloped them in a welcoming yet foreboding embrace. Somewhere in its heart it held the prize of a lifetime. At the same time, it was under siege from so many angles and so many people that the prize could be lost. Rayne couldn't help but make the comparison to their situation. If, as Pablo said, Chase was a different kind of treasure, finding a way to her was barred by Turner's pursuit and by Rayne's past actions. What would she have to do to make sure Chase wasn't lost to her forever?

***

Pablo sided the boat to the pier, and Effi jumped onto it, mooring rope in hand. Despite being a wooden structure, it had survived the arson attack. There was a sand bank between the main building and the pier that had presumably stopped the fire from spreading naturally and destroying it. But Rayne wondered why it hadn't been razed separately anyway.

Effi secured the rope to the dock and beckoned them to join her. "Come on. It's perfectly safe."

She bounced up and down on the wood to demonstrate her point. It creaked under the strain of Effi's weight before part of it snapped loudly and her right leg disappeared up to her knee in the jagged gash.

Pablo laughed and slapped the side of his boat repeatedly. "You silly woman! Not so safe!"

Tonyck was quick to Effi's side, while Effi held up her middle finger toward Pablo and scowled. Ginn went to Effi's aid too, and the twins slowly began to disentangle Effi's leg from the broken floor. Tonyck took out her utility tool, unfolded a saw from its twenty plus accoutrements, and set to work on the board that had given way. Ginn mirrored her sister, and once through the wood, they were able to pull Effi out.

Rayne wasn't surprised to see large splinters had pierced Effi's leg, but she *was* impressed that Effi hadn't screamed or cursed in pain. The twins helped Effi onto the ground.

"Throw me the first aid kit hanging on my bag," Tonyck said to no one in particular.

Rayne turned but Chase already had it unclipped and was halfway off the boat. Tonyck took it and gave Chase a curt nod. Rayne joined them on the deck, careful to check her footing as she did. She knelt down and put her hand over Effi's. "Are you okay?"

Effi shrugged. "I feel a little stupid. It's not very impressive when your guide can't even negotiate an old dock."

Rayne squeezed Effi's hand and smiled. "It was funny though." She released Effi's hand and turned to Tonyck. "Chase and I will take a look at the buildings while you fix Effi up. Maybe Pablo and Ginn could come with us and cover more ground." Rayne inclined her head to the darkening sky filled with ominous black-gray clouds of rain. "Daylight's fading, and it'd be best if we were settled in before that deluge hits."

Tonyck tapped the radio clipped to her belt. "Let us know when you've found somewhere suitable." She looked at Ginn. "Keep her safe."

Ginn grinned and tugged on the strap across her chest that held her AK47. "Sure thing, sis."

Pablo offered the boat keys to Tonyck. "And *you* keep her safe."

"The boat or Effi?" Tonyck asked.

"My boat, of course," Pablo said. He pulled the minute remnant of his cigarette from his dry lips and crushed it underfoot. He jutted his chin toward Effi. "*She* is very good at taking care of herself."

They each grabbed their backpacks and headed down the pier to the FUNAI building. The smoky scent of dead wood assailed Rayne's nostrils as they drew closer, but the more nauseating odor of death overpowered that and any other forest fragrance that might otherwise have been pleasant.

"Smells like death," Chase said, and she pulled her scarf up to cover her nose.

"Chase and I will take the outer huts, Ginn." Rayne pointed to the collection of constructs of varying sizes beyond a small clearing. "You and Pablo scope the main building."

Ginn laughed and shook her head. "*Or* Pablo and Chase hit the outer buildings, and we'll take the main structure." She alternated her pointing finger between herself and Rayne. "I can't keep you safe if I can't see you."

"The only threat we might come across here are Indians. If that happens, I want someone by my side who can communicate with them, not someone who can shoot them." Rayne motioned to the rifle Ginn had moved into ready position.

"You don't know that for sure." Ginn looked far from convinced.

"She is right," Pablo said. "There are no other boats docked, so the only other people who might be around are the ones who belong here. They will respond better to those not carrying the tools of death. Ms. Rayne is safer with Chase."

Rayne smiled when she saw what looked like slightly smug validation crossing Chase's expression. Rayne was aware the situation would pander to Chase's chivalrous nature, and while that was a bonus, Rayne's reasoning held true. They stood a better chance taking a non-aggressive stance than thrusting an assault rifle in the air.

Ginn shrugged and tilted her head. "If you're sure. You're the boss." She pulled her radio from her backpack strap and checked the display. "Channel five?"

Rayne and Chase looked at their units. "Channel five." Chase pressed the talk button and everyone's radio registered the communication.

Rayne turned her arm to check her watch. "It's nearly half past six. Let's check in with each other every fifteen minutes."

"Will do, lady boss." Ginn saluted and slapped Pablo on the back. "Let's go, Pablo," she said, exaggerating the end of his name to emphasize the rhyme.

Rayne looked to Chase. "Ready for our adventure, hero?" Rayne smiled at Chase's bashful grin that said she knew Rayne was playing up to Chase's vision of herself but loving it anyway.

"Sure thing, lady boss," Chase said and wiggled her eyebrows.

Rayne felt herself swoon at the seductive look in Chase's eyes. It was an expression Chase had never given her before, but by God, did she love it.

They made their way across the sand onto the bamboo walkway that connected each of the outer huts. As they progressed and inspected each one, the gravity of what had happened here impressed itself on Rayne's consciousness. Dried blood sprayed in strangely artistic arcs, a visual record of callous cruelty, bloodthirsty and barbaric. The ground bore dark inkblots where the lifeblood of FUNAI agents had pooled before being absorbed into the dust, feeding the forest in death as they'd tried to protect it in life. Doors hung from hinges, kicked inward with extreme force. Splintered shards of wood were strewn across the floor, its pale flesh speckled with the spilled blood of those who sought refuge from the attack. Every piece of furniture in each hut had been shattered or demolished, made impossible to reuse or repurpose.

Rayne and Chase wandered silently amongst the man-made wreckage as if words shared would cause further damage. Rayne felt a reverent reluctance to speak where the FUNAI agents and their families had been slaughtered, and it was similar to how she'd felt walking around the Holocaust Museum in DC. It was like pushing through the thick aftermath of evil that had passed through, exacted its will, and moved on. This was the will of men; evil men whose greed had eaten their inherent goodness alive from the inside and left a hole that could only be filled with violence and wealth.

Rayne finally came to one hut, inexplicably unmarred by the horrific events that had transpired. It was just a shell, empty and apparently unused.

"A food store maybe," Chase said quietly, walking past Rayne to enter the hut.

Rayne nodded as she looked inside. "Makes sense. Whoever attacked this place must have stripped it clean after everyone was dead. Pablo says the gold prospectors are still using local children from families steeped in debt bondage. If they were tasked with acquiring the food, they'd have no reason to destroy it after they'd finished. Just an oversight, I suppose."

Chase emerged from the hut, rested against the outside wall, and knocked her head against the bamboo. "How is the Brazilian government letting this happen, Rayne?" She kicked at a tuft of vegetation. "People have been exploiting, enslaving, and slaughtering these innocent tribes since the eighteen hundreds. Why isn't the US government doing something about it? Aren't we supposed to be the leaders of the free world? Aren't we responsible for protecting people who can't protect themselves?"

Rayne reached out and took Chase's hand, seeing the last of the retreating sun's rays glisten in her tears. Her heart ached for how deeply Chase was clearly affected by everything around her. "There's no glory in helping these people, no oil to be drilled for and no religious freedom to protect."

Chase lifted her free hand to cover her eyes, but Rayne still saw the escaping drops of liquid sorrow fall from Chase's face onto the ground. "I'm sorry I made you work so hard to get me to come with you for this."

She wiped her eyes and looked up at Rayne, who saw the distress mix with determination in Chase's expression.

"You don't have to apologize for that. Most people have no idea of the war that's raging in this rain forest." Rayne stopped herself from drying Chase's tears. There was such beauty in her vulnerability.

"*You* did."

Rayne pressed her lips together and sighed. "But I'd forgotten." When Turner approached Rayne's firm and said he was a logger, and though Jenny had suspected his business had been an illegal one, they couldn't find anything to confirm their suspicions. She'd been uncharacteristically blinkered by the lure of the Golden Trinity. "It's been a few years since I was last here." Rayne's breathing hitched when Chase squeezed her hand.

"The last time you were here, was that when you saved Pablo?"

Chase's expression was so pure, so open and unguarded, that Rayne took a moment to gather herself and answer. Rayne never thought she'd see that again. It was as if Chase had begun to push back all the walls she'd constructed to keep Rayne from being part of her life again.

"'Saved' is a bit of an exaggeration," Rayne said, the splinter of failing to save his wife and daughter pushed deeper into her soul.

Chase pulled Rayne closer. "Will you tell me what happened?"

Rayne steadied herself, taken aback by Chase's sudden intimacy. She was so used to being the predator that Chase's movement knocked her off balance in more than just a physical way. "I was here looking for the Golden Raft of Fonte and I'd barely begun my search when I came across a terrifying scene. The gold prospectors were just trucking out." Rayne closed her eyes for a second, trying to stop the memory recollection from turning into a full color movie playing in her head. "Maybe twenty, thirty people. Severed limbs, bodies hacked haphazardly, their blood stark and red against the lush green of the forest palms where they'd been slaughtered." Rayne felt Chase's grip tighten, and she moved her other hand to rest of Rayne's waist. "I thought everyone was dead. Women. Children. Animals." She clenched her jaw and swallowed against the sickening bile rising in her throat. It had been such a long time since she'd thought about that day in detail, but it still triggered the same response. "I fell to my knees and vomited. I'd never seen anything like it." Rayne shook her head slowly. "I never want to see anything like it again. I was about to leave to report it to FUNAI when I saw a movement in the distance. I picked my way through the bodies and found Pablo with his wife and daughter crumpled in motionless heaps, his eyes looking up at me in horror." She put her hand over her mouth, unsure if she might actually be sick.

"They were already dead?"

Rayne nodded. "I patched Pablo up as best I could, did a quick transfusion, made a rudimentary stretcher from some bamboo and paracord and dragged him to my Jeep."

"Wait." Chase raised her eyebrows. "You gave him a blood transfusion?"

"I'm a golden blood. I can donate to anyone."

Chase smiled. "How did I not know about this?"

Rayne glanced at the ground. "You don't exactly follow my social media stream."

"That's where you're wrong." Chase pulled Rayne to her and pressed her hard body to Rayne's. "You just never publicized it."

Rayne felt Chase let go of her hand, but the loss was fleeting because she cupped Rayne's face instead. Chase leaned in and kissed Rayne gently. Rayne pulled back slightly, her eyes searching Chase's to interpret what the kiss signified. The flood of desire washed across Chase's expression, and Rayne let out a short breath as she realized Chase wanted more. Rayne wrapped her hand around the back of Chase's neck to pull her in for a deeper kiss.

Rayne heard the whistle of an arrow a millisecond before its tip buried in the bamboo wall of the hut only two inches to the left of Chase's head. Someone shouted something in a language she didn't comprehend. Rayne closed her eyes and prayed Chase understood.

CHAPTER SEVENTEEN

CHASE BROKE AWAY from Rayne, startled. She glanced to her right to see an arrow level with her eye line. Warning shot. "Put your arms out, splay your hands, and reach for the sky…very slowly," Chase whispered, beginning to do as she'd instructed herself.

Rayne's eyes opened gradually. "What did they say?"

Chase shook her head. "Don't speak. And no sudden moves, okay?"

Rayne blinked instead of nodding and raised her hands precisely as Chase had advised.

"Friends," Chase said in Tupi-Guarani, hoping their language sat within that family of tongues. She sidestepped Rayne to face a line of six Indians, each of them with arrows nocked and strings at half tension. "Friends."

The one in the center of the line lowered his bow and came two steps closer to her. He said a string of words extremely fast and pointed to the machetes hanging from Chase's belt and on a strap across Rayne's chest.

Chase nodded and lowered her eyes, not wanting to appear confrontational. "Take off your blade and place it on the ground, slow enough for moss to grow on you," she whispered. Chase unbuckled her belt, slid the sheath from it, and squatted to the floor to discard her knife.

The leader waved his hand decisively. Chase took it as a demand to stay down so she went to her knees and laced her fingers behind her head. Rayne followed suit. Chase's heart, already racing for different reasons, was now banging against her chest like it wanted to escape. Wait in line.

Two of the others approached, lowered their bows, and collected their weapons one-handed. They stuffed the sheathed blades inside the waist of body wraps around their butts and upper thighs that looked only slightly thicker than paper. The leader barked another instruction, directed at the two closest to them. Chase made out the words, rope and bind.

"Don't struggle. Let them tie you up. Everything's going to be fine." Chase made sure her voice sounded calm though she knew Rayne wasn't someone who panicked. If the Indians were inclined to instant violence against *brancos* she and Rayne had jumped the first hurdle. Now she had to hope she could convince them that, unlike most white people they crossed paths with, their intentions were good.

Chase had a theory that, despite their tendency to span across thirty plus thousand square miles of the rain forest, they somehow communicated across tribes to keep each other safe. She hypothesized that all of the Indians were from a single original tribe, and the names given to them by white intruders or FUNAI protectors were crude misunderstandings of the interlinked nature of the whole indigenous population. If her postulations were correct, this unexpected meeting would turn out to be exactly what they needed to help keep them out of Turner and Owen's way.

Another of the Indians removed Chase's backpack, then Rayne's, and took them back to the leader. He emptied them both of everything, inspected it all, and nodded, apparently satisfied. The other guy repacked them and threw them both over his shoulder.

Chase remained compliant and as motionless as possible as her hands were pulled behind her back and thin, wiry vines were wrapped around the wrists. They were guided back to their feet and pushed forward.

The leader headed along the bamboo path and Chase and Rayne followed, with the rest of their party close behind. Within moments, they were out of the FUNAI compound and enveloped in the dusky darkness of the forest.

"Checking in, lady boss. You find anything?"

Ginn's voice crackled in over both their radios. The leader jumped before he spun around and looked at them for the source of the noise. Chase pushed her right hip forward to offer her radio.

"Friends," Chase said again, then said she needed to answer them or they'd try to find them. It wasn't quite that fluent, but the leader seemed to comprehend because he unclipped Chase's radio from her waistband and put it up to her mouth. His other hand held the tip of his arrow to her throat. He pressed the talk button, indicating that this group had not only come across white people but was also familiar with their technology.

"There's a hut at the back that should work," Chase said. "We'll come back to the boat shortly. Meet us there." Chase felt the arrow point nick the underside of her chin, caused by her jaw movement when she spoke. The leader withdrew both the arrow and the radio. He looked slightly apologetic when he saw her blood on his arrow, but he wiped it on his wrap and said nothing. He put the radio in the animal skin knapsack hanging over his shoulder, nocked the arrow back onto his bow, and turned back into the forest.

They walked silently for another fifteen minutes before the radio disturbed them again.

"Have you guys gotten lost?" Ginn asked.

Chase didn't know Ginn at all, but she could hear the worry poorly disguised in her casual tone. The leader turned and repeated the same process.

"Sorry, Ginn. We'll be there in ten minutes."

The leader nodded, and Chase began to wonder how much of what she was saying he understood. She remained relaxed. If they were going to kill them, they wouldn't have trekked them all the way into the forest to do so.

Ten minutes of quiet progress was made before the radio rumbled into life again.

"Tonyck is so pissed with me. Where are you? I'm at the huts. Fresh tracks. More than just you two. We'll find you."

The leader turned again, his expression more irritated now, and shook his head. "Nah. No follow."

He retrieved Chase's radio once more and offered it to her mouth. This time, his arrow tip was absent.

"Ginn, we're okay. Don't try to track us." Chase looked at the leader, trying to figure out his intentions, but his face might as well have been made of clear glass. Nothing.

"What the fuck are you talking about? Where the hell are you?"

Chase hadn't missed Tonyck's particularly unfriendly way of communicating with her. "We're with a small group of natives. We're safe, and we'll be back in the morning." Explaining why they were there would take some time. If they were being taken to the tribe's home, she wouldn't be in a hurry to try to leave tonight and undoubtedly offend them. She pinned her hopes on the bindings and bows being mere precautions.

"Fuck that. Where's Rayne? Why isn't she saying anything. If you've let anything happen to her, I swear to—"

The leader pressed the talk button. Apparently, he had as much patience for Tonyck's attitude as Chase did. She smiled in thanks.

"I'd never let anything happen to Rayne." Chase bit her lip, glad that

Rayne could only see the back of her head. "We're both fine."

The leader took the radio and walked past Chase to Rayne. Chase turned slightly to the side so she could see what was happening but didn't move enough to kickstart the others into action. Rayne looked to Chase for guidance, and she nodded. "Calm her down," Chase said quietly.

"Tonyck, I need you to relax." Rayne kept her eyes on Chase, who simply continued to nod slowly. "Make camp, and we'll join you…" She raised her eyebrow at Chase. She smiled and winked. "We'll rejoin you in the morning. We're where we need to be. This an order, Tonyck. I need you to stand down."

The leader depressed the talk button, again evidencing he understood at least enough English to know that Rayne had said what she needed to or all he was going to allow her to say.

"This isn't cool, Rayne. We're supposed to be wherever you are," Tonyck said.

Chase heard the anxiety in her tone, just as she had with her sister's. Ginn was probably kicking herself for letting Rayne go without her, or Tonyck was kicking her anyway, and Chase sympathized. But when Rayne made a decision, little would deter her from that choice. Chase would rather *she* was here with Rayne and not either of the tank twins anyway. She suspected neither of them would have had the sense to go quietly to their knees, and the situation could have ended up bloody.

The leader twisted the volume switch to the off position and slipped it back into his knapsack. He must have noticed Rayne also had one when he approached her, and he took that one too, switching it off, before dropping it into his pack. He returned to the head of the group, and Chase picked up the pace he set. She could feel Rayne almost vibrating behind her. Rayne wasn't used to being told what to do, and so far she'd had to do everything Chase had instructed her to do. Chase felt sure she'd pay for it later, somehow…when they were no longer trussed up like rodeo calves.

***

Darkness fell in the rain forest, making it virtually impossible for Chase to see the end of her nose. When she stumbled and nearly fell for the sixth time, she stopped walking and Rayne collided into her back.

"Oh, bugger."

Rayne stayed close. Chase liked the feeling of Rayne's body pushed against hers, and she pushed back at her. The five behind them didn't join the pileup, making Chase think that they had some kind of clever jungle-vision developed from generations of navigating its blackness without fire torches or flashlights.

"I can't see," Chase said in English, then repeated it in Tupi-Guarani. The leader said something about releasing them, and their bindings were removed. Chase rubbed her wrists, but the indentations from the vines weren't particularly deep. If she'd been inclined or if it had become necessary, she could've escaped, but the group had needed them bound to feel safe, and that was okay with Chase. Under different circumstances, she might've happily been tied up when Rayne was close.

The leader took her hand and placed it on his shoulder as he turned. He'd either concluded they were no threat, or he was convinced they wouldn't be able to find their way back to the FUNAI HQ in the pitch-blackness that enveloped them. Chase reached behind and found Rayne's hand. "Put your hand on my shoulder and stay close."

"You're enjoying being in charge, aren't you?" Rayne asked quietly, her breath warm on Chase's ear.

Chase grinned, happily aware Rayne couldn't see. "Shh. No talking."

They continued like a human train for another mile or so before Chase saw several small huts in the distance, outlined in the shadows provided by dancing firelight. As they drew closer, Chase made out at least another fifteen people, men, women, and children, moving around the small encampment or sitting beside the fire. Three women began to move toward them, but when they saw Chase and Rayne, they stopped in their tracks.

A heated conversation ensued, and Chase didn't need to know the language to understand that the women weren't impressed by their impromptu visitors. Anger transcended the need to comprehend words. Chase suppressed the desire to smile as the leader bowed his head, and she heard the word for sorry repeated too many times to count. She did love a good matriarchal setup. She heard the words friends and help too. Chase figured the leader had come across enough white people to know that some of them could provide some assistance, and she guessed it was a medical emergency that had brought them to the FUNAI HQ. That also explained why he'd inspected the contents of their packs before taking them captive. Maybe they'd been searching for a first aid kit, but what injury could've befallen one of them that they couldn't cope with themselves with their usual methods?

The women scowled but stepped aside to let them pass, and the leader beckoned her and Rayne to follow. Chase took Rayne's hand and pulled her close as they walked past several huts and the inquisitive stares of the tribe's children. The leader stopped at a hut and carefully peeled back the door, made from vines and bamboo and tied to the structure. He motioned into the hut, and they went inside. Lying on a bed of palm leaves was a young girl no older than eight. A bloody rag wrapped around her upper arm gave Chase the answer to her question—a bullet wound.

"You fix," the leader said in English. "Make better."

"How long ago?" Chase asked and accompanied her words with the charade of her hand as a gun.

He held up a finger. "One day."

Chase searched her memory for everything Noemie had ever told her about the operations she'd had to do on her tours. One day wasn't specific, but given how long it took them to get here, it must've been at least three hours ago. That meant the kid, though unlucky to have gotten shot, *had* been lucky enough that the bullet hadn't busted through her brachial artery. Otherwise she'd already have bled out and they might've reacted by killing the closest white people to them in revenge. Bonus. Chase had read about bullets being left inside the body for fear of doing more damage by removing them, but long term, lead poisoning had been recorded. *Shit.* She also suspected that they'd want the bullet removed simply because the thing inside her was the work of white devils.

Chase turned to the leader, about to say that she needed her backpack, to find him already holding both of their packs. Chase put her hands together and lowered her head. "Thank you." She upturned her bag and let the contents empty to the ground before sorting through them and picking out her first aid kit. Noemie had packed that piece of luggage, one of her own combat med kits, and conscientiously checked that each item was present and fresh. She'd listed them out loud, but Chase hadn't paid too much attention. Her mind had been on why she'd agreed to go with Rayne on this crazy adventure. She wished she'd paid a little more attention.

Chase knelt beside the little girl and held her palm over her forehead. She had a fever. "Wet. Water," Chase said and gave the leader a piece of cloth from a mound of them by the girl's head. He passed it to another man waiting behind him and repeated the instruction in his own language. The exchange reiterated that the tribe must have had some sort of prolonged contact with white people or at least people who spoke English.

She felt the warmth of Rayne's hand on her shoulder, and she crouched down alongside Chase.

"Do you have any idea what you're doing?" Rayne moved her hand to Chase's thigh.

"I used to watch *Scrubs* reruns when I was a kid. Does that count?"

Rayne punched her thigh. "This is serious, Chase. You can't just go poking around in there."

Chase looked up at Rayne and smiled. "Don't worry. Noemie's shown me a trick or two, and she gave me a quick med combat lesson before your limo picked me up—thanks for that, by the way. Nice way to travel."

"Chase…"

Chase placed her hand over Rayne's. "I told you everything was going to be okay, and it will be. I'm trying to make you laugh to calm you down."

Rayne huffed and withdrew her hand from beneath Chase's. "I'm calm. I'm always calm."

"Okay then." Chase turned her attention back to the girl and asked her name.

"Mutapi," she whispered.

"I'm going to help," Chase said in the same language the girl had understood. "But you have to be brave. It will hurt."

Mutapi nodded and held out her hand. The leader dropped to his knees and clasped her tight enough for his knuckles to whiten. Chase realized he was Mutapi's father. She reached out and touched his forearm gently. "It's going to be fine. I'll fix her."

He touched his free hand to his chest twice and once to his forehead. Chase didn't need words to explain. His daughter was everything to him.

"Muscles *and* medical expertise. Two more things to love about Chase Stinsen."

Chase stiffened. *Love?* An innocent turn of phrase or a deeper meaning? She shook it off, stupid to consider, even briefly, that it was anything other than Rayne being flippant. She stopped her mind from wandering back to the kiss they'd shared. She'd parse that out later. Right now she had to concentrate on digging a bullet out of an innocent little girl's arm. This was fast becoming Chase's most interesting adventure yet.

CHAPTER EIGHTEEN

CHASE KNELT AT Mutapi's side and dabbed the wet cloth on her forehead. She'd cooled considerably since Chase had removed the bullet and closed the wound. Mutapi's father, Jabuti, hadn't left her side since, though he had panicked slightly when Chase gave Mutapi a light anesthetic to knock her out while she stitched the wound. There'd been no other visitors to the hut, causing Chase to assume Mutapi's mother was no longer around. With Mutapi taking a bullet, Chase wondered if her mother had met a similar fate and hadn't made it.

Rayne hadn't left the hut either, and though there was nowhere she could really go, Chase had been grateful for the company. Rayne, now perched on top of a small chair in Chase's eye line, became more of a distraction. Chase couldn't resist quick glances up at her, and every time she did, Rayne met her gaze and smiled. Rayne's initial smile had been innocent, but each time Chase looked up, Rayne's smile got a little bigger and a little more knowing. Confident was probably a better description, as if she could see Chase was thinking about their earlier kiss.

It was some kiss, but Chase was already partially regretting it. Not the kiss itself as such—that had been electric—but their situation. She'd instigated it, and took full responsibility for that, but she'd been reckless to succumb to her feelings for Rayne here. Of all the places it could've happened, Rayne had chosen this one to reveal the only piece missing in making her the perfect woman—a heart.

Chase wrung out the cloth in the bowl, dipped it again, and replaced it on Mutapi's forehead. "She's going to be all right," she said to Jabuti. On cue, Mutapi stirred, focused her dark brown eyes on Chase, and grinned. Her smile spoke of everything it should—childhood innocence, hope, and unguarded openness. How she could be that way after taking a bullet likely from a white man, Chase didn't get, but she was thankful Mutapi was that way. "She's a tough kid." Chase gently pinched Mutapi's nose and was rewarded with the cutest of giggles before she stepped away to give Jabuti unfettered access to his daughter.

Rayne stood up and joined her, while Jabuti and Mutapi chatted quietly. Chase felt Rayne's hand on the back of her neck, and she shivered at the touch.

"Sensitive?" Rayne asked, drawing light patterns with her fingers.

"I think it's the sun. Maybe I didn't put enough protection there." Chase didn't want to accept that such a simple caress could affect her that much.

Rayne didn't rebuke Chase's excuse, but Chase could feel her silent disagreement.

"That was all very impressive."

"Oh yeah?" Chase couldn't deny she wanted to impress Rayne and show her that she hadn't made a mistake in asking her to accompany them on this adventure. In all honesty, she'd impressed herself. She would enjoy regaling Noemie with the tale on her next official leave too. And she owed her a giant burger since Noemie had bet Chase would need her kit before the end of the third expedition day. "Not dead weight after all?" They hadn't been Rayne's words, but they still stung, and Chase was having trouble letting them go.

"I never called you that." Rayne began to play with Chase's hair and twist it into little tufts. "But, fear not, I'll make sure that Tonyck hears all about your heroics tonight."

Rayne's nonchalant intimacy was making Chase want to sink to the ground, pull Rayne with her, and continue their interrupted make out session. *Think serious thoughts.* She rolled her neck, and Rayne's hand fell away.

"We have to tell him why we're here and warn him about Turner and Owen." For a few hours, Chase had managed to put those two things to the back of her mind. While they kept a good pace, it seemed logical that they should easily reach the Golden Trinity before them. They had a head start *and* the map. And coming across this small tribe so early might be even more fortuitous if Chase's theory about them all communicating proved to be correct.

"What do you expect them to do? They're being threatened by outsiders left and right," Rayne whispered. "Why should anything you say make them live their lives any differently? Or be any more terrified than they already are?"

Did Rayne want to hear this? "Because I've got a plan." A very loose one, ambitious and extremely difficult to pull off. One that had only just dropped into her brain like a penny in a wishing well. But if they *did* find the Golden Trinity, Chase was certain that the lure of such a bounty would garner the necessary support and expertise.

"Do tell." Rayne stepped off to one side and waited for the big reveal.

Rayne had shown Chase that she was capable of altruistic actions, but what was formulating in Chase's mind was something far more widespread than helping one guy. What if they could help the whole nation? As far as Chase knew, Rayne's heart was still set on claiming the Golden Trinity as her discovery and taking a portion of the riches. They hadn't really discussed what they'd do if they found it, possibly because neither of them thought they would or, that if it was real, it wouldn't be as extensive as folklore promised it was. What would Rayne think of using the treasure to broker a deal between the Brazilian government and all of the tribes in the rain forest? What if it was possible to use the gold to buy every inch of the Amazon and protect it from drug dealers, illegal loggers, gold prospectors, and animal traffickers? It was a formidable prospect, but the more Chase thought about it, the more excited she became.

"I have a theory about all the tribes maintaining some sort of communication system. How else have so many of them managed to stay unconquered and away from the constant invasion of all kinds of people desperate to exploit them?" Chase paused to gauge Rayne's reaction.

"Makes sense. Go on…"

"I think that the outliers, the tribes closest to the groups of non-indigenous people, have learned a degree of English so they can understand the 'enemy.' Maybe they pulled the short straw when they had a meeting. I don't know, but they decided they needed to be able to understand what the hell these invaders were up to. With me so far?" Chase tapped on her thigh repeatedly, the energy of her ideas too much to contain and keep physically still.

Rayne nodded. "You think that if you tell this tribe what's coming, every Indian in the rain forest will be informed?" She rubbed her forehead. "That's a long shot, Chase."

"If this was your home, and someone warned you that there was danger far worse than anything you've ever experienced, wouldn't you listen? Could you take the chance not to?" Rain began to lash down hard enough for Chase to check the roof and hope the tribe had figured out waterproofing. Outside the hut, Chase could hear the unhurried footsteps of the tribe retreating into their huts.

"I suppose you have the added respect after saving Mutapi. They might be more inclined to hear what you have to say."

Chase shrugged. "I didn't save Mutapi, I—"

"You did in his eyes." Rayne motioned toward Jabuti, still holding his daughter tenderly. "If you're right about outlier tribes being the eyes and ears for all tribes, these people will have seen their own die from bullet wounds before now. We have no idea about their understanding of biology; to them, a bullet anywhere might be seen as a death sentence. You also might be the first white person they've come across that *hasn't* abused them in one way or another. Put those things together, and maybe it'll be enough for them to heed your words... For them to go any farther on an *actual* jungle grapevine, I guess we just have to hope your theory is right."

Chase hooked her finger in Rayne's belt and pulled her into a hug. "Thank you."

"For what?"

"For trusting me." Chase knew it was no small thing. Earning Rayne's trust was virtually impossible. The walls she'd built around her heart *and* her head were all but impenetrable. Chase had seen plenty of people try and fail in the years they were friends. Her parents, the people every child *should* be able to trust implicitly without condition, had failed her in that regard and unknowingly fostered a self-imposed isolation in Rayne. They had a lot to answer for.

Rayne held Chase a little tighter, then broke away. She looked toward Jabuti and Mutapi. "Do you think he's the tribe leader?"

"Maybe." Chase laughed, remembering the way he'd been greeted back into camp with her and Rayne in tow. "But after seeing those women in action when we got here, maybe this is a matriarchy."

Rayne made an approving sound. "Wouldn't that be a refreshing change?"

Jabuti rose and turned to them. "Sleep now. Talk tomorrow."

Chase looked around at the palm leaves three or four deep on the ground and weighed it against going out in the rain to put up her tarp and hammock. There was one other bed, which must have been Jabuti's. She motioned toward an empty space at the rear of the hunt, close to where the embers of a fire remained. "Here?" she asked in Tupian.

Jabuti shook his head and pointed at his cot. "There."

Chase held up her hands. "No, we couldn't."

"You must." He sank back to the ground and lay beside his daughter, turning his back to them and saying no more.

Chase appraised the makeshift bed, about two foot wide and six foot long, just long enough for Rayne's toes not to hang over its edge. "You take the bed. I'll take the floor."

Rayne grinned and shook her head. "No. You heard the man. We both take the bed. You wouldn't want to offend him now, would you?"

Rayne squatted down and began to remove her boots.

"There's not enough room for both of us." Chase tried again, but there was no conviction in her persistence.

Rayne pulled back the thin gauze-like sheet and rolled onto the bed. She lay sideways and patted the empty space beside her. The tiny space was barely big enough for Chase's ass.

"Quit your whining, Stinsen, and get your beautifully shaped butt in here."

"Fine." Chase unlaced her boots. She sat on the edge of the bed with her back to Rayne, kicked her boots off, and swung her legs onto the cot. She shifted onto her left butt cheek and lay down, trying to keep some distance between her ass and Rayne's crotch.

She felt Rayne's hand on her hip before Rayne pulled her closer so they were spooning. Chase didn't resist.

"It's gotten cold. We should share body heat."

Rayne's warm breath caressed Chase's neck, and it felt like her lips were hovering over Chase's bare skin. Chase squeezed her eyes closed and willed herself to ignore the wonderful feeling of Rayne's body pressed against hers, struggled against the part of her mind that would happily flip over and pick up where that kiss left off. She reminded herself that Jabuti and Mutapi were there too…a douse of cold water on her inflamed desire.

Rayne draped her arm over Chase's waist and sighed. "Night, Chase."

"Night, Rayne." Chase concentrated on her sleep mantra. *Black is black, white is white.* But sleep seemed as likely as a Lotto win when Rayne was this close. Chase pulled the sheet over them and resigned herself to the fact that this was going to be the longest night of her life.

***

Chase woke to an empty cot and pushed away the immediate conflict of being both relieved and melancholy. At least Rayne wouldn't have to endure Chase's morning breath. Conscious of the taste of dry air and dirty teeth, Chase pulled a box of Altoids from her pocket and popped one in her mouth. Had Rayne been beside her, Chase might've been tempted to knock back the whole pack. She pushed the tin back into the side pocket of her cargo pants and stretched. She became aware of the smell of her armpits and reached for her backpack. No one else was in the hut. Should she be worried? She opened her shirt and swiftly applied the deodorant she kept in the side pocket of her pack. She sweated plenty on a regular day; a day in the jungle alongside Rayne was a test for any antiperspirant.

Marginally concerned for Rayne's safety, Chase was quick to check her boots for critters before pulling them on to head outside. In the light of day, the little camp was more impressive. She hadn't really focused on taking much of it in last night. There were around ten huts, each capped with vegetation that looked naturally waterproof. At the head of the camp was a much larger hut that she thought might serve as a communal space. In the center of the bamboo shelters was a huge firepit surrounded by many small wooden seats, but only a few of them were currently occupied by tribespeople who looked like they were trying not to stare at the pale intruder in their inner sanctum.

Mutapi appeared between two huts, ran toward her, and threw herself into Chase's arms. Chase picked her up and swung her into the air, careful not to touch the dressing on her arm. Mutapi smiled so widely that her eyes were barely open.

"He-ro," Mutapi said in what was clearly an early attempt to speak English.

"Hero," Rayne said slowly.

Chase had been so enamored with Mutapi's greeting that she didn't register Rayne's approach. "You're teaching her English?"

Rayne shook her head. "Not really. While you were sleeping like the dead, she pointed at you then touched her mouth. Then she pointed to herself, said 'Mutapi,' and touched her mouth again."

Chase waited for more explanation but none was forthcoming. "And you didn't just tell her my name was Chase?"

Rayne shrugged and looked up to the sky. "Hero seemed more

appropriate."

Chase smothered a smile. She liked being thought of as a hero, even to a skinny kid she'd probably never see again. She placed Mutapi back on her feet and checked her watch for the first time that morning to see to it was past seven. "We need to talk to the elders or the leader, then we've got to get back before your tank twins ignore your order and come searching for you."

Rayne held up her radio. "Not to worry. Jabuti gave us our radios back. I've already spoken to Tonyck and told her about your plan."

Her heart rate fluttered a little higher. Chase blew out her breath, conscious she'd have to resume their ongoing confrontation soon. This had been a pleasant respite. "And how badly did she take that?"

"Surprisingly well, actually. She thinks it's a good idea if your theory turns out to be fact."

That was unexpected but not unwelcome. If she and Tonyck could find some common ground, maybe this expedition wouldn't have to be a daily battle. "Excellent. Do you know where Jabuti is? Time to find out who runs the show."

"I think he's gathered most people in the communal hut, ready for you."

Chase felt Mutapi's hand slip into hers, and she began to tug Chase toward the large hut. "Looks like this little one is a quick study."

Rayne laughed and came up alongside Chase. "Did I already tell you how grateful I am that you agreed to come on this trip?"

"Maybe you did yesterday, but you haven't today." Chase shoved Rayne's shoulder gently, resisting the temptation to put her arm around her shoulders. Whatever was going on between them took a back seat to this right now. "And since I can count on one hand the number of times I've heard you use that word, I'd be happy to hear you tell me all over again."

"Well, now I'm now saying it."

They reached the hut to find the door open. Chase scanned the area and estimated twenty people assembled in a circle with the three women from last night their obvious focus. So it *was* a matriarchy. Each of the women held a staff with an orb of some description at their head. From the distance they were at, it was impossible for Chase to tell what the orbs contained or signified. She was struck by how strikingly similar the women looked, again something she missed last night. Jabuti sat close by, but it was clear he wasn't a first-tier decision maker. Mutapi ran over and sat with him.

The woman in the middle of the three leaders beckoned her and Rayne forward. Chase lowered her head in deference and entered their space. The central leader held up her hand to indicate when they were close enough and waved at them to join them on the floor.

"Jabuti tells us you have a warning," she said in a version of Tupi Chase was able to comprehend.

Chase held her hands together to offer a thank you. In a mixture of Tupi and English for names, she explained that Turner was coming to raid the rain forest of the Golden Trinity. At the mention of their treasure, everyone in the room made a sound, some surprised, some angered.

"We will not allow that," the woman to the left said and struck her staff into the ground.

The leader in the center placed her hand on the other woman's staff and pushed it away, showing Chase she was the overall matriarch.

"Turner will bring a well-armed force." Chase pointed to Mutapi. "Every one of them will have bigger guns than the one that shot Mutapi. Your arrows won't stop them, and they've sworn to kill anyone who stands in their way. With the FUNAI currently out of action, no one can stop their assault on your home."

"What do you propose?" the old woman asked.

"That you send out your warriors to warn the other tribes. Spread the word as far and wide as possible. Tell them to keep a lookout and stay out of the way. Under no circumstances should they try to fight these people... or everyone will be massacred." Chase waited for a response. She felt like she might've been a little over dramatic. The whole thing had begun to seem almost unreal, like she was auditioning for a part in a movie.

The old woman looked at Chase without words for a moment. "And what are you going to do?"

Chase glanced at Rayne. Knowing she didn't understand the language made it easy to keep Chase's end game to herself. "We're going to get there before them." Chase focused her attention on the central leader. What she was about to say probably wouldn't be well received by the staff-shaker on the left. "We want to use the Golden Trinity to help you, to keep you and all your people safe...forever."

The leader smiled. "A grand gesture. But the Golden Trinity already keeps everyone safe."

THE GOLDEN TRINITY

Chase hadn't anticipated this, but she should've seen it coming. Christ, if she was that tired that she wasn't considering all the options already, it didn't bode well for the rest of the trip. The uncontacted and non-Western civilizations often believed there were spiritual connections between their people and the treasures their land held and how those spirits protected the treasure. "The men coming won't stop until they have the Golden Trinity. If they need more people to conquer this land, more will follow. They *will* take it away."

"Many have tried before. Many have failed."

The old woman must have been referring to the small groups of adventurers, like Percy Harrison Fawcett, who'd set off into the jungle in 1925 and was never seen again. But they didn't have the weapons to wipe out a whole tribe in thirty seconds. Turner was well financed. Owen was an animal. The only way it ended for them was glory or death. Chase would settle for them rotting in jail forever, though how they were supposed to achieve that, she had no idea. Something else they hadn't considered before setting off on this expedition.

"These people don't know what failure is." Chase clasped her hands together, imploring the leader to understand the magnitude of what was coming. "They're killers. They'll cut you down. And yes, you might kill a few of them, but for every arrow you let fly, their guns shoot sixty bullets." That seemed to get the message across. They had no immediate response, so Chase pressed on. "They'll slaughter anyone and everyone who stands in their way."

The central leader inclined her head and narrowed her eyes. She stood, with the help of the other two, and made her way to Chase. Last night Chase had thought she was maybe in her forties, but now she looked much older, and her progress toward Chase was slow.

She came to stand in front of Chase. "*You* are standing in their way."

Chase looked up at her and nodded. The leader placed her hands on Chase's head and pressed quite hard, to the point of some discomfort. Sensing this could be an important part of their decision, Chase remained still. She closed her eyes and waited. The leader removed her hands and put them on Chase's shoulders to steady herself as she squatted to the ground. Chase opened her eyes to meet the leader's gaze. She was clearly searching for something. Without words, she pushed aside Chase's shirt to put her hand on Chase's skin, over her heart. The leader stayed that way and closed her eyes, as if she was shutting every other stimulus from her mind to concentrate purely on the sound of Chase's heart. What was the old woman trying to discover from her heartbeat? Chase waited. She closed her mind to the room and concentrated on the woman's hand on her heart. Whatever she was trying to find, Chase wanted to help her do so.

She didn't count how many minutes the two of them were in that position, but the woman finally removed her hand. She used Chase as a leaning post to get back to her feet, then put a finger under Chase's chin to raise her head. Once again, the woman looked as though she was scouring Chase's eyes for some deeper motivation for her actions. Or maybe she was just looking into Chase's soul. The leader had a kind of aura that made Chase think that it might actually be possible.

"We will warn our people of this impending threat."

"You're able to warn *everyone?*" Chase wanted confirmation her theory was correct.

She nodded. "You are intuitive, Chase Stinsen. We *are* able to warn *everyone.*"

Chase smiled at the leader's use of English for her name, then the implications of what she'd just said began to sink in. If she hadn't already been sitting down, she would've sunk to the floor. All of the tribes across the whole of the rain forest, crossing the arbitrary borders of nine nations, were linked and quite possibly factions of one much larger people. The ramifications for anthropological study were huge and blew away all previous understanding of the indigenous communities scattered across over two million square miles of the Amazon.

"This journey will lead to a personal discovery," the woman said before she turned and ambled back to her sisters.

Rayne nudged her. "Verdict?"

The leader announced her decision to the gathered tribe, and it was greeted with tentative murmurs. She went on to describe the magnitude of the threat, which stirred more vocal rumbles. Chase hoped they'd be able to communicate the deadly nature of the incoming group, and that the message wouldn't be watered down like in a game of telephone.

"They've agreed to send people out across the forest." Chase swiveled on her knees to face Rayne. "I was right. All the tribes maintain a communication system of some kind."

"Do you think they use monkeys or pink dolphins as well?"

Chase laughed. "No, but I would like to see that."

Jabuti approached them with Mutapi clinging to his hand. She and Rayne stood.

"Go safely, Chase Stinsen."

He held out his other arm, and Chase clasped it tightly. "We'll certainly try," she said in Tupi.

"Two of our scouts will take you back to your boat." Jabuti scooped Mutapi into his arms and kissed her forehead before turning back to Chase. "Thank you for saving my little girl."

Chase ruffled her hair. "Look after your father, Mutapi," Chase said in Tupi.

Mutapi nodded. "Yes, Hero. I will," she said, half in Tupi, half in English.

Chase smiled. *Hero.* Was this expedition forging her into the person she'd always dreamed of being?

CHAPTER NINETEEN

RAYNE COULD HEAR the turning of Chase's mental cogs over the monkey calls echoing through the dense forest. She'd barely said anything in the past half hour since Rayne, Chase, and their two-person escort had left the camp. Rayne knew her well enough to know that kind of silence equaled intense cogitation.

"Are you going to share your concerns, or are you just going to continue to overthink them until your head explodes?" Rayne gave Chase a little shove to emphasize her point.

"What?" Chase asked and looked blank for a moment. "What? No, nothing…well, something. But I'm not all that good at walking and talking when it's something serious."

Rayne began to swipe at vines with the stick she was carrying. They weren't in her way, she just wanted to distract herself if Chase's sober ponderings revolved around what was going on between them. "Maybe you could try? We're going to be nonstop from here on in, Chase. We've lost time with this detour, and as beneficial as it certainly was, it narrows the gap between us and Turner."

Chase stopped. "That's what I'm thinking about."

Rayne took Chase's arms and pulled her forward. "We have to keep moving." A wave of relief washed over her only to be replaced by a slight petulance that Chase *hadn't* been thinking about them. "Walk and talk."

"Have you thought about what happens when Turner and Owen get to the Golden Trinity?"

Rayne heard Chase's worry loud and clear, and she didn't blame her. So much could go awry on this adventure. There were many deadly obstacles to navigate to get to the treasure but the deadliest they might have to face was Turner and Owen. Turner didn't strike Rayne as a particularly forgiving person, and she *had* drugged him, tied him up, and stolen his priceless ancient map to arguably the largest treasure the world would ever see. And then there was Owen, and he said that he'd kill her if they ever crossed paths in competition again. There was no law here, and no protection other than their weapons. This wouldn't be a situation she could talk them out of. Turner could kill them all and the rain forest would never reveal his crime.

"What makes you think they'll find it at all? We have the map."

Chase laughed, but it sounded more mirthful than humored.

"From what you told me about him, Turner isn't a stupid man. He'll have a copy of the map. But even if he didn't, all he has to do is buy the best trackers in the business and track *us* instead of following the map." Chase ran her hand over her hair and scrubbed at the back of her head. "All the time I was imploring the tribe to get out of his way, I was thinking, how are *we* going to get out of his way? Have you got a plan you're not telling me about?"

"Hey." Rayne touched Chase's forearm. "I'm trying to be honest with you about everything. We can't plan for something when we don't know what it looks like… That didn't make any sense…" Rayne dug her hands into her pockets and played with the small hag stone she always took on expeditions. So far, it had bought her plenty of luck. "I mean, we don't know what the Golden Trinity will be. We can't know the extent of it. We can't anticipate how big it might be." She pulled out the hag stone and began tossing it in the air. "We have a satellite phone, and we've got a chopper pilot waiting in Leticia. As soon as we find it, we get out of here. We can always hire more pilots if we need them."

Chase snatched her stone midair and inspected it. "What's this old thing?" She twisted it over in her hand and closed her fist over it. "Why do you carry this? Tell me and take my mind off Turner and Owen."

Rayne raised her eyebrows and glanced at Chase. It wasn't like her to let something that big go, at least not until she'd analyzed it to the nth degree. But Rayne wasn't about to push it or pass up the opportunity to discuss something lighter. "You want the whole story?"

"Sure. We've got time."

Chase smiled at her, so unguarded and open, making Rayne smile back. This reminded her of all those long conversations they used to have that extended deep into the night.

"The magic of hag stones is three-fold—protection, healing, and seeing beyond what appears to be there. I found that one in a cute little cottage I rented in New York. I probably shouldn't have taken it, but I left a note and some money." Rayne drifted to the unusual little place on top of a boring old apartment block. It had been such a perfect location for a weekend-long booty call with…with whom she couldn't recall.

"Pleasant memories?" Chase asked.

Rayne thought she heard a tinge of sharpness in Chase's voice. Was she jealous of a memory that wasn't even fully formed? The sad fact was that Rayne barely remembered any names of the many women she'd enjoyed over the years. It seemed rather ironic that the woman she'd never managed to get in bed was the one woman she struggled to get out of her head. "It was a nice break from reality," Rayne said and tried to grab her stone, but Chase wasn't giving it up yet. She batted Rayne away and kept it in the hand farther away from her. "Anyway, every adventure I've been on since I…rehomed it has been a huge success."

"I didn't peg you as the superstitious type." Chase handed the stone back.

Rayne thumbed its smooth surface and peered through its hole at their two scouts. "Lucky they're not trolls."

"That *is* lucky. What do you see if you look at me through it?"

Chase wiggled her eyebrows. What Rayne saw was Chase looking incredibly sexy, and Rayne fought the rising urge to jump on her, wrap her legs around Chase's waist, and kiss her again. Chase in adventure-mode ramped up her overall attractiveness still further.

Rayne held the stone to her eye and studied Chase for the briefest of seconds before she stumbled and nearly fell. Chase was quick to intercept her fall, and her arms felt sure, strong, and sturdy around Rayne's waist.

"Careful. We don't want you spraining or breaking anything," Chase said as she released her grip on Rayne slowly. "So, did you see anything extra through your special stone?"

"Yes, actually." Rayne adjusted her backpack that had skewed slightly when she lost her footing. "I see someone who's unbelievably kind and altruistic. The sort of selflessness that's extremely difficult to find in a person. So many people do good deeds simply to look good, score points, or please their god." Rayne glanced at Chase and saw her cheeks had flushed, giving her a glow like she'd been in the sun a little too long.

"I like the way you see me." Chase met Rayne's look briefly before she concentrated on the forest before her.

"It's not just me that sees you that way." Rayne thought back to all the times she'd seen Chase and Noemie together. "Noemie doesn't use a hag stone, and she thinks the sun rises and sets with you."

Chase laughed. "I'm not sure about that."

"I am." Rayne swiped at another vine, fending off the melancholy that always nibbled at her when she got into discussions about parents or guardians and their kids. "She's got you so high on a pedestal you must be dizzy from lack of oxygen." And that was how it was supposed to be, so she'd been told, at least until the kid reached thirty and finally began to realize their idol was really only human.

"How do you work that out?"

"You forget I saw her with you when she was just a skinny runt of a street kid. The way she looked at you when you were imparting life lessons, she hung on your every word, Chase. The way she uses your life and achievements as her yardstick for success. Whenever she was around you, it was like she wanted to crawl inside your kangaroo pouch and absorb all that you are." Rayne smiled at the memories of Chase and Noemie on the couch when she'd go visit. Noemie would lie with her head on a cushion in Chase's lap while Chase stroked her hair. Knowing the life Noemie had endured, it was a miracle she allowed anyone to get close to her, physically or mentally, but it was clear she'd made a special connection with Chase, and it was a special thing to catch a glimpse of.

Chase shrugged, perhaps uncomfortable with the idea of being held in such high regard.

"What about you? Do you want a kid if you ever grow up?"

Rayne shoved Chase away, faking offense. "Did you?"

Chase shook her head. "Absolutely not. I never planned or wanted children. Noemie…she just *happened*. Things went really bad for her, and she had no one. We went from her spending a few nights a week on the couch to me converting the attic space into a bedroom for her…"

Chase's voice had grown softer as she recalled her past. Rayne fought the thought that she should've hung around to see all that happening for herself. "She was lucky you were around."

Chase didn't respond, and for a few moments, the only sounds were the calls of the forest's inhabitants and their footsteps squelching on the sodden ground. Rainy season might be coming to an end, but it had had a hell of a leaving party last night.

"You deflected my question." Chase finally broke the silence between them.

"What question?" Rayne knew damn well what Chase was referring to and reprimanded herself for not doing a good enough job of the deflection. But even though the conversation had been directed to its current topic by Rayne, she was reluctant to discuss her own thoughts on the subject.

Chase nudged Rayne gently as they walked. "Nice try, Rayne. I'll play along though and ask again. Do you want kids if you ever grow up enough to have them?"

Rayne waited for something, anything, to interrupt them, drug traffickers, another tribe, a giant anaconda, anything would have been more welcome than where this conversation was heading.

"Rayne?"

"No." Rayne recognized her sharp response. It wasn't Chase's fault she'd asked the question. It was a perfectly innocent inquiry. "No," she said again, less aggressive this time. "I can't have kids."

Chase reached out and held Rayne's arm. "Aw, crap. I'm such a dweeb. I'm sorry. I shouldn't have pushed."

Rayne continued walking, and it took her a second before she realized where Chase's mind had gone logically after Rayne's statement. "Oh no, I don't mean can't as in biologically unable." She touched Chase's hand. "I mean, morally I can't have them." She glanced at Chase, who looked somewhat confused.

"What do you mean, morally? Did you go all religious since we stopped being friends and think it's wrong for lesbians to have kids?"

Rayne snorted and shook her head. "Definitely not. I'm an atheist, just like you." Chase's words stung. *Since they stopped being friends.* Weren't they at least friends again now?

"I'm agnostic, not atheist. What do you mean by morally?"

Christ, Chase was like an investigative journalist with a lead she just wouldn't let go of, except this story wasn't all that interesting. "I don't want to mess up a kid's life. I don't want to make the same mistakes my parents did." Damn it. She didn't want to talk about this again. Chase already knew more than anyone except her highly paid shrink. She didn't want to bore her with more details. "I'm not like you, Chase. I'm selfish. I don't have the capacity to care for a little person." Rayne hoped the last sentence would be the one Chase heard out of everything she'd just said. It was the one thing that should resonate as "in character," and might distract

Chase long enough for this trek to be over. She could see the outer FUNAI huts in the distance beyond the edge of the jungle.

She felt Chase's touch firmly at the base of her spine, comforting and intimate. Was this what emotional support involved?

"History doesn't always have to repeat itself. Parents teach us how *not* to be just as much as they teach you how *to* be in this world."

Rayne clenched her jaw. She wanted this conversation to be over. She tapped the shoulder of one of the scouts. "We'll be okay from here, thanks."

They glanced over their shoulder and looked at her blankly then looked to Chase for interpretation, who said something she didn't understand. She should've asked Jenny to find her a phrase book but was doubtful Lonely Planet published a version in Tupi.

They turned and disappeared into the dense forest from where they came. Chase caught Rayne's hand and pulled her closer.

"You get to choose your path, Rayne. No one gets to push you down a road you don't want to go anymore."

Rayne broke away. This was all too much. "Did you get that out of a fortune cookie?" Rayne turned away from Chase's hurt expression and started back along the path to FUNAI. She was making a mistake. She could be no more to Chase than a fun couple of nights of hot sex. Rayne couldn't—wouldn't—be anything more. She didn't have that capacity. And Chase deserved better…far better than her.

Chapter Twenty

"How is it you say? The wanderers return?"

Pablo greeted them with what Chase now understood as his trademark grin. It was almost big enough to make Chase forget about his very recent past. But the scene Rayne had described automatically popped up in her mind, and she admired his ability to be so full of life when the memory of his family's death could never be far from his thoughts.

"Boy, am I glad to see you back, lady boss." Ginn helped Rayne board the boat.

She looked relieved. No doubt Tonyck had given her hell for letting Rayne go off without her.

"I should hope so," Rayne said, sitting beside Pablo at the helm.

"Can we maybe not do that again?" Tonyck said and looked only at Chase.

Chase readied to defend herself, and Rayne's decision, but neither a contemptuous glare nor an angry tirade followed. Chase nodded. "Let's stick together from now on." She jumped into the boat, dumped her bag, and sat beside Effi. "How's your leg?"

Effi rolled her eyes dramatically. "Tonyck looked after me." She glanced at Tonyck and gave her a meaningful smile. "She stitched it up, but I'm going to have to be careful around the water." She lifted her trouser leg up to reveal most of her shin covered in camouflage duct tape. "This should keep anything from getting in there."

Chase smiled at the tape. She would've chosen that over regular black any day of the week. "Let me know when it needs redressing; I've got rainbow-colored tape in my pack."

Effi narrowed her eyes. "You have?"

Chase laughed and shook her head. "No. Just plain old black, I'm afraid. You should stick with Tonyck strapping you up." Chase caught another secret smile Effi threw Tonyck's way and figured she'd done more than tend to Effi's wounds.

Robyn Nyx

Chase saw Rayne glance over her shoulder at them, too briefly for Chase to make eye contact. Rayne had said nothing since her smart-ass "fortune cookie" comment, and Chase allowed the silence. She knew damn well what Rayne was trying to do, but Chase wasn't fooled. Rayne always lashed out verbally when she felt exposed and vulnerable. The discussion about her folks and potential parenthood had clearly freaked her out, which Chase expected. Rayne might try to push her away, but with them having to be in such close proximity for the next God knows how long, there was nowhere for Chase to be pushed to. Rayne had revealed more than a glimpse of something Chase liked, and she wouldn't be letting her escape from further scrutiny so easily. Chase had kissed her. She'd crossed the line that she'd sworn not to, and she'd been right to hold back. Chase had known that if they kissed, it wouldn't be *just* a kiss. It wouldn't stop there…at least not for her. The attraction, the connection Chase had resisted had been unleashed the moment their lips met. And Chase owed it to herself to explore it. Maybe not in the rain forest but definitely when they returned.

The clicking and spluttering of the engine drew Chase's attention.

"*Filho de puta.*" Pablo slammed his fist on the dashboard and the boat kicked into life.

Rayne and the tank twins exchanged a glance Chase couldn't interpret with one hundred percent certainty, but it was somewhere between relief and expectation as if they'd figured something had to go wrong somehow. Effi looked relaxed and remained unaffected, but something passed over her expression briefly, and Chase wondered if her overall cool exterior masked a panic that might bite them on the ass at some point.

Pablo pulled into the center of the river. "Away we go."

Chase tapped Rayne on the shoulder after a few silent minutes had passed, hoping the soft lull of the water might have assuaged her mood. She turned and smiled, but her eyes spoke of an anxiety Chase had never seen before. She'd been relatively blasé about Turner and Owen's pursuit, but Chase felt sure it must be bothering her at least a little bit, and the look in her eyes backed that assumption.

"What do you need?" Rayne asked.

Chase ignored the sharpness. "We should take a look at the map together." Chase tapped the map's hermetically sealed case with her foot. "We need to have some idea of what it means when we get to the tree."

THE GOLDEN TRINITY

Rayne turned on her seat. "That makes sense. Let's do it."

Chase hoisted the heavy glass case onto the empty bench section beside her before retrieving a paper copy of the map and a journal from her bag. She'd made a few notes in it from the time she'd spent with the map on the plane journey. She had a feeling it wasn't the map Rayne or Turner thought it was. The way Rayne had spoken about it was as if the map alone would lead them to the Golden Trinity. Chase was pretty sure it would turn out to be only the first piece of a much larger puzzle.

She rolled the paper map out and used a couple of pieces of duct tape to stick the top edges to the glass case so she could lift it up to look at the original if necessary. It might be that they hadn't needed to lug the original all the way here, but Chase didn't want to take any chances. It could easily be that they'd need the real map to feed a jaguar that would lead them to the next puzzle piece. Wasn't that always the way with treasure hunts?

"Sit with Pablo. I need that seat."

Rayne and Effi exchanged seats, with Effi showing no reaction to being spoken to so firmly. Chase buzzed at being physically close to Rayne again.

"Can you move so I can see the map?"

"Sure." The proximity was all too brief, but it made sense to shift for Rayne's comfort, although Chase would've been happy having Rayne lean across her lap to look at the map. *Behave.* Nothing had changed. This still wasn't the time to act on their attraction. Chase stood and swapped places with the map.

Rayne ran her fingers over the symbols beneath the laminated plastic. "Mayan glyphs have never been my thing. I should've paid more attention to them, then maybe more of this would make sense." She twisted to look at it from a different angle. "It looks so different from the other codices that still exist. Even the colors vary dramatically."

Chase nodded and swept her hand across the map, still slightly in awe of being this close to such an ancient artifact. That feeling never grew old. "I think the colors relate to how the Mayans saw the world as a quincunx."

Ginn laughed. "That sounds like a curse…or maybe a sex toy. I can't decide."

She and her twin giggled like a couple of college boys seeing naked titties in a porn magazine for the first time.

"Behave."

Rayne said the word but looked as if she could barely stop herself from joining their joke.

"What does it mean then, Doc?"

Tonyck's use of Chase's formal title came as a surprise. More surprising that she sounded respectful rather than mocking. Had she had an attitude adjustment while Chase and Rayne were deep in the forest with the tribe? "It's a similar system to the four traditional points on a compass with four colors representing north, east, south, and west. The fifth 'direction' is the space in the center of the quadrants. It's thought to represent the sun."

"How did you figure out that we had to begin this journey from the tree this was found inside?"

Rayne smiled as she asked the question, and Chase realized she was giving her the opportunity to score some credibility in the eyes of the tank twins. "Generally, Mayan texts are read left to right and top to bottom in columns. And the whole text fits into an invisible grid. That doesn't apply here, which makes sense. The scribe needed to protect the Golden Trinity at the same time as providing a route to it." Chase became aware her hands were flapping around and telling the story. She tried to rein them in. "The map, if it was ever found, was only to be read by the Maya elite so it appears to be constructed in a circular fashion. It was rare that they wrote this way, and it was usually to keep things from a more general audience." She pointed to the two green signs at the center of the map. "This is the symbol for tree, along with the sun god or sun-faced ruler. The sun god allows everything to grow and has encouraged the tree to develop in order to protect the secret within it. Everything around it moves outward in increasingly smaller circles, with each ring of signs giving less and less information."

"How do the colors play a part?"

Effi, who'd initially seemed disinterested, had now turned back to the group and was intrigued enough to ask a question.

"They'll tell us which direction to go until we get to the next marker," said Chase.

Tonyck shifted her gun and laid it across her lap. "We better hope all the markers aren't trees or we're fucked. It could be they've already been chopped down."

Tonyck's concern was well placed, but Chase hoped it would be unwarranted, especially since the symbol for tree repeated almost ten times on the map. She figured some were bound to be subterfuge. "From what Turner told Rayne, he was the deepest logger in the area. I think it's highly unlikely that, in the timescale from him discovering the map to now, anyone else has made significant progress beyond the origin tree." Chase looked beyond the boat to the horizon. Lush green trees stretched into the sky for miles. It was hard to believe that within the forest, there'd been vast swaths of it chopped down or burned to make room for crops, or worse, burned in retaliation by criminals so that no one would benefit. From the river it looked untouched and untamed. But if the Brazilian government continued to release large chunks of it to logging and agriculture, how long would it be before this vista was destroyed? Unless the Golden Trinity was real enough to broker a deal to keep the Amazon safe forever... Sitting in the boat, on the world's second largest river amongst nearly four hundred billion trees, Chase suddenly felt too small and ineffective for this challenge. She gave herself a mental motivational kick. *Screw that.* Plenty of world-changing ideas started with just one person.

"Unlikely but not impossible," Rayne said. "And that's what will make it interesting." She nudged Chase. "You didn't want an easy ride, did you?"

Rayne winked, and Chase thought of all the sexual comebacks Rayne would have responded with if she'd asked the question. Chase was tempted to try one of her own, but it'd probably be an epic fail like a T. rex trying to high-five a pterodactyl. "Has it ever been an easy ride with you?"

Rayne raised her eyebrow; the left one, the one that seemed to be directly connected to the dirty part of her brain. Chase had seen her do it to other women, and Rayne had often used it on Chase too…when Chase had been adamant she wouldn't fall for Rayne's considerable charms. Now that she'd opened that door, Rayne's small action had a big impact, and Chase was aware of the reaction in her shorts. She couldn't hold Rayne's gaze and focused instead on the map, hoping that the cornucopia of color might distract her from only seeing the beauty in Rayne's eyes.

"Do you want it easy?"

Rayne's seductive smile made Chase clench her pussy *and* her jaw, but neither stemmed the desire to pull Rayne onto her lap and do unspeakable things to her.

Pablo laughed. "You women need to get a room."

Truth. But since that wouldn't be happening for a good while, Chase needed Rayne to…well, rein it in because the hammocks they'd packed definitely wouldn't stand up to the two of them going at it like horny rabbits. And Chase was never quiet when it came to having sex.

Chase glanced at Tonyck. Still no glare. A questioning raised eyebrow but no obvious disgust or rage. Chase didn't know what Rayne had said to her, if she'd said anything at all, or if something had happened while they were gone, but this was a much-preferred atmosphere. There was almost a camaraderie building, something Chase had never experienced before. She'd only ever worked with Rayne and that hadn't turned out so good last time. Chase could only hope that this time would be different.

CHAPTER TWENTY-ONE

CHASE HAD JUST closed her journal and stuffed it back into her pack when the engine began to billow smoke. She tapped Pablo on the shoulder and nodded toward the dark black plumes heading toward the clear sky. "I'm thinking that probably isn't a good thing?"

Pablo turned and promptly began to curse loudly in Brazilian Portuguese. He pulled open the engine lid, and a pungent heat hit Chase's nostrils. That *definitely* wasn't good.

"This isn't an abandon ship moment, is it?" They'd made solid progress upriver, and Pablo had estimated they were a half day from the point where they'd transfer to the smaller boat and paddle to the headwaters before starting their land journey to the origin tree. Chase was beginning to question the logic of *not* going in by Jeep or chopper, though a potential army of Turner's loggers would have been alerted to their presence. Chomped on by a caiman or held captive by Turner's terrorist tree choppers? It wasn't an attractive choice.

"Would you be angry if I said yes?" The skin around Pablo's eyes creased as he scrunched his face apologetically.

"I wouldn't be surprised." Chase elbowed Rayne gently. "Are you so against an easy ride that you've sabotaged your own boat?"

Rayne winked. "You'll never know." She stood and moved up the boat to stop behind Pablo. "Are we paddling the rest of the way?"

Effi joined Rayne. "No. The current is too strong for easy progress. We'd be better off paddling to the shore and beginning our overland trip immediately."

Pablo stopped the engine and looked at Effi, clearly not convinced. "Are you sure?"

Effi waved her hand dismissively. "You're the boat man. I'm the guide." She pulled a map from the leg pocket of her hiking pants. "We're here." She tapped on the map, her impatience evident. "The water level has already dropped far lower than it ever has by this time in previous years. We shouldn't waste our energy battling the current when we can head west on land and cut this section off."

Effi drew her fingers across the map in a small triangle. What she said looked like it made sense so Chase didn't understand Pablo's reluctance.

Rayne looked to Tonyck. "What do you think?"

Tonyck shrugged. "Both options have pros and cons. But at least the land is more predictable." She smiled. "And you know I prefer feet to boats as a mode of transport."

Chase seconded that logic. If their luck was bad enough that the second boat sprang a leak, getting everyone and everything safely to shore was problematic and fraught with danger. "We'd also be easy pickings for those boat bandits you told us about. We wouldn't be able to out-paddle an outboard motor." Even with her and the tank twins rowing. "We'd be too vulnerable out here."

Rayne nodded slowly. "But we were avoiding land so we didn't run into Turner…"

Tonyck scratched at her forehead before gesturing toward the jungle. "Yep. It's a risk. But at least this way, we'll be better able to tell if they're in front of us or behind us."

Ginn whistled. "I agree with those three, Rayne. The jungle suits us two far better than a wooden bowl in the middle of an alligator-infested river—and don't correct me on whatever animals are lurking in this murky water. I don't give a shit if it's an alligator or a crocodile. They've both got big fucking teeth, and they both eat humans. That's all I need to know." She hefted her AK47 over her shoulder. "And this baby works better on dry land."

Tonyck lifted her rifle and smacked it against Ginn's. "Hooyah, sister."

Chase didn't care much for the macho display, but they'd backed her and that was progress. Rayne clearly held their opinion in high regard, and why wouldn't she? They had extensive military service. Why bother having that on the payroll if she wasn't going to listen to what they had to say?

"So you just want to abandon *both* boats?"

Pablo still needed convincing.

"You were hired to get us upriver as far as you could, Pablo." Rayne put her hand on his shoulder. "You've done that. It's not your fault the boat has failed us. You can stay with it, fix it, and head back to Tabatinga.

THE GOLDEN TRINITY

Consider your contract fulfilled."

Chase recognized Rayne was giving Pablo an easy out. She leaned forward to get a better look at Pablo's face, interested to see if he took it. Did he have nothing left to lose or had he given enough?

Pablo patted Rayne's arm. "My contract to you will never be fulfilled. Do you not know that by now?"

"Going overland wasn't part of our deal, Pablo. That's why you found Effi for me."

Gentleness and humility seeped from every word Rayne spoke. Chase couldn't grasp why Rayne hadn't shown this side of her before. Unless she just hadn't been around to see it…or didn't want to see it.

"I can handle it from here," Effi said.

Pablo shook his head and put his finger to his mouth without looking at Effi. "No more of this, Miss. Rayne. I am coming with you all. I wish to be part of the team that discovers the Golden Trinity."

Effi clenched her jaw, and it was the first time Chase had seen anything other than casual nonchalance on her part since she'd told Chase her FUNAI story. Chase didn't know whether Effi was irritated more by Pablo's dismissal of her insistence that she could handle it or that he thought she couldn't handle it because she was a woman. Chase didn't think Pablo was sexist. He'd chosen Effi in the first instance, was clearly indebted to Rayne and didn't begrudge her gender, and he seemed completely comfortable being surrounded by strong and powerful women, of mind and body. Chase figured Pablo had never intended to leave Rayne to it and simply hadn't shared that with Effi. Perhaps he thought Rayne wouldn't have let him come at all if he'd told her he was in it for the whole journey.

Rayne sighed and looked slightly exasperated, but she had a small smile that told Chase she was quietly glad that Pablo was insisting on going with them. Rayne had something that made people want to be with her, over and above the call of duty, and she suspected the tank twins would follow Rayne to the inner core of the earth if that's where the adventure took them, whether Rayne paid for the services or not…And it was that same "thing" that had ensured Chase was here by her side now too.

"There's no getting rid of you?" Rayne smiled a little more.

"Not a chance."

Pablo tugged his ball cap lower over his eyes, his emotions clearly getting the better of him. Chase shared Rayne's relief at Pablo's insistence.

With Turner and Owen behind them, and with no idea how close they might be or who else they'd brought with them, an extra body on their side of the fight was welcome.

"Now that that's sorted, can we get on dry land before this piece of junk completely gives up the ghost and sinks?" Tonyck tossed a bag onto the paddle boat. "I've never fancied swimming with dolphins, let alone piranhas."

She had a point. Chase hefted her backpack onto her shoulders, picked up her water bag, and dropped it into the other boat. She went to grab Rayne's bag, but Rayne waved her away.

"I've got it. Get the map." Rayne lifted her pack with relative ease and threw it to Tonyck's waiting arms.

Within a few minutes, everything and everyone bar Pablo was safely off his failing craft.

He pocketed the keys and patted the steering wheel. "Good-bye, old friend. I hope that you will be here on my return."

Chase raised her eyebrows at Rayne. The proliferation of banditos meant his boat would be long gone and stripped for parts or fixed up and sold within the day.

"If she isn't, you can buy a new one with your share of the treasure."

Chase tried not to react visibly to Rayne's declaration, even though her words jarred. Rayne still intended to make some kind of profit from the find. "I thought we'd decided we would discuss what we did with the Golden Trinity *after* we found it. We shouldn't be talking about shares of something when we don't even know what it is yet."

Rayne smiled and held up her hands. "Apologies, Chase. Old habits, etcetera."

Chase tried unsuccessfully to get a read on Rayne's seriousness. Had Chase fallen for a tall tale again? Did Rayne have every intention of trying to broker the treasure to the highest bidder?

"I'm serious, Chase. Stop looking at me like that."

Chase might be struggling to read Rayne, but it clearly wasn't a mutual problem. Chase never had been good at hiding what was going on in her head...especially from Rayne.

"If we find this treasure, I'll make so much money from the fallout, I won't need to sell it to anyone." Rayne tugged at Chase's shirt. "And you can install it in the Brazilian National Museum...if they have room for all of it."

Rayne's laugh eased Chase's tension a little. Old betrayals died just as hard as old habits, but Chase had seen a whole new side to Rayne over the past few days. The near-death Syrian experience had clearly triggered something in Rayne and maybe even left the old Rayne behind altogether. Chase hoped so, because every moment they were spending together was bringing them closer to each other. And Chase didn't want that to end.

Chapter Twenty-two

RAYNE WATCHED CHASE and Effi work together to figure out a route to the origin tree based on the Mayan map and Effi's modern one. They operated quickly and smoothly, as if they'd been doing it together for years. They rolled up their respective scrolls and motioned the team forward into the depths of the rain forest. Rayne allowed herself to drift to her earlier conversation with Chase. She pulled at the straps on her backpack to stop the friction at the base of her spine and moved on, following Effi but slightly to her side so she could see ahead. She didn't want to miss a moment of this.

Rayne had meant it. She was sure she'd meant what she'd said on the boat. But when they were face-to-face with the most iconic and sought-after treasure in history, would she be able to resist? She wanted to resist, she was certain of that. She wanted to be the kind of person Chase was interested in…the exact opposite of everything Rayne had become since falling under the spell of her mentor, Lauren Young. But even after Lauren was gone, Rayne continued to be that person. She swiped aside a vine with her machete, taking comfort in its violent efficiency. She didn't know how to be anyone else for fear of being seen as vulnerable and open to being taken for a fool. There'd been small acts of altruism here and there—looking after Pablo being her most impressive—but for the most part, she'd been the treasure hunter Lauren had molded her into—self-interested, ruthless, and single-minded.

Rayne glance back at Chase, who seemed to be concentrating hard on something. Maybe she was puzzling the map in her mind. Chase did have a photographic memory after all. Rayne hadn't mentioned that to G&T, because she didn't want them thinking they were lugging the original map around for nothing. What was it about Chase, though? In her presence, Rayne wanted desperately to be a better version of herself. For years, she'd hidden and denied that fact, poked fun at Chase whenever their paths had crossed, taken pleasure in beating Chase to every prize they competed for. But under longer term exposure, Rayne seemed powerless to deny a deeper attraction to Chase than a simple one night conquest. Rayne just had to stop fighting with herself and let it be. Maybe Chase deserved someone better, but what if Rayne *could* be good enough? And if she was, how could she win Chase over and convince her she really was the woman Chase needed her to be?

The feeling of complete weightlessness hit sudden and hard. Rayne threw her arms upward, desperately trying to get a hold on the ground as she rushed past it. Damp soil wedged beneath her nails as she clawed at the walls of the hole she was falling into. She hit the ground a little softer than she'd expected considering the height she'd come from and felt around to discover she'd landed on a bed of vine leaves…far better than a series of buried spikes designed to skewer the plummeting victim.

She looked up to see the heads of Chase and G&T peering over the small entrance she'd unwittingly discovered.

"Rayne? Rayne? Are you okay?"

Chase's voice seemed clearer than the shouts of her bodyguards.

"Peachy, thanks." Rayne turned her flashlight on but left it clipped to her pack straps and looked around. "Any chance of a rope pull before I get attacked by a clan of vampire bats?"

"Sure thing, lady boss," Tonyck called down.

Rayne shuffled and backed up against the wet wall of the hole and wondered about its purpose while she waited. It didn't seem to lead anywhere, and the absence of sharpened points led her to think that it couldn't be an animal trap.

"Coming down now."

Tonyck again. Shame it wasn't Chase. Being rescued from the depths of an oubliette by Chase held a certain romantic appeal, and Rayne was sure it would have crossed Chase's mind. She would relish the opportunity to be the hero. Rayne knew that anything less offended Chase's chivalrous inclinations.

Rayne grasped the end of the rope as it came into sight and secured it around her back and under her arms. She held onto it to reduce the tension under her armpits and pushed her feet against the squishy wall, ready to climb. She gave the rope two short tugs to indicate she'd tied it. "Okay. I'm harnessed up."

"Pulling you up now," Tonyck shouted.

THE GOLDEN TRINITY

Rayne began a relatively rapid ascent toward the bright sky about twenty feet from where she'd landed. When she emerged, Chase enveloped her in a hug and held tight. Chase relaxed the embrace but still grasped Rayne around her upper arms, her eyes telling Rayne exactly how she felt.

"I'm okay." Rayne swallowed against the unfamiliar ball of emotion rising from her chest and threatening to escape from her throat. Chase's raw vulnerability, her yearning innocence was devastating.

"From now on, you should really stick to following in my footsteps," Effi said over Chase's shoulder.

Rayne gathered her composure, looked beyond Chase's searching gaze, and laughed. "Where's the fun in that?"

Chase released her grip and took a step back. She seemed almost dazed and shook her head quickly as if to sober herself. Rayne looked at her, but Chase avoided her eyes and began to gather the rope. Ginn held out her arms, and Chase wound the rope around them. Rayne turned off her flashlight and nodded to the pit. "What's the purpose of that anyway?"

Effi grinned. "Man traps. The tribes dig them to catch loggers and bandits."

"To do what with them?" Rayne expected a brutal answer.

"To torture and send a message," Effi said. "Killing them would be too easy, and they can't kill them all. This way the broken man goes back to their little company or gang and warns them to stay away from that area."

"Does it work?"

Effi tilted her head to the left. "Sometimes. Sometimes not. It can provoke a terrible revenge."

Relieved she hadn't been left to be discovered by a local tribe, Rayne motioned to Effi. "Lead the way, McDuff."

Effi wrinkled her nose and looked confused. "McWhat?"

"McDuff. Shakespeare." Rayne saw that Effi had no idea what she was talking about. "Never mind. Just go."

Effi shrugged, turned, and headed west.

"There's a lot to be said for a classical education," Chase said as she came up alongside Rayne. "*I'm* a fan of his work."

Rayne raised her eyebrows. "Really? Do you have a favorite play?"

"I always loved *Romeo and Juliet.*"

"Surprise." Rayne nudged Chase as they walked. "I suppose you see yourself as Romeo?"

"Of course."

Chase smiled, and there was no sign of the awkwardness of her reaction to Rayne's mishap.

"But you would have written a different ending?"

Chase ran her hand through her hair and adjusted her sunglasses before she answered. "There's a lot to be said for happy endings. Every reader loves them."

Rayne considered her own messed up family, not dissimilar to the Capulets or Montagues. Reputation and social standing meant everything to them, more than the happiness of their only child. The sadness of the memory weighed heavy and each step became a little harder. She fought against it. They'd done their damage, but they were out of her life. Why couldn't she cut it loose? "Not everyone can have a happy ending, Chase, no matter how much they want it."

"Maybe they can if they start living for the future instead of in the past."

Rayne clenched her jaw. "You do love your fortune cookie philosophies, don't you?" She reached out, instantly regretting the comment, and Chase didn't pull away. "I'm sorry. This is hard…It's new."

Chase nodded. "I know. There's baggage and history to deal with." She shrugged. "Now probably isn't the best time to start unpacking all of that."

Rayne let her hand drop and tried to concentrate on watching the path again. Her body began to ache from the fall. The adrenaline released when she'd endured her unscheduled descent into the pit had dulled her pain receptors only temporarily. Another misstep wouldn't be welcome. But she pondered Chase's words silently.

If not now, when? They had no way of knowing how this expedition would turn out. Maybe now was *exactly* the right time. Rayne resolved to talk to Chase more when they stopped to camp for the night. By day, they could focus on the Golden Trinity, but by night, Rayne wanted to focus only on Chase.

CHAPTER TWENTY-THREE

TWO FULL DAYS of jungle hiking had been as much fun as Noemie had warned her it would be—zero. The team was so focused on getting to the origin tree as quickly as possible that the journey had been functional and lacking in any real interaction. The previous two nights, Chase had been sure Rayne was trying to engineer some alone time, but the tank twins had insisted on everyone sticking close and sleeping under one giant patchwork tarp. The only alone time Chase had managed over the past sixty hours was with a freshly dug hole and some biodegradable toilet paper. Her feet constantly ached, and she feared she might develop foot rot. Then there was the monkey meat. She'd been over-exposed to its unique flavor and was seriously considering becoming a vegetarian. And the exposed parts of her body were like a dot-to-dot page from all the bug bites, and it was all she could to stop herself itching her own skin off. No matter how much bug spray she applied, they still kept munching on her. Chase didn't want to even acknowledge the hallucinations she'd been having late into the day as the sun began to disappear and the forest became more secretive. She swore she'd caught glimpses of the three old women from the Indian camp. She'd half expected to see some of their people in the trees beyond them, keeping an eye on their progress from a safe distance. When it was the matriarchs she saw, Chase feared fatigue was playing tricks with her mind.

She rubbed her eyes and focused on the present. Under usual circumstance, huge chunks of silence would be welcome, but social etiquette demanded that small talk be made in situations like this. It wasn't something she was good at, but the lack of it was making her more anxious so she'd taken to mimicking birdcalls. Tonyck put a stop to that pretty quick. She'd cited the need for stealth and silence. Chase suspected she was just plain irritated by Chase's poor imitation skills. Rayne had glanced back a few times and smiled. It'd been worth it just for those.

Effi raised her arm with a closed fist, the sign for them to halt immediately and stay completely silent. She waved her other hand to the ground, indicating for them to crouch down and take cover. Chase checked behind her to see Tonyck bear-crawling her way toward Effi and Pablo. Ginn had her rifle poised and aimed beyond them all. Chase probably wouldn't care too much for what Ginn could see through the custom super sight she'd fixed onto it.

Chase stayed low and quietly moved to Rayne's side. "We're close to the origin tree. Do you think that Turner has some men guarding it, waiting for us?"

Rayne nodded. "Most likely."

"Then it's an opportunity to find out how close he is…if we outnumber them." Any knowledge they could gain now would be an advantage.

"I like where your head's at," Ginn whispered into Chase's ear.

Chase jumped and tried to cover up her surprise by shifting her weight from one knee to the other. Ginn's approach had been completely silent, and Chase couldn't help but be impressed. Ginn smirked but said nothing about her reaction.

"I'm on the right track, yeah? If we can grab one of them and…" Torture him? What lengths would they have to go to get the information they wanted? "ask him a few questions. They're probably just locals who work for him. They won't owe him anything."

Ginn tilted her head to one side and sucked a breath of air through her teeth. "I guess there's only one way to find out." She grinned and wiggled her eyebrows before quickly crawling over to Tonyck.

They were both surprisingly agile despite their outhouse-like builds.

"If G&T can secure one of them, they'll talk…whether they want to or not."

Rayne accompanied her words with a warning look. Chase didn't regret her suggestion. They would've thought about it anyway. The logger would be given a choice—talk willingly or talk painfully. The tank twins wouldn't have to raise a hand if he made the right decision.

Rayne tapped her finger on Chase's forehead. "What's going on in there?"

Chase batted Rayne's hand away gently. "They'll only do what they have to." She recalled the aggression in Tonyck's eyes at the hotel after Syria when it was aimed at her. She had to admit she was relieved that Tonyck had calmed her ire. "And if they start to go overboard, you can

always stop them. They're *your* employees, Rayne. They'll do as you say."
Rayne looked back over to the twins with Effi. "Let's hope they don't have to."

Tonyck waved them over to join them and made it clear they were to stay low and remain quiet. When she and Rayne got to their position, the view that assaulted her eyes shocked her soul. She was kneeling on the soft, lush green carpet of vegetation associated with the Amazon, but she looked down on naked, burned, and arid ground. A cruel circle of charred earth, scarred and hardened from mechanical attack, stretched out across several miles. In the foreground, the agents of destruction idled, an ugly and comically contrasting yellow mass of metal and rubber. Just to the left of those machines, on the edge of the abused land, a lone lupuna tree remained. It stood tall and over thirty feet wide, looking arrogant and unbowed by the devastation in its midst.

The origin tree. It had endured hundreds of years, impossible to tell exactly how many because tropical trees lacked identifiable growth rings, but it alone had remained steadfast for centuries, holding its secret behind its calloused wood. There was a certain spiritual poetry to its resistance, as if it were destined to resist the exploitation of its home.

Awe and disgust dueled for Chase's attention. The wanton rape of this land had profited white men with no legitimate claim to its bounty. And because of that, it had given up the key to perhaps its greatest secret: the Golden Trinity. Only now, in sight of the origin tree, did Chase feel, truly feel, the possibilities of truth behind the legend.

She reached out and grasped Rayne's hand without overthinking it. This was a moment that had to be shared, because its impact was too great to witness alone. And in that second, Chase realized there was no one else in the world she'd rather experience something so monumentally and concurrently positive and negative. Dark and light. Tears burned the back of her eyes, and she was grateful for the blackness of her Oakley lenses, shielding out the sun and blocking in her emotion.

Rayne squeezed her hand in return. "It's real…"

"It's a fucking tree," Tonyck said, her face expressionless until she grinned.

Chase suppressed the strange desire to jump up and hug everyone. Tonyck may have been joking, but she was absolutely right. The origin tree was simply the beginning of the true journey, though according to the map, the cave was only a few days' trek away via the other trees.

Chase blinked away the combination of unreleased tears and unabashed wonderment and took a second look at the scene. A Jeep parked alongside the tree. One guy in the driver's seat with his feet on the dash, another guy lying across the back seat with his head propped up on the door, and two guys sat on the hood. Four of them, six of us. They were decent odds if it weren't for the rifle barrels Chase could see positioned within reach of each of them. What were the tank twins plotting? Did they think nothing of taking a life? Had they already decided which three they would shoot and which one looked most likely to sing? Could they make that kind of judgment from four hundred feet away?

They had the forest to cover them for the most part, but if they all moved, they'd surely alert the loggers. Only the tank twins were trained to navigate the terrain noiselessly. Chase wanted to be in on the action, but she had to be realistic and accept her current limitations. Flashes of Indiana Jones movies played in her head. His recklessness usually paid off, but that was Hollywood. This was real life, and those guns would be loaded with real bullets.

"There's no cover," Tonyck said. "We can't circle around and come up behind them."

Ginn shook her head. "Is it sniper time?"

When Tonyck nodded, Chase moved forward. "You can't just kill them. You've got to give them a chance to do the right thing."

Tonyck eyeballed her. "We don't 'got to' do anything you say. Do you know military tactics? Do you know how to ambush a group of armed men? Do you know what it is to take a life?"

Chase despised rhetorical questions. Tonyck knew damn well that she couldn't answer in the affirmative to any of them. She rubbed her forehead and pushed her ball cap up. Being out of Tonyck's firing line had been nice while it had lasted. "I didn't come on this expedition to be involved in killing *anyone*."

Rayne put one hand on Chase's thigh and the other on Tonyck's shoulder. "No one did, Chase."

Ginn reached into one of the ammunition packs on her webbing, pulled out a bullet, and dangled it in front of Chase's face like a hypnotist would with a pocket watch.

"Rubber." Ginn grinned before pulling a small revolver from its holster.

"Non-lethal."

"Ah." Chase rubbed hard at her forehead as if that would scrub away her error in jumping to the wrong conclusion. She'd misjudged the twins' intentions completely. "I'm sorry…"

"Don't worry about it." Ginn winked before she loaded six bullets into the chamber and quietly snapped it back.

"We'll need to get closer before we take the shots." Tonyck addressed only Rayne as retrieved her own revolver and did the same. "Fifty meters should do it." She turned to look at Chase and Pablo. "As soon as all four are down, we converge on them, but you two need to stay behind us in case they're not fully immobilized and they attack." She tapped the barrel of her gun on her knee. "We've only got six rounds each. It should be enough, three bullets per guy, but be careful." She glared at Chase. "And no heroics. You got it?"

Chase rolled her neck. "I got it." She motioned to Rayne and Effi. "What about…" She stopped herself from saying "the girls." It seemed particularly patronizing and disrespectful especially after seeing Rayne handle a gunfight with consummate composure in Syria.

"You two stay here. Look after the map." Tonyck glanced at Rayne's sidearm. "Give us cover if we need it. Save our ass if you need to."

Rayne smiled and scrubbed the heel of her hand over Tonyck's closely shaved head. "You know I will."

Chase peeled off her pack and removed her machete, hat, and sunglasses. Pablo watched her and then followed suit. His eyes darted here and there, and he seemed fidgety and restless. Chase caught his attention. "Are you up to this?" she asked.

He licked his lips then pulled at his bottom lip with his teeth and sighed. "I guess I will have to be."

Chase looked to Tonyck and saw she'd witnessed Pablo's growing anxiety. "Tonyck, maybe Pablo could stay to protect Rayne. Effi could come with us instead."

Tonyck nodded. "Makes sense. Effi's probably lighter on her feet. We don't want you cracking any twigs with your size thirteens, do we?"

Tonyck handled it well, and Chase saw Rayne's puzzled expression change to understanding as she realized what had happened. It hadn't been that long since Pablo had lost his whole family and village at the business end of machine guns and machetes.

"Yes, yes. I stay and protect Ms. Rayne."

Tonyck offered a quick nod toward Chase. She took it as a small sign of approval at noticing Pablo's discomfort and probably saving them from his freezing at go time. Effi's raised eyebrow suggested she wasn't quite as impressed. Unexpected. Chase thought she would have jumped at the chance to prove herself to Tonyck. They seemed to have gotten quite cozy over the last couple of days.

As Chase went to follow the tanks twins, Rayne caught her wrist.

"Be careful, Stinsen."

Chase smiled at the small show of concern for her well-being but didn't milk it. Instead she took Rayne's hand and squeezed it gently. "I'll be back."

"You better be."

Chase couldn't see Rayne's eyes behind her glasses, but she heard the sentiment in her words.

Chase joined the twins and Effi as they began a slow descent toward the Jeep and its armed occupants. She became aware of her heart thudding at the wall of her chest. It seemed louder than any one of the bird calls or monkey conversations bouncing between the trees that dwarfed them. She knew she was being stupid. No one could hear the mix of adrenaline and mild panic thump-thumping in her veins. But it was something to concentrate on and calm her.

They got to about a hundred and fifty feet away, when Tonyck motioned to halt their progress. From this angle, all four of the guys were visible. The twins divided up their targets and took aim.

"When they're down," Tonyck whispered, "run like hell at the ones on the hood. We'll take the two in the car."

"Get their guns as far away from them as possible first." Chase looked at Effi to ensure she'd heard her. She nodded, but she was wringing her hands. Chase resolved to deal with her guy quick then assist Effi with hers. She and the twins had all assumed Effi had the ability to fight. Given Pablo's reaction, there was little other choice. Rayne needed to keep the map safe in case there were others in the forest they hadn't seen. No doubt Tonyck had registered Effi's lack of enthusiasm and planned to pick up the slack too.

"Ready."

Tonyck waited until everyone had nodded before she and Ginn began firing. The loggers fell back or to the ground, and they broke cover. Chase overtook the tank twins and launched herself at one of the guys on the hood who was already getting to his knees. She kicked him in the gut, and the force sent him into the grill of the Jeep. She picked up both rifles and caber-tossed them back the way they'd come, before she turned, grabbed the guy's head, and knocked it onto the bumper twice. She released her grip, put her knee in the center of his back, and yanked each of his arms behind him.

She was about to pull out zip ties to secure his wrists when she was grabbed from behind and tossed at the Jeep, knocking the breath from her. She turned in time to see Effi on the ground holding her face. Chase ducked the second guy's punch and brought her fist up under his chin. As he rocked back, she kicked out at his chest. Ginn came around at speed and threw herself on him. Chase took the window of opportunity to stamp on the back of her own guy to stop him from rising. She pulled a zip tie around each wrist and one through both ties to fashion them into plastic cuffs. When she looked up, Tonyck had brought the other two guys out of the Jeep and thrown them to the ground.

Effi rose from the dirt and rubbed the back of her head. "I'm not much of a fighter."

Pablo and Rayne emerged from the forest. Chase straightened her back and stood a little taller. She didn't quell the slightly barbaric hope that Rayne was impressed by the way Chase had handled herself. Rayne threw a smile her way and raised her eyebrows. Yep, she'd seen Chase in action, and she'd liked it.

Rayne set the map case and her pack down by the front wheel of the Jeep. "Good work." She winked at Chase. "Pablo, would you translate our questions for me, please?"

"Of course, Ms. Rayne."

"Thank you." Rayne looked at the four roughed up guys on their knees. "Who do you work for?"

Pablo repeated the question and relayed their response, confirming their employer was Turner.

"What are you doing here, and why are you armed?" Rayne asked, one hand on her hip and the other on the handle of her machete.

Chase's baser instincts fluttered, and she hopped onto the hood of the Jeep to watch the show. Rayne in interrogator mode was quite the spectacle.

"They said Turner ordered them to stay with the origin tree until he gets here. They're armed only to protect themselves because Turner said dangerous people would be coming and would hurt them to get to the tree." Pablo shrugged and gestured to their captives. "They are local people, not mercenaries."

"You believe them?" Rayne smoothed some loose hair from her forehead and tucked it behind her ear.

Pablo tilted his head to the side. "I think that mercenaries might not have been so easy to capture and subdue."

Pablo's observation was rich considering he hadn't been involved and had watched from a safe distance. But he was probably right. Once their guns were gone, they hadn't drawn the knives hanging from their belts. They'd tried to defend themselves with their fists even though they'd been shot at.

"Ask if they know when Turner will get here."

Tonyck's question cut through any fading hope that Turner might not be coming at all because he no longer had the map.

Pablo did as requested. "They say they have no way of knowing that."

Chase frowned. When she'd studied the scene from above, hadn't she seen something on the dash? She shook her head when she spotted the satellite phone, stood on the hood, and reached over the windshield to retrieve it from the dash. "No way of knowing?" She tossed the phone in front of the kneeling locals.

Rayne glanced back. "Nicely done, Chase." She unsheathed her machete and used its tip to lift the chin of the guy who'd been doing all the talking. She motioned to the tank twins with her other hand. "They're trained to ask questions in a very different way to how nicely I'm asking them." She waited while Pablo translated her words. "They'll use their fists, and they'll use their knives…and their guns if they have to. Is that what you want? Is your loyalty to Turner worth spilling your blood?" She returned her machete to her hip when all of them shook their heads. "When will Turner get here?"

Pablo paled and his eyes widened when he heard their answer. "He is due in a couple of hours. He is coming by helicopter."

Chase ran her hand over the back of her head and whistled. "We need to get out of here." The map led them west from the origin tree. They needed to establish as much ground between them and Turner as possible. They had little hope of any leftover downpours covering their tracks. "Turner won't need the map. His plan will be to track us and take it back."

"And use you to find the Trinity."

When Rayne looked at Chase this time, the playfulness in her eyes had disappeared and had been replaced by fear. Chase knew it wasn't Turner that scared her. Rayne's distress set off Chase's fight response. She jumped off the hood, scrambled across the ruined ground between her and the loggers, and grabbed the talkative one by the front of his dusty white tank. "Is Owen with them? How many of them are there?" She shook him when he didn't answer quickly enough following Pablo's speedy repeat of her questions. "Answer me."

"Yes, Senhor Owen is with Turner. He thinks they have at least six people with them and these four had been told they would be going with them."

Pablo rested his hands on Chase's forearms, and she looked down at them. Her arms were as tense as the rest of her had become at the news Turner was so close.

He patted her arms softly. "We do not beat the people we fear by becoming them."

Chase relaxed her grip, released the man's shirt, and backed away. She felt Rayne's presence but didn't turn to look at her. Rayne's terrified expression had stirred something deeply dormant in Chase's psyche, and despite letting go of the kneeling guy, her mind had already gone to a darker place. Her instinct to protect had played a pre-vision of Chase snapping the guy's neck. She hadn't acted on it, but the power that surged through her in that moment had begun to wash away any reluctance she had against doing whatever might be necessary to keep Rayne safe.

She tried to blink it away and reclaim a calm objectivity. When she refocused, she met Tonyck's eyes and recognized understanding in them. Tonyck gave one short nod. There was no need for words. It was clear that Rayne was the priority for both of them.

Would there be *anything* Chase *wouldn't* do for Rayne?

Chapter Twenty-four

Tonyck motioned to their four temporary prisoners. "What are we doing with these guys?"

Each of them now had identical purple-blue lumps on their foreheads, evidence of G&T's exemplary shooting skills. They'd cooperated to a degree, but they were set to join Turner and Owen's team when they landed. Having six people on their backs was six more than Rayne wanted. She didn't want to gift them another four.

"Pablo, ask them if they have families." Rayne considered the best course of action while he conversed with the captives.

"They do not, Ms. Rayne. They've only recently moved to Tabatinga to find work."

"Okay." Rayne closed her eyes to think for a moment. *How much would it take?* "Tell them I'll give each of them ten thousand US dollars to get in this Jeep, head back to Tabatinga, pack up their lives, and move to another town." She looked at Pablo. "Is that enough?"

He chuckled. "That is a king's ransom to people like them, Ms. Rayne."

"And you don't think Turner will be paying them more than that?"

Pablo shook his head. "White businessmen have exploited local workers for centuries. It will be a miracle if Turner is paying them anything at all. I will give them your offer."

The resulting expressions on their faces told Rayne what she need to know. Forty thousand dollars bought these men a whole new life, free from slave labor under men like Turner. Disbelief, relief, and gratitude. The emotions were easy to identify.

"Are you sure about this, lady boss?" Ginn hitched forward from her seat on the roof of the Jeep. "How do you know they won't come back?"

Rayne turned and patted Ginn's thigh. "I am." She addressed Tonyck. "Give them some money now to get going, and I'll pay the rest when we return from this expedition. Look at them." The kneeling men were all but vibrating with the possibilities of the new life her money would mean for them. "They're desperate to escape this life. Would you get the rest of our packs, Tonyck? Ginn and Pablo can handle these guys." After Tonyck nodded, Rayne wandered over to Pablo and asked him to gather details so she could transfer their money to them. She explained her plan then left Pablo and Ginn to execute it while she went to see how Chase was getting on with the origin tree.

Chase was on her knees alternating between quick glances at the map and longer inspections of the hole in the tree where the map had been removed. Effi stood over her with her hands on Chase's shoulders. Rayne bit back the desire to use a rubber bullet on her. There was nothing in Effi's motivations to worry about. Tonyck seemed to be the focus of her intimate intentions. And the attraction between Rayne and Chase was obvious to everyone. Still, Effi was touching Chase, and Rayne didn't like it.

"Are we ready to go?" Rayne knelt beside Chase. She looked up and nodded, the delight of discovery obvious.

"We're heading west until we come across another lone lupuna tree in the midst of a whole load of aguaje palm trees and scarlet macaws." Chase pointed to a series of symbols in the first circle on the map and tapped three. "These means red, yellow, and blue, like the colors of the macaw. They nest in the holes of trees, and this collection of symbols indicates there's a particular place where they congregate in their thousands instead of the usual small family group or pairs."

"And we're hoping that hasn't changed in nearly one thousand years?" Rayne couldn't keep the mild disbelief out of her words.

"People have been farming in the Amazon for nearly ten thousand years, and we're talking about areas of forestation that remain untouched by the industrial revolution. It won't have changed because people haven't been anywhere near it."

Chase's excitement made Rayne smile and reminded her again how much she enjoyed working with her. She'd missed out on so many joint adventures through her own greed and blind ambition. When they managed to get out of this, preferably unscathed, she hoped they'd be able to work together on future projects…if they could agree on what to do when they found *this* prize.

Chase jumped up and pulled Rayne with her. "Plus, I think the next tree will be scarred in much the same way as this one was."

Rayne didn't let go of Chase's hands and was pleased to see Chase's sudden movement had dislodged Effi's grip on her shoulders. "You think there might be another map?"

Chase wrinkled her nose. "I don't think so." She waved the map in her hand before rolling it up. "After we've been to all the trees, this map should lead us to a cave if I've read it correctly. But there could be something else in the tree that might help us gain access to the treasure...not keys as such, obviously, but you never know."

Rayne smiled widely at Chase's rapid-fire way of delivering information. She always spoke at three times her regular speed when she was mid-discovery, like her mouth had to keep up with how fast her brain was processing the puzzle pieces. "Enjoying yourself?" Somehow Chase's unbounded pleasure made the expedition even more fun and pushed away the imminent threat of Turner and his dog, Owen.

Chase pulled Rayne close. "I'm having the time of my life."

Rayne waited. Would it come, even with Effi as an audience? Chase had never been a public display of affection person, not that Rayne had seen her with that many women. Chase didn't seem interested enough to pursue a medium-term relationship, let alone a long-term one.

Chase moved an escapee hair from Rayne's face and gently pushed it around her ear. She wrapped her hand around Rayne's neck, her thumb rested on Rayne's cheek, and Chase gazed into her eyes. For the first time, Rayne relaxed at being looked *into*, not looked *at*. Chase didn't make her feel like a sex object, a conquest, or an ambition. When Chase looked into her eyes, Rayne's heart wavered at the possibilities of being loved simply for who she was, not what she could offer someone, not what she could do for them or their reputation, and not for what she could buy them

Chase's lips were warm on her own, and Rayne closed her eyes. She couldn't let Chase see what this kiss was doing to her, what it might mean...not yet. Chase was gone too soon. Rayne opened her eyes to a smile she wanted to keep on seeing.

"Let's go find the Golden Trinity." Chase traced her fingers over Rayne's mouth as she withdrew her hand.

Effi coughed and pointed into the rain forest to the left of where they'd come from. "That's west." She smirked and fanned herself with a free hand. "Hot. Very hot."

And all for me.

Chase picked up her packs and slung them over and across her body, and Rayne lost herself for a moment imagining finally being able to see Chase fully naked, being able to touch her super hard body. Rayne let out a theatrical sigh. She had to wait a little while longer, and that was okay. They'd started this journey with Chase a begrudging traveler, still burning hot and angry at Rayne's treatment of her. This was definitely movement in the right direction.

Tonyck emerged from the trees with half of the rest of their gear and dumped it on the ground at Rayne's feet. "One more trip should do it. Care to help?"

The question was directed at Effi, who grinned and immediately followed Tonyck back into the forest. Rayne looked over in the direction of the Jeep to see the four men climbing in to leave. They gunned the vehicle into the distance, dark dust spiraling toward the sky. Ginn and Pablo retrieved the loggers' rifles and rejoined Rayne and Chase as Tonyck and Effi brought down the last of their luggage.

"Anyone want one of these…in case things get a little rough?" Ginn asked, offering the rifles she had stacked across her arms.

Rayne shook her head. "I'm happy with what I have."

"I will take one." Pablo lifted one from Ginn's arms. "I will not shoot a man, but I can shoot the ground just fine."

Ginn laughed. "Sometimes that can be all you need, Pablo."

"For me too." Effi raised her hand and Ginn passed her one.

"I'll take one." Chase stepped up and grabbed a rifle. "Is there any extra ammunition?"

"Unfortunately not. Whatever's in the clip is all you have, so no practice rounds," Tonyck said. "You have shot something like this, haven't you? All of you?"

Chase nodded, but Pablo and Effi said they hadn't. Ginn ran them through a quick guide to the rifles, paying plenty of attention to the safety catch. She took the clip from the unused one before throwing it as far as she could into the forest.

Rayne checked the time. Almost a half hour had passed since they'd been told that Turner might only be a few hours away. "We need to move."

"Sure thing, lady boss. Which direction, Stinse?" Tonyck asked.

Rayne saw the briefest flicker of a smile before Chase responded with their heading. It was good Tonyck had done as Rayne had asked and eased off Chase. They could learn a lot from each other if they were willing to park their stubbornness long enough.

Rayne followed Effi as she and Tonyck led the way. She glanced back at the origin tree one last time. Majestic though it was, it now looked out of place, lonely even. Having served its purpose, would it now die? Rayne shook off the thought of death. With Turner and Owen so close, she didn't have the time to entertain such morbid musings. And besides, the not-yet-written history books were calling her name.

Chapter Twenty-five

Chase leaned back and looked up. From this angle, this close to the tree, she couldn't see a single speck of sky. The trunk of the tree stretched up into the heavens before fanning out a protective umbrella of branches and leaves into the emergent layer of the rain forest. Almost reverently, Chase pressed her palm to the smooth bark then crouched to her knees, never losing contact with the tree until her hand touched the large circle of calloused wood she was looking for.

"This is it, Rayne. This is the one." Chase reached for Rayne without turning and didn't have to wait long to feel her warmth. Chase pulled her down to join her at the base of the gigantic tree.

Rayne placed her free hand on the scarred trunk. "You can almost hear the heartbeat of history."

Chase glanced at Rayne. "You can be pretty poetic sometimes."

Rayne swatted the peak of Chase's cap. "Shut up." She tapped her knuckles on the bark. "It's going to take a while to get through that."

Chase nodded. "Might be a good idea to send your tank twins backward. They could walk off some other tracks and maybe slow Turner down."

"Any tracker with half a mind for the job wouldn't be fooled for long with their trails. They'll know they weren't loaded down with enough weight and packs." Rayne beckoned Tonyck over anyway.

"What do you need, lady boss?"

"Chase needs some time to get into the tree." Rayne stood and leaned against it. "We're thinking you and Ginn could track back and lay some alternate tracks to put the dogs off the scent. What do you think?"

"I'll take Effi. Ginn can stand guard and patrol the perimeter. We're not leaving you alone."

Chase focused on getting the right tools from her pack and didn't answer to say that wouldn't be the case. Chase had a rifle, and she'd use it if she had to—not to kill, obviously—but she'd been a damn good shot on the range against paper targets. She could easily wing them if necessary.

Put that on top of the fact that Rayne was well enough equipped to look after herself and Tonyck really had very little to worry about.

"I'm not alone." Rayne placed her hand on Chase's shoulder and squeezed. "I've got Chase."

Tonyck laughed. "Your little weekend warrior? I guess you're right." Chase didn't look up at Tonyck's half-compliment but quietly appreciated it. They'd reached an understanding without really having to talk to each other, a perfect scenario for Chase, and Tonyck now seemed to accept Chase's presence far more than she had originally. Chase's initial suspicion that Tonyck had a thing for Rayne had been unfounded. She'd concluded that beyond Tonyck's professional responsibility for Rayne, a deeper family-like connection had been established. Rayne seemed as close as she'd let herself be to the tank twins, but Chase wondered how Rayne felt about it; suffocated, probably. Rayne's parents had raised her to ensure she never needed anybody or at least never to admit to it.

"How long do you think you'll need, Stinse?"

That was the second time Tonyck had shortened her name, another subtle indication of her tacit acceptance of Chase's value to the expedition. This time, Chase looked up before standing and stretching out her legs. "The scarring was quite deep on the origin tree. I expect they were all cut around the same time so they should be similarly sized. An hour or so should do it." She pointed to the reciprocating saw, chisel, and hammer she'd gotten from her pack. "We should have another two of these holes to cut out so I've got to conserve the battery."

Tonyck raised her eyebrow and looked unconvinced. "You'd better get to it. I'm betting that'll take closer to two hours."

Rayne's expression turned serious. "We don't have two hours."

Tonyck saluted and began to walk away. "I hear you, lady boss. I'll let Ginn and Effi know what's happening, and I'll position Pablo on lookout up a tree somewhere."

Rayne turned to Chase after Tonyck left. "I can't wait to see what's inside here."

"We'd better hope this lupuna doesn't contain a spirit. It might not take kindly to me slicing it open."

"So long as you don't pee on the tree, we should be okay."

Chase had come across a folktale of a woman falling ill after peeing on a spirited lupuna tree. Rayne had obviously read the same thing. "I'm jumping straight to the point where I slice it open, although I feel like that should offend the spirit more than a little urine."

Rayne smiled and motioned to Chase's tools. "You should get on." Her eyes darkened slightly. "We don't have a lot of time."

Chase nodded and returned to her position at the footings of the tree. Turner didn't have to dig around for clues or try to translate the map. All he needed to do was find and stay on their trail. Chase hoped Tonyck and Effi could at least delay their progress with some false tracks. They'd been happy to see few signs of any tribes other than a few crossed branches that acted as a warning not to venture farther into their forest. Unfortunately, Chase knew that a few twigs wouldn't stop Turner and Owen.

Chase used the chisel to edge out the vaguely circular chunk of wood she'd carved around. She'd been careful to keep checking when the depth of her incision hit space. The map gave no clues as to what was contained in this tree so Chase had used the electric saw sparingly to limit the possibility of slicing through anything secreted inside.

She eased it out as if she were opening the most eagerly anticipated Christmas gift ever. Rayne knelt by her side and put her hand on Chase's thigh. Her touch felt even hotter than usual. She blinked away the physical distraction and placed the wood on the ground before focusing her flashlight on the newly exposed hole.

"What is it?"

Chase smiled at the impatience in Rayne's voice. She'd gotten used to being first to everything. This was a little payback for the last couple of finds Rayne had beaten her to. "Wait." Chase reached in and carefully grasped the object, unsure of its fragility. She dropped the flashlight to the ground and used her free hand to close around the relatively solid shape.

"What does it feel like?" Rayne tapped Chase on the back.

Chase shrugged her off. "I've got to be careful with it. Relax." If it wasn't for the knowledge that Turner was bearing down on them, Chase would've drawn the process out. But they didn't have time for games. She pulled the box out and placed it on top of a small waterproof bag she'd laid out. Chase unclipped her utility knife from her belt and used the blade to scrape away the sap seal. "Looks like they used latex sap to stick the two halves together." She slipped the knife end into a small hole she found and gently pried the halves apart. Inside was a small and strangely-shaped carved piece of mahogany wood.

Rayne knelt beside Chase. "You did say it could be a key of sorts. Maybe it's shaped to fit in something?"

Chase nodded. "There doesn't appear to be any distinctive markings, though the wood itself is beautiful." She took some time to thoroughly check the box over. "Look at this. It matches." Chase lay one half of the box on the laminated map copy and tapped a series of symbols on the first circle of them.

"It's definitely the right piece then." Rayne took a few photos, first with Chase's camera and then with her own. She handed Chase a marker. "You'd better label this as number one. If there *are* any more of them, it could be that the order might matter when we get to the cave."

Chase took the pen, numbered the bag, and placed their find inside. "Time to roll." She checked her watch. "That took just under an hour. Tonyck and Effi should be back any minute."

Rayne got to her feet. "I'll see where they are."

Chase started to gather her tools while Rayne wandered off to call for Tonyck on the radio and wave for Ginn and Pablo to rejoin them.

Pack up complete, she hitched her bags up onto her back and looked over to Rayne. Ginn and Pablo were with her, but there was clearly something wrong.

"What's the problem?" Chase asked as she approached.

"We can't get hold of Tonyck or Effi," Rayne said.

Chase glanced at Ginn and back to Rayne. "Maybe the radios are out of range?" It was a long shot considering they'd been able to keep in touch when the tribe had taken her and Rayne away for the night.

Rayne shook her head. "Tonyck had one of the sat phones. She's not answering that either."

The unspoken explanation hung heavy in the space between them all. Pablo scratched at the scar on his chest, making it clear what he thought had become of them both.

"What do you want to do?" Chase addressed Ginn. Tonyck was *her* sister. It had to be her call. She had to be the one to decide a plan of action regardless of her employment status with Rayne. Ginn didn't respond immediately, and her conflict was clear.

"I…I don't know." Ginn looked at Rayne then in the direction Tonyck and Effi had gone just over an hour ago.

"You have to go after them, Ginn." Chase adjusted the rifle strap across her chest, reminding herself that she had the means to protect the rest of their diminishing team.

Rayne nodded and put her hand on Ginn's shoulder. "Chase is right. You've got no real choice, G. You need to go after your sister."

Ginn shook her head, then nodded, then shook it again before rubbing both hands over her head as if she were trying to scrub the situation from her mind.

"I can't let you go ahead on your own. Tonyck would…" Ginn dropped her eyes to the ground and kicked at the vegetation beneath her feet.

"Tonyck's not here to make a decision, Ginn." Chase couldn't be sure she'd leave Rayne if she were in Ginn's position either. "It's an almost impossible choice, we know that. But you're not leaving Rayne alone, and Pablo and I are armed." Though neither of them had any inclination to shoot anyone. Chase pushed that challenge to the back of her mind for now. She'd really hoped that level of violence wouldn't come to pass. But with Tonyck missing, Chase couldn't escape the inevitability that it already had. "We'll take care of Rayne. Go get your sister and Effi and come back to us." Chase punched Ginn's upper arm. "We finish this together."

Ginn nodded, more convincingly this time. "You've got this," she said and looked directly, and only, at Chase. It was clear she wasn't entrusting Pablo to keep Rayne safe. Ginn loaded up her packs then pointed to the original map. "We'll follow your trail. Move as fast as you can."

"We'll be so fast we'll be at the cave before you catch up." Chase didn't feel the emotion she tried to portray in an accompanying smile.

"Don't go in without us," Ginn said then turned and headed back toward their original trail without looking back.

There were a few moments of respectful silence before Chase tapped the map box with her foot. "Do you want to take first shift on this?" she asked Pablo.

"Absolutely. Which way are we heading?"

"White means north, Pablo, until we find the next tree." *Surrounded by a moat that may or may not still be writhing with anacondas…*

CHAPTER TWENTY-SIX

CHASE WOKE FROM a deep sleep with the feeling she was being watched. She sat up and looked around but could see only Pablo, lit by a neon glow stick, perched on guard just as he had been when she reluctantly fell to sleep. Rayne was still lost to the sandman, and Chase enjoyed another few moments watching her, so peaceful and relaxed. She wondered if she'd get the chance to wake up next to Rayne in normal circumstances or if this adventure would end and sweep away all of their heightened feelings, leaving them both alone again and both unwilling to cross the bridge between them.

Chase rubbed her eyes and withdrew from her sleeping bag. There were more pressing issues to concern herself with right now. Like what the hell had happened to Tonyck and Effi? And had the same fate befallen Ginn? The team had been halved in one easy step, and with no idea how close Turner might be, the rest of them were forced to press on, taking a three-hour sleep burst before getting back on the trail.

Chase checked her watch. She'd only been asleep thirty minutes after taking the first hour on stag. She peered into the darkness, unable to lose the feeling of being observed from a distance. She pulled on her boots, grabbed her machete, and ventured slowly toward the inner forest.

"Thank you for the warning."

Chase spun around at the sound of a partially familiar voice. The three women she'd spoken to when she and Rayne had been taken from the FUNAI camp stood before her.

"What the hell?" she said in English and lowered her machete. "Why are you here? How are you here?" Chase asked in Tupi.

"To thank you. You were right. These men are…a different beast from those who have come before them," the central one said.

"You've seen them? Are they near here?" Chase took a breath and quelled the threat of rising panic. She didn't have the time or the capacity for it, but if these old women could find them so easily, Turner must be close.

"The rain forest sees and hears everything. But no. They are at least a day without rest behind you…" She reached out and rested her hand on Chase's head as she had done before. "They have prisoners, and those prisoners are doing their best to slow them down."

Chase didn't move away from the old woman's touch, not wanting to offend her. "Tonyck and Effi? What about Ginn? Never mind." Chase knew the women couldn't know their team, but at least she now knew they were alive. "How do you know this?"

"Our communities have disappeared into the farther reaches of our home where the white men will not follow, but we are still watching them."

"Have you seen a lone traveler between our two groups?" Chase didn't know how Ginn would have reacted to seeing her sister captured by Turner. Had she tried to rescue her and failed?

The old woman shook her head. "She is no longer alone. We have heard there was a small battle. She was hurt, but she is alive." She increased the pressure on Chase's head. "You must not allow them to get to the Golden Trinity. Their disappointment will lead to destruction."

Disappointment? The Golden Trinity promised to be the largest treasure haul in history. How on earth could Turner be disappointed? "We're trying to get there as fast as we can, I promise you that." Chase could neither promise nor guarantee what the old woman asked for. She didn't make promises she couldn't keep.

"Protect the Golden Trinity. It is no longer safe." The old woman let go of Chase's head and began to step back, engulfed in the blackness of the forest.

"Wait. Is that all you can tell me?" Chase slammed her palm on the tree closest to her. "Why can't you just lead us there and save us the trouble?" She shone her flashlight after the women, but they were gone.

"Who are you talking to?"

"Fuck," Chase said when Rayne startled her. "Does anyone else want to stealthily appear from the shadows?"

"What are you talking about?" Rayne caught hold of Chase's wrist. "Are you sleepwalking?"

Chase allowed Rayne to pull her closer. "No. I'm wide-awake, but it did feel like I might've been dreaming." Chase slipped her arms around Rayne's waist and kissed her forehead. "Because I couldn't possibly have had a full conversation with that old woman from the Indian tribe, could I? Especially in the dead of night in the middle of a jungle."

Rayne placed her palm on Chase's chest. "Your heart's pounding out of your ribs, Chase."

Chase's heart *was* banging hard, but it wasn't in response to what may or may not have been another jungle hallucination. Rayne's hand on her skin felt like it might sear into Chase's body and wrap around her heart. In the dying moonlight, Rayne looked almost ethereal, achingly beautiful. Rayne was always stunning to look at from a visually shallow point of view, but now, Chase could see so much inner beauty within Rayne that she'd never been able to see before, beauty that Rayne had never allowed her to see.

Chase kissed her and guided her gently to rest against a tree. Real or not, the old woman voiced Chase's fears that Turner probably wouldn't think twice about ending them once he had what he sought.

At some point their meeting was inevitable, and there was no way to predict how that scenario played out. Chase didn't want her life to end. She had no intention of giving in to Turner or Owen. But if the worst did happen…if they were captured and killed, Chase couldn't die having never truly *known* Rayne.

"Chase…" Rayne broke away and put her fingers to Chase's lips. "What are you doing?"

"What I've been wanting to do since we kissed at that hut." Chase pushed her body against Rayne's. "Will you let me?"

Rayne pushed back and grabbed Chase's ass. "I thought you'd never ask. Yes. Yes, goddammit."

Chase drew her hand through Rayne's hair before clasping the back of her neck to pull her in for another kiss. The fire they'd started a few short days ago spread from Chase's lips to her toes. All the longing, the uncertainty, the desire, and the wishing that Rayne could be the woman Chase needed, smashed together inside of her and melded into something solid, something real.

Rayne's response was urgent and desperate. She moved her hands over Chase's body, grabbing, stroking, dragging her nails across Chase's skin. Trails of heat remained wherever Rayne's hands had passed, and Chase became so lost in the kiss that she was barely cognizant of where Rayne's hands were at all. So deep was their impact that it felt like they were everywhere at once.

Chase slipped her hand beneath Rayne's shirt and squeezed her breast. Rayne gasped and dug her nails into Chase's butt.

"Harder," Rayne whispered, her breath light against Chase's neck. Chase sighed hard into Rayne's hair and as she happily obliged, Rayne murmured louder. Chase unzipped and opened Rayne's pants with her other hand, before she pressed the heel of her hand against Rayne's clit. Chase absorbed Rayne's moan and slipped her finger between and inside the wet lips of Rayne's pussy. Rayne gripped the back of Chase's head with one hand and her ass in the other, silently encouraging her to drive deeper. Chase let her tongue explore Rayne's mouth, and Rayne sucked on it, before she broke away and put her mouth on Chase's neck. Rayne bit down hard, and it was all Chase could do to stop her own scream.

"More," Rayne whispered.

Chase did as requested, and her three fingers filled Rayne, making her whisper curses and threats into Chase's ear. Rayne hitched her leg onto a low hanging branch, and she opened up even more. Chase's final finger entered the warm inner folds of Rayne's sex, and Rayne bit her again, this time surely hard enough to draw blood.

"Fuck." Chase growled into Rayne's mouth. But it was everything Chase wanted, a woman who knew what she wanted, a woman who liked it hard and deep, rough and instinctive. Rayne. The woman Chase had fought her desire for since they'd first met.

"Please, Chase. Harder. Fuck me like—"

"It's the only time we'll ever get to do it?" Chase gave Rayne exactly what she wanted. She twisted her hand in Rayne's hair and thrust into her with everything she had, gave Rayne all that she was, physically. As Rayne rose and fell with the power of her orgasm and muffled her scream on Chase's chest, Chase knew this couldn't be the last time. She'd hesitated too long for this, and Rayne had waited too long to reveal her true self to Chase. The fates couldn't conspire to give Chase everything she'd ever wanted in a woman only to take it away after the briefest of tastes.

Chase withdrew her hand and clutched Rayne tight to her body, shuddering with her as she drifted down from the peaks of her pleasure. For some reason, Chase thought of the three old women who'd just visited her and their similarities to the Greek Fates. It didn't matter if it had really happened or if it was just in her head. They'd implored her to continue, to protect the Golden Trinity, to stop Turner. Chase closed her eyes. They were asking a lot of her. But right now, after what she and Rayne had just done, she kinda felt like she could do anything, felt invincible almost. *"This journey will lead to a personal discovery,"* the old woman had said when they first met. Was this what she meant? Chase looked into Rayne's eyes and searched for the bond she believed they'd just sealed, an unbreakable connection only realized through a strong and intimate meeting of bodies, minds, and souls. Did Rayne feel the same? Her soft expression implied that she did. And if that was the case, maybe together they were enough to do exactly what the indigenous Amazon people needed them to.

CHAPTER TWENTY-SEVEN

"YOU'RE THE ONE with the tools. *You* should do it." Rayne put her hands on her hips and looked at Chase, before she glanced over Chase's shoulder to see the water moving with a carpet of anacondas. There was no way she was going anywhere near them or the tree.

Chase raised her eyebrow and leaned against a tree after dropping her pack to the ground. "We need the second piece of the puzzle."

"Screw the second piece of the puzzle. It's probably only another chunk of wood anyway." Rayne twirled her buck knife in her hand. "Chop a tree down, and I'll whittle a replica right now."

Chase laughed. "The amazing Rayne Marcellus actually has a weakness." Chase clapped Pablo on the back. "How much are you going to pay us to keep quiet and not tell the world that you're scared of snakes?"

Rayne pointed her knife at Chase. "Oh, okay then, Mister. I suppose you're not afraid of anything?"

Chase's grin slowly disappeared and she looked contemplative. "I wouldn't say that."

"So…what *are* you afraid of?"

Chase pushed her ball cap back and wiped her forehead with her scarf. "Failure." She pushed off the tree and began to dig around in her pack.

"Drop the mic, why don't you?" Rayne gave Chase a playful shove, realizing that she'd never intended for Rayne to tackle the tree.

Chase looked up and smiled. "It's the truth."

"Nothing else?" Pablo asked. "Spiders? Heights? Small spaces?"

Chase shook her head. "Nope, no, and no. My mom was fearless, and she raised me to be the same." Chase put her tools into a smaller bag and strapped it across her chest. "Life's too short to waste it being scared of things. Face it all head-on and never back down. If I had a tag line, that'd be it."

Rayne smiled, but the mention of Chase's near-perfect childhood stirred the memories of her contrasting formative years and reminded her that Pablo wouldn't have the chance to raise his children at all. She glanced across at him and saw the faraway look in his eyes that probably meant his thinking aligned with hers. A change of subject was required. "This is a good opportunity for you to be all heroic then, isn't it?"

Rayne didn't miss the boon of satisfaction in Chase's expression. She loved being the hero, and strangely, Rayne was happy to let her. Rayne had spent a lifetime working hard to be taken seriously, to not be treated like the little woman unable to do the heavy lifting. And it wasn't just the typical men she had to convince. It was female colleagues and lovers too. Challenging deeply embedded, socially intrinsic misogyny was sometimes harder with the women who propagated it than the men who initiated it.

Chase did it differently. Chase clearly understood and acknowledged that Rayne was more than capable of doing whatever she needed to do. It was just that Chase seemed to *want* to look after Rayne. And last night, when Chase had taken her, possessed her, loved her, brief though it had been, she'd promised much and the encounter resonated deeply within Rayne in a place she'd believed she was built without.

All they had to do now was get out of this alive. *And* save Tonyck, Ginn, and Effi. *And* discover the Golden Trinity. *And* protect it from Turner and Owen.

One thing at a time. Rayne wasn't sure quite what to make of Chase's tale regarding the old women in the night, but she did hope what they'd supposedly said was true. If G&T were alive after Turner and Owen had found them, maybe Owen wasn't such a sadistic swine and wouldn't make good on his threat to kill Rayne if they crossed paths again.

"Will you suck the venom out of my body if I get bitten?"

Chase's question sounded far away and echoed in a distant part of Rayne's mind. She came back to the moment and placed her hand on Chase's chest. "Of course I will. But don't let that happen just because you think that's what it'll take to get my mouth on you." She leaned in closer and whispered, "I'll suck on you any time you want. All you have to do is ask nicely." Rayne smiled when Chase's eyes half-lidded and she let out a low and long sigh. Rayne liked the sound of that. She longed to hear what other sounds she could make Chase elicit. "Now go. Get the next chunk of ancient wood so we can stay ahead of Turner and his goons." Rayne smacked Chase on the ass after she'd grinned and turned to head toward the moat. "Do shout if you need any help."

Pablo shook his head. "Some might ask how you two could be so distracted with each other under the circumstances."

"But not you?"

"Not me, Ms. Rayne. When the threat of death looms large, the need to celebrate and cherish all that is good about living is strong."

Rayne patted Pablo on the back. "I do love your jungle philosophy, Pablo. You should have your own YouTube channel, like a Brazilian version of Jason Silva."

"I have no idea who that is, but you make it sound like a compliment. I will take it."

"It *is* a compliment." Rayne looked over to Chase, who was already halfway up a tree. She watched, engrossed, impressed, and turned on, as Chase snagged the lupuna tree branches with the climbing rope she'd fashioned into a lasso. She would've made a damn fine cowboy in the Wild West. Chase swung across the moat with consummate ease and landed on the strange man-built island that hosted only the lupuna tree. The moat of anacondas didn't seem in the least bit interested. Chase looked across and waved, obviously wanting to ensure her audience was being suitably attentive to her prowess. Rayne clapped and blew her a kiss, before she sat on a nearby branch to watch the rest of the show.

The shrill sound of her sat phone ringing took some time to place. They'd been just over a week without technology and unnatural noise, and Rayne hadn't missed it one iota. Only two people had this number though—Jenny back home and Tonyck.

Rayne pulled it from her pack and closed her eyes for a moment before checking the number displayed, not a hundred percent sure who she wanted it to be.

"Tonyck?"

"Your not-so-gentle giant is currently in no position to make a phone call, Ms. Marcellus."

"Turner."

"Second time lucky. Yes, it's me."

"What do you want?" Stupid question. He wanted the Golden Trinity. He wanted Chase to get him there.

"So many things, Rayne. Too many to go into over the phone… I'd much rather talk in person, if you're agreeable?"

Rayne jumped up and turned three hundred and sixty degrees to scope the trees. Were they already here? Were they watching them? "No. I'm not agreeable." She slumped back onto the thick branch. "I'd very much like never to see you again."

"Then perhaps you shouldn't have drugged my people, assaulted me, and stolen my property...You could simply have declined my very generous offer, Rayne, and I could have employed someone else. No harm. No bad feelings."

Rayne scoffed. "And let you ride through the Amazon in a tank, crushing everyone and everything in your way? I couldn't let that happen, Turner. Even I have to draw lines in the sand."

"You didn't draw a line. You kicked the sand in my face." Turner dropped his conversational tone. "You took what was mine, and I want it back. If you want what's yours back, you should wait for us to find you, and we can make a civilized trade."

"How do I know they're all still alive?" Rayne didn't want to entertain the notion that G&T or Effi had already been dispatched by Turner, or more likely, Owen. And she was sure he'd know they were currently more valuable to him alive than dead. But she wanted more proof that the whispered words from Chase's hallucination-cum-dream-cum-freaky vision.

"*You* don't trust *my* word? That's rich after what you did, Rayne. But I'll play along if only to fulfill the crazy idea you've gotten in your head about me being the bad guy and you being on the side of good...as if you ever could be."

Rayne heard muffled grunts and the flat, crunching thud of fists on bodies. She shut her eyes to stop the sounds from initiating an accompanying movie and reminded herself that G&T had both spent time in enemy hands. The twins were no strangers to brutality, but Effi was another matter entirely.

"Hey, lady boss," Tonyck said. "Don't worry about us. This is a picnic."

More noises that she didn't want to match with actions followed before Turner coughed into the phone.

"Satisfied?" He gave a short laugh. "Owen is having so much fun with your bodyguards that he's joked he won't need to be paid for this job."

Rayne swallowed against the sickening thought of what the twins and Effi were going through. She tried to focus on the bigger picture, the greater good. It was a noble sentiment until it was put to the test with the people she cared about. They were beginning to feel like a chosen family, and Rayne had allowed them to fall into the lap of a psychopath.

The distant sound of Chase's saw reminded her what they were doing here and that the twins knew when they were signing up that being in Rayne's employ could be dangerous. She looked up and saw Pablo had crouched in front of her. He said nothing, but the look in his eyes indicated he understood who she was conversing with. No doubt he was feeling the same guilt about bringing Effi to this shit show.

"Have I lost you?"

"I'm here," Rayne said. Her mind was flicking through the range of possible actions and plans. She wished Turner had called when Chase was down here.

"Do we have a deal?"

Turner's question implied they were talking about stocks and shares rather than people's lives. What was she supposed to do? Half the reason she and her team were here at all was to protect the indigenous tribes. They'd done that by warning them. The communities had communicated, and they were all safe and out of Turner's way. Rayne had wanted the glory, of course, of being the treasure hunter who led a team to discover the largest and most iconic treasure haul in history. That wasn't a consideration when it came to three innocent lives. But what had those old women meant when they'd told Chase that Turner's disappointment would lead to destruction? It didn't make sense. How was she supposed to make a decision based on nonsensical information?

She had to trust. For the first time in her life, she had to have faith in other people and rely on someone other than herself. *So how did that go exactly?*

"We're going to keep moving, Turner." Rayne ignored Pablo's quizzical expression. "The map is leading us to other trees, and we're collecting artifacts that may or may not help when we get to the Golden Trinity. I'm not a patient woman, and I have no intention of sitting around in this humid hellhole that time forgot, waiting for you." She took a breath, waiting for more words to come out rather than thinking too hard about what to say. Everything sounded good thus far. "We'll press on, finding the trees, and heading inexorably toward the Golden Trinity. At some point, you'll find us because all *you're* having to do is follow our tracks. What we're doing will take more time. When we find the Trinity, we'll exchange the knowledge to access it for our friends." Rayne imagined power animals, peaceful brooks, anything to prevent the panic that was trying to bang down her calm visage and take over. "That's the deal, Turner."

"Mm. So you're proposing to do all the heavy lifting, and we can just walk in when it's all done?" Turner cleared his throat. "Owen will be disappointed, but I'll take the deal, Rayne. Don't try to fuck me again. I'm a forgiving man, but you've gone way beyond what I could possibly endure. Another transgression and I'd have no choice but to allow Owen to…do what Owen does best."

Rayne rubbed her hand over her face and tried to stop herself from thinking about that in graphic detail. "You need to keep your dog under control, Turner. I want my people healthy and unharmed."

Turner chuckled in a way that made Rayne want to rip out his throat.

"Your people? From what Owen tells me, you have no people. I'll see you very soon, Rayne."

Turner ended the call, and Rayne looked to Pablo for his reaction, choosing not to analyze Turner's "no people" comment until later. Later as in, never.

"'Humid hellhole that time forgot?' This is my home, Ms. Rayne."

Rayne smiled, relieved for a little levity but still tense and on edge. "Have I done the right thing, Pablo?" It seemed alien to ask for justification for her actions. She never had before.

Pablo patted Rayne on the knee softly. "When there are so many pieces on the board, the right play, the right thing, is different for each of them, Ms. Rayne. This is another impossible choice, just as it was for your Ginn." He shrugged and shook his head. "You have managed to keep the people you don't know safe, but they still need more from you. I do not understand what it is they mean by 'protecting' the Golden Trinity, and I do not know how you are supposed to achieve that *and* rescue our friends. But you are a formidable woman, Ms. Rayne." He motioned toward Chase. "And she is extraordinary. Together, you will fix this."

Rayne tilted her head back and looked toward the sky peeking through the canopy of trees. It seemed a richer shade of blue here, deeper than any sky she'd seen in the many other parts of the world she'd visited. She pondered Pablo's description of them both. She agreed with his assessment of Chase; she *was* extraordinary and could do anything she applied herself to. Maybe that would be enough, even in the face of Turner and his little band of merc men. She hoped Pablo was right. She couldn't foresee how this played out, how they were supposed to save everyone and get the treasure…the "disappointing" treasure. This was one of those situations she'd spent her whole life avoiding, one that couldn't be planned for or fully controlled. She had to trust the solution would present itself when they really needed it.

Rayne took a deep breath of the freshest air on earth and focused on Chase. She was still hard at work on discovering what secrets this lupuna tree had held in her belly for many hundreds of years. If Rayne *had* to rely on other people, Chase Stinsen would always be her first choice.

CHAPTER TWENTY-EIGHT

"I KNOW HUNTING treasure is supposed to be hard, but I think the Mayans took this particular one a little too seriously."

Chase grinned at Rayne's comment as she stepped to the edge of the ravine and looked down. Six hundred feet, rocks, and white water…and a lupuna tree halfway down the cliff face. Nothing like this had ever been found in the Amazon, and no satellite imagery had hinted that anything like this was possible. And yet, here it was, and here they were, facing the final challenge to get the third artifact before the map led them to the cave.

"I thought you said you didn't want it easy?"

Rayne poked Chase in the chest. "You misremember what I said. I asked you if *you* wanted it easy." Rayne crossed her arms and peered over the cliff top. "*I* like easy."

Chase shrugged. "Whatever you say. I still have to go down there and retrieve the final artifact." Chase dropped to her knees and began to pack the tools she needed into the smaller bag, as before. The snakes had been surprisingly easy, but this one would require even more concentration and the strength of Rayne and Pablo. Chase could definitely have used the tank twins right about now, but they were otherwise engaged as Turner's prisoners. Not for much longer, she hoped, but she and Rayne had yet to figure out how they were going to free them, get the treasure, beat Turner, avoid death, *and* make it home.

"And you think this one will be made of maize somehow?"

"Yeah, it makes sense." Chase tugged her pack closed and began to unravel the three-hundred-foot climbing rope. "The Mayans believed the gods had three attempts at making mankind—wood, clay—"

"And maize." Rayne picked up one end of the rope and looked around for a tree to secure it to.

"Exactly. The first tree yielded the chunk of wood, the gods' first material to fashion humans. The second tree contained the clay pot, their second material. Logically, this tree will give up something made of maize or corn." Chase joined Rayne in checking the trees closest to the cliff edge. They needed something strong and tall with not too thick a trunk to wrap the rope around. Unfortunately, those kinds of trees didn't seem to grow around here.

They'd brought three ropes with them, and if they could've connected them together, this wouldn't have been a problem since the taller trees were only fifty feet away. But the tank twins had been carrying the other two. With them gone, they only had one rope, and Chase knew it wasn't quite long enough to reach the tree. In the absence of a laser measure, there was only one way to find out.

"But the map doesn't give any clue as to how we'll need to use the three objects to access the cave or the Trinity?" Rayne hugged a tree to the left of the lupuna tree location then gave it a shake. "This one seems like the best of them."

Chase pushed at it and blew out a heavy breath when it moved easily. "I hope you two are feeling strong. I don't want to trust my life only to the steadiness of this tree."

Pablo flexed his skinny arm. "I am stronger than I look."

"I hope so," Chase muttered under her breath, "because your limbs look like dried twigs." She looked back at Rayne who was still waiting for an answer. "Sorry, no. The symbols on the map match the ones on the wood and clay, but I can't see anything else other than directions. I expect we'll have to figure it out when we get there. Like you said, they've not made it easy for us."

Chase's mind drifted to the old woman and what they'd said about protecting the Golden Trinity from Turner. "*Their disappointment will lead to destruction.*" Did they mean that if Turner didn't get what he wanted, if they somehow managed to stop him from getting to the treasure at all, that he'd go berserk and try to destroy...what? The tribes were safe and the treasure would be out of his reach. The rain forest? Even with the logging machines at his disposal, the authorities could stop him before he managed to do too much damage.

Rayne placed her hand on Chase's shoulder. "We could wait until Turner catches up. The rope isn't long enough, is it?"

Chase took up the other end of the rope Rayne was holding. "It'll be long enough." She avoided prolonged eye contact and began to wrap the rope around the tree and knot it. She didn't want to wait for help from

Turner and his men, and who knew what condition the tank twins would be in after a couple of days in Owen's company. She could do this. *They* could do this.

Chase stood, gathered the remaining rope, and casually dropped it over the edge of the cliff. She didn't want to look to see how short the rope was in relation to the tree just yet.

"You're not securing yourself to the other end?" Rayne didn't look impressed.

"Nope." Chase pulled the carabiner and brake bar from her pants pocket. "I'll use these to rappel down."

Rayne shook her head and began to pull the rope back up. "No. No, you damn well will not. There's no need to make this any more dangerous than it has to be."

Pablo smirked. "You should do as Ms. Rayne commands." He motioned toward the ravine. "An angry woman is more dangerous than any fall from a cliff."

Chase stuffed her hands in her pockets. "I'll be fine."

"Yes. Yes, you will be fine, because you're going to do it properly." Rayne held out the end of the rope when she'd finally pulled the length of it back to the top of the cliff.

Chase took it and fashioned a swami belt around her waist. Rayne was right of course, and Chase was begrudgingly glad for insistent intervention. She'd gotten carried away in a macho moment and suddenly the rope was over the cliff.

Rayne came closer and tugged at the knot, checking its tightness. "It's taken me a while to get back to you, I'm not losing you to an unnecessarily heroic stunt, do you hear me?"

Chase wrapped her hand around Rayne's neck and pulled her in. Her lips tasted salty but the sweetness of the kiss was succor for Chase's soul. It felt good to allow herself to be cared for in this way. "Okay. Whatever you say," Chase said. Rayne would know that was the closest she'd get to saying Rayne was right.

"That's right. Whatever *I* say." Rayne stepped away, before pulling some utility gloves from her pack and telling Pablo to get his.

Chase checked the knots around herself and the tree once more. She strapped her pack of tools tightly to her back, stood at the edge of the cliff, and put on her gloves. "Ready?"

Rayne took up the rope slack and wedged herself with her feet against the tree. Pablo picked up the rope behind Rayne and secured his feet against another tree.

"Ready."

Chase leaned backward into the arms of nothingness until she was at a ninety-degree angle, her feet flat against the rock. "Lower me down." *Nice and steady.*

Chase walked down the cliff with relatively large strides, and the end of the line came faster than she'd expected. She heard Rayne shout, "That's all there is," from above. She looked to her right. The tree was ten feet away. She'd have to unravel the rope harness to gain an extra three feet. The side of the cliff was made up of the roots of the trees above ground and small rocky outcrops. Chase walked her feet down to get closer to the cliff face and fixed her toes onto a rock to hold her weight. She thumbed out the dirt around a root and gave it a pull.

It held firm. She looked at the remaining distance between herself and the first decent sized branch of the lupuna. She could do this. Chase began to untie the knot around her waist with one hand, holding tight to the exposed roots with her other hand. With the harness unraveled, Chase climbed down the extra few feet the rope allowed. She threaded the end of it through a root to keep it from swinging once she let it go.

Chase looked down at the raging water and jagged rocks beneath her. One wrong move, one weak root, and her life would be over in seconds. She straightened up, kiss-close to the cliff, and worked a second handhold. One hold at a time. She lifted her right boot to the next rock, felt for stability, and pulled herself along. Progress was slow, digging out each handhold tedious, but Chase resisted the temptation to rush and make a mistake.

Chase pushed off her right foot to reach for a rock handhold. The ground crumbled beneath the pressure, she lost her footing, and her right hand gripped fresh air. Her body swung out and away from the cliff, jarring her left shoulder as she held on with just her left hand. Plumes of rock dust invaded her eyes and mouth. The roaring of her blood rushing around her head was louder than the racing water beneath her.

"Shit." Chase steadied her body and caught hold of a jutting rock with her right hand and eased the pressure from her left shoulder. She found holds for her feet and stayed there, eyes closed, prone and spread-eagle for a few moments, steadying her breath and heart.

She opened her eyes and kissed the root her left hand was hooked into. "Thank you." Chase continued cautiously, triple-checking each foothold and handhold before relying on it fully and applying her body weight. Finally, the lupuna tree was within reach. Chase grabbed hold of a branch with her right hand. Content it was strong enough, she leaned across the cliff face and grasped it with her left hand. Her right foot followed onto a lower branch, and lastly her left foot. She traversed her way along the branches to the trunk and gave the tree a quick embrace. "And thank you."

Chase made her way down the trunk to its base and the strange piece of cliff it was stranded on. There was no way this tree was ever there accidentally. It had to have been deliberately planted years before the Mayans hid the secret path to the Golden Trinity. That fact alone destroyed current understanding that Mayans were barely in Brazil. Chase wondered if they were only here to keep their treasure safe, hundreds of miles away from rival tribes and eventually, the Spanish conquistadors.

Chase quickly located the scarred wood circle, prepared her tools, and began the task of retrieving the final puzzle piece needed to enter the cave of the Golden Trinity.

CHAPTER TWENTY-NINE

RAYNE LAY ON her belly with her head peeking over the edge of the cliff to watch Chase's progress. Her heart had jumped up from her chest and out of her throat to dive into the ravine when Chase had slipped. That was the only thing stopping her from screaming out, which was never helpful in any situation.

"It is a good thing her arms are strong, Ms. Rayne. That slip would have snapped my body from my shoulder." Pablo lay beside her, also looking down.

Rayne nodded, her voice still playing hide-and-seek. Fatigue had kicked in, and she'd almost fallen unconscious with exhaustion while Chase cut into the tree, but sheer bloody-mindedness kept her eyes open. She convinced her body that there was no way she could fall asleep right now.

"I've got it."

Chase called up from below, but her words were barely whispers on the wind. Rayne couldn't see what she held up from so far away, but as long as she had something, it had been worth the risk...or maybe not. Was anything worth the risk of losing Chase now that she finally had her?

A tug on the rope beneath her body alerted her to Chase's positioning. She looked down to see Chase had already secured a harness around her waist and was ready to begin what would be a steady and slow ascent to rejoin them. "She's ready to come up," Rayne said to Pablo, and they resumed their positions against their respective trees to take up the slack. Rayne tugged twice on the rope to indicate they were ready.

As the rope slackened, she and Pablo pulled it up, ensuring that if Chase were to lose her footing again, they'd hold the tension. The climb seemed to take hours, but in reality, was probably only sixty minutes or so. Every now and then Chase would call up to say she was okay, and each time, Rayne was glad to hear her voice sound louder and thus, closer to the top of the cliff.

Rayne heard a noise that sounded like Darth Vader on steroids and glanced behind her to its origin. "Oh, fuck!" An anaconda emerged from the water and dived toward her. Rayne jumped backward and released her grip on the rope. Pablo cursed and threw a rock at its head, and the snake turned on him, hissing and rising, ready to attack. It launched itself at Pablo, wrapped around his chest, and locked its jaw onto his face. He let go of the rope, and Rayne heard Chase's exclamation as the excess slack tumbled over the cliff. Rayne jumped to the right to avoid being caught by it and pulled over the edge.

"What the hell's happening?"

Relief flooded through Rayne as she heard Chase's voice so close, but she was unable to help her. The anaconda had slid around Pablo's chest, beginning to crush him. He clutched at it, but it wasn't giving him up easily. He screamed out as the snake continued to encircle his chest and neck, and there was easily another twenty feet of it not yet attached to him.

Rayne withdrew her machete and looked for a point of attack. If she sliced it too low down, it could loosen itself from Pablo and launch at her. She had no idea how agile they were, and given its size, it should be rather cumbersome. But its attack on Pablo had been impressively fast.

Come on, Rayne. She was wasting time. Pablo was losing consciousness.

"I'll grab its head." Chase rushed past Rayne. "You slice through its neck."

"Okay." Rayne raised her machete and slowly approached the snake while Chase came around the back of it. In milliseconds, Chase had grabbed both halves of the beast's open mouth.

"Now!"

Rayne brought her machete down on its neck, chopping halfway through it. The rest of its ridiculously long body writhed and thrashed, catching Rayne and sending her thudding to the ground.

"Babe, get up. Finish the job," Chase yelled, still hanging onto its head as it struggled.

Rayne jumped up and began to hack at the snake's neck. Its blood splattered all of them with the force she struck it with, and she continued until she'd finally chopped its head off. Chase pried its jaws from Pablo's face and neck and tossed it aside before beginning to loosen its considerable length from around his body. Pablo had passed out, and it was only now that Rayne saw that the snake had bitten into his cheek and neck. His blood soaked his tank top.

"Get the first aid kit." Chase removed her scarf, bundled it, and pressed it against Pablo's neck to stem the bleeding.

Rayne emptied her pack hurriedly all over the ground and plucked the kit from it. She turned just as Pablo opened his eyes.

"That was a…big snake…Ms. Rayne."

He held out his hands, and Rayne dropped to her knees in front of him and clasped her hands over his. "You saved my life," she whispered, then looked at Chase and the scarf she was holding to Pablo's neck. It was already crimson and sodden with Pablo's blood.

Chase took hold of one of Rayne's hands and held it to his neck. "Apply pressure."

Chase opened the kit and pulled out a chunk of gauze. She returned to Pablo and removed Rayne's hand, along with the scarf. Rayne gasped at the size and number of puncture wounds in his neck as Chase tried to stem the blood pulsing from all of the holes from the snake's teeth.

Pablo squeezed Rayne's hand. "Now we are even, Ms. Rayne…Now I go…to see my family."

"No." Rayne shook his hand. "Not yet. It's not your time."

Pablo smiled weakly, his face becoming paler by the second.

"It is…okay, Ms. Rayne. I can see my family."

He released her hand and reached out as if he were reaching for something or someone beyond Rayne. She looked at Chase. "Do something. Please." Rayne took another piece of gauze and held it on the many other teeth wounds on Pablo's check. As it soaked up his blood, she saw how badly his flesh was torn, and she could see his teeth through the gaping hole.

Chase shook her head slowly. "I'm so sorry, Rayne."

"No…No. Fix it, Chase. Fix him…You can do it. I know you can."

Rayne followed Chase's gaze to settle on Pablo. His eyes, usually so full of life and mischief, were vacant and glassy. Rayne's chest heaved, and she fell backward onto the giant length of the snake's body. "No…" Her scream eviscerated the silence of the jungle. She picked up her machete and chopped wildly all around her. Her blade sliced the snake's flesh and stuck inside it. She pulled the machete from it and continued, wanting the wet slapping noise to drown out the words in her head. But Rayne still heard them whispering, *It should have been you. It was your time.*

Chase's arms around Rayne stopped her manic hacking. Her grip was firm as she circled Rayne.

"Baby, stop," Chase whispered.

Rayne dropped her machete to the ground and her knees gave way. But Chase held on and didn't let go. As Rayne's breathless convulsions evolved into body-racking sobs, Chase's embrace held firm.

Rayne let herself go. All of the pain. All of the hurt. All of the regret. The consuming grief. The overwhelming feeling that she hadn't done enough. She released it all and knew, in that moment, Chase would catch her as she let herself fall, not just physically but emotionally.

"I've got you," Chase whispered and brushed her hair, wet with tears, gently from Rayne's face.

Rayne didn't hold back. Any time before this, she would have "pulled herself together" as constantly commanded to do by her parents every time she fell, physically or metaphorically. She didn't try to hold back her emotional response to the loss of Pablo, as strange as that was to do. She didn't hide the pain deep in the recesses of her heart and mind for fear of ridicule, of being seen as weak and vulnerable, easy prey. She made no attempt to withhold the tears, the physical proof of her grief, for the sake of appearances. She had nothing to prove to Chase. She released the screams, although their intensity and volume bounced painfully around her head.

"I've got you, baby."

Chase's repeated phrase settled in Rayne's conscious this time, and she realized, completely, that Chase was solid and true. Her support wasn't conditional or fickle. Her words weren't uttered just for something to say; they were honest and meaningful. As Rayne allowed Chase to guide her to the ground, her embrace never faltering, Rayne opened herself up to the possibilities of a life with Chase beyond this adventure. She glanced at Pablo and wished with all that she was that he *did* get to be with his family again. All Rayne wanted was to be here, in Chase's arms, feeling like she was cocooned in the safest place in the world.

CHAPTER THIRTY

RAYNE SORTED THROUGH Pablo's pack, taking what they might need from it. Somehow, it felt wrong, like they were stealing. Chase didn't want to be a part of it so she excused herself and began to wash out her scarf in the stream. As Pablo's blood colored the river before disappearing and becoming part of the murky brown water, Chase thought of the impermanence of life. They'd expected to finish this adventure together. The danger should only have been in the form of Turner and Owen. Pablo's life wasn't supposed to end that way. She shrugged and rubbed the material hard between her fists. Who decided how a life was supposed to end anyway? She glanced across at Rayne and shuddered. She couldn't lose her. She couldn't let anything happen to her. She had to stop Owen, no matter the cost.

Chase returned to Pablo's makeshift stretcher and tied off the last knot around to make sure the tarp was secure around his body. She sealed a small gap with yet another piece of duct tape to make sure nothing could get inside. Rayne had been almost hysterically insistent that they couldn't bury or leave Pablo's body there. Chase hadn't protested; taking him with them seemed like the only option and the decent thing to do. She hadn't known Pablo for that long, but she didn't want to think of him being eaten post-mortem by jaguars, snakes, and insects. Carrying him with them would slow them down considerably, but they were in no real hurry anyway. They had the three pieces the map had led them to, and the journey to the cave promised to be only a relatively short way from the third tree. Turner and Owen's imminent arrival was a double-edged sword. They'd get Effi and the tank twins back but would have to give up the Trinity…unless they could figure out a way to keep it from them and still rescue their trio. Maybe the old women had some magic up their sleeves they could share…

"Ready?" she asked

Rayne rose from her position on the ground. "Almost."

Chase smiled, but the atmosphere shrouded them both in unspoken sadness. Chase strapped the original map and its case to the stretcher she'd made slightly longer than Pablo's body to accommodate it. Now it seemed they were only transporting the artifact so that they could get it home. Thus far, it hadn't been needed. The laminated copy had gotten them where they needed to be and continued to do so now that they were on their way to the cave.

"This way?" Rayne pointed upstream.

Chase nodded. "We'll run parallel to it, but let's stay away from the edge." Chase had expected trouble with snakes at the second tree, not this one. Anaconda attacks on humans were rare. While it was unlikely to happen again, Chase didn't want to take any chances. She saw Rayne clench her jaw, but she didn't respond.

Rayne led the way, following Chase's directions, and other than those instructions, there was very little conversation. Rayne seemed particularly introspective, and Chase didn't quite know what to say. She'd never lost anyone close to her so she couldn't empathize with any authority. All of those hackneyed clichés about being in a better place and God having a plan had always seemed trite and lacked veracity. So Chase simply let Rayne be what she needed to be. Silent.

After a few miles, Chase needed to rest from pulling Pablo. He wasn't heavy, but negotiating the wooden stretcher over the jungle terrain was awkward and tiring.

Rayne settled on a rock and patted the space beside her. "Would you like some water?"

Chase licked her dry lips and realized she'd become a little hydrated. "Sure."

Rayne pulled a water bottle from her pack and offered it to Chase as she sat on the rock. "Bet you're wishing you'd stuck to your guns and not come with me…"

Chase turned to look at Rayne. She put the water bottle down and took Rayne's face in her hands. "No, babe. Not at all." She kissed Rayne's forehead. "I don't want to be anywhere else in the world." She kissed her nose. "I want to be right by your side." *Now and always?* Chase kissed Rayne, and she responded, pulling Chase closer. Chase ran her hands over Rayne's back and rested on her hips.

Rayne withdrew and looked at Chase, her expression serious. "This was supposed to be a lot easier than how it turned out."

Chase smiled and caressed Rayne's cheek. "It's not over yet."

Rayne puffed out her cheeks. "You think it can get worse?"

"God, I hope not." In all probability, it *was* going to get worse, but Rayne didn't need to hear that, not when her dead friend was wrapped up in a tarp a few feet away and her bodyguards were in the hands of a psychopath. Shit had definitely gone sideways. Chase had never envisaged it being just the two of them finding the Golden Trinity. Chase thought about the old women again. She didn't want to dismiss their utterings as crazy talk, but she was struggling to grasp how Turner would be disappointed by the Trinity…and how they were supposed to stop him, Owen, and their team of armed assholes.

Rayne put her finger beneath Chase's chin and lifted it up to face her. "Where's your head at?"

Chas took Rayne's finger and kissed it. "I'm thinking about the future… and where this adventure leaves us." It wasn't a complete lie. At the back of her mind, since they'd had sex in the middle of the night, their future— if they had one—had been a constant question.

Rayne withdrew her finger, picked up her water bottle, and gave it to Chase once more. "Where do you want it to leave us?"

"In a better place than we were before." Chase emptied half the bottle in a few swallows and passed it back to Rayne She'd finally let Rayne's betrayal go and it had liberated her, allowing her to move forward freely. "We should purify some more water while we've got it running past us so freely."

"Good idea." Rayne drank the rest of the bottle before retrieving the Guardian purifier from one of her packs.

She wandered over to the water's edge. The snake attack still fresh in her mind, Chase quickly joined her, rifle at the ready, safety off. They said nothing while Rayne dipped the pipe into the stream and pumped it into their bottles. When she was done, they retreated back to the rock and packed the bottles.

Chase laid her rifle on the ground and pulled Rayne into her arms. She sensed that she'd have to be the one to open up her heart. If she was waiting for Rayne to offer up her true feelings first, Chase would likely be disappointed. "Are you ready to find that better place?" She was all too aware that Rayne carried her history with her and let it inform her present and future in unhealthy ways. She didn't have to be a psychotherapist to know that. Unlimited, shallow dalliances with sexual partners; no close friends with whom she trusted her secrets and her fears; no emotional connections to speak of at all. Rayne had the tank twins and clearly their adoration, but they were on her payroll. It was only during this adventure that Rayne had appeared to begin exploring the possibilities of deeper relationships. Chase felt Rayne smile against her chest.

"You know, I pay damn good money to a Harvard-educated therapist. You shouldn't have to 'therapize' me too."

Chase laughed and held up her hands. "Busted..." She pulled Rayne back in. "Well? Are you?"

"I think so...I hope so. This has been a relatively short trip, but I've learned a lot about myself, about what I actually want from this life." She traced small circles on Chase's chest as she spoke. "About what I need."

Rayne looked up, and once again, Chase saw the vulnerable beautiful soul that Rayne really was, the person she'd hidden and kept protected from the world. She slipped her hand around the back of Rayne's neck and kissed her, hoping that everything she felt for Rayne could be conveyed between their lips.

"Aww, isn't that just such a pretty picture?"

Chase had never seen Turner or heard his voice, but she guessed it was him. They both turned to see a posse of people behind them. Chase glanced at her rifle and back up at the group. This wasn't a time for suicidal heroics. She didn't make a grab for it. "That was a helluva kiss not to hear all these people stomping through the jungle twenty feet behind us," Chase muttered to Rayne.

Rayne smiled then faced Turner. "I'd say it was lovely to see you again, but it isn't...so I won't."

Turner held his hands to his chest. "That hurts, Rayne. What have I ever done to you other than offer an extremely lucrative contract?"

As he spoke, Chase felt like a thousand leeches were crawling all over her body, and she shivered. Turner's creepiness reached her even though he stood twenty feet away. Chase took a moment to assess his group. She recognized the guy from the bar in Tabatinga and his three flunkies. Nose-ring woman was still sporting a fading black eye, which Chase found surprisingly satisfying. There was one other guy but no sign of the tank twins or their guide. All of Turner's people were armed with a machete, a gun, or both.

"Where are Ginn, Tonyck, and Effi?" Rayne asked.

Turner smirked. "Your bodyguards are with Owen, where they'll remain until you come through on your half of the deal. Effi is right here." He stepped sideways and she came into view. Chase could see she didn't seem to be restrained in any way.

Turner tilted his head in Chase's direction and laughed. "Looking for signs that Effi is my prisoner?"

He put his arm around her and pulled her close. She didn't resist. In fact, she put her arm around his waist.

"What the hell?" Rayne took a step forward.

"Effi works for me, Rayne. Not you. She *never* worked for you...or Pablo Araújo." Turner reached for the guy from the bar. "Speaking of him, Nicolai still wants his piece of whatever it was you paid him to get you upriver. Effi tells us he was with you and didn't stay with the boat she sabotaged, so where is he?"

Chase reeled from the revelation that Effi had played them *and* sabotaged the boat, forcing them into the jungle...clearly so she could lead Tonyck straight into an ambush and weaken their team. Rayne went to move forward. Chase felt her anger and stopped her from advancing. Turner needed them to lead him to the Trinity, but that might not keep him from hurting Rayne, given the opportunity.

Chase motioned to Pablo's body. "Anaconda attack."

Effi laughed, and Rayne struggled against Chase's grip on her wrist.

"You fucking bitch." Rayne stayed put, but she didn't hold back a verbal attack. "He was your friend."

Effi shook her head. "I don't have any friends. But if I did, I wouldn't have chosen some skinny runt widow with a bad habit of dishing out pseudo-philosophical bullshit."

Chase liked Pablo's jungle philosophy. Now she felt the need to slap Effi down. She resisted, hoping she'd get a chance to make her pay for it later.

Rayne stopped straining against Chase and squeezed her hand. "She doesn't get away with that," Rayne whispered quietly enough so that only Chase heard.

"No. She definitely doesn't."

Turner motioned to Pablo's body. "You're carrying him with you so that you can give him a proper burial?" Rayne nodded. "At least you have some honor…"

"You're holding on to the fact that Rayne stole the map from you like you're some paragon of propriety. But you're not." Chase waved her hand at Turner dismissively. "You're a thief, a criminal." Chase recalled the article she'd read about families of orangutans being slaughtered by illegal loggers. "And probably a murderer. Where do you get off acting high and mighty and beyond reproach?"

Turner chuckled and stepped closer to them, and the whole group followed as one. "We had a compact, a gentleman's agreement. There is supposed to be honor among thieves. If we don't have that, then we *are* just unruly and lawless thugs." He raised an eyebrow, removed his hat, swept his hand through his hair, and replaced it carefully, just so. "I wouldn't expect you to understand, Ms. Stinsen. You're not like us. You don't live and move in our world." He shook his head and smirked as he moved forward to within spitting distance of them. "You shouldn't really be here, but Rayne isn't all she professes to be, is she? She *needed* you because *she* wasn't good enough. *She* couldn't do the job I was paying her to do."

Rayne slapped him, hard, before Chase could react and stop her. Turner held his jaw before he smiled and took a step back.

"Hit a nerve, did I?"

"I said I'd get the job done. I never said anything about the team I'd use."

Turner *had* triggered Rayne, though he probably had no idea why his words struck so deeply. Chase knew the accusation of not being good enough, simply not being *enough* was a scar she carried from childhood. "I want to be here," Chase said. "And Rayne is *nothing* like you."

Turner shrugged. "Whatever. Enough of this chitchat. *You* have to lead me to what's rightfully mine." He poked Chase in the chest then turned to his heavies and motioned to Rayne. "Tie this one up. She's like a wild animal."

Chase had pushed down the desire to break Turner's finger when he prodded her in the chest. She'd always hated that for reasons she'd never pinned down. His sense of entitlement to the treasure irritated her even more.

Nicolai stepped forward. "That would be my pleasure," he said, touching his nose.

"Still sore from getting a beatdown from a girl?" Rayne asked.

He curled his upper lip. "When Mr. Turner is finished with you, we will have a rematch."

He pulled Rayne's arms behind her and secured her wrists with paracord. He held on to the considerable length remaining and tugged it. "On a leash, just like a bitch should be."

Rayne jerked forward, but he jumped out of the way and laughed.

"I'm assuming you're able to navigate *and* convey your friend's body?" Turner asked.

"Yeah, I can." Chase felt a certain responsibility to ensure Pablo's corpse was respectfully treated. She had no intention of letting anyone else pull the stretcher. They wouldn't be as careful as she'd been so far.

"Tia, José. Remove their machetes and pick up the extra packs." He pointed to the original map on Pablo's stretcher. "It's good that you've brought my map. I would've hated to have to send Owen to pick it up from San Fran after this little adventure is over…Let's go."

Nicolai tugged Rayne away after her machete had been taken. Chase clenched and unclenched her fists before giving up her own machete. She gathered her packs and moved to Pablo's stretcher. She picked up the rope and began to pull. The cave was another half day's trek at the pace she could manage. Maybe that'd give her the time to figure out their ingenious escape plan…

CHAPTER THIRTY-ONE

EVERY BUG IN the Amazon had received the memo that Rayne was unable to defend herself against them. With her hands tied behind her back, her only option was to employ a Parkinson's disease-like tic to keep them from feasting on her flesh. Every hour or so, Chase had stopped moving forward to insist on giving Rayne water. Turner had allowed it, and she was grateful he wasn't being a complete asshole. In between those small and welcome exchanges with Chase, Rayne had retreated internally in an effort not to focus on the insects, or the humidity, or the distinct discomfort from her boots. Instead she used the time to drift off and think about all the things she wanted to do to and with Chase if they got out of this in one piece. Now, she'd decided to continue an imaginary conversation with Chase that picked up where Turner had interrupted them.

"I need you, Chase. It feels like I might always have needed you, but I was too much of a coward to entertain that idea, never mind embrace it. Needing someone feels like a weakness, like not being a whole person without you is a failure…I can't be a failure, Chase. But I can't be without you."

Rayne sighed. She should have said all that and more after the third tree. They'd had the time to talk, but Pablo's death had hit hard. Instead of talking about it, which might easily have led to talking about where she and Chase might lead, Rayne held her own internal monologue. And in her head, it was simple and so easy to talk about her feelings and emotions, her fears and her hopes, even her dreams. None of which she'd ever shared with anyone other than her therapist. If she were being totally honest with herself, she'd never completely cooperated with her therapist either. Chase made her feel safe in ways she never knew existed and made sharing her truth a real probability, not just a vague possibility.

Rayne brought herself back to reality and looked at Chase from behind. Her shirt was drenched in sweat and stuck to her body. Rayne could admire the bunching and relaxing of her back muscles visible around her pack as she pulled the stretcher. *Pablo.* Rayne closed her eyes briefly. It was small comfort that he might have rejoined his family and left no one else behind to increase Rayne's guilt.

"This should be it." Chase stopped, dropped the stretcher rope, and tossed her packs to the ground.

They'd come to a small clearing before the rise of what Rayne could only describe as a cliff face. Lupuna trees, sixty feet tall, patrolled its base and reached up to the sky, almost in prayer. Chase unrolled the map copy and studied it for a long moment before she rolled it back up and stuffed it in the leg pocket of her cargo pants. She approached the trees, and Turner followed. Nicolai tugged on Rayne's rope, and she briefly wondered how easy it might be to flip the slack around his throat and pull until he fell unconscious.

"I need Rayne. I can't do this without her." Chase stuffed her hands in her pockets as if to emphasize she was done unless she got what she wanted.

Turner nodded to his goons, and they trained their rifles on Chase. "Do not try to fuck me…Let her go."

Nicolai roughly untied her before shoving her forward. Rayne rubbed her wrists as she strode across the clearing to join Chase. "You need me?" she asked, unconvinced.

Chase nodded. "I do. You're an expert with the Mayan supernatural world. I'm not. And I need your analytical brain to work this riddle out." She pulled out the map, knelt down, and opened it across the ground. Rayne joined her. "The map says there are stone plaques all around here carved with the heads of gods and *ways*—"

"Spirit companions."

"Great." Chase pointed at a section on the map. "But this doesn't tell us which ones to follow. They were color coded to give directions to the next one."

"The color couldn't possibly survive in the elements for seven hundred years, surely?" Rayne looked over Chase's shoulder to see Turner had moved close enough so that he could hear everything they were saying.

"Please continue, Rayne. Don't mind me. I'm just keeping eyes and ears on my investment," Turner said. "Once bitten, etcetera."

Rayne turned her attention back to Chase and the map. They'd still not figured out how to get out of this mess, other than relying on Turner's good will, and she trusted his word about as far as she might be able to spit him. If they couldn't get away from him, how were they supposed to come up with a plan? Added to that, they had no idea where Owen was holding G&T, though she suspected they wouldn't be too far away.

"Rayne?"

"Sorry. You were saying that the stones might be colored…"

"Yeah, but we've got to figure out which ones to follow: the *ways* or the gods. Thoughts?" Chase sat back on her butt, clearly waiting for Rayne's input.

"The obvious answer would be to follow the stones of the gods. The Mayans were deeply religious and modeled their behavior to suit a huge pantheon of deities. It's said that the Golden Trinity was their finest tribute to the gods—"

"But I've also read that it was the gods who gave the Mayans this treasure in the first place."

"But if the treasure is physical, if it's gold and silver, that can't be true, can it?" Rayne asked. "No gods really give anything to their followers, do they?"

Chase shrugged. "As an agnostic, I'd tend to agree, but what if—"

"If their gods weren't gods at all. What if they were aliens?"

Turner laughed. "What are you talking about? Aliens? You can't be serious?"

Rayne waved him away. "You need to let us work. That means thinking about the impossibilities as possibilities."

He shook his head then shrugged. "I guess you're the experts. But we're not looking for crystal skulls, ladies…and I use the term loosely."

Chase waved him silent. "Please. Be quiet."

He raised his hands and sat down. "Fine. Just be quick about it. It's nearly nightfall."

Turner told Nicolai and his gang to set up camp in the trees close by. Rich positioned his rifle across his chest, finger poised on the trigger. Rayne briefly closed her eyes and tried to ignore all of the external distraction. When she opened them, Chase was looking at her and smiling. "What?"

"This is most likely the worst situation we've ever been in, together or apart, but it's still fantastic to be working like this with you again."

Rayne tapped her fingernail to the map. "Then let's get it figured out so we can move on to the next big adventure." Rayne prayed there was conviction in her voice, because there was none in her heart.

Chase grinned and ran her hand over Rayne's cheek. "Okay, baby."

Rayne liked the way that sounded almost as much as the way it made her feel. "So I was saying that the obvious choice would be to follow the gods' stones, as if the Mayans left the trail to be followed *by* their gods."

Chase nodded. "That makes perfect sense. The Golden Trinity is the biggest collection of treasure *un*known to humankind. It was their greatest offering. But…"

"What if the map is for mortals?" Rayne asked. "What if they constantly moved the treasure to keep it from being discovered—"

"That's why it ended up here, so far away from any known Mayan settlements. This could be the fourth or fifth time they'd moved it to protect it from people like him." Chase motioned toward Turner. "And each time they moved it, it was farther away from their settlements."

"Exactly. You said the map was complicated, with much of it written with syllabograms rather than just logograms, meaning that it was only ever to be read by the elite, the most scholarly. So certain people were tasked to move it…until—"

"Until the whole Mayan civilization collapsed and no one was around to move it anymore." Chase nodded and bounced on her butt.

"Okay." Rayne placed her hand on Chase's and squeezed, barely able to contain her excitement. "That would mean that the *way* stones are the spirit companions of the elite group who buried it here."

Chase smiled. "That's genius. Then we should follow the *way* stones to locate the cave, yes?"

"Yes! The gods wouldn't need a map. The Mayans would have faith that if the gods ever wanted to collect, they could find it and take it whenever they wanted." Rayne paused and tapped the map. "What if we're wrong? It'd be relatively easy to follow one path to its conclusion, and if that conclusion wasn't the cave, what's stopping us from simply trying the alternative?"

Chase pointed to a particularly dense section of writing in the bottom left corner of the map. "That's what this talks about. Following the wrong stones will take the follower around and around until they go mad or they step on the wrong one and fall to their death."

Rayne became aware of how heavy-footed they'd been. Was it possible that this whole area was karstic, and they were delicately balanced above a whole world of fissures, undergrounds streams, and caves? "So the Mayan elite were also exceptional geologists?" Rayne didn't hide her admiration. It was so easy to assume the modern world had all previous civilizations beat for knowledge when in fact, the opposite often proved to be true.

"It certainly looks like it, baby."

There it was again, rolling from Chase's tongue as naturally as if she'd been addressing Rayne that way for years. Rayne looked up to the sky. They'd been so engrossed in deciphering the map that she hadn't noticed dusk was quickly giving way to the comforting darkness of nightfall. She looked at Turner. "We'll have to pick this up at dawn. It's getting dark, and if we make mistakes in this lack of light, they could be fatal."

Turner stood and brushed at his trousers. "Okay. Camp should be ready by now." He nodded toward Rich. "Can I assume that being held at gunpoint will be sufficient incentive not to try anything stupid?" Rayne and Chase nodded. "Good. Tying you up again would make dining and toileting more difficult than is necessary."

He smiled and showed the white teeth Rayne remembered had stood out when they first met. She had the desire to knock them all out, more so than ever. Rayne held out her hand, and Chase nestled her own hand in it. There was little point to not being affectionate with each other. Turner had stumbled across the nature of their relationship when he caught up with them earlier that day. Rayne needed Chase close, almost clamored for the safety her proximity provided. Turner seemed relatively levelheaded, and his anger toward her seemed to have cooled considerably. Dare she hope that he'd honor his end of their deal? The Golden Trinity in exchange for G&T…and all of their freedom. Turner was proving himself to be a greedy, ambitious criminal, but there were no signs of sadistic tendencies. He hadn't hurt them even now that he'd had ample opportunity to do so. To murder people, even to sanction it, took a certain kind of person, and maybe Turner didn't have it in him.

Owen was a different prospect entirely. Without Turner to keep him in check, he could already have…No. Rayne didn't want to think about that. Turner held all the cards. "We want proof of life, or we go no farther." Rayne stopped walking toward the camp on the edge of the clearing.

"I'm surprised that it took you this long to ask." Turner pulled the radio from his belt. "Owen. It's me."

"I was beginning to worry about the radio silence. Everything going according to plan on your end?"

"Yep. We've stopped because they need daylight for the next stage... Can you put one of her bodyguards on for me? A sign of my goodwill is required."

Owen chuckled down the radio. "Is that so?" Another laugh. "Well, sure."

The ensuing silence stretched on for an age.

"Hey, lady boss," said Tonyck.

Relief washed over Rayne. Losing Pablo had been devastating. She didn't know how she would have coped if G&T had fallen too. "Are you both okay?"

Tonyck laughed. "You don't need to worry about us, Rayne. We're fine. Owen's hospitality has belied his reputation."

Rayne recalled the unpleasant sounds she'd heard when they'd spoken last time. Owen seemed to be living up to his reputation just fine.

"See? All good," Owen said. "Anything else?"

"Not for now. I'll radio with coordinates later." Turner clipped his radio back onto his belt. "Can we proceed?"

Rayne nodded and continued toward camp. Hearing Owen had unsettled her somehow. He was a ruthless mercenary acting like a good shepherd. She hoped Turner had offered a good enough deal for him to keep his gun holstered.

CHAPTER THIRTY-TWO

SHE AND RAYNE had been watched all night by one or the other of Nicolai's goons, but Chase felt like they were being watched by something or someone else. She'd half expected a visit in the night by the three old women, but they hadn't materialized. She nudged Rayne awake. "Time to discover the largest treasure haul in the history of the world."

Rayne turned onto her back and yawned. "Can it wait? I could really use another couple of hours of beauty sleep, *and* I was having a *very* enjoyable dream featuring you." She put her hand on Chase's thigh, and squeezed.

Chase removed Rayne's hand and kissed her knuckles. "*You* don't need beauty sleep. If you were to get any more gorgeous, I'd never get any work done. And we'll have all the time in the world to make those dirty dreams into reality once we're out of here."

Rayne turned onto her side to face Chase. "How do you feel about what's most likely going to happen?"

"What do you mean?" Chase asked.

"We'll find the treasure—because that's what we do—but you won't get to give it to the Brazilian government, and I won't get to keep or sell any of it." Rayne put her finger on Chase's lips when she went to respond. "Wait, sweet lover, I'm not done."

Chase swallowed. *Sweet lover.* That. That right there had become far more important than any treasure. Her growing feelings for Rayne had crept up on Chase. She'd barely realized it had been happening, but as Rayne raised the issue of the treasure's fate, Chase discovered that it was secondary to them getting back to America to explore their new relationship. It made sense, of course, that the treasure should be secondary to them actually surviving this adventure, but having met Turner, Chase no longer feared for their lives. He was no murderer. Chase had quietly accepted that they were most likely going to lose this treasure in the moment. The three old women spoke in riddles and made no sense.

They'd managed the most important part of this expedition, ensuring the indigenous people were safe, and Chase had been thinking that once they were back safe on US soil, there was nothing to stop them from exposing Turner and revealing everything. The Brazilian authorities would do the rest, and most of the treasure would be restored to them. They had to play a longer game than they were used to, but that was okay. They still had a chance of winning in the end.

Rayne punched her arm. "Well? Did you hear any of that?"

Chase grinned. "Sorry, you sent me on an engaging train of thought with your 'sweet lover' comment. What was the gist?"

Rayne raised her eyebrow and looked decidedly unimpressed. "The *gist* was that you and I never resolved how we were going to handle our competing agendas when we finally discovered the Golden Trinity. It looks like that conflict is no longer going to happen, mainly because that bitch, Effi, fucked us. I wanted to know if that might stand in the way of you and I moving forward."

Chase caressed Rayne's cheek and smiled. She cursed so infrequently that it always sounded funny when she did. "It won't." She leaned closed and whispered, "And I have a plan. Not for now or here, for when we're home. I don't know why I didn't think of it earlier."

"Is it heroic? Or dangerous? Or brave?"

Chase tilted her head and shrugged. "No. It's none of those things."

Rayne smiled and tapped her finger on Chase's forehead gently. "Then that's why you didn't think of it earlier. You're in the last chance saloon of bright ideas, and we don't have the winning hand." She sighed and sat up, pushing her sleeping bag down as she did. "And let me tell you, that sucks. And it hurts like hell."

Rayne was right, as often seemed to be the case when she analyzed Chase. Chase had lost a few artifacts to Rayne in the past year, and they'd been sold to the highest bidder or some idiot who believed they were distant descendants of great queens or kings. Each occurrence *did* hurt like hell, and this one was no different. It was rather ironic that Rayne would now get a taste of her own medicine and didn't like it at all. Chase didn't want to dwell on that, on what might or might not have happened if they'd been in control of the destiny of the Golden Trinity instead of Turner. She'd figure that out before their next joint adventure if it was meant to be.

Turner came into Chase's peripheral vision. "The curtain is up, people.

THE GOLDEN TRINITY

Time to make me the richest man on the planet."

Chase nodded and got up. *Lap it up while it lasts, asshole.*

***

Chase stood in front of the first lupuna tree at the far left of the cliff base. "Black, west. Three hundred feet west should be our first stone." Chase rerolled the map and put it in her pocket. "We're on our own from this point. The stones should hold all the information and direction we need."

Rayne adjusted the pack across her chest and pulled on the strap. "I've got all three artifacts from the trees right here."

Turner pointed to his mute buddy, Rich. "And we've got the original map should it be needed."

Chase nodded. She couldn't anticipate why they might need it, but she wasn't about to dismiss its potential usefulness until they had the Trinity in their sight. She just hoped they could keep it in its sealed state if they did end up needing it. Exposing it would deteriorate it rapidly, so fast that it might turn to dust within minutes.

Chase slipped her arm and head through the climbing rope and let it drop across her chest. "Let's go," she said as she began to walk forward with Rayne at her side.

Chase stopped at just under three hundred feet and scanned the ground, covered with waist-high grass. "I'm going to need my machete," she said to Turner. He nodded to Nicolai, who gave it to her before stepping back quickly. Chase said nothing but she had to admit that she liked his wariness of her. The bar fight was clearly fresh in his mind. She dropped her climbing rope to the ground to mark two hundred and ninety-five feet from the lupuna tree. "Stand back, baby." She winked at Rayne before beginning to hack at the stubborn grass, slowly moving forward, and attacking a two-foot wide strip.

Chase dropped to her knees when she saw the first stone and beckoned Rayne to join her. She heard Turner speaking, but his chatter was distant and muted from her pulse pounding in her ears. The Trinity *was* real. "The first one, Rayne. It's the first one."

Rayne knelt beside her. "Oh my God…"

Rayne pulled on her utility gloves and dug at the stone along with

243

Chase, to clear the grass growth. It took ten minutes before Chase could brush away the last of the dirt to fully uncover what the stone might tell them.

"That's impossible...It's maintained its color." Chase used a wide brush to fully clear the stone. "God or spirit companion?" Rayne traced her fingers over the top logogram. "*Nupuul*...counterpart, right?"

Chase nodded. "Yeah. Not bad."

"No, then. Along with the three other logos, I think that it reads, 'Counterpart jaguar, the *way* of the Holy King of...'"

"K'inich Janaab Pakal." Chase filled in the gap after a short silence. "The last known ruler of the largest Mayan city-state before the whole civilization collapsed."

Rayne tugged at Chase's shirt repeatedly. "Then our theory is right. This is the last time they moved the Trinity because they no longer existed after Pakal."

"This is truly amazing." Chase looked up to see Turner's reaction, and he seemed just as wide-eyed and awestruck as they were.

"Where is it directing you to next?" he asked.

Chase returned her attention to the stone. "These bars equal five, but see how decorative they are, rather than a simple bar?" Rayne nodded. "This oval shape with the lines here," Chase pointed to the stone, "and here, plus what looks like an eye; that's zero."

"Sixty feet then?" Rayne asked.

"Yep, exactly right. And yellow means south, so we're walking parallel with the cliff face." Chase stood and addressed Turner. "I need photos." She motioned to the stone. "It might be that this whole clearing will collapse. I can't just leave it. We've got to properly document this discovery. It's the biggest one since Arthur Evans uncovered Knossos."

Turner glanced at Rich, who simply shrugged. Chase supposed that if he had an opinion, he'd make Turner aware of it through sign language, though she hadn't seen them use it yet. All of their communication had been written on erasable electronic tablets. She wondered how recently he'd lost his tongue. Rayne mentioned something about drug traffickers, but she didn't know when it had occurred.

"Okay, but make it quick. I don't want to run out of daylight again." He scratched at his neck. "I'm being eaten alive by these bugs, and I want to get home."

"Not a problem." Chase pulled her camera from her backpack and quickly took some shots, wide to include the location, before switching lenses for close-ups to capture the intricate detail of each logogram and the writings that accompanied them.

"Part of your plan?" Rayne whispered.

Chase hadn't thought of it that way. She'd been too excited in the presence of the stones to think about the photographs being evidence for the exposé she had in mind. She shook her head. "I just want to have something tangible to look back on in the years to come, you know? Photographs are physical memories that the brain can't possible re-create. When my memories inevitably begin to fade and lose definition and color, I want thousands of camera shots to remind me what a glorious and adventurous life I've led."

Rayne smiled and caressed Chase's cheek. "You're a soppy moose... South then?"

Chase gave Rayne a gentle shove. "*You're* soppy...and yeah, south." She shoved her Canon back into her pack and began to walk the sixty feet south.

They got to that one, deciphered and photographed it, and moved to the third one. At the fourth, Chase began to wonder exactly how many stones there might be. She'd been rooting for three, after the number of trees and the fact they were after the Golden *Trinity*, but it wasn't to be.

"The distance of the directions can always be divided by three," Chase said to no one in particular at stone number eight. She looked back at the path they'd taken. The Mayans seemed to be leading them a merry crisscross dance of directions, and Chase could feel the rising tension in the group. She'd noticed Nicolai's grip on his rifle had moved from the handle to the trigger. As a precaution, Chase ensured she was always situated between him and Rayne.

Stone nine was located at the very edge of the clearing, and as she began to hack at the grass once more, she casually wondered about switching arms. She didn't want to end up with one arm looking like Popeye's while the other was a twig. She probably should've alternated at each stone. She noticed figures walking toward them through the jungle and ceased her progress to see who it was. Surely the three old women hadn't decided to take matters into their own hands?

"What's the matter?" Rayne placed her hand on Chase's shoulder.

"Someone's coming." Chase pointed toward the movement in the trees.

"G and T!" Rayne jumped up from the ground.

She looked as though she was about to race forward, but Owen appeared at their side, and she stood stock-still, gripping Chase's wrist tightly.

"What are you doing here?" Turner asked. "I told you I'd radio you when I had the Trinity."

"Change of plan."

Everything happened so much slower than it ever did in the movies. Owen raised his handgun to shoulder height and squeezed off one round. He adjusted and aimed again, letting off a second shot. Chase launched herself at Rayne, and they fell to the ground in super slow motion. Moments after Chase covered Rayne's body with her own, Turner dropped to the ground beside them. A perfectly circular, ebony-black hole marked the center of his forehead, scarlet blood began to seep from it, and his mouth fell open in a frozen yell. Milliseconds later, Rich fell beside Turner, similarly and perfectly executed.

Chase looked up to see Owen grinning as nonchalantly as if he'd just shot two coconuts at a fair and was about to claim the teddy bear prize. His gun, and that of his companion, who flanked the other side of the tank twins, was trained on Effi, Nicolai, and his three goons.

"I'm going to need help carrying this immense treasure from the cave it's hiding in onto Turner's helicopter," said Owen. "You have five seconds to decide whether you'd like to earn ten thousand dollars or chew on my bullets…And, go."

Nicolai nodded to his three people, and they all lowered their weapons. "We don't care who pays us, as long as we *do* get paid."

Owen grinned. "I'm a man of my word, and I will pay for your services."

Effi looked down at Turner and Rich, and Chase couldn't see if she actually had any feelings for Turner, or whether it had always been for the money.

Effi raised her hands. "I'm up for the ten K."

"Too late." Owen patted the chest pocket of his jacket with his left hand. "I only have forty thousand."

He shot Effi in the chest. She dropped to her knees, clutching desperately at the hole swiftly relinquishing her life. Chase watched, helpless, as Owen loosed another round into her head.

"Die already. I'm not giving out Oscars for best performance."

Owen and his buddy laughed, and they were soon joined with nervous-sounding laughter from Nicolai and his gang.

"Chase Stinsen and Rayne Marcellus. Working together again." Owen came to stand before them, his boots almost touching Chase's head. "This is like a McCartney and Lennon reunion, except you're both alive...for now. This is such a huge occasion. Let's celebrate by finding the Golden Trinity." He reached down, grabbed Chase's shirt, and pulled her to her feet. "What do you say, Stinsen?"

Chase swallowed and took in all the carnage around her. Owen had been there less than three minutes, and there was a dead body for each one of those minutes. Rayne slowly stood, and Chase felt stronger for her nearness. But what good was that strength when faced with this level of careless violence? "I think we're close," was all she could think of to say.

Owen moved closer and pressed the barrel of his gun under Chase's chin. "You and the pretty woman are supposed to be the best treasure hunters and archeologists in the world. You'd better do more than think. You'd better *know*, or you'll find yourself lying in the dirt next to this greedy, stupid prick and his dumb boyfriend."

Chase nodded as best she could against the hard metal of Owen's gun. Rayne had asked if this expedition was going to get worse. Owen showing up and murdering Turner without any apparent provocation definitely fell into that category. She closed her eyes briefly and tried to hold on to the disappearing thread of hope that they really were going to make it out of this alive.

Chapter Thirty-three

RAYNE SMILED AT G&T, and they smiled back from a distance. Knowing they were here relieved some of the pressure but being in such close proximity to Owen again counterbalanced that relief. They weren't in too bad a state considering they'd spent time with Owen, but their black eyes, cut lips, and bruised cheeks were evidence enough that they were at the mercy of a twisted and sick individual.

"Are you worried about me making good on my threat, Rayne?"

His breath brushed across her neck as she leaned over Chase to study the ninth stone. She tried to dismiss the menace behind his words as macho rhetoric. "Are you going to let us concentrate? If you want this done, you'd be better off to stand back and gives us space to do our job." Rayne faced him with a sparky confidence she had to work hard to fake, then turned away before he could recognize the terror bubbling beneath her skin.

"Fine. We'll talk about your future later."

In her peripheral vision, he drummed his fingers on the hilt of his gun which he'd carelessly positioned in the front waistband of his trousers. She thought about making a lunge at him and pulling the trigger. Shooting his appendage off might make him less of a vicious dick...for the few hours before he bled to death.

"Breathe, baby," Chase whispered. "We'll get through this."

Rayne wanted to believe that. She really did. And maybe, just maybe, if she hadn't witnessed Owen's brutal, nonchalant murder of Turner, Rich, and Effi, she could roll with that tiny ball of hope that they *could* get through this. But she and Chase were only useful until they found the Trinity. Christ, he was already toying with her emotions by reminding her of his threat when they'd last crossed paths.

Chase pulled her camera from her pack, and Owen practically jumped across the space between them.

"What the hell, Owen?" Chase stumbled back as Owen grabbed at her.

"I'm just getting my camera."

He tugged it from her hands and began to flick through the photos on the back screen.

"You don't need your camera."

Rayne put her hand on Chase's thigh. "Leave it."

Chase ignored her warning and stood to challenge him. "Yes, I do. I need to document this discovery."

Owen laughed. "To what end?"

Chase frowned, as if confused by Owen's lack of understanding. "This discovery belongs to history."

Owen stepped into Chase's space and poked her in the chest. "This discovery belongs to *me*."

He took two steps back, threw Chase's Canon high into the air, withdrew his gun, and shot at like it was a clay pigeon. He missed, but the camera still hit the ground with an ugly and unhealthy thud somewhere in the grass behind them. He leveled his gun at Chase's head.

"Think carefully about your next move, Stinsen. Maybe Rayne's good enough to find the Trinity solo."

Rayne tugged at Chase's belt and pulled her backward. "Chase, please. I can't do this alone." Rayne didn't mean finding the Trinity, though that *was* probably true too.

Chase looked down at Rayne, then across the clearing in the general direction of where Owen had tossed her camera. She stepped back, and Rayne relaxed a little.

"We head toward the cliff face and the lupuna trees," Chase said, not looking Rayne in the eye.

"For what distance?" Rayne asked, trying to catch Chase's gaze. Was she not looking at her because she'd chosen to back down or because Rayne had *asked* her to back down?

Chase gathered her things and began to walk without waiting. "Until something exciting happens."

Rayne caught up easily, and she gave Chase a gentle push. "Hey, what's with you? Are you keeping me in the dark for a reason?"

Chase glanced sideways and looked irritated, but her brow relaxed and she smiled. "I'm sorry. I shouldn't take this shit out on you...I just feel so fucking *helpless*."

"I know, baby, me too." Rayne wanted to stop Chase and pull her into an embrace. She wanted the power to think of a place and be there instantly, away from this situation and the pervading sense of hopelessness. "But we're better side by side. You know that, right? You know that we're stronger when we face something and work it out together."

Chase nodded and stood a little straighter. "At least we know where your tank twins are now."

Chase motioned behind her to G&T. They were bound together with their hands behind their backs, and Owen's buddy prodded them forward from behind. Rayne wondered about the rage simmering in them. They'd left the military behind with the expectation that being in a hostage situation again would be unlikely. They probably wanted to rip out their captors' throats with their bare hands, if such a thing were possible. She'd watched some guy do it in a movie once, but she wasn't convinced it could be done in real life. "I wonder how Tonyck's coping with Effi's death? They'd gotten close."

Chase gave a short laugh and shook her head. "I wouldn't imagine she'll lose any sleep over it. Effi used her to get what she wanted, and that's never a nice feeling, regardless of what becomes of the person who used you."

Rayne looked away and focused on the lupuna trees ahead. It seemed like Chase might be referencing what had happened in Florida, and she didn't want to engage in that conversation and have it dragged up again. It really felt like they'd moved on.

Chase touched Rayne's forearm gently. "No."

Rayne waited for more, but nothing came. "No, what?"

Chase grinned. "No, I wasn't thinking about Florida. That's in the past, Rayne, and I'm not about to start dredging it up again. I'm all about moving forward."

Chase stumbled, and Rayne turned to see Owen behind her.

"Less talking, more hunting. Find me the Trinity, or I start shooting again." He nodded toward G&T. "I'll start by putting one of your dumb animals out of their misery, the really stupid one who fell for that black chick's charms."

Tonyck gave no visible reaction, of course. There was no way she'd give Owen any pleasure from that. Rayne winked at her, and she returned the gesture. Owen nodded to his cohort, who smacked the butt of his gun against Tonyck's head. She staggered forward but didn't lose her footing.

Ginn tumbled with her but also managed to stay upright.

"You should keep that smug smile off your face, or I'll be throwing your dead body on top of your would-be girlfriend and setting fire to you both." Owen snarled, and his fingers twitched against his gun.

Rayne looked back at the path ahead. Owen clearly had control issues over his violent tendencies, so they needed to avoid provoking him. Chase threw her a warning, wide-eyed glance as if to say the same thing.

"Okay, take it easy, Owen," Chase said and held her hands up in an effort to placate him. "I promise we're doing everything we can to get you to the Trinity."

Owen clenched his jaw and waved them on. "Good. Then let's go."

Chase turned and continued walking, always looking at the ground intently.

"What are you looking for? More stones?" Rayne asked.

She didn't look up. "I don't think so. The last stone implied it was just that, the last stone. But between that and the trees…where's the cave? We walked along the cliff face, and we didn't find anything. And now we're less than a hundred feet away from the trees again." Chase lowered her voice to a whisper. "I'm beginning to wonder if this is the 'disappointment' the old women were talking about. Maybe they knew that even after finding all the trees and following all the clues we still wouldn't be able to find the Trinity." Chase scratched at her head through her ball cap. "It makes sense, doesn't it? That's how a treasure stays hidden and undiscovered for over seven hundred years. You make it absolutely impossible to find."

"Then why provide a map at all?" Rayne asked though Chase had a point. "The Mayans went to a lot of trouble with hiding the three artifacts in the trees, and not just laying the stones, but carving them. And if our theory is correct about the treasure being moved on a reasonably regular basis, then there *must* be a way to it."

Chase sighed. "You're right. I know that you're right. And I *do* think that our theory stands the test of logic. But maybe I'm missing something. Maybe what we think we know about the Mayan language isn't as accurate as we believe it is, and because of that, I'm misinterpreting vital logograms and words."

Rayne grinned when she felt the hardness of rock underfoot. "Or maybe you've interpreted everything with one hundred percent accuracy, and you're standing over the entrance to the cave *right now*."

THE GOLDEN TRINITY

Chase stopped and narrowed her eyes. "What are you talking about?"

Rayne pointed to the ground beneath her feet before she knelt and began to pull the grass aside. As she did so, she uncovered a triangular-shaped stone with more carvings.

"Oh my God!" Chase dropped to her knees and took Rayne's face in her hands. "We're nearly there."

"Get on with it." Owen stepped into view. "I want to be out of here and buying my own island before dark."

Once again, Owen's interruption brought home the stark reality of their situation and squashed the momentary joy of coming one step closer to the Golden Trinity. Rayne didn't bother to look up. "What does it say?"

Chase was already dusting off the soil and dirt after hacking the grass down.

"Belief...hurdle." Chase took off her ball cap and ruffled her hair, slick with sweat from the humidity. She looked around and shook her head. "Believe that this is the final hurdle? When it isn't...Have we missed something on the map? Maybe we need to take a look at the original."

Rayne put her hand on Chase's knee to stop her from rising. "Wait. What if you were a little bit right about common understanding of the Mayan language not being completely accurate?"

"Nuance?" Chase nodded quickly, catching on to Rayne's train of thought. "Differences in the style of scribes?"

"Exactly. Synonyms," Rayne said. "Think of the English language where one word can mean three things, or there are fifteen words for the same thing. There's no way to *know* that the Mayan language has been translated perfectly, just as you say."

"Okay. Belief, conviction." Chase pulled her cap back on and continued to dust off the stone.

"Principle, code."

"Acceptance, trust."

As Chase worked out the hundreds of years of growth that had settled within the intricate lines of the carvings, Rayne saw a god. "K'awiil."

Chase looked up and frowned. "What?"

Rayne pressed her finger to the logogram Chase had just completely cleared. "The god K'awiil was the principal deity of the Maya royal line. Can you see how one foot *isn't* a foot and is actually an open-mouthed serpent? He personified abundance, usually thought to be agricultural abundance. But we're talking about the Golden Trinity, an abundance of treasure for the gods. Giving to them, instead of the other way around."

"God equals faith...A *leap*, not a hurdle, of *faith*." Chase grinned, but it soon faded. "To where?"

Rayne shook her head. "That's the faith part, silly. We're not on the top of the cliff where the leap would be obvious. I think you have to run, *leap* off the stone...and have faith."

"What about speed? And weight? And stride length? There are so many variables."

"*Faith*, baby."

Chase sighed as she stood and took her climbing rope from her shoulder. She fashioned a rope harness around her waist and thighs. "I'm going to need Tonyck and Ginn to hold the other end when I jump."

Owen laughed. "Jump where?"

Chase shrugged. "I guess we'll see. But I'm about a hundred and fifty-five pounds, and I need those two to anchor me if this leap of faith sees me dropping hell-bound."

Owen raised his eyebrows but nodded at his buddy, and in turn, he untied their hands from behind their backs and retied them at the front before he shoved G&T forward to Chase.

"Are you doing okay?" Rayne expected nothing more than they'd given her when she asked the same question before.

"Stop worrying about us, lady boss," said Tonyck. "Just concentrate on working with Stinse to get the Trinity."

The subtext was clear. Get the Trinity, then we'll make a break for it. Owen and five goons. Nicolai and his gang were saying nothing, but their presence was menacing enough. The odds would've been manageable if not for the presence of guns and Owen's apparent glee in using them. *A leap of faith.* Rayne hoped the Trinity would provide the solution to their problem.

CHAPTER THIRTY-FOUR

CHASE CHECKED THE knots on her swami belt despite feeling foolish for doing so. This leap of faith was a long shot, even for her, but then the clue to that *was* in the phrasing. She found it hard to believe that after going to so much trouble with the map, the trees, the artifacts, and the stones that the entrance to the cave could be found by jumping from a stone onto solid ground. Tonyck and Ginn had tied one big loop around themselves and were sat on the ground, heels dug in and hands wrapped around the rope, giving Chase around twenty feet of slack. Chase could see they were taking their role seriously because they'd both put their utility gloves on.

Chase tracked her path backward in the precise direction they'd come from. She stopped and turned after counting twenty paces. Rayne nodded slowly at her, her hands clasped together as if she were praying, and Chase could see the trepidation and excitement battling for supremacy in her eyes.

She pulled the straps of her backpack tighter over her shoulders and took a deep breath before setting off. As she ran, her mind flicked back to college days and the long jump. Her best friend beat her consistently, making Chase crazy and determined to win. So Chase trained and trained until finally, at one college event, she jumped farther than her bestic by two inches. It didn't matter that it was only two inches. It didn't matter that beating her best friend signified the end of their friendship. All that mattered to Chase was the win.

And that's all that mattered right now. The win. Finding the Trinity. Her right foot hit the stone. She launched herself into the air and closed her eyes. For a brief glorious moment, she was weightless and could've imagined she was anywhere in the world instead of being forced to work for a maniac.

Then she hit the ground with a thud and rolled.

Nothing.

The ground didn't shake, and it didn't move beneath her. So much for the leap of faith. Why didn't the map just say it was another ten feet forward? Chase closed her eyes, sighed, and lay back onto the grass, knowing that she'd disappear from view.

But instead of the soft cushion of vegetation, Chase's head hit something hard, really hard. She flipped over onto her belly to look upon not just one but three triangular stones. All carved with the same god. The central stone featured a circular hole in the clutches of the serpent's jaw, and it was carved with additional words. *Lay map here.*

Chase jumped up. "I need the map! Bring the map."

She watched Rayne grab the original map from Nicolai's hands and run toward her. Chase allowed herself a small smile despite the circumstances. She liked seeing Rayne run toward her, and it made her want Rayne to jump into her arms when she got there so she could spin her around like the hero does in all the great movies. She shook her head to snap out of the daydream as Rayne reached her.

"This goddamn thing is heavy," Rayne said. "I'm glad I haven't been the one to lug it around the jungle this whole trip…Why do you need it?"

Chase grabbed Rayne's other hand and pulled her around to the ground to face the three stones. "Look."

"More stones. Same god…I'm going to make an assumption that the middle stone wants you to roll up this ancient and priceless scroll and stick it inside that hole." Rayne wiped her fingers across her forehead. "Please tell me that I'm wrong."

"You're wrong."

Rayne blew out a breath and sank lower to her butt. "Oh, thank God."

Chase grinned and shook her head. "Rayne. I'm lying. You're absolutely right."

Rayne sprang back to her haunches and slapped Chase hard across her shoulder. "You swine. Are you serious? We've got to crack this open and shove it in a grubby stone?" She shook her head and pulled the case to her chest. "No. There's got to be another way…Put the duplicate copy in there and see what happens."

Chase laughed. "I'm not going to insult your intelligence or waste my breath explaining why that clearly wouldn't work."

"What do you want us to do, Stinse?"

Tonyck's shout reminded Chase they were still on the ground, hunkered down waiting for Chase to fall. "Stay exactly where you are…and be ready for anything. I'm going to connect Rayne to my harness so you could do with some help from anyone strong enough to hold the rope."

"You've found the entrance?" Owen asked as he walked toward them. Chase held up her hand. "Maybe. But I need you to stay right where you are. When we put the map in this stone, we don't know what's going to happen. The other side of the last stone is most likely the safest place to be."

Owen tapped his gun. "You'll still be in range from back there, you know?"

Chase clenched her jaw and waved him away. "Yeah, sure." His long-distance accuracy didn't seem up to much against moving targets if Chase's camera was anything to go by. It was Tonyck and Ginn who should be most concerned. She returned her attention to Rayne, who'd relinquished the map and laid it on the ground. Chase pushed it closer to Rayne. "I can't do it. You have to do it. You're the one with less respect for history."

Rayne raised her eyebrows and punched Chase square in the chest. "Wow. If that's what you think, Mister, we've got a problem."

"I never realized before how easy you are to tease. You're like a little wind-up toy. Wind her up and watch her go."

"And *I* never realized how you used humor in tremendously serious situations where some might perceive it as completely inappropriate," Rayne said.

"So you won't do it?" Chase gave Rayne a little push.

"No, Miss Morals and Conscience." Rayne crossed her arms over her chest. "*You* do it."

Chase sighed and pulled the case onto her knee. "Fine…do you know how sexy you are when you go all indignant like that?"

Rayne tapped her fingernails on the map. "Shut up and open the damn thing."

"Yes, ma'am." Chase plugged in the six-digit combination. Did she really have to do this? She supposed if the Trinity was really here, the map had been the cherry on the cake they'd no longer have. "Maybe we'll be able to take it out and put it back in the case when it does…whatever it needs to do."

"We can hope."

As she opened the case slowly, Chase could almost hear the degradation of the bark begin, and it was like a tiny hammer hitting the same place over and over. The more it degraded, the more painful it became. She shook it off and took one end of the map. This had to be done quickly. They didn't know what the map was required to do, and if it deteriorated too much too soon, perhaps it wouldn't be able to fulfill its task. The Mayans hadn't designed it to last this long.

Chase ignored the cracking in the bark as she rolled it into the circular shape the stone required. "Throw the case back toward them. If the ground gives, we don't want that heavy thing falling on either of our heads."

Rayne did as Chase asked. "Stick it in the hole then, Chase."

Chase grinned at Rayne's unsubtle innuendo. "Oh, I will." She remembered Rayne wasn't harnessed to her yet. "The ground might give. Maybe it would be safer for you to join the others, then follow on my rope."

"No way." Rayne removed her paracord bracelet, unfurled it, and tossed one of the ends to Chase. "Harness me up, honey."

Chase shook her head. "How come you can be all sexual in this situation, but I can't be humorous?"

"Oh, Chase. You've got so much to learn about women. When your hair is *this* long," she flipped her ponytail over her shoulder, "you can get away with anything you damn well please."

Chase's body responded to the look Rayne gave her. Who was she to argue with Rayne's logic when it was absolutely true. Chase fed the cord through the loops of Rayne's cargo pants, tied it off, and attached it to her own harness with a figure eight knot. "If we drop any kind of distance, this stuff is going to hurt. You're going to have to try to hang on to me to support your weight when we fall."

Rayne raised her eyebrow and smirked. "You only have to ask if you want me to hold you, Chase."

"Seriously…Are you ready?"

"I'm ever-ready, Chase. You'll learn that."

"Wow, you can just flip a switch, can't you?" Chase grinned, then remembered the company they were in. This was supposed to be this much fun, but with Owen so close, something could go wrong at any moment. She wished they could be doing this under better circumstances.

Rayne caressed Chase's check and looked at her seriously. "I know, Chase. I feel it too."

Chase nodded before she shouted to the tank twins that they were a go. Chase retrieved the rolled-up map and began to carefully place it into the central hole of the middle stone. "There's no resistance. Shall I just keep pushing?" Rayne nodded, but Chase wasn't sure. "What if the map falls through the hole completely?"

"Then that's what it was supposed to do." Rayne wrapped her arms around Chase's waist and pressed her face against her shoulder. "Make the earth move, baby."

Chase would've shaken her head, but her focus was pulled when she felt something against the map. "Another hole?" she whispered, more as a question than a statement. She continued to gently push the map downward until it felt like pushing it farther might snap it. Only about three inches remained above the triangular stone. "Can you hear that?" Chase pressed her ear to the stone. That was whirring and grinding, for sure. It was slow, steady, but it was there. The ground beneath her feet began to vibrate. Chase turned and held Rayne just as the ground disappeared completely and she felt weightless once again. Chase heard the surprised shouts of the tank twins before the slack in the rope tautened, and she and Rayne jolted to an abrupt stop.

Rayne's grip around Chase's waist didn't falter, but Chase reached around. "Come around the front so I can hold you."

Rayne did as Chase instructed without a quip.

Chase figured the drop might have given her more of a shock than she'd anticipated. The tank twins began to let the rope down little by little. "Reach into my pocket and pull out a glow stick."

"How am I supposed to resist responding when the setups are coming thick and fast?"

"I don't know," Chase said. "You've had them under control for most of this expedition."

Rayne felt around in Chase's pocket, got the glow stick, snapped it, and dropped it. They both looked down as it fell into the vast darkness. It came to rest far enough down that its light was dim.

"What can you see?"

Chase looked up to see Owen peering over the edge of the crater they'd just created, and it was then that she saw just how big it was. She glanced left and right and calculated it must be a hundred feet wide. She could hear chunks of the earth thudding to the cave floor below them. "Not a whole lot yet," Chase said. "Tell them to keep the rope going nice and steady."

"Pull on the rope when you've reached the bottom, and I'll follow," Owen said.

"Bring down another rope with you; we may need to go deeper." Chase focused on Rayne. "How's the harness holding up?"

"I'll be glad when I can loosen it." Rayne kissed her. "You think this is what they meant by a leap of faith?"

Chase smiled, the taste of Rayne fresh on her lips energizing her. "The Mayans or us?"

"Either." Rayne tilted her head slightly. "Both."

"It worked for the Mayans. I'm prepared to make the same leap with us.I have no intention of using any safety rope with us." Chase saw that vulnerability and shyness slip out again in her responding smile.

"That's a bold promise, but I guess that's okay since we don't know if we'll be around to make an 'us' after we've found the Trinity."

"Hey, don't say that," Chase said. "We're going to get through this."

Rayne nodded, though Chase could see there was little belief behind her eyes. She couldn't let her down. She wouldn't let her down. There'd be a way they could all get out of this alive, and Chase would find it. She had to.

CHAPTER THIRTY-FIVE

HITTING THE GROUND was a welcome distraction from the intensity of their conversation. For a brief moment Rayne had allowed herself to believe they could get out of this, but then she remembered the callous way Owen dispatched Turner, Rich, and Effi. Now that they were deep underground in previously uncharted territory, killing them would be even easier because he wouldn't have to worry about hiding the bodies.

For now, she needed to push those thoughts from her mind and focus on finding the Trinity. She and Chase untied themselves from the rope, and Chase pulled on it to indicate they'd reached the bottom. Rayne wrapped the paracord and stuffed it into her pocket. They both retrieved flashlights from their packs. When they turned them on and looked around, Rayne's breath caught. Large stone steps led them deeper into the cave, and at the bottom of those steps was a Mayan temple, a much smaller version than El Castillo for sure, but amazing nonetheless. There were four large stepped platforms shaping the body of the temple and the typical flight of steep stone steps split the platforms symmetrically. Where the stone was once bright, it was now damp-looking and dark green. Rayne focused her flashlight on the ground beneath the temple to see it was flooded.

"That doesn't look ominous at *all*," Rayne said. "Me first." She began to jog down the steps toward the temple. She heard Chase's footsteps behind her and upped her pace. When she got to the bottom, she paused at the water separating them from the temple by a hundred feet and no indication as to the depth.

Chase grabbed her waist and pulled her close. "We're going to have to address your competitive streak."

Chase kissed her, and Rayne relaxed into Chase's strong embrace. "I just want to see it first. I want to get there before Owen catches up with us and spoils the fun." She kissed Chase once more and pulled away. "Fancy a swim?"

Chase pointed to the slightly raised stone at the edge of the steps they'd just come down from. "The slab topping that stone, it doesn't look like it's attached with mortar. The Mayans used mortar for every building."

"You're thinking that it moves?" Rayne asked as she walked toward it. Chase nodded. "I do. We're in proper adventure mode now, Rayne."

She grinned, and Rayne couldn't help but smile. Chase was full of life any time, but she vibrated when she was on a trail. Rayne took a deep breath at the beauty of it all and tried to push away the sadness that tugged for her attention and scolded her for wasting so much time without Chase.

Chase got to her knees and pushed at the slab. It crunched loudly over the stone but began to give, exposing the stone beneath it. Rayne joined Chase and helped her push until the slab fell away and splashed into the water.

"The wood piece?" Chase gestured toward the strangely-shaped hole in the center of the stone, positioned in the jaws of the serpent leg of K'awiil as with the previous stone. She swung her backpack around, opened it, and pulled out the artifact they'd found in the first lupuna tree. "Do you want to do it?"

Rayne took the carved wood from Chase's hand and maneuvered it a few times before she found what she thought would be the right position. She carefully placed the artifact into the hole and pressed it down when she met with resistance. There was a click as it pushed down and sprang back up slightly before the ground grumbled beneath their feet. Mechanisms they could hear but couldn't see lumbered into action, droning and creaking as they did. The glass-like appearance of the water shattered as whatever they'd started rumbled upward.

"It's a bridge," Chase said as they watched and waited for it to reveal itself.

Rayne squatted down after a few minutes. "How deep *is* this bloody moat?"

"A temple underground!"

They turned to see Owen at the top of the stone steps, a climbing rope over his shoulder and across his chest. For the first time, he looked somewhat excited instead of just plain menacing. Rayne preferred the menacing version; excitement seemed all kinds of wrong on his face. He jogged down the steps and slapped Chase on the back as if they were best buddies just as a stone bridge broke the surface of the water. Rayne wondered if he could swim, then wished it could have been a moat of boiling acid instead.

Chase looked back up the steps. "Just you?"

He shook his head. "Larry's coming down shortly, don't worry. And don't get any stupid ideas."

He tapped the gun in his waistband as a warning, but Rayne was busy trying not to laugh at the name of Owen's colleague. Whatever a Larry was supposed to look like, it wasn't the guy holding a gun to G&T. Larry seemed like a name for a cuddly kind of guy.

Chase held up her hands. "I'm just asking. We don't know what's inside and may need more hands."

"Nicolai and his gang are looking after her bodyguards right now; tying them up nice and tight to one of those big trees. They'll come down for the treasure when I radio them. If the radio doesn't work, I'll just pull on the rope." Owen motioned to the bridge. "After you."

Chase tested the first step of the bridge then turned to Rayne. "Let me get all the way across, then you come over. Okay?"

Rayne suppressed the desire to raise her eyebrow, knowing that Chase was right to make sure the bridge was safe enough for one to cross before she tried. Still, she was used to being first, and it was a habit she wouldn't give up for anyone.

Chase reached the other side of the bridge and before she'd turned, Rayne followed.

"Are you coming?" Rayne asked Owen.

"I'll wait until Larry gets down here," he said. "Keep going."

Rayne shrugged and whispered to Chase, "Do you think he's scared that we might overpower him?"

Chase turned her back to the bridge and began to walk toward the temple. "Maybe. And if we get the chance, that's exactly what I have in mind."

"We'll have to choose our time very carefully. If either of us get shot, the nearest hospital is eight hours away even with my pilot." Still, escape suddenly seemed entirely feasible.

"Then we'd better not get shot. Just be ready." Chase wrapped her hand around Rayne's wrist. "I won't put you in danger, but I'll risk *everything* to make sure you're safe."

Rayne swallowed against the ball of rising emotion in her throat. Was this what love was? Caring for someone so strongly that they'd put everything on the line for the woman they loved? Did Chase actually *love* Rayne or was it simply her heroic proclivities rising to the fore? Rayne pulled her arm away and motioned toward the temple entrance. She'd ask Chase soon enough, but she didn't want to share such an intimate and petrifying moment with Owen as their audience. "It's K'awiil again." The double doors to the temple were six feet tall and six feet wide, and K'awiil was intricately carved across the entire expanse of heavy stone. Even with the light covering of moss, the god was easy to distinguish. This time, his serpent leg stretched across the base of the doors to come up at their center where a handle or door opening would usually be located. Again, its jaws wrapped around another odd shaped hole.

Chase opened her backpack on the ground and pulled out the clay and maize artifacts from the second and third trees. They were both identical to the naked eye.

"Clay or maize?" Chase asked as she held one in each hand as if she were trying to ascertain their weight.

Rayne didn't hesitate. "It has to be clay. If all of these artifacts are keys, the order appears to be the same as the order in which the Mayan gods tried to create humans. They succeeded with a dough made from yellow and white corn, so it makes sense that the corn artifact will be the final key to the Trinity once we're inside the temple." She reached out and touched both of them. "Can you feel any difference in the weight?"

"Yep. The clay is solid. It's substantially heavier." Chase placed the artifacts on her backpack and used her flashlight to investigate the hole in the door. She tentatively placed her fingers inside.

"You probably shouldn't do that. You won't be much good to me if they get chopped off."

Chase laughed and shook her head. "I could still cuddle you." She withdrew her hand anyway.

"That just wouldn't do." Rayne wiggled her eyebrows. "I need it *all*."

"I think there's a lever just here." Chase pointed a few inches below the hole. "We drop the clay sculpture through the hole, and its weight will set off a chain reaction to open the door. It's probably set so that only the exact weight will begin the process."

"And clay wouldn't increase or decrease in weight since its creation." Rayne picked the clay artifact from the ground and gave it to Chase. "Your turn."

THE GOLDEN TRINITY

Chase proffered the sculptured shape to the hole and pushed it in. Rayne heard it drop onto the latch Chase had identified, and sure enough, ancient machinery clicked and clunked into place. Owen and Larry approached them just as the doors began to open.

"You girls are doing amazing." He and his buddy laughed. "We'll wait here until you've finished the job for me."

Neither she nor Chase responded to his patronizing comment, and Chase picked up her backpack. Rayne's heart was pounding hard against her chest, and she could barely breathe as the doors fully opened. The enormity of what they were in the midst of achieving became tangible. This was no longer just another adventure following a map. This was the greatest undiscovered treasure in the history of the world. She and Chase had been the ones to figure it out.

They used their flashlights to check inside. If there were once jaguars in here protecting the Trinity, Rayne was confident they were long gone. Nor was she expecting any seven-hundred-year-old Mayan priests to come stumbling out of the temple brandishing an obsidian dagger trying to kill them. She'd raided enough tombs and discovered enough hidden treasures to know that stone creatures coming to life once you removed their token were the folly of fictional characters and movies alone.

She and Chase stepped into the darkness cautiously. Rayne shivered like an ice-cold blanket had been wrapped around her. "Do you feel that?"

Chase nodded. "The temperature change? Yeah, I feel it."

Rayne tracked her flashlight over the ground and the walls. "Look at these carvings," she said, her light focus on the 3-D sculpted columns along the walkway. "I can't believe they did this over and over to relocate the Trinity."

"Maybe that's what some of their original temples were for. This could be the one and only temple built beneath the ground. As their civilization became more unstable with the constant battles between city-states, perhaps underground was their safest bet."

Rayne approached the wall and traced her hand along the bodies of the gods and imagined how many years of hard work had gone into creating each sculpture, let alone the whole temple.

"Be careful," Chase said. "This is usually the part where the spears shoot out and the walls start moving in."

"Let's hope they save that until Owen and his ridiculously-named friend come in."

Chase laughed. "You've got something against that name."

"I didn't until I met this guy." Rayne walked back to the path. "This temple doesn't look big in the scheme of Mayan temples. Could it be that it goes deeper underground?"

Chase focused her flashlight on another door, singular this time. "I guess we'll see soon enough."

"Three holes, three keys." Rayne waited while Chase dipped into her bag to retrieve the final artifact molded from corn. "This has all been reasonably easy, don't you think?"

Chase stopped what she was doing and looked up at Rayne, an incredulous expression on her face. "*Easy?* Cutting into ancient trees, rappelling down a cliff side, and falling down a giant sinkhole. You're calling that easy?"

"You know what I mean." Rayne shoved Chase's shoulder gently. "Given that the Trinity has remained undiscovered for so long, I was kind of expecting a whole line of the dead bodies of previous treasure hunters somewhere, you know? I've read about plenty of people who tried to get here and were never seen again."

Chase smiled. "Maybe they were dealt with by the head bashers or the arrow people. Remember that the old women took some convincing that they needed to get out of the way of these guys. And we were the only ones who ever had the map. No one else could've gotten this far." Chase pulled the final artifact from her bag. "Do you want to do this one together?"

Rayne placed her hands over Chase's. "Here's to discovering the most famous treasure in the history of treasure hunting…together."

Together. Rayne liked the sound of that. They pressed the maize sculpture into the hole, felt it drop, and listened to the lever catch and the door mechanism begin to heave itself open. After all the centuries of inertia, that it moved so smoothly amazed her. Chase reached for Rayne's hand and grasped it tightly as the door began to slowly open to reveal its long-held secret.

CHAPTER THIRTY-SIX

WALLS COVERED WITH stucco. Previously bright paintings in primary colors faded but not lost. All of the symbols Chase had seen on the stones, the map, and the artifacts replicated in multitude around the whole area. In the very center of the room positioned on a thick column sat a giant sculpture of K'awiil on his back, his serpent leg stretching to reach the ceiling as if holding it upright. In his right hand was a dagger, and his left hand held a small bowl. The statue wasn't stone; it was verdigris, indicating that it was made from copper. Around the column was nothingness. Chase walked into the room slowly, checking her footing on the stone floor as she did. There was only ten feet of ground before a gaping abyss beckoned between the edge of their walkway and the column. She snapped a glow light and dropped it into the black pit. Its bright luminescence swiftly disappeared, and Chase heard nothing to indicate it hit the floor. Chase let out a deep breath and shook her head. "So not the last key then." She felt Rayne's hand on the base of her back, hot against her wet shirt and cool skin.

"And not so easy."

Chase turned back. She could see Owen and Larry hovering around the opening of the temple and wondered why they hadn't ventured in. Maybe *they'd* watched too many inaccurate archeologist adventure movies and were expecting to be chased down a tiny corridor by a gigantic circular stone. "Owen. I need the other climbing rope."

"Come and get it."

Chase glanced back at Rayne. "The guy can murder three people in as many minutes, but he's afraid of a dark underground temple. Are we calling that irony?"

Rayne shrugged. "Or cowardice."

Chase jogged back to the entrance of the temple and took the rope from Owen.

"Wait. What's up there?" he asked.

"Why don't you come and take a look?"

Owen pulled the gun from his waistband then hung his arm by his side.

"Answer the question, Stinsen."

Chase acknowledged the quiet threat with a shrug. "The room is empty but for a mammoth statue in the center. I need the rope because there's twenty to thirty feet of fresh air between the entrance to the room and the column holding the statue, which I'm assuming I have to get to in order to reveal where the Trinity actually is."

Owen dismissed her with a wave of his hand. "Off you go."

Chase raised her eyebrow at him and then looked at Larry, who shrugged. Clearly, he didn't understand why Owen wouldn't enter the temple either. She turned and headed back to Rayne.

"Is he still not coming in?"

Chase shook her head. "No, he's staying put like something's spooked him."

Rayne looked vaguely amused. "What's the new plan?"

Chase pointed to the door. "We're going to tie one end of the rope through the keyhole of that door, then I'm going to lasso any part of the god's body that will hold under tension of me crawling across the rope." She pulled her scarf across the back of her neck and mopped up the sweat she attributed to the environment rather than any tension or nerves. "Sound good?"

"As long as everything holds, it's a solid plan."

Chase pulled off her cap, threw it to the ground, and ran her hand through her hair. "Then let's do it." Chase took one end of the rope, threaded it through the hole where they'd placed the final artifact, and locked it off loosely with a bowline knot. At the other end, she tied a honda knot, making the loop large enough for the statue's head.

"You're very impressive with all the knots," Rayne said and winked. "Do you ever use them…at home?"

"You mean, to tie someone up with?"

Rayne nodded. "Yes…" she said, her voice dropping a little husky.

"I don't need to tie my lovers up." Chase jutted her chin. "They tend to stay willingly."

Rayne grinned. "Still…could be fun."

Rayne raised her eyebrow the way that drove Chase wild. "Okay." She turned away after quickly, squeezing her thighs together to repress her response. "I need to concentrate now."

Chase nailed the head after three attempts and pulled the loop tight. She went back to the door, untied the bowline, and dragged the excess rope through the hole to ensure a taut line before retying the knot. Chase walked to the edge of the abyss then stepped back, slipped her arm around Rayne's waist, and pulled her into a kiss. When they parted, Chase said, "Just in case something goes wrong, I want you to be the last thing on my mind and my lips."

Rayne raised the back of her hand to her forehead and bent her knees slightly. "Swoon." Then she struck Chase across the chest. "*Nothing* will go wrong…I won't let it."

Chase released Rayne and took hold of the rope. She hitched both her ankles over it and began to work her way toward the column. "You should probably step back to the entrance in case that walkway collapses."

Rayne said nothing but did as instructed, and Chase worked her way toward the column one hand at a time. By the time she felt the stone of the column beneath her back, her forearms were ablaze with tension and about as stiff as the stone itself. She unhooked her feet and rubbed at her lower arms, trying to loosen them up. She finally stood and edged around the statue three hundred and sixty degrees to take it all in.

"What do you see?" Rayne called from the doorway.

"One second." Chase held up her hand as she translated the writing and logograms on the god's belly. "Divine blood. Life-giving. Abundance. Blood is our blood." Chase followed the god's arm to the dagger she'd seen from the walkway. From there, it had looked as though it were part of the statue, but this close, Chase could see it separated from the god and was made from obsidian rather than copper. "So, in true Mayan style, I have to do a little bloodletting ritual." Chase checked the bowl in the god's other hand and saw there was a small hole in the bottom. The god's hand cupped the bowl. Chase figured she had to put her blood into the bowl and it would drain off somewhere until a required weight was reached to set off the mechanism as it had with the doors. *Simple.* Except she had no idea how much blood, and the inscription was strangely reticent on that score.

"You've got to what?"

"Give the god my blood in exchange for the Trinity. Seems like a fair trade to me, don't you think?" Chase grasped the hilt of the dagger and slowly removed it from the god's hand. She wasn't going to use it. She had a field blood transfusion kit in her pack, but it could be that the lack of weight in that hand might also contribute to the process.

"I suppose it makes sense," Rayne said. "Is the dagger made of obsidian or is it a shaped shark's tooth?"

"It's obsidian. Why? Would that tell me something I need to know?" Chase flipped through her mental notes on Mayan culture and couldn't recall anything about the importance of either material.

"Nope. I was just curious…How much blood do you have to part with?" Rayne stepped forward as if she were going to approach the edge but pulled back.

"It doesn't say." Chase sighed. "Another leap of faith. How much blood can I lose before I lose consciousness?" Chase climbed up onto the belly of the god, shoved her shirtsleeve up, and held her arm over the bowl. She leaned her chest against the other arm to see if she could fall unconscious and still stay in position for the blood to fall where it was needed.

"People donate one pint easy enough, so I'd guess at two. I can't say for sure, Chase."

Chase thought about the Mayan rituals. Bloodletting and sacrifice were a huge part of their culture. Would they expect all the blood from one person, or even two or more? There was no way of predicting it. Nothing in the map or on the stones gave any hint as to this final process.

"Be careful, Chase."

"Sure thing." Chase placed the dagger on the bowl, pulled the first aid kit from her backpack, and tossed the pack to the ground. She removed the transfusion kit and placed it in the bowl. She pushed the elastic band over her hand and up onto the widest part of her left forearm. The vein she always donated blood from responded immediately and pushed up to the surface. Chase fitted the tubing to the needle and used the dagger cut the tubing to a more reasonable length. She used a small piece of tape to secure the open end of the tubing to the edge of the bowl before replacing the unused portion of the kit into its bag and dropping it to the ground on top of her backpack. She paused. She'd given blood religiously every four months almost her whole life, even if she was in another country. Every time, she watched with fascination as her vein came to attention obediently and the nurse gently pushed the sharp needle into it. And every time, she tried to push out a pint faster than she had on the previous occasion. Her personal best was eight minutes and three seconds. She had this. Plus, Noemie had given her an emergency lesson on doing a full blood transfusion before she'd left the city. How hard could it actually be on herself?

Chase offered the needle to her vein and pressed it through the skin. Blood coursed out of her, turning the translucent tube scarlet red. She rested her arm on the bowl and began to clench and unclench her fist. She watched her blood trickle from the open end of the tube and down into the hole of the god's bowl. That's when she realized she had no way of knowing how much blood she was parting with other than an estimate of time based on past experience. She checked her watch and was only thirty seconds in. Still, she should've connected the blood bag to the tube, collected the blood, and then emptied it into the bowl. *Shit.*

Chase glanced across the pit and couldn't see Rayne. "Where are you?"

"Right here, baby."

She sounded too close. Chase peered over the belly of the god to see Rayne inching toward her on the rope. She was already close to the column. Chase sighed. There was no telling this woman what she could and couldn't do. "I thought you were staying at the doorway in case the walkway fell away."

"And I decided that the safest place would be here with you. Also… if this contraption needs more blood than you can give, we'd better be prepared." Rayne hitched up and gave Chase a quick peck on the cheek. "And lastly, if this whole place collapses, I want to be right by your side."

"So if we die, we die…together?"

Rayne shook her head. "No. Because we'll have a better chance of surviving if we work together."

Chase smiled. "You're so romantic." She refocused on pumping the blood from her system and keeping an eye on the time.

Rayne leaned against the statue and placed her hand on Chase's thigh. "I've got you."

Chase closed her eyes and rested against the god's arm. *She's got me.*

Eight minutes passed. Then ten. At twelve, Chase began to feel a little dizzy but a quick protein bar seemed to right the problem. Rayne was beginning to look a little concerned when, as Chase's watch indicated it had been fifteen minutes, something loud dropped deep within the belly of the statue. Gears clunked, the god vibrated, and the whole column started to shake.

"Oh, shit." Chase pulled the needle from her arm, and Rayne fixed a wad of cotton over it and secured it with medical tape. Chase got down from the god. "Get back over there." Rayne didn't move. "Now! I'll be right behind you."

"Fuck, Chase. That's what they say in all the movies and you turn around. Pfft. Gone."

Chase guided Rayne to the rope. "Super. Great talk. Go."

Rayne did as instructed and looked to be making quick progress along the line. She reached the other side and ran to the doorway. Chase pulled her backpack tight and grabbed onto the rope. The column shuddered and the statue rocked. Chase grabbed hold of the rope and worked her way across the pit as fast as she could, glad for that extra training she'd done with Noemie. She was halfway across when the column began to sink and the rope along with it. *This is gonna hurt.* Chase unclipped her buck knife from her belt and began to saw through the rope. Progress was slow with her left hand, but she wanted her stronger arm to hold her weight when it eventually separated. She heard the creaking of the stone door as it struggled under the pressure. It was a new rope, but the point at which the pressure would become too much and it would snap at its weakest point could be anywhere.

The rope became impossibly taut, too tight to withstand the strain for much longer, just as Chase sliced through the last strand. She shoved the knife into her waistband and clutched at the rope with her left hand as it swung toward the side of the pit. Chase smashed into the stone wall, her left side absorbing the brunt of the impact. She grunted as the pain ripped through her shoulder but kept her grip tight. She heard Rayne's scream then saw her appear over the edge of the pit.

"Baby."

"It's okay, Rayne. I'm okay." Chase looked down before she began to climb the rope. From the vast darkness, something was rising. She scrambled upward and thrust her hand over the edge. Rayne helped her over and she lay on the ground, breathing hard. "Counter balance. Look." Chase moved across the floor on her stomach as Rayne looked into the pit.

"Oh my God, Chase. You're right. Something's coming up."

The raised floor came to rest two feet below the one Chase was prone on.

But the vast circular stone floor wasn't heaving with gold or layered with riches and gems. She heard the thud of footsteps heading their way, and in her peripheral vision she saw Owen and Larry.

"What the FUCK is that supposed to be?"

Chase swallowed and refocused on the new floor. Maybe she'd missed something. Maybe the floor itself was solid gold. Around the hole where the column had disappeared looked to be a simple, circular stone altar.

Owen kicked Chase in the ribs. "Find out what that is. *This* can't be it. There has to be more."

His disappointment will lead to destruction. The old woman's words echoed in Chase's head as she got to her feet and stepped tentatively onto the stone floor. Chase caught hold of Rayne and pulled her with her toward the center. They reached the stone altar to discover a circular wheel around twenty-five feet in diameter. Its rim was around six feet wide and the well inside around eighteen inches deep. At each point at zero, one hundred and twenty, and two hundred and forty degrees lay what looked to be a life-size human effigy. From first glance, one was made from wood, the second from clay, and the third from maize dough. Chase blinked, wondering if she was delirious from the combination of blood loss and the pain from the fall. But when she opened her eyes, the picture hadn't changed. She began to laugh. There was nothing else *to* do.

"What the fuck is it?" Owen yelled.

"The Golden Trinity," said Chase, turning to him as everything fell into place in her mind. "The Mayans believed the gods had three attempts at making humans—two failed attempts with wood and clay, and the final, successful attempt, with a dough ground from corn." She gestured to the altar. "These are those attempts. The Golden Trinity isn't the treasure haul of a lifetime. It isn't riches beyond all comprehension. It's a belief system, an idea, something far richer, far more important than gold or silver. It's a treasure because *ideas* are the greatest treasure of all. They don't die."

Owen stormed across the stone floor and pushed Chase out of the way. "You're lying. That can't be."

He slumped over the altar as he saw Chase wasn't lying. Chase pulled the knife from her waist, grabbed a handful of Owen's hair, yanked his head back, and pressed the knife against his throat. Larry went for his gun. "Don't do it. I'll slit his throat faster than you can pull that out of your pants." Larry raised his hands, and Chase nodded toward him. "Rayne. Relieve Larry of his weapon."

Rayne rushed across the floor and pulled his gun from its holster. She stepped out of his reach and aimed the gun at his head. "Any other weapons we need to know about?" He shook his head. "Do a twirl for me. I'd like to see for myself."

Chase smiled at Rayne's immediate control of the situation. She saw a bowie knife stuck in the back of his trousers as he turned. "Knife. Back of the pants," Chase said, keeping just enough pressure on her knife to keep Owen compliant. She pulled his gun from the front of his trousers then quickly stepped back and leveled the gun at him from a safe distance. She'd seen too many movies where the bad guy had been able to disarm the hero because they stood too close to them. Chase wasn't about to make that mistake.

"Got it," Rayne said. "Reach down with your left hand, pull the knife out, and throw it in the opposite direction to us as far as you can."

Rayne had obviously seen Larry with the gun in his right hand, and Chase was even more impressed. Larry withdrew the knife and tossed it.

"Lie down on the floor and cross your hands behind your back."

After Larry got to the floor, Rayne pulled the paracord from her pocket. Deftly, considering she had a gun in one hand, she tied a slipknot in the cord. She got closer to him, but still not within his reach, and threw the knotted end toward his hands.

"Catch that and slip it around your right wrist."

Larry did so, and Rayne pulled the rope over his body toward his left side. She then stepped in, and dropped her knee into his back. She swiftly tied the rope around his left wrist and got to her feet.

"Nice roping, cowgirl." Chase smiled. *Now what?*

"What's your next move, Stinsen?" Owen asked. "Are you going to leave us down here to rot? Or are you going to shoot us? Do you have that in you?"

He took a step closer to her and Chase backed off a step. "Stay exactly where you are, Owen. You have no idea what I'm capable of in the wrong circumstances. And goddamn, these are the wrong circumstances." Chase felt something unfamiliar bubble beneath her usually calm demeanor, and she fought to control it. It was exactly that which separated someone like Owen from someone like her. "Walk over to your buddy and lie facedown."

Owen laughed. "I don't think so." He took another step closer to her.

Chase shifted the gun slightly to the left and fired. He jumped, only a fraction, but he still reacted, and that might be enough. "Don't make me repeat myself."

His nostrils flared and he clenched his jaw, but he slowly walked over to Larry and got down beside him.

"Link your arm through Larry's and stay completely still." Chase moved slightly closer and kept the gun aimed at Owen's head. Rayne looked nervous, but she knelt on Owen's back as she had with Larry and secured him to his friend in seconds. Chase heard footsteps. She rushed over to Rayne, and they pressed themselves against the wall, both with their guns directed at the doorway.

"Get in here!" Owen shouted.

"Shit," Chase whispered. "We should've gagged him."

"Too late, baby. Are you ready?"

Chase blew out a breath. "To go down in a hail of bullets like Butch Cassidy and the Sundown Kid? Not really…I had plans…with you."

Rayne smiled and kissed her, deep and hard, like it could be…Chase terminated the thought and responded with everything that she was. If it was the last kiss, she wanted to remember it in the afterlife.

"So you didn't need backup after all?"

Ginn. She and Tonyck came into view, rifles at waist height, ready for action. Rayne pushed off the wall and jumped at them both. Tonyck caught her and swung her around like a rag doll.

"How?" Rayne asked.

But the question became moot when she and Rayne saw the three old women come into view, along with twenty or so of their tribe.

Ginn motioned at them with a thumb and a wide grin. "Backup."

Chase smiled and sank to her knees, the weight of the past few days pushing her down. "Better late than never."

Ginn came over and dragged Chase up and shoved her camera at her chest. "Thought you might want this. Now stand tall, Stinse. You're a hero now."

"You're *my* hero." Rayne came into view around Ginn's hulking frame. "I bet you like the sound of that, don't you?"

Chase nodded, then pulled her into a hug and held her tight. "Let's go home and see what other sounds you make that I like."

Rayne leaned back slightly and caressed Chase's cheek. "And the Golden Trinity?"

Chase met the gaze of the three old women. They nodded in that powerful, old wise-woman kind of way. Chase sighed and focused on Rayne. "Let's leave that right here, where it belongs."

Epilogue

Two months later

CHASE WRAPPED HER legs around Rayne's waist and slipped down into the bathtub behind her. "Mm, perfect temperature. You're going to have to run all my baths from now on. I can never get it right in the tub at my place."

Rayne closed the magazine she was reading and placed it on the in-wall shelf. "Perfect article, baby…Maybe you should move in so I can do just that. You spend most of your time here anyway."

Chase moved Rayne's long, wet hair from her chest and began to trace light circles around her nipples. "You liked it? If I moved in here, where would Noemie go when she's back from the army?"

Rayne tugged Chase's foot from the water and gently massaged it. "I think it's even better than the Zenobia piece. I've got a fifth bedroom. She could make it hers. You know, if she wanted."

Chase grumbled. "Okay, too much. One conversation at a time, please. It wouldn't be hard to better the Zenobia piece since I couldn't tell the whole truth because of your mean ass lawyers."

Rayne laughed softly, leaned down, and kissed the top of Chase's foot. "You didn't tell the *whole truth* on this one either."

"That's different. We had to protect the tribe." Chase squeezed Rayne's nipple between her thumb and forefinger. Rayne rocked back against her and murmured. "What do you think the tribe did with Owen and the rest of them?"

Rayne leaned farther back into Chase's body. "I have to say that I don't care, I don't want to know, *and* I don't want to talk about him."

"Plausible deniability, eh?" Chase thought about the work Rayne had commissioned and paid for, including a safe walkway down to the temple. "I don't mind saying again how much you surprised me with your idea to make the site safe for the indigenous people, especially rebuilding most of the ground with a wooden floor and covering it with artificial grass so the site isn't visible from satellites."

"You make it sound like it cost millions of dollars." Rayne placed her hand over Chase's. "With all the local tribes providing the labor, I paid barely a hundred thousand for materials."

"Still, that place could've been a tourist trap and raised a lot of money for the indigenous people." Chase guided her other hand between Rayne's legs and circled her clit.

"Is that what you wanted to write about? Did you want to give the place to the whole of Brazil and the rest of the world?" Rayne asked between gasps of pleasure.

"No. I'm just saying, the absence of greed impressed me. I love that the Trinity still belongs to the people who believe in it. And I have to admit that I like being one of only four people in the world beyond the tribes that know exactly where it is." Chase gave Rayne small kisses from the nape of her neck and along her shoulder while her hand continued to play between Rayne's legs.

"Would you be doing these delightful things to me if I had tried to sell the whole place, effigies and all, to the highest bidder?" Rayne raised her hips and pushed against Chase's touch, demanding more.

Chase pressed a little harder on Rayne's hardening center. "Absolutely not. Well, I don't know. Maybe not. It's a tough call. You kind of bewitched me in the rain forest."

Rayne laughed, took Chase's hand from her breast, and kissed her palm. "*I* bewitched *you*?"

"Yes. Take responsibility for making me completely powerless against your charms." Chase slipped her finger between Rayne's soft folds of flesh but Rayne grabbed her wrist and stopped her from exploring farther.

"Number one, my charms took years to work on you. And number two, you are not making love to me in the bath. I do *not* want a soapy foof." Rayne flipped herself over and faced Chase. "Once this feature hits the newsstands, you'll be inundated with job offers and people offering you obscene amounts of money to reveal the location of the Trinity."

Chase leaned down and kissed Rayne. "I don't need obscene amounts of money. I have you."

"Ha!" Rayne slapped Chase's chest and splashed water all over the floor. "Just because you're ridiculously amazing between the sheets does *not* mean I'm going to be your sugar mommy."

Chase frowned and stuck out her bottom lip. "Are you sure?" She tracked her fingers along Rayne's back, into that insanely sexy dip at the base of her spine, and rested her hand on Rayne's butt cheek. "I could give up lecturing and be your sex slave. I could wander around the house all hours of the day and night completely naked, and furnish you with ridiculously amazing sex whenever and wherever you wanted it." Chase squeezed Rayne's ass. "Doesn't that sound tempting at all?"

Rayne nodded and licked her lips. "It *does* sound tempting. Very tempting. And I do love it when you walk around the house naked. You have the best ass in the world...but you also have other great talents, like being one of the top archeologists and the second-best treasure hunter in the world."

Chase smiled and ran her fingers through Rayne's hair. "I don't mind being second best to you...but you do usually cheat *and* you have the tank twins to help you out, so it's not really a fair comparison."

"We should settle this once and for all. A treasure hunt to end all treasure hunts. You versus me. No team. Just you and me." Rayne lifted herself from the bath and wrapped a giant towel around her waist.

Chase sat up. "I'm intrigued. What are we hunting?"

Rayne padded out of the bathroom, swishing her hair and her hips, giving Chase her all.

"So," Chase called out as she climbed out of the bath and grabbed a towel, "what are we hunting?"

"Each other's hearts."

Chase grinned, ran into the bedroom, and tackled Rayne to the bed. "Winner takes all?" She pulled open Rayne's towel and sucked a nipple into her mouth while her fingers slipped into the welcoming wetness of Rayne's pussy.

Rayne gasped. "Yeah," she whispered, breathless against Chase's neck as she fucked her. "Winner takes all."

Chase moved from Rayne's nipple to her mouth and kissed her. "That's completely uncharted territory. It's widely understood that you don't have a heart."

"Then you don't accept the challenge?" Rayne asked between hot, passionate kisses.

Chase drove her fingers deeper inside Rayne and nibbled on her neck, the feeling of being inside and around her the most exquisite thing she'd ever experienced. "Oh no, I accept your challenge, Rayne. But you have an unfair advantage."

Rayne pushed her hips from the bed and onto Chase's fingers. "What's that?"

"You already *have* my heart."

What's Your Story?

Global Wordsmiths, CIC, provides an all-encompassing service for all writers, ranging from basic proofreading and cover design to development editing, typesetting, and eBook services. A major part of our work is charity and community focused, delivering writing projects to under-served and under-represented groups across Nottinghamshire, giving voice to the voiceless and visibility to the unseen.

To learn more about what we offer, visit: www.globalwords.co.uk

A selection of books by Global Words Press:
Desire, Love, Identity: with the National Justice Museum
Aventuras en México: Farmilo Primary School
Life's Whispers: Journeys to the Hospice
Times Past: with The Workhouse, National Trust
Times Past: Young at Heart with AGE UK
In Different Shoes: Stories of Trans Lives
From Surviving to Thriving: Reclaiming Our Voices
Don't Look Back, You're Not Going That Way

Self-published authors working with Global Wordsmiths:
E.V. Bancroft
Valden Bush
Addison M. Conley
Dee Griffiths and Ali Holah
Helena Harte
Karen Klyne
Ray Martin
AJ Mason
Emma Nichols
Robyn Nyx
John Parsons
Simon Smalley

Other Great Books
by Independent Authors

The Copper Scroll by Robyn Nyx
When love and ambition collide, will Chase and Rayne's fledgling relationship survive the fallout?
Available on Amazon (ISBN 9798711238386)

Call to Me by Helena Harte
Sometimes the call you least expect is the one you need the most.
Available from Amazon (ISBN 9781838066802)

True Karma by Karen Klyne
Love moves to its own rhythm, if only you stop long enough to hear it.
Available from Amazon (ISBN 9781916444393)

Elodie by Emma Nichols
There's such a thing as a perfect life so why won't she let herself live it?
Available from Amazon (ASIN B08WRFXGRG)

Addie Mae by Addison M. Conley
At the beginning of a bitter divorce, Maddy meets mysterious Jessie Stevens. They bond over scuba diving, and as their friendship grows, so does the attraction.
Available from Amazon (ISBN 9780998029641)

What Happens in Vegas! by Claire Highton-Stevenson
A one night stand changes everything.
Available from Amazon (ISBN 9798676460181)

The Women and the Storm by Kitty McIntosh
Being the only witch in a small Scottish town is not easy.
Available from Amazon (ISBN 9798654945983)

Nights of Lily Ann: Redemption of Carly by L L Shelton
Lily Ann makes women's desires come true as a lesbian escort, but can she help Carly, who is in search of a normal life after becoming blind.
Available from Amazon (ISBN 9798652694906)

Heatwave by Maggie McIntyre
"A seductive age-gap story of love and loss, danger and delight."
Available from Amazon (ASIN B08GJ6YXZD)

Printed in Great Britain
by Amazon

19392256R00169